THE
POISONED
THRONE

TINTAGEL BOOK II

By M. K. Hume and available from Headline Review

King Arthur Trilogy
Dragon's Child
Warrior of the West
The Bloody Cup

Prophecy Trilogy
Clash of Kings
Death of an Empire
Web of Deceit

Twilight of the Celts Trilogy
The Last Dragon
The Storm Lord
The Ice King

Stormbringer's Voyage (e-novella)
The Last Dragon's Voyage (e-short story)
The Emperor's Blood (e-novella)

Tintagel Trilogy
The Blood of Kings
The Poisoned Throne

M. K. HUME

THE POISONED THRONE

TINTAGEL BOOK II

headline
review

First published in 2015 by
HEADLINE REVIEW
An imprint of HEADLINE PUBLISHING GROUP

1

Cataloguing in Publication Data is available from the British Library

ISBN 978 1 4722 1584 0 (Hardback)
ISBN 978 1 4722 1583 3 (Trade Paperback)

Typeset in Golden Cockerel by Avon DataSet Ltd, Bidford-on-Avon, Warwickshire

Printed and bound in Great Britain by CPI Group (UK) Ltd, Croydon, CR0 4YY

MIX
Paper from
responsible sources
FSC® C104740

Headline's policy is to use papers that are natural, renewable and recyclable products
and made from wood grown in well-managed forests and other controlled sources.
The logging and manufacturing processes are expected to conform to the
environmental regulations of the country of origin.

HEADLINE PUBLISHING GROUP
An Hachette UK Company
Carmelite House
50 Victoria Embankment
London EC4Y 0DZ

www.headline.co.uk
www.hachette.co.uk

This book is dedicated to my son, Brendan Niels Hume, with my love and best wishes.

Brendan has experienced his fair share of life's glories and adversities. With an adventurous bent during his youth, he lived the hard imperatives of military life and found a way to reconcile his ethical reservations about war with the demands of voluntary service in the armed forces. Later, he learned the harsh realities of surviving in the modern world of business and raising a family. Despite the difficulties he has faced, Brendan always reminds me of how much can be achieved if we nurture our ambitions and persevere with the pursuit of a good and happy life.

I am so very proud of him.

Ave, Brendan.

M. K. Hume
December 2015

ACKNOWLEDGEMENTS

As well as dedicating this book to my second son, Brendan, I would like to thank him for the enormous amount of his help with this novel. He has returned to the hearth at a time when I needed him most and assisted me with this book when I was lost in a wilderness.

I must also thank the girls and guys from The Coffee Club of Albany Creek in Brisbane. On too many days to count, I would arrive with writing materials in hand, and then order a Brekkie Hot-Pot (hold the chorizo) and numerous cups of English Breakfast tea. For the next three hours or so, I'd work like a demon while the staff saw to my culinary needs. Their friendliness, support and pure niceness helped me over a difficult time. Ave, The Coffee Club.

Clare Foss and Emma Holtz, my minders at Headline, have been very patient with me as this novel has unfolded. Unfortunately, I can't flick the blame for my slowness on to the Roman, Constantine, because I'm afraid that the fault was truly mine. Although Clare and Emma could have been impatient at my tardiness, they have, as always, been wonderful. My thanks also go to the rest of the editorial staff, artists and cartographers at Headline who always manage to make sense of my meanderings. What can I say other than thank you!

As always the covers for these Tintagel novels are a dream!

My beautiful agent, Dorie, is always in my thoughts and I miss her gorgeous smile. Talking on a phone isn't as nice as face to face chats.

My thanks also go to my older son, Damian, and my friends Pauline, Penny and Roger who helped to keep me sane during the hard times when the going got tough.

I also thank my little dog, Rusty, with lots of smiles and love. When the days were hard to face, Rusty's unconditional love gave me the heart to enter the world of the Dark Ages.

That which doesn't kill us, friends, makes us stronger.

Ave.

M. K. Hume

DRAMATIS PERSONAE

Adolphus (Father)
: The healer from the religious community at Glastonbury.

Aeron
: Aeron ap Iorweth. The king of the Dobunni tribe. He is married to Queen Endellion, and is the son-in-law of King Caradoc, the deceased king of the Dumnonii tribe. He is the father of Pridenow.

Andragathius
: A senior officer who served in Gallia under Flavius Magnus Maximus.

Ardunn (Queen)
: The wife of King Cadal, King of Cornwall. She resides at Tintagel.

Cadal
: The king of the Dumnonii tribe. The son of King Caradoc, he is married to Queen Ardunn. He rules Cornwall from Tintagel.

Cael
: A wagon driver who is hired for the journey from Corinium to Tintagel.

Calindre
: A special knife given to Severa by Cael for her protection.

Caradoc
: Caradoc ap Ynyr. The deceased king of the Dumnonii tribe. He is the father of King Cadal, Prince Cadoc and Queen Endellion.

Cassivellaunus
: An advisor appointed by Tribune Maximo to assist the newly crowned Constantinus in his role as High King of the Britons.

Cledwyn
: The son of Conanus and, later, the ruler of Armorica (Brittany) in Gallia.

Clidna	The madam at a Corinium brothel where Marcus Britannicus is murdered.
Conanus	A British survivor of Maximus's campaigns in Gaul who becomes the ruler of Armorica (Brittany) in Gallia. Severa's uncle, he is the father of Cledwyn.
Constans	The eldest son of Constantinus who is domiciled at the legion headquarters in Cymru. He moves to Venta Belgarum to live with his father when Constantinus becomes High King of the Britons.
Constantinus	Later, Emperor Constantine III. As a centurion in Roman Britannia, he is appointed as adjutant to Marcus Britannicus, the original suitor of Lady Severa. Constantinus accompanies Marcus to Corinium and assumes command of the detachment after Marcus is assassinated.
Constantius	The general who escorts Constantine back to Ravenna. He kills Constantine on the orders of Emperor Honorius.
Crispus	One of Constantinus's junior officers.
Dilic	Severa's serving-maid after she arrives in Tintagel.
Drusus	A Roman scout who accompanies Constantinus and Severa in their escape from Glastonbury.
Elen (Queen)	Deceased wife of Magnus Maximus. She is the mother of Severa.
Endellion (Queen)	The wife of King Aeron of the Dobunni tribe. She was the illegitimate daughter of

King Caradoc and Saraid, the Wise Woman of the Red Wells.

Gerontius — One of Constantine's ex-Roman generals in Gallia.

Gregorius — An advisor appointed by Tribune Maximo to assist the newly crowned Constantinus in his role as High King of the Britons.

Gregory (Father) — The abbot of the religious community at Glastonbury.

Gwennan — A prostitute in the brothel where Marcus Britannicus is murdered.

Hibernians — The native tribesmen of Ireland.

Honorius — Western Roman Emperor from 393AD to 423AD.

Jesus of Nazareth — Icon of the Christian Church. He is reputed to have travelled to Britannia as a child with Joseph the Trader.

Joseph the Trader — Joseph of Arimathea. A Jew who travelled throughout Britannia and is believed to have spent some time in Glastonbury. His wooden staff is believed to have been the source of the famed thorn tree of Glastonbury.

Justinianus — A Frank who joins Constantine's revolt against the power of Rome.

Lachie — The kitchen-hand at the brothel where Marcus Britannicus is murdered. He is the brother of the simple-minded Nudd, one of two guards at the brothel.

Llian (Queen) — The widow of King Llew ap Adwen of the Dobunni tribe. After Llew's death, she

	continues to live with King Aeron's family as a dowager queen.
Macsen Wledig	The Celtic name for Flavius Magnus Maximus.
Marcus Britannicus	A Roman aristocrat who serves as a senior officer in the legions. He is selected as a candidate for marriage to Severa, the only daughter of Flavius Magnus Maximus, who is unwed. If successful, Marcus will be entitled to claim the vacant throne of the High King of the Britons and, hopefully, unite the British tribes. Marcus is assassinated at a brothel in Corinium.
Maximo	A tribune and commander of the Roman forces in Britannia. The superior of Marcus Britannicus.
Maximus	Flavius Magnus Maximus. A deceased Roman tribune who became the Roman governor of Britain. He eventually became the Emperor of the Western Empire in Rome and was assassinated by Theodosius, Emperor of the Eastern Empire in Constantinople.
Nebiogastes	A Frank leader who joins Constantine in his revolt against Rome.
Nudd	A simple-minded guard who works at the brothel in Corinium where Marcus Britannicus is murdered.
Paulus	Constantinus's decurion.
Picts	The native population of Northern Britannia.

Pridenow	The son of King Aeron and Queen Endellion of the Dobunni tribe. He is an important personage as his line will lead to the birth of King Artor, High King of the Britons.
Rusticus (Decimus)	A Praetorian who replaced Apollinaris as Constantine's prefect.
Saraid	The Wise Woman of the Red Wells. She is the birth mother of Queen Endellion but abandons the child as an infant. She is a white witch and a notable healer.
Sarus	A Visigoth commander who fights for Emperor Honorius and Rome.
Severa	The daughter of Flavius Magnus Maximus and Queen Elen. She marries Constantinus and bears two sons, Ambrosius and Uther Pendragon, who become High Kings of the Britons. Later, as a widow, she marries Vortigern, who also becomes the High King of the Britons. She bears him one son, Vortimer.
Stilicho	A distinguished Roman general in the service of Emperor Honorius. He fought at the battle of Valentia in Gallia.
Vortigern	A young British soldier of the Demetae tribe who serves under Constantinus. He later becomes the High King of the Britons.

Major Roman Settlements
in Britain (c. 360 AD)

■ Roman Fortress and Legion
◉ Roman Settlement

Bremenium

Vallum
Hadriani

Onnum

Magnis

Vinovia

Bravoniacum

Lavatrae

Verterae

Caractonium

Eburacum

Bremetennacum

VI Victrix

OCEANUS HIBERNICUS

Melandra

Mamucium

OCEANUS
GERMANICUS

Mona

Canovium

Deva

Lindum

Segontium

XX
VICTRIX

Aquae

Venta Icenorum
(Cerdicsand)

Margidunum

Letocetum

Ratae

Causennae

Viroconium

FOREST
OF
ARDEN

Durobrivae

Venonae

Salinae

Bannaventa

Camulodunum

Moridunum

Venta Silurum

II AUGUSTA

Isca

Glevum

Corinium

SABRINA AEST

Abone

Londinium

Aquae Sulis

Calleva
Atrebatum

Lindinis

Venta Belgarum

Glastonbury

Sorviodunum

Cadbury

Noviomagus

Tintagel

Durnovaria

Anderida

Isca Dumnoniorum

Vectis

BARBARIAN ATTACKS ON ROMAN BRITAIN (c. 383-410 AD)

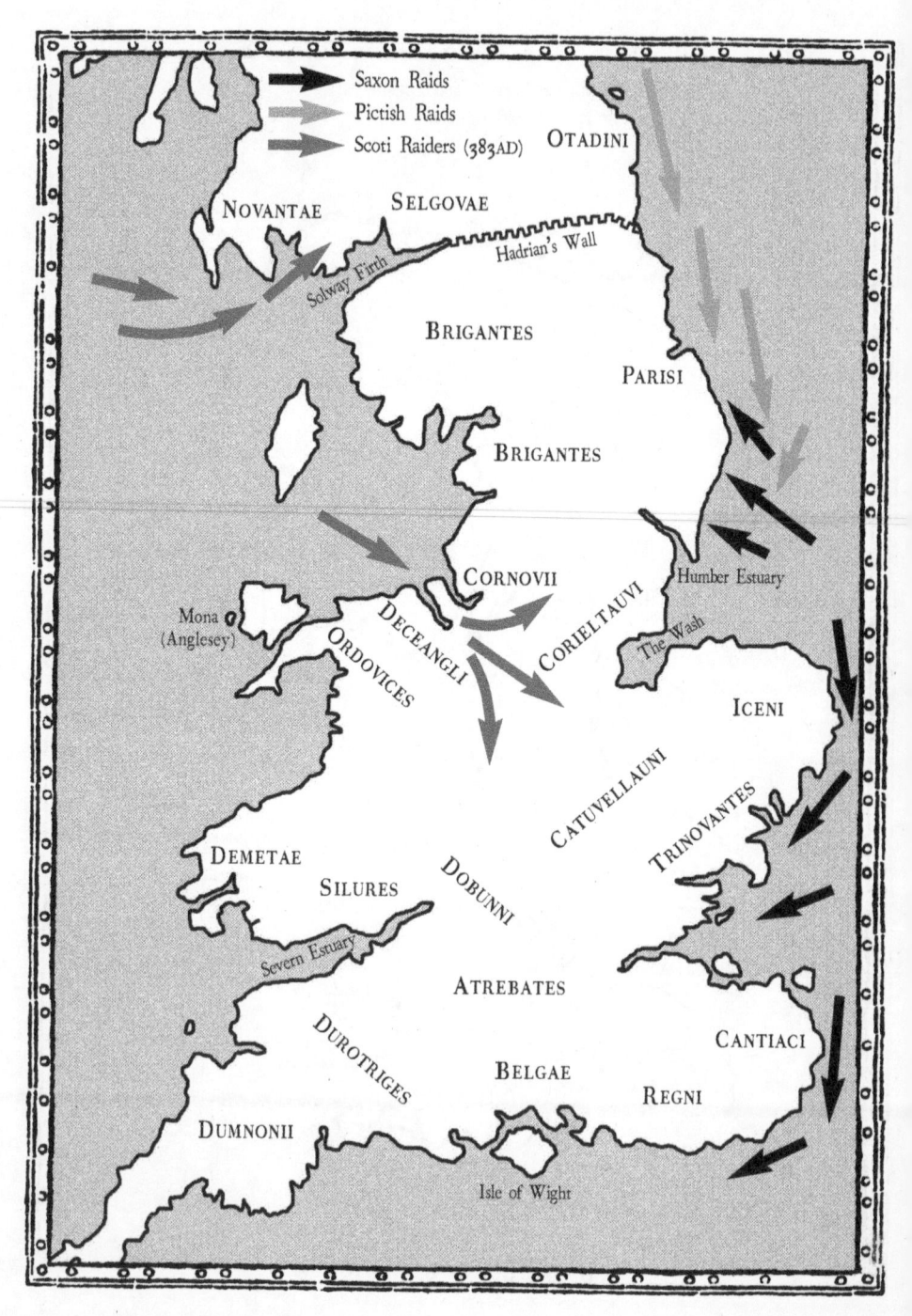

Saxon Raids
Pictish Raids
Scoti Raiders (383AD)

OTADINI

NOVANTAE

SELGOVAE

Hadrian's Wall

Solway Firth

BRIGANTES

PARISI

BRIGANTES

CORNOVII

Humber Estuary

Mona
(Anglesey)

DECEANGLI

ORDOVICES

CORIELTAUVI

The Wash

ICENI

CATUVELLAUNI

TRINOVANTES

DEMETAE

SILURES

DOBUNNI

Severn Estuary

ATREBATES

CANTIACI

DUROTRIGES

BELGAE

REGNI

DUMNONII

Isle of Wight

PROLOGUE

'My hands are filthy,' Constantinus observed as he stared down at them, crusted and sticky with half-dried blood. The battle madness was gradually fading from his eyes as they scanned the field with the constant vigilance of a trained Roman cavalryman.

Critically wounded soldiers were moaning and twitching around him as large snowflakes began to fall and nature blanketed the gore and the filth of the pitifully small expanse of ground where the Picts had made their final charge. The commander rose slowly to his full height, stretching his back and shoulder muscles, cramped from crouching in the front line of combat for many weary hours. His sword arm was so tired he could barely raise it, but he masked his exhaustion. Erect, his tall frame towered over those of his soldiers who were still standing. Around the Roman fighting square, the defensive formation called the Tortoise, a swathe of Pictish corpses were lying in untidy piles.

'Stand down!' Constantinus ordered in a clear, steady voice, indicating he was in total control of the situation. 'Drink and eat while you can. Paulus! Take four men and clear a path so we can carry our wounded on to solid ground.'

Several of his soldiers snapped to attention and began to clear a walkway through the tangle of corpses. As Constantinus calculated the numbers of enemy casualties, he estimated that the Picts had fielded a force of a thousand warriors. However, many of that number were lying dead on this small expanse of firm earth, surrounded by a dangerous expanse of swamp and sucking mud. Quickly, the disciplined legionnaires constructed a path through the corpses to allow the survivors of Constantinus's three centuries to drive their trembling muscles into a determined trot.

A few crisp orders from the commander and his surviving men moved stolidly through the muck as they followed a pathway that Constantinus had marked out earlier in the day with strips of cloth torn from his own red cloak. When he had realised the size of the horde aligned against his force, he had selected the best place available for their stand, although many of his infantrymen were nervous about defending a solitary patch of firm ground so close to quicksand and treacherous swamps.

Only an experienced commander such as Constantinus, an officer who had been promoted through the infantry ranks, would have the imagination to appreciate the tactical advantage of such an unpromising area. Fortunately, his men trusted his agile mind and courage, so they had followed him into the defensive positions he had selected. Constantinus had always led his troops from the van so, like those legionnaires who preceded them in the days of the Caesars, these well-disciplined soldiers were prepared to follow their centurion to their deaths.

This strategy had provided his outnumbered force with a slight edge that had served them well against the sheer size of the Pictish army and the resources available to their king. Rome's last major garrisons, apart from Venta Silurum in Cymru and the legionnaires of the reinforced Dracos Legion, had already been stretched thin when Constantinus made his valiant attempt to prevent the northern invaders from tearing the south of Britannia to pieces. The number of trained soldiers available to his command was insufficient to provide any worthwhile opposition to the Pict advance, or so it had seemed, so he was well aware of the inadequacies of his tactical position. Three hundred legionnaires, plus seventy-five native auxiliaries, were unlikely to mount a successful defence against a horde of victorious Picts who had gained confidence with each battle, destroying every town and hamlet in their wake.

The Picts had charged at Constantinus's defensive lines in wave after wave as they tried to smash their way through the interlocked shields of the Tortoise manoeuvre in a vain search for weakness. It was one of a number of tactics that had served the Romans well for centuries, but it demanded grit, patience, stolid discipline and grim determination. During the many hours that they had spent in the cramped positions demanded by the Tortoise manoeuvre, Constantinus's foot soldiers had proved themselves to be indomitable. Once again, their commander had demonstrated his ability to lead from the front.

'I refuse to die in this pissant dung-pile at the end of the known world,' he snarled until his words were passed onwards to every man in his force. 'We are fucking Romans, and we're proud to have been suckled by the She-wolf. My soldiers will not be defeated by bare-arsed savages with painted faces.'

A weak cheer was raised from the men around him, but Constantinus simply grimaced.

'We are *Romans*!' he yelled again in a louder voice. 'We don't run from anyone, regardless of how many of these blue-faced bastards are lined up against us.'

The responding cheer was louder this time, so Constantinus took the opportunity to scream the same words in their own tongue toward the Pictish warriors who were splashing around in the swamp, although the barbarians responded with catcalls and obscene gestures. Some of them had already been dragged down into the sucking sands after the Romans had pushed them away from their safe bastion, while a number of others had exhausted themselves when they tried to find some purchase on the firmer patches of ground. As Constantinus had hoped, the murderous swamp had killed scores of Picts before they had reached his defensive positions. Even more were to meet their deaths as they desperately tried to settle into their combat formations and join battle with the legionnaires. His fighting words were intended to antagonise the enemy rather than inspire his own men, who knew that angry men make mistakes – and sometimes reckless decisions.

The hours seemed to lengthen as the barbarians threw themselves against the slowly contracting Tortoise formation, but the Picts had been forced to absorb up to ten times the losses inflicted on the trained legionnaires whose weapons had been designed for confrontations such as this. The Roman gladius, or short stabbing sword, had no hilt that could become caught in woven shields or in cloaks. Without exposing themselves, and while their heads were covered by the second row of shields from the defenders behind them, the Roman infantry presented iron walls to the Picts, whose shields were made of wood or even light wicker.

'We have to make ourselves hard to kill until these bastards are screaming with frustration and taking insane risks to reach the points of our swords,' Constantinus reminded the men nearest to him. The commander had explained his strategy and tactics when they had first set foot on this small, oblong patch of dry earth. The legionnaires could make their own judgement of their success as the day wore on for, although the defenders could only concentrate on the men who appeared in the press of human bodies in front of them, the increasing frustration and desperation of the Picts was unmistakeable.

Finally the tattooed savages pulled back with the onset of dusk, but three-quarters of their number would never leave the swamp.

Behind the defensive line, a new perimeter was constructed on another area of firm earth that would protect the Roman force during the hours of darkness. Paulus, Constantinus's deputy, would assume command while Constantinus had a short period of rest. Here, surrounded by earth and tree-trunk walls, the wounded legionnaires could be protected and the fitter of the infantrymen could gain a little much-needed sleep.

Meanwhile, scouts were despatched to keep track of the Pict survivors and, hopefully, gain intelligence on their intentions. Still more men were allotted the familiar and necessary task of stripping the dead of any valuables as well as any useful weaponry. By full darkness, a bivouac had been established. A number of tents and improvised shelters had also been raised for those men who needed cover from the elements. No Romans were permitted to sleep until their defensive position was prepared, regardless of the weather conditions or the surrounding terrain. Such attention to detail had long been the way of the Roman army, and lay at the very heart of their invincibility.

A light coating of snow had fallen during the late afternoon, sufficient to lay a thin shroud of white over the flat expanse of land that included the swamps along the coast near Metaris Aest. The nearest large town was Causennae, but the walls of this unfortunate township had been breached by the Picts, so its buildings had been stripped of their valuables. After their victory, the Picts had pillaged and burned nearby farms to the ground, while dragging away many of the British peasants as captives. But they sought no refuge behind the smashed gates of Causennae. Somewhere in this wet and wintry landscape, the northern invaders had hidden themselves among the networks of rivers, tributaries, marshland and the ever-changing coastline that shifted with the region's heavy tidal flows. Here, trees were rare and troop movements should have been obvious in the grasslands and reeds, yet the Picts were adept at vanishing into them.

Despite the film of snow, the fields of sere grasses hid the tracks of the retreating Pict warriors. Constantinus's forward scouts found their spoor heading into the north, for wounded warriors were abandoned if they were unable to maintain the pace of their comrades. Information extracted from those who had chosen to remain alive revealed that the enemy was hastening towards its refuge at the Abus Flood.

At dawn, Constantinus ordered his legionnaires to strike camp.

'We'll follow the Picts into the north, Paulus,' he told his senior officer. 'Those of us who are fit will chase them as far as the Wall, but I'll not risk our wounded men. They can travel to Causennae where they can be cared for by our surgeons. The lightly wounded can travel with the wagons and supplies that will slow my fighting column. I want best speed, so our legionnaires will carry minimal loads.'

When the Picts had begun their retreat, they abandoned several wagons laden down with the spoils of Causennae and several other towns further to the north. One of the wagons contained dried meat, grain and other supplies to augment those necessities that they would normally have scavenged from the pillaged countryside. The Roman infantrymen would now take some to replenish their individual food stores.

One of the other wagons gave Constantinus cause for anger when a close inspection revealed looted spoils from churches, country villas and farmsteads. The hoard contained a large cache of women's jewellery, and even the tiny bangles, birth gifts and bulla amulets of small children. Many of these precious objects were stained with dried blood, mute witness to the violence inflicted on innocent victims. Blood-spattered religious relics showed that priests had been cut down at their own altars. Constantinus, neither a romantic nor particularly religious, was even so a man of integrity, sickened by the deaths of innocent non-combatants. He accepted that civilians must die during times of conflict, even merchants and townspeople, but women and children should, ideally, be shown some mercy, even if indignities were inflicted on their bodies.

Still, he had won a remarkable battle and had acquired fresh reserves of food and a tidy sum in captured treasure. As his legionnaires had come to believe, he had been favoured by the smiles of Fortuna.

Paulus, his deputy, was one officer who accepted that his commander was a lucky man, an able leader and a courageous soldier, but in his view pursuit of the retreating Picts might be begging for trouble. These barbarians had inflicted massive losses on their enemy but, of the three hundred elite legionnaires who had woken to a bleak dawn a day ago, only one hundred and seventy remained fit for a forced march that would take them into harm's way. However he knew better than to argue.

At the head of the Roman column, Constantinus led his men from their temporary shelter in the swamplands in the bone-jarring march favoured by the legions. These infantrymen could move with remarkable speed, considering that each man was required to carry his personal sleeping tent, digging tool, tinder box, cooking utensil, food supplies, beer and a small axe, along with a shield and spear, in a pack on his back. This fighting kit had scarcely changed since the time of the Great Caesar and, before him, Marius the inventor-consul, whose planning had turned the Roman infantryman into the greatest foot soldier of all time. Each step was in time, for Roman armies fought as a cohesive group.

By any yardstick, Constantinus was an unusual specimen of manhood, for his physique and colouring spoke of barbarian ancestry. He was tall, broad-shouldered and narrow-hipped; his hair was neither black nor brown, but seemed to be the colour of rich mahogany, that exotic timber rarely seen to the west of Constantinople. Red lights, barbarian in colour, danced through his locks when the sun was reflecting light. Although he wore his hair in the clipped style of the military, a natural curl appeared when it grew to the length of a finger joint, a fact that annoyed him greatly. In contrast, he was smooth-skinned over the rest of his body, unlike many fellow officers who were forced to shave or pluck theirs.

His face was as handsome as that of a Greek statue, with a straight nose and high cheekbones above a well-shaped chin. His eyes were greenish-brown and he was fortunate enough to possess abnormally long lashes. Only his mouth, seemingly bee-stung in its fullness, might be described as a flaw. It was as mobile as his dark, arched eyebrows. All these exceptional features were offset by golden, easily tanned skin.

The men in the ranks often joked about their commander's effect on women in every stratum of society. The camp followers fell over their own feet in their efforts to gain his attention, while the wives and women of his fellow officers were quick to invite him to any entertainment that was proposed within the garrison. Similarly, women of the British aristocracy clustered around him like moths to an incandescent flame. He also drove the effeminates within the Roman bureaucracy half-demented with desire. Oblivious to the blandishments of the lovesick and the lustful, he managed to pass politely through their ranks and caused no humiliation or pain to darken his reputation.

If only he had been born of patrician blood, his advancement would have been certain.

As far as Paulus was aware, his commander had no romantic entanglements and he never frequented the whores who flocked to the garrisons.

'The man isn't human,' one of the young British auxiliaries stated pugnaciously when the subject of Constantinus's love life was discussed during a campfire gossip. 'Maybe he's got no balls, although he's like no castrato I ever met. In any event, I've heard he has a brat!'

'I'd keep a civil tongue in your head when you speak of our master if I were you. If he's choosy, it's just a sign that he's a better man than both of us,' his Roman companion replied. He gave his friend a light cuff around the ears, despite being a foot shorter than the younger man.

Now, with his armour dented and dull, the commander was still cutting a handsome figure in his helmet with its scarlet horsehair ruff, although he was grimy, unshaven and foot-sore from the many miles travelled each day in their pursuit of the elusive Pict raiders. The unlined skin under his eyes was blue and bruised with weariness, but his eyes were as clear and as sharp as ever; in them his men detected a fury, for this particular Roman hated to lose and the Picts were successfully eluding him.

The second day of their fruitless pursuit began to try Constantinus's patience.

'Send out the scouts again, Paulus. The Picts can't have been swallowed up by the earth when they had so little start on us.' He grinned then, with a sudden flash of wry humour. 'I'd match our legionnaires against the barbarians every day and twice on Sunday, so the blue bastards must be trying to link up with the larger group of invaders near the Abus Flood. We'll find them first. We'll winkle them out, even if I have to wear my feet off at the knees.'

I know you will, Paulus thought sourly. As well as mine, so it's best that we get on with it. 'Should we continue to march into the night?'

'No! Even the best of our soldiers have to sleep sometime. Exhausted men can't produce sudden bursts of speed. Until such time as I decide otherwise, my men will rest, eat and sleep during the hours of darkness.'

During this long explanation, Constantinus scarcely looked at his decurion, but Paulus wasn't insulted. Such occasional consultations were unusual within the Roman hierarchy and Paulus was always flattered by such intimate moments.

Constantinus was unique in one other quality. The Roman knew that destiny had promised him a future, one that could elevate him above ordinary humans for the rest of time.

Few educated men believed the maundering of prophets or crazed soothsayers, but many Roman legionnaires were super-stitious, so Constantinus had achieved some fame within the ranks after a wise man had prophesied that he would rise far above the rank to which a soldier could normally aspire.

A year earlier, he had been part of a patrol that had ranged far from their home garrison at Venta Silurum. The legionnaires had marched north across Hadrian's Wall and entered the dangerous territory ruled by the northern Celtic tribes. There, in a small, unnamed village beyond Castra Exploratorium, Constantinus's troop had been halted by a capering travesty of a man, a Wilde Man from the Woods who foamed at the mouth as if he had the dreaded disease carried by crazed forest beasts. Normally, this lunatic would have begged for coin or food and would have threatened bad luck to his audience if his pleas were ignored. The pragmatic Romans would have given this strange creature a wide berth.

The Wilde Man had walked unerringly towards Constantinus, his scowl and his blank, unfocused eyes suggesting that he meant to cause some harm to the Roman commander. Two guardsmen stepped forward to restrain the madman, but the centurion stayed them with a raised hand when the hermit addressed him by name.

'Constantine! Emperor that will soon be! Prepare yourself for a time when your soldiers elevate you to the purple! Take care whom you wed, master, for your son is in need of a true mother.'

The old man's voice was cracked from disuse during his years as a hermit in the wild forests, so the words were dragged over his rarely used vocal cords as if a corpse was speaking from deep inside a grave. Constantinus was startled by the hermit's reference to Constans, the lad of twelve years who lived in the centurion's quarters at the garrison in Cymru. The boy's mother had died during childbirth many years earlier.

'I have no aspirations towards such a future, old man. Such ambitions are mere hubris and fire the blood with treasonous thoughts. Begone, unless you have something to tell me that might be useful.'

The Wilde Man grinned maliciously and Constantinus's hair

rose on the back of his neck. 'You are marked for greatness, Centurion. The wife of your destiny will be one who is prized for her bloodline, for she is the child of Macsen Wledig, Emperor of Rome. Will you dare to take her to your heart? She is a briar rose, and only the bravest of men would dare to grip her thorns and the poison in them that sours the blood. But, if your heart remains free of greed and jealousy, then you will rule Britannia lifelong. If you should be poisoned by avarice, then you will have glory beyond your imagining, but your sons and their sons will be the greater men. You will lose the child you love best. Be careful, Constantine. For every step you take will be dangerous and every move you make will be measured against the judgement of the Lord of Order. Will you dare to stand in the clear light of His all-seeing eyes?'

'I fear nothing that I can see, or hear, touch or taste, old man. If I can feel the hilt of my gladius in my palm, or smell the scent of battle on the wind, then I will believe I go to war. All else is nothing but idle talk.'

Constantinus lifted his handsome head proudly. The Wilde Man could see no fear in the dark eyes of the centurion, but he sensed a pulse in the throat of the Roman, an indication that he wanted to make his mark and ensure that his name would be remembered in the wash of time.

The old hermit laughed cynically, so the rattle in his throat sounded like the judder of dry bones in an earthenware mug. 'You are fated to find glory, Constantine. But you must always consider the child of Macsen Wledig, for it is she who holds the key to your destiny.

'I'll leave you now, Centurion. I am done here, for the scent of human flesh sickens me.'

The Wilde Man turned away and took a single step off the

edge of the Roman road, then with his next his figure blurred quickly into the background of trees and underbrush. Despite the many pairs of sharp eyes that followed his movements, he vanished into nothingness.

The impenetrable woodland swallowed the hermit into its dark substance as if he was made of earth and tree roots rather than flesh. The superstitious infantrymen crossed themselves surreptitiously and mumbled prayers to ward off evil, but the centurion laughed with genuine amusement.

Constantinus was left to wonder at the meaning of the Wilde Man's prophecy. Nor was he alone in being struck by the strange promise of future greatness. Even when the incident seemed forgotten, the hermit's words still lingered in the soldiers' memories as the men waited for that time when Constantinus would claim his own.

CHAPTER I

A VERY PROPER WIFE

The legions comprised a strength of six thousand men each and were divided into ten equal tactical units, known as cohorts. The cohorts, in their turn, were divided into six centuries.

Carl Roebuck

The trees shivered with the first of the autumn chills and, in Corinium, Endellion looked up from her pile of homely mending to see the first yellow leaf fall from the atrium tree and float to earth. She bent to retrieve the large, still-pliant leaf. Now, adrift, its perfect shape had already begun to curl.

Autumn was always a time of introspection for the Dumnonii-born queen of the Dobunni tribe. This still-warm season remained busy with the harvest and the bounty of growing things, yet it always reminded her that death was waiting for the last leaves to fall. Insidious and patient, winter took everything it wanted without pity. Still, there could be no change without the slow march of the seasons.

Like her father before her, Endellion had pondered the

inevitability of old age. The first lines of age had crossed her eyes and the back of her neck; her hands were more bony than before and childbearing and gravity had caused her breasts to sag a little. She had no wish to live forever, though, even if she could be promised the wonders of eternal youth.

'Many persons would welcome such a life – but it's not for me,' she murmured without thinking.

'Your pardon, Endellion?' Severa asked seriously, as she raised her head from a length of linen that she was valiantly attempting to hem. Most girls and women of quality learned to sew beautifully by their tenth year, but Severa's strong hands had proved to be an exception to the rule.

'I'm sorry, Severa, I was just thinking aloud. A spent leaf fell at my feet, so I couldn't help but notice its beauty, even though the poor thing was about to die. So many people want to live forever, but I'm sure that our bodies would wear out and cause us terrible pain that would last throughout our interminable, deathless lives. My father, who lived to a great age, would often say that we should be wary of the dreams that we hunger after. He believed we would rue the receipt of God's gifts if we were granted our hearts' desires without some qualification.'

Severa glanced around at the soft green grasses, the pear tree heavy with ripening fruit, the wildflowers, and the cabbages growing thickly along the atrium path. With careful eyes, she surveyed the two-storeyed palace.

'Living forever in this palatial home in Corinium would be very comfortable, Endellion, but to spend eternity in a dirt-floored and verminous hovel would be a different proposition. Imagine having to labour long and hard for all eternity.'

'It would be horrid, Severa – a particularly cruel Hades. I can't really imagine what it would be like to slave in the darkness of the lead mines or to fish in the rough seas of the ocean for long periods of time. I've never experienced true hunger or the agony of thirst. I can understand the suffering of others, but I've never had to suffer myself.'

The queen sighed as she considered her own good fortune.

'My father believed that the old gods were tricksters who offered the people what they *thought* they wanted. At any road, girl, I've done enough moaning and groaning for one day. Still, I wish that Aeron was safely at home.'

With a feeling of regret in the pit of her stomach, Endellion recalled the many years of separation in those years when Aeron had followed Magnus Maximus on his campaigns into Gallia. Maximus had been the long-time friend of her father, King Caradoc of Tintagel, so Endellion was familiar with the background of the Roman commander who had been executed by his enemies some twelve years earlier. Her father had been a tribal king noted for his statesmanship, his expertise as a military commander and his success as regent of Britannia during the period that Maximus had carried out his foray into Gallia. Caradoc's reputation had endured for the twelve years that had elapsed since his death.

Those twelve years had passed in the blinking of an eye. Endellion still struggled to accept that both her father and Flavius Magnus Maximus had been dead for all that time. Aeron had told her that these two very different leaders had been favoured by Fortuna and were gifted, or cursed, with mercurial powers. The gods had loved them, but both men had paid a price for the favours of Heaven.

The queen glanced around the atrium of the Roman-style villa that was used as Corinium's royal palace. Endellion could recall the features of Llew pen Adwen, the king of these lands, who had been no older than her present age when he had died at the hands of the wild savages from Hibernia. His dowager queen, Llian, was still domiciled within the palace. The death of Llian's much-loved husband had meant that Endellion's own husband, Aeron, had reluctantly assumed the throne, despite the resultant loss of his freedom.

'After all, I had adventures enough during those years when I was dragged along in the wake of Maximus's army. I knew sufficient excitement to last a lifetime,' Aeron had told his queen during a quiet and contemplative conversation. 'My sleep is still disturbed whenever I have dreams of my escape to Britannia, after Maximus was defeated in Italia. I thought at the time that you had been irrevocably lost to me.'

'My father admired the words of Socrates, the Greek philosopher, who said that the throne of a kingdom was a burden that could be compared with a cup of poison,' Endellion had responded. 'It seemed crazy to me that any man could steal that cup willingly, but he convinced me that possession of a throne seems wonderful as long as you don't have to bear the responsibilities that go with the task. The ruler is expected to serve as well as rule and the poisoned cup can destroy those who sip from it.'

Endellion possessed firm views on duty and responsibility, and she recalled how she had lain with Aeron in one of the grand rooms of the villa before the commencement of King Llew's funeral and the presentation of her husband to the Dobunni people as their new king. Aeron had refused to take immediate possession of the king's quarters. 'I think it's best for the grieving queen to have a short period of normalcy before we ask her to move to her new abode,' he had said with his usual compassion. Endellion had agreed without hesitation but, as events transpired, Llian had been invited to dwell with Aeron's queen as a permanent resident in the palace, where she would remain as an honoured guest comfortably ensconced in her own suite of rooms. Her old servants were permitted to serve her in her widowhood and she was able to instruct Endellion in the multitude of tasks that a queen must learn to embrace.

Now, four years after those sweeping changes in their circumstances, Endellion and Aeron had settled into Corinium with dutiful hearts, as they worked hard to earn the love of the Dobunni tribe. The servants were soon reporting to the citizenry that the queen worked at menial tasks just like any poor housewife would have done, while she spent hours of her day reviewing the many duties involved in organising the household in an earnest, practical fashion. The population of Corinium were gratified too to learn that the dowager queen was blooming as she cared for Endellion's growing brood.

Endellion's pleasant reverie was interrupted by the entry of a slight, boyish girl of some ten years, who skidded to a halt on the stones of the atrium as she tried to slow her headlong run.

'Mother, please order Pridenow to leave my hair alone,' Endellion's eldest child, a daughter called Orla, demanded once she caught her breath. 'Please tell him to stop! He's already cut off a part of my plaits.'

Orla was yet to grow into the beauty that her facial bones promised. Long-legged and boyish, she had the black hair of her mother and the same green eyes. She had recently taken an interest in more feminine pursuits for the very first time, so the mutilated plait was a matter of some hot and impatient tears.

A little boy pounded through the room in chase of his older sister, head down like a charging bull as he attempted to keep up with her. He was so angry that he didn't realise his mother was present until he ran headlong into her wicker mending basket and, with a sudden gasp of pain from a scraped shin, realised that he was in trouble again.

Pridenow was seven, an active little boy with a chubby, arresting face and mobile features. Endellion's heart almost stopped with love and the fears she felt for his future.

Pridenow possessed a pair of clear, light-grey eyes that were so unusual that those persons who met the boy for the first time were often confused by those deceptively transparent and colourless windows into the soul. Endellion had first seen those eyes when the child was presented to her, still covered in blood and mucus, immediately after his birth. She remembered her father's repetition of the prophecy made on the night of Endellion's conception by her birth-mother, Saraid, the Wise Woman of the Red Wells, who had long since passed into the shades. The crux of the prophecy had been passed down to Caradoc's sons and, in turn, would be repeated to Caradoc's grandsons, for Saraid had assured the great king that a grey-eyed man would, one day, enter the court of one of the Dumnonii kings. All of Caradoc's male heirs must be dissuaded from travelling to Armorica, or following any leader who promised glory in the wars that were waged in Gallia. The grey-eyed man must be dissuaded from precipitate actions, or the Dumnonii tribe would suffer untold disasters, as would the other tribes of Britannia. Caradoc had left a short but deadly message for those men of his clan who would follow him into the future.

Would Pridenow grow into that grey-eyed man? At seven, he was far too young to carry the fate of the nation on his chubby shoulders if Saraid's prophecy had been true.

Like most men, Aeron was inclined to make light of Endellion's fears. 'There must be more grey-eyed lads in Britannia, especially in those tribal outlands where northerners had mated with British women,' he reminded her. 'I doubt that Pridenow would be the boy your mother referred to when she described the hero destined to become Britannia's saviour. It's more likely that the witch-woman was speaking of later times in the future of the British people.'

She had nodded, unable to find any flaw in her husband's reasoning. Aeron was such a logical man that she had been persuaded by his certainty. But she was Pridenow's mother; she had kissed his scabbed knees better when he fell and she had spread arnica on his bruises. She had chided him when he tumbled out of trees, even as she anxiously checked his sturdy little body for broken bones. Even now, his clothing made up the bulk of the mending in her basket, for he tore his shirts and outgrew his trews so quickly.

Despite Aeron's best intentions, Endellion had arrived at her own decision regarding Pridenow's wellbeing. Even if the whole world might suffer as a consequence of her actions, she would never permit her son to travel to the continent. She had heard the stories about her mother's gifts of the Sight and she knew, from bitter experience, that this inherited talent was real. Her own dreams had seemed threateningly real, even when she couldn't understand their meaning, because they were either revelations from an unknown past or predictions of a distant future.

Saraid had been presumed dead long before Endellion had met her future husband, for the Wise Woman of the Red Wells had vanished into the depths of the forest leaving her neat little house a deserted shell. When Endellion was ten years old, Caradoc had sought Saraid only to find her round stone cottage was in ruins, the remains open to the sky. Storms and inclement weather had torn away the thatch and rotted the rafters. But Saraid's carefully tended roses had grown wild, to clamber over the stone walls in a fountain of scarlet and heart's-blood red.

In his infancy, Endellion had been certain that her changeling son would die. Yet here was her grey-eyed boy, alive and well. Moreover, he belonged to a bloodline that should exist long into the future. But if Pridenow was invited to Gallia, Endellion would know that Saraid had truly seen the shadows of days that had not yet dawned.

As Endellion considered her children's squabble, a ripe pear fell from one of the branches of the tree in the atrium.

'Come here, Pridenow. Why are you tormenting your sister? Orla is so much bigger than you that she isn't allowed to strike you back. I had thought better of my young man.'

The little boy blushed resentfully and scowled with rage. Although incensed with his sister, he felt a sense of shame because he had been too angry to consider that Orla had been forbidden to retaliate.

'I'd forgotten, Mother. Orla told me I was a runt with fish eyes. She said my eyes are the same colour as some of the dead pilchards that are laid out in the baskets at the marketplace. My eyes aren't like those of a dead fish, are they?'

Endellion knew she mustn't show any partiality if he was to develop into a strong and honest young man. 'That's not an excuse, Pridenow. You must never harm a girl, no matter what they might say or do.'

'But that's not fair!' Pridenow exclaimed. 'She's bigger than me!'

'But you'll grow faster than she will, so now is the time when you must learn to treat women with care and respect. Never believe that men's size permits them to beat their wives and abuse their daughters.'

Pridenow shook his head miserably.

'I still don't think it's fair,' he muttered, but Endellion could tell that her son had understood everything she had said and so she was confident that Pridenow would gain something worthwhile from her lesson.

'Just look at Orla's hair!' Endellion held up the offending plait. 'A girl's hair is a reflection of her physical beauty and you've managed to mar hers by chopping pieces out of it. It will take years to grow back again. Did you mean to make her unhappy?'

'No, Mother! But she made me really, really angry...' Pridenow's excuses trailed away into silence.

'Right, young man, I have a small task that you will carry out for me. But, before that, I want you to apologise to your sister for your rude behaviour.'

Endellion waited while the small boy kicked restlessly at the tiles on the floor of the atrium until finally he apologised to Orla with a sheepish smile.

'Now, young Pridenow! I want you to climb the tree and pick the last of the pears for me. You can also gather the bruised fruit lying on the ground.' Endellion pointed imperiously at an old, plaited basket. 'But, before you begin, I want you to listen while I speak to Orla.

'What really happened, Orla? What made Pridenow so angry? He's not normally spiteful!'

'Nothing much, Mother. He's always very touchy, so it's difficult to joke with him.'

Orla was attempting to look guileless, but the girl was unable to lie worth a tinker's curse.

'Is that the truth, Orla?'

'Nearly, Mother...' She twirled her cut plait around her forefinger and searched her mind for a plausible excuse.

'Tell me, Orla, or perhaps I should ask your brother for his version of this tale.'

Orla capitulated. Her mother watched and waited as the girl explained what had really transpired.

'He was upset when I made some jokes about his eyes. I heard Gwyneth talking to the other servants about wolves' eyes. She was joking, but she said that Pridenow was a very nice little boy, considering he carried the blood of the wolf god in his veins. I was only repeating the maid's words, Mother, so I couldn't have known that he'd be upset. When he yelled at me, I said his eyes reminded me of a dead fish.'

Endellion's lips twitched, but she forced herself to raise one eyebrow and look sternly at her daughter. Orla suddenly realised how cold her mother's green eyes could be.

'What am I to do with you, Orla? You've called him a wolf and a dead fish at the same time. Pretty insults to throw at your younger brother, aren't they?'

'I'm sorry,' Orla whispered.

'Pridenow has heard the same thing said by thoughtless servants for as long as he can remember. I've heard many stupid insults over the years about any number of people. I've heard that blue eyes are cold, brown eyes are lusty, black eyes are wicked and hazel eyes are indicators of a foolish nature in their owner. I've also been told that blond hair is a sign of barbarism, in which case your Aunt Severa is barbaric. Black hair like yours has often been compared with the tresses of witches, while red hair is universally believed to belong to those with an evil disposition. Do I need to explain this nonsense any further?'

'No! Not at all, Mother,' Orla whispered in a contrite voice, while Pridenow hid a grin behind his hand.

'You'll have to learn to ignore gossip because it's usually

unkind and often wrong. Yes, wolves do have grey eyes, but they are creatures of the wild and they live in families, just like we do. Like us they also live together in love and loyalty. Your family is the most important thing in your life, and your family members will always come to your defence, so you must do your very best not to hurt your brother's feelings.'

'I'm sorry, Mother. I didn't stop to think.' Orla turned to her brother. 'I'm sorry, Pridenow. I was trying to irritate you because you are always following me around. I don't really think you're like a wolf at all. Or a dead fish.'

Now that honour had been satisfied on both sides, Pridenow began to collect the last of the fruit from the pear tree, his furious anger now forgotten.

Once Pridenow had picked the last of the pears, both children presented the fruit to Endellion and accompanied their mother to a long, separate room where all cooking for the villa was carried out. Fire was one of the great enemies of family life, with the exception of Saxon attacks and disease, for the flames that baked their bread and roasted their meat could easily kill them if it escaped from the stone fire pits and ovens.

In the warmth of the stone-floored kitchen, Orla and Pridenow peeled the pears which were cooked and made into a honeyed treat with some of Endellion's precious condiments, odd little aromatic sticks from far-off eastern lands. As the concoction was placed into a fire-blackened pot of water and swung over the hot coals, she prayed soundlessly that her brood would always remain safe.

'It's time that Severa was wed, Endellion, but who will take her?' Aeron asked his wife one night as they were sharing some companionable silence in the scriptorium. Like Endellion, he was extremely fond of the well-born orphan who had always been the responsibility of the Dumnonii people, firstly in the capable hands of King Caradoc and, after his death, in the care of the only mother she had ever known, Endellion.

'Yes, husband. She has passed her nineteenth year and should have been wedded for several years by now, but waiting for the right man never caused me any harm.'

Endellion was referring to the long courtship between herself and Aeron that had resulted from her husband's adventures with Severa's father, Flavius Magnus Maximus, during the emperor's forays into Gallia and Italia. Although Endellion had met Aeron when she was barely eleven years of age, Maximus's ambitions had kept them apart until she was, in the eyes of her world, an old maid.

'You've always been the perfect wife,' Aeron responded and nuzzled his wife's neck as she cross-checked the household accounts. He considered himself to be a fortunate man, for his wife was not only literate and numerate, but accomplished in many other areas as well. A pleasant companion and loving bedfellow, she had borne him five children who were growing like weeds, living proof of God's favour.

'I believe that Severa will prove to be a dutiful and doting wife, if she is fortunate enough to marry a man who is kind and prepared to overlook her unfortunate birth. But she could become the tool of an ambitious man who would use her to further his own plans. Even the crown of the Western Empire could become a part of her dowry if the right political conditions existed. We can only hope that God will stand at her side and protect her.'

Aeron crossed himself quickly, for he had seen for himself what hubris and rampant ambition could do to usually civilised and sensible men. He shuddered at the memory of loyal servants who went to their deaths rather than leave their masters to ignominy and execution. He could still see the face of Andragathius, the captain of Maximus's Horse and his most loyal servant, who obeyed his master's instructions and led Aeron to safety. Andragathius's need for revenge on his Roman enemies was such that any delay in resuming the battle was like a knife in his side; he and his remaining companions had ridden away joyously at the prospect of making an insane, suicidal attack against their Roman masters.

Both Aeron and his queen sighed for the past and the loved ones who would never return.

'Perhaps you should let the council of kings know that you have decided that Severa should be wed. When do they meet again? I know the council has been inactive for some years, but the current Pictish invasion in the north could be a good reason to call a meeting in the near future. I believe the Roman centuries have dug the enemy out of their rat-holes along the east coast, but I heard old Huw talking about the Picts and how they've lodged themselves into the mountain spine of northern Britannia, just like ticks in an old man's blanket.'

'I thought you didn't listen to gossip, woman?' Aeron quipped. 'Didn't you punish Orla and Pridenow for that very same sin?'

'Aye! But I don't pretend to be perfect! Besides, old Huw served my father for many years and he's forgotten more about the northern savages than most of our kings will ever learn. Besides, the old man is right, isn't he?'

Her husband nodded glumly.

'I've been told that the Picts have set up an encampment to the north of Eburacum, so they seem to have settled in for the

winter. This is a new strategy on their part and it could bode ill
for our forces in the north. When the legions were stationed
in the garrison at Eburacum, such arrogance would never have
been permitted. But, since the Roman command abandoned the
fortress, the Picts have been permitted unrestricted entry to
the northern lands of Britannia. The population there is unprotected. Small parties of raiders are collecting food, gold and
slaves to take north, so we believe the spring attacks will be
earlier than normal. The fighting will be vicious and might
penetrate further into the south than their usual efforts. Even
now, what's left of the legions is wasting Roman blood in a vain
attempt to isolate some of the barbarian war parties. God help
them! There has been some talk of reinforcements returning
from Gallia, but I fear that the emperor, Honorius, is ready to
cede Britannia, Gallia, Hispania and Northern Africa to the
barbarians, rather than throw away good Roman gold on what
he sees as lost causes.'

Endellion paled. A world without their Roman overlords was
hard to imagine. The legions had protected this fertile island
from the northern savages for more than four hundred years.
The British people had given up their autonomy when the first
Roman sandals had stood on the pebbled beaches of Dubris, but
the Romans had brought civilisation, trade and wealth with
them, so that no Britons alive could remember a time when
their people were slaves fated to live out their days in ignorance
and filth.

'We face an uncertain future if we can't depend on the protection of the Roman legions. My father accepted that the sheer
number of raiders in our lands would ultimately allow them to
rule over the British people. Although he hated the thought,
he believed that the Saxon barbarians would ultimately prevail,

and these new masters would be far less hospitable than the Romans.'

'We'll have little control over the disasters that will befall us, wife, so I'm reluctant to fear what I can't change.' He pulled up her chin so he could stare into her troubled eyes. 'It's time to put your labours to one side, Endellion, and come to bed.'

His wife resisted him momentarily as she imagined a war-torn world that her children might be forced to endure. But Aeron, familiar with her introspective fits, gripped her hand and turned her face up to his with his other palm.

'Smile for me, sweet Endellion, and we shall make our way to rest. I've lived long enough to know that the wisest men snatch their pleasures while they can. Perhaps your sweet flesh will ease my troubles ... and, perhaps, an old man can do the same for you.'

Despite herself, Aeron's mock-lasciviousness triggered a giggle from Endellion. She eyed him quizzically.

'We're an old married couple, not passionate young lovers, my lord,' she said seriously. But then she spoiled the whole effect by giggling again.

'Perhaps I should take you into the stables. The hay is soft and sweet in the storage loft, so I could show you how a man should treat a heartless and teasing wench.'

'You wouldn't dare, you fool,' Endellion retorted, and then drew in her breath as her husband squeezed her sensitive nipple with one familiar hand.

Aeron knew by her flaring eyes that her lust matched his.

'No, Aeron! We have a perfectly good bed along the corridor ...' Endellion's voice faded away as Aeron swung her over his shoulder with a mocking groan of feigned pain. 'I'm far too heavy, my love,' she protested.

'Come on, wench! I refuse to waste a harvest moon worrying about verminous Picts or heathen Saxons. Have I ever told you that I married the most wilful, carnal and imaginative woman in all of Britannia?'

'How dare you accuse me of carnality? You've taught me everything I know!'

And then the respectable, middle-aged rulers hurried into the stables. The guardsmen watched their giggling progress with knowing complacency, for the ways of the aristocracy were very strange. Why would the king choose to pleasure himself with the queen in the straw?

'I wouldn't care to leave a comfortable bed to sleep in the stables,' one of the younger guardsmen said emphatically. 'I sometimes wonder if the Great Ones have sex in the same way as we lesser men.'

'You daft pillock! How many ways can men and women pleasure each other?' his friend replied with a friendly cuff to the side of the head.

Both of these watchful guards knew that the world of Corinium was safe and well under such benevolent and carefree rulers. Meanwhile, in the straw of the stables, Endellion could see a square of stars, as brilliant as shards of glass, through an opening in the loft. She wondered if God lived in one of those shivering stars and then, as her husband's body became more demanding, she thought of nothing sensible at all.

CHAPTER II

A MEETING IN DEVA

The unbelieving husband is sanctified by the wife.

Corinthians, 7:14

Winter passed slowly as the population of the south shuddered and shivered through the throes of war, periodic flurries of violence reflecting the ongoing campaign in the even colder north. This was a strange experience for the people of Britannia, because conflict during this dark and inhospitable season was a rare experience. These Pict invaders must have planned their raids over a long period of time if they were prepared to winter inside hostile terrain surrounded by enemies. Accustomed to the freezing cold to the north of the Wall, the Picts had caught the Britons and Romans completely off guard.

The Romans dug their way into the mountain ranges of Britannia as they searched for remnants of the original Pict army that had disappeared into the landscape. The three centuries of legionnaires under the command of Constantinus had proved successful against one large group of hostiles who occupied Navio, a deserted fort abandoned by its Roman occupiers in bygone days and allowed to deteriorate. Other deserted Roman camps from yesteryear had offered some protection to isolated cadres of the enemy, so the entire winter had been taken up with the dangerous and tedious task of weeding out and crushing them.

As the Pict warrior force spread throughout the northern parts of Britannia, the British kings found that they were reliant on the last remnants of the Roman legions to defend them. Throughout the winter and the unseasonably wet spring that followed, the Roman forces had been thinly stretched on the ground as they struggled to keep the groups of Pictish fighters from coalescing into a large and efficient army.

But Constantinus and his force of legionnaires and native auxiliaries had weakened the backbone of the invading Picts. His fierce and uncompromising pursuit of the infiltrating warriors had been the deciding factor in a series of battles fought mostly on the run. Then, by denying the invaders an opportunity to regroup, the centurion had pursued them until they were run to ground.

Then, through a combination of luck and good strategy, Constantinus had managed to decimate them.

The Pictish strategy had been risky at best, for finding suitable places to hide for the winter, not to mention their difficulties with supply lines, had been a calculated risk for the Pictish commanders who had decided to remain isolated from their comrades. They had taken the precaution of sending advance parties into the north-east during the preceding twelve months, with the specific purpose of secreting caches of food and weapons in isolated caverns and hidden encampments but, even so, the northern warriors had been forced to carry some grain with them and live off the land whenever the opportunity occurred. It had proved to be a cold and miserable winter for Picts and Britons alike. Famine had gripped the land and hunger hollowed the bellies of the combatants, as the local farmers lost their stores of winter grain to warriors on both sides.

At the same time, the Roman Eagles had no intention of leaving Britannia under the cloud of a military defeat. Despite the moderate size of their force in the disputed area, the young men who served under Constantinus in this arse-end of the Western Empire were eager to prove that they were worthy of promotion and transfer to softer, more profitable commands. Every legionnaire in the Roman army was aware that the empire was contracting back into the Sacred City of the Seven Hills, so they contrived to achieve maximum profit from the retreat.

Spring died and the heat of summer baked the fens and the swamps under steel-blue skies by the time the Picts were finally defeated outside Eburacum. The rivers ran red and the citizens of that august city believed at first that their troops had failed. The Picts had thrown themselves against the Roman troops and their native auxiliaries with the desperation of homesick men who were hungry to return to their kinfolk in the stark mountains of the north.

Finally, defeat became inevitable when the Picts made the strange decision to attack the Romano-Britannic army frontally, a strategy that was bound to bring out the best tactical defences of the legionnaires. In tried and true fashion, Tribune Maximo and his Roman troops stood their ground in the centre of the field, while their light native cavalry was used to smash and harry the Pictish survivors before they could escape.

* * *

Word had come quickly to Corinium.

As the sun began to descend into the afternoon sky, a small troop of British cavalry rode southward along the wide Roman road that connected Corinium and Ratae. The weary riders were covered with a thick coating of white dust from the many miles they had travelled. The commander of the Dumnonii column was Ynyr, son of Cadoc of Tintagel, Endellion's brother. When her nephew was ushered into Endellion's presence, Ynyr threw himself negligently on to a stool and drank the proffered mug of beer, after kissing his aunt soundly and tossing Pridenow into the air like a cloth toy.

'I had hoped you and the children would be here and not seeking relief from the heat beside the sea, Aunt Endellion. I fear that my men are near to done and, although it's only a small push to reach our homes, I doubt that the horses can last without a long rest to recover their strength. We've been away for almost six months on this campaign.'

Endellion ruffled her nephew's hair with affection. 'You've been absent for far too long, young man, so rest a while. A week in Corinium will make little difference to those who wait for news of your return, so we'll send a courier to keep them informed. There's no need to put exhausted men and animals at risk, and my husband will want to speak with you when he returns from his mission to Ratae.'

'So Aeron is representing our interests with the kings of Cymru and the tribes of the north? Good! Those of us who live in the south-west are often forgotten and unrepresented. My father will be pleased that Aeron has decided to attend their discussions. Was he specifically invited?'

Ynyr's expression was as cynical as ever, so Endellion was certain that Cadoc had been displeased with the undue influence of the Cymru tribes on past decisions affecting future security. The shores of Aeron's kingdom were well protected and his tribal villages and towns were shielded by the great ranges of mountains to the east, so the Dobunni tribe was less vulnerable than the Atrebates and Cornovii, populations whose survival depended on the protection of their Roman masters.

'No! My lord wasn't invited, which would have come as no surprise to your father, but Aeron had already journeyed to Venta Silurum where his younger brother rules. He received sketchy details of the meeting from his brother and, as he had been eager to attend such a gathering for some time, he chose to travel to Ratae and force his way into the meeting of the council. He was certain that none of the other kings would object to his presence. I hope his endeavours were successful.'

Ynyr gazed suspiciously at his aunt. 'Why?'

Endellion was acutely aware that her father's male kin had little guile in their natures, so they could be bluntly spoken at times when diplomacy was needed. But she also knew that plain speaking could be a virtue.

She nodded in the direction of Severa, who was playing with the queen's youngest daughter, an infant not yet twelve months old. Ynyr's face lightened immediately.

'Was King Aeron in Corinium for the birth of your youngest child, Aunt Endellion?'

'No!' She shook her head regretfully. 'He had planned to return to me, but word then came of the meeting at Ratae as soon as the Picts were put to the sword. He waited and waited, but my time of confinement couldn't be delayed for any political outcome. And you?'

Something in her nephew's face suggested to Endellion that

Ynyr's new wife might have been pregnant when he departed on this last campaign.

'Aye! A courier reached me outside of Eburacum. I have been told that I have a son, a boy-child who will be named Gorlois after one of my kinsmen who lives in Armorica. I will meet the babe when I return to Tintagel. I must admit to some anxiety because I was absent at a time when I should have presented my son and heir to my people. I should have had the opportunity to hang his birth gift around his neck and give thanks at the Chapel of the Sacred Springs for God's gift of a boy who will one day become a king. Instead, I was far away, securing the safety and wealth of other kings, as well as the security of their heirs and their acres. Sadly, too many of our young people have perished in recent times, and our tribes can ill afford the loss of their best warriors.'

'I'm afraid that destiny is cruel and uncaring.' Endellion's voice was laced with bitterness. 'We are required to relinquish almost everything we love for the sake of our lands and our people. Your grandfather, Caradoc, gave everything willingly, but I have always resented some of Fortuna's demands. What of you, Ynyr?'

The young man nodded, but he refused to answer. Clever as she undoubtedly was, Endellion couldn't fully understand complex matters such as duty and the exigencies of rule. Like it or not, she was only a woman.

Unaware of his thoughts, Endellion tried to lift the spirits of her young nephew, whose face was far older and more careworn than the features of any twenty year old should have been.

'Britannia demands that we pay a high price for our freedom,' she mused. 'When did our lives begin to go so wrong?'

* * *

Although Severa was the subject of the thoughts of both Endellion and Ynyr, she scarcely noticed their concerns. Nor did she realise that she was the cause of some discussion at the conference of the British kings in Ratae, the armed Roman camp that sat at a critical junction of the well-maintained arterial roads servicing the northern outposts of Britannia. As the discussion flowed to and fro, the British rulers were forced to recall their experiences at the hands of Flavius Magnus Maximus, the assassinated High King of Britannia and ruler of the Western Roman Empire. Many of the kings remembered that Maximus had bequeathed something of inestimable value to them in the form of an unmarried daughter through whom a claim to the title of High King could be made. The more acquisitive and ruthless among them had already realised that she could be the means of achieving the ultimate reward, the laurel wreath of Rome.

'Remember,' Aeron shouted over their bleats and howls, 'there are some matters that must be taken into account before you make fools of yourselves and press your own claims. The tribes must arrive at a unanimous agreement, if you are determined to anoint a High King. Unanimous! Nor could one of you steal Severa and hope to foist her off on us, pregnant from rape. Such perfidy would be treated with the contempt that such vileness would deserve by me and by those rulers who are of high moral fibre. My wife raised Severa and she would never permit this girl to be abased for political ambitions.'

Many of the kings thumped on table tops and insisted that they should be heard. For these men, women were without rights or dignity, chattels respected only for the quality of their menfolk, their fertility and their personal wealth.

'In case you have forgotten, my wife was the daughter of King

Caradoc of the Dumnonii tribe and was begotten on the Wise Woman of the Red Wells. I've heard tell that there has been much gossip about this union, but you should understand that Severa's mother was a woman of considerable power and prestige. Your own safety and comfort could be endangered if you were to flout her wishes. My wife is a strong and intelligent woman who will not permit harm to be visited on Severa. Such foolishness would only result in dissension and civil war.'

The torrent of jarring noise rose up towards the rush roof of the hall as the more raucous of the rulers continued to argue. A flock of pigeons that had been sleeping in the rafters rose from their roosts in a sudden flourish of wings.

'You may shout from now until Our Lord comes to judge us all, but nothing will change. Severa is half-Roman, so she should be promised to one of the coming men from the legions. However, I admit that I'm ignorant of anyone who would be acceptable as a bridegroom.'

The argument generated within the audience increased in volume. The British kings needed their Roman overlords, especially in these lawless times when barbarians were destroying everything that was good in the isles, yet they resented the career Roman warriors who ensured their safety. The British kings, seduced by Maximus on an earlier occasion, had watched their best warriors follow that Roman to fame, glory and an early death. A memory of failure, bitter as aloes, reminded them of everything that had been lost.

'Our people will find themselves at war with each other if they cannot solve the problem of Severa and her association with the throne of Britannia. Don't blind your eyes to reality. My family has kept her safe for twenty years, but the time has come when she should be married to a suitable husband.

Any fool can imagine what might happen if we continue to pretend that she doesn't exist.'

Aeron was aware that rich and peaceful Corinium would be caught up in the midst of a major conflict and he feared that such a catastrophe was imminent. For their part, the assembled kings remained silent while each mulled over the complicated problem.

The silence was sullen with affront, resentment and thwarted ambitions. Each king eyed his neighbour with a palpable distrust.

'I suggest that you search for a suitable Roman aristocrat who could perform the duties of the next High King of the Britons. Once you arrive at your decision, you should pass on your recommendations to Tribune Maximo, who is the representative of the Roman emperor. Your choice must be a man who can represent our interests as well as the requirements of Rome. Such a candidate will not be easy to find, because Maximo will demand that any person nominated must be a patrician and an officer under his command. You must ensure that the interests of our people are protected. There is one certainty! If the gossip filtering through to us from the east is to be believed, the Roman domination of Britannia will not last much longer. We will need a strong military hand and willing allies if we hope to hold back the Picts and the Saxons, let alone any other opportunists such as the Hibernians, savages who hunger to steal what our tribes have amassed over the centuries.'

'What's in this plan for the Dobunni tribe?' the Brigante heir snapped, causing a howl of complaints and protests. In such a fraught and volatile situation, Aeron struggled to bring these selfish and intractable men to some kind of common ground.

'You may shout and rant against the situation all you want, but Severa is a real woman in need of a real husband. None of you wanted the responsibility when Caradoc was appointed as regent by Flavius Magnus Maximus. Then, after the emperor was executed, none of you volunteered to take over her care, either before or after Caradoc's death. You were happy to maintain the status quo. And now you have the effrontery to accuse *me* of chicanery by using Severa as a pawn in a search for power. Think! Would I speak of my personal reservations if I had ulterior motives? Hardly!'

Aeron's forceful voice silenced some of the criticisms, but the long-suffering kings of the east coast tribes were opposed to his plans. Eventually, Aeron realised that further argument was fruitless, so he rose to his feet and pushed his stool back so hard that it tipped over with a great clatter.

'I'm sick of the whole fuss with you fools, so I'm off to my bed. Should you arrive at a viable solution, I would be pleased to hear of it. Otherwise, I intend to leave for Corinium in the morning. It may have escaped your notice, but some of us have been fighting your battles for many months now, while others in your midst are doing nothing to protect their own lands. My wife gave birth to my latest child months ago and I have yet to meet my newest daughter. I find that prospect more attractive than discussing unworkable strategies with those idiots among you who show minimal foresight and even less strategic nous. I bid you goodnight!'

As he turned away, Aeron heard a single plaintive voice inquire: 'Why is he in such a hurry to see an infant daughter? Girls don't matter anyway, so this Dobunni upstart must have some ulterior motive.'

Aeron's shoulders squared and his neck muscles bunched as he paused and considered whether or not to challenge the oaf who had spoken with such derision. But common sense prevailed;

such stupidity warranted no answer. He passed through the hall door and slammed it shut behind him.

Honorius, the Roman emperor, was a ruler of limited talent and insatiable avarice. As the supreme monarch, he had inherited the immeasurable accumulated wealth of the Roman world, including the possessions of Nero, Tiberius, Constantine and Claudius.

During his reign, Honorius had surpassed Gratian in his opulent lifestyle and his decadent lusts. Unfortunately, his wilful waste of the gold and jewels in the national treasure chest had left a shortfall in the amount of coin available to pay public servants and soldiers in the service of Rome, both at home and abroad. Honorius would never deprive himself in order to pay his debts.

Such reluctance to part with his wealth to ensure the viability of his workforce and his legions contributed to further problems within the Roman hierarchy. In Gratian's time, the legionnaires had eventually raised Maximus to the purple after wearying of months and years without pay during their service in the far reaches of the empire. Honorius must have expected that his garrisons in Britannia might cast around for an ambassador who would represent the province's best interests when negotiating with Rome.

The officer in charge of the depleted Roman forces in Britannia, Tribune Maximo, was a distant scion of a Claudian family with a long history of madness and political chicanery. In recent years, a succession of Roman emperors had sprung from this powerful family, but Maximo was, at best, more of a politician than a warrior. He had several wives in several countries and was cautious by inclination. He knew he would never be a prospect for marriage to Severa, morganatic or otherwise. However, one of his immediate subordinates, the young and rather effete aristocrat, Marcus Britannicus, had the ambition and the necessary wherewithal for such an elevation. After making a long list of promises of preferment to Maximo and his fellow officers, if he proved to be a successful suitor for Severa's hand, Marcus eventually persuaded his commander to proffer him as a candidate for potential glory.

Unenthused by the prospect of having the aristocratic and dissolute Marcus as a potential High King of Britannia, the troops in the ranks cheered half-heartedly, but they were further inspired when they were given extra rations of beer after receiving a promise of pay and allowances forthcoming by the end of the year.

'Who the hell is Marcus Britannicus? I've never heard of him,' Endellion snapped grumpily.

Aeron had responded by recounting the general accolade given by the troops with a cynical jibe at the young man's lack of talent or distinction. The fact that the tribal kings had found him to be an acceptable candidate was also a source of suspicion. Still, any candidate was better than none and Aeron comforted himself with the fact that a decision had been made. Perhaps a weak man would be compliant to both sides. Unfortunately, the only person likely to suffer by such a decision was Severa.

'But he is of good birth, beloved, and he *might* turn out to be a worthy suitor for Severa. From what I've heard, this young man has proved acceptable to most of the kings, so he'll be here to meet Severa within the week. You will then have an opportunity to judge his character for yourself.'

Despite his comforting words, Aeron knew that the betrothal would proceed whether Endellion liked it or not.

He was a brave and logical man, but the problem of their ward had been weighing heavily on his mind. An unwed girl was rather like an unridden and untrained horse. It ate and drank, but it had no purpose for its existence. And so it was that the twenty-year-old Severa would remain in a state of flux until the situation was resolved. She was neither a child nor a woman and, as such, was a drain on the dynamics of her family.

Endellion loathed this commonly held viewpoint. Through many years of care, she had come to love Severa, although the child had not always been particularly lovable. Prickly by nature, she was quick to fall into periods of sullen resentment or to make arrogant demands. For one brief period, under the spell of Decius, her father's old decurion, Severa had blossomed as she learned about her family, warts and all, from this loyal retainer. Perhaps all that Severa had ever really needed was love, plus a sense of place and importance.

'Why should Severa marry this man? She knows nothing about him and nothing has been done to convince us that he'll make a worthy husband. I'm not prepared to hand Severa over to a stranger without knowing a great deal about him and his future prospects.'

Aeron grinned at his wife with open approval.

'I warned the tribal kings that you'd have to be convinced of the necessity for this union. I don't know much about him myself. But it wouldn't be in his best interest to treat Severa badly, for she's the key to his future wealth and power, especially if he aspires to the purple.'

Endellion snorted contemptuously.

'The way Severa's father treasured her mother, I suppose. She was beaten so severely that she almost died.'

Aeron had the grace to be shame-faced at Endellion's

accusation. Many good men had failed Elen, who was the daughter of an Ordovice king. She had been Maximus's route to the throne of the Western Roman Empire. Friendless, and miles from her home and the bosom of her family, she had died in childbirth.

'I'll ensure that no such disaster will overcome Severa,' Aeron insisted.

'You can be assured that such a shameful occurrence won't be allowed to happen again, my lord. I'll make sure that it doesn't! This Marcus will have me to answer to if he treats Severa harshly. Meanwhile, I'll order the maids to ensure that rooms are prepared for his visit.' She grinned at her husband. 'I can only hope he's house-trained.'

'I'd like to think so, Endellion. After all, he is a Roman patrician.'

'So was Nero, and numerous tales have been circulated about his household manners. So too, for that matter, was Maximus. The man may have been your friend, Aeron, but you never fully trusted him.'

Endellion persisted in stepping beyond the boundaries that were laid down for well-bred, tribal wives, so her pronouncements often set Aeron's teeth on edge, although he respected his wife sufficiently to listen to her opinions. In the eyes of many of his neighbouring kings, he was too weak to school her properly, but Aeron knew Endellion was one of the most intelligent Britons, male or female, that he had ever met.

Heaven help this Marcus if he tries to patronise Endellion, Aeron thought seriously. Maybe I should warn him. No, we'll let this Roman candidate find out for himself, if he is foolish enough to adopt airs and graces around my uncompromising wife.

Severa was much easier to convince of the merits of this marriage contract than Endellion. She was more than ready for marriage, having become tired of the nursery and her lack of status in the king's household. Every one of her childhood acquaintances were wed now and blessed with children of their own, so Severa was prepared to accept any inadequacies in Marcus's appearance or manners if it meant she could leave Corinium with pride in her step.

'I love you and the children, Aunt Endellion. I really do! But what am I in this pretty house? I can't organise the household duties, although you've trained me to carry out these tasks if the necessity should arise. Nor am I a mother or a wife. I'm nothing, really! Your maids and every peasant in the household have more earthly purpose than I have.'

Endellion hugged Severa with a sudden surge of sympathy. 'I want you to be happy, my darling, but marriage isn't the only way to achieve fulfilment in what can be a life of tears and trouble. You don't have to wed a man whom you might come to detest. Some girls are given no choice in the husband who is selected for them, but I'll swear to you, with my hand on my crucifix, that you will never be forced into an unacceptable union.'

Severa looked deeply into Endellion's lambent green eyes. She had never felt so cherished.

'Thank you, Endellion. I'm grateful for your support. As for this Roman suitor who will soon arrive, I'll do my very best to like him. But I don't think I have the liberty to be too selective, do I.'

'You are the daughter of an emperor, so you mustn't bow your head to any man who is not your equal,' Endellion stated unequivocally. 'Our family loves you, darling girl, so I hope this

Marcus Britannicus will make a perfect husband, one who will present you with many children and a long and happy life.'

As promised, the small Roman contingent arrived in Corinium within the week. The youngish officer at the head of the column was Marcus Britannicus, as he was known by his few friends, or Marcus Shit-head, as he was described by his detractors. This particular patrician was not well liked by his men, or respected by his peers.

Constantinus, Marcus Britannicus's adjutant, had won some measure of fame as the centurion whose troops had crushed the Pictish invasion and forced the invaders to flee to the safety of the lands beyond Hadrian's Wall, so he was riding at the flank of his commander's horse. This promotion, although well deserved, was far less than Constantinus's due, but his plebeian birth closed the higher ranks to him. Many of the farmers and townsfolk who gathered to throw flowers at Marcus's feet had also come out of curiosity and a desire to see this Constantinus, a new Roman hero.

Aeron gazed at the handsome, chiselled face and noted the deference and respect that was seemingly accorded to him by the Roman cavalrymen who rode behind the senior officers. The king sighed with frustration. Constantinus had more charisma than the patrician he was protecting.

As he observed the mixed cavalcade of thirty-two Roman and British cavalrymen and a half-century of forty infantrymen, Aeron approved of the hard-bitten, determined expression on the faces of these men who followed in Marcus's wake, even if they seemed to defer more to Constantinus than Marcus Britannicus. At least the proposed High King would have battle-hardened men at his back.

From among the troops one boyish face stood out, causing Aeron a brief shiver of presentiment. This dark-haired lad was thick in the body, unlike many of the tribal warriors. Aeron could feel the boy's cold regard as he assessed Corinium, its people and its king.

With a clash of arms and a military salute, the troop came to a halt in the forecourt of the king's residence. Then, once Marcus Britannicus had dismounted and stitched a wholly false smile on to his face, Aeron invited his guest into the villa's atrium where his wife awaited them.

From a narrow window in the scriptorium, Endellion had been given time to examine the potential bridegroom's face and form before bowing deeply when she was introduced by her husband. From her vantage point, the queen's gaze had also been drawn to the boy in the furthest rank of the native cavalry.

A shadow seemed to pass across the sun and Endellion's odd gift of precognition meant that for an instant, she thought she could see a dead emperor with a boy's face; but it wasn't familiar to her. Then, as Severa entered the vantage point to peer out at the new arrivals with her foster-mother, the girl's shoulder came in contact with Endellion's arm and a sudden flash of insight burned across the back of the queen's eyes. Just for a moment, she saw a bloody babe as it wailed in equally bloody hands. Then Endellion regained her composure and descended to meet her guest at the forecourt.

Marcus was no taller than Endellion, but his frame was much heavier and, unlike many of his fellow officers, he was plump and soft around the belly. The extra flesh on his torso and neck blurred his jawline and padded the back of his hands whose short fingers were also sprinkled with sprays of ginger hair. At first glance, Marcus was more epicure than warrior.

His thick ginger hair was one of his vanities, so precious oils darkened the colour and kept his curls in place in a rigid line across his low forehead. Marcus was evidently a man for whom superficial appearances were important.

Endellion could smell the heavy, cloying scent of precious oils that had been laved into Marcus's skin and had permeated a fragment of cloth tied around his neck in order to protect his tender flesh from the rough edges of his armour. As she expected, the armour worn by the Roman was more ceremonial than practical. After a lifetime of living among fighting men, she was contemptuous of the overblown images of satyrs, nymphs and bunches of grapes that rioted across it. Even the Roman's helmet bore a representation of Medusa scowling out from its crown. Every item of armour seemed to be excessively decorated, so much so that Marcus was forced to carry his headdress under his arm. If the helm was designed to add to his height, as Endellion supposed, it failed because its awkwardness made it almost impossible to wear comfortably for extended periods.

With an arrogant nonchalance, Marcus bowed perfunctorily to the queen of the Dobunni tribe and stared around the atrium with a desultory glance that spoke of his scorn for these bucolic provincials. While the pear tree seemed to satisfy Marcus's expectations, it was obvious that the entire area lacked the dignity and beauty to which he was accustomed. Then, as he listened to Aeron's descriptions of Severa's virtues, Marcus gave a bored kick at one of the stones edging the garden bed and succeeded only in smearing fresh manure across the clean terrazzo floor. With a muffled oath, he cleaned his sandal on the same garden edging, muttering under his breath in irritation.

The king paused. He was aware that his guest was paying little attention to his host's welcome, so Aeron's mouth and brows scowled with displeasure.

'Should I send for a servant to clean your sandals?' Endellion asked scornfully.

'No! It's just some muck from your vegetable patch,' Marcus replied, although the suggestion that ornamental cabbages were planted for human consumption caused Endellion to bite her lip. Aristocratic villas in Italia often grew edible plants in their atriums; Marcus's scorn indicated his ignorance. Endellion was beginning to dislike Severa's young swain.

Surprised at the tone of the discussion, Aeron's face stiffened with his own insult. Either Marcus was partially blind, or he was determined to provoke the sensibilities of his hostess.

Constantinus, Marcus's adjutant, stepped forward and spoke tersely to Marcus. The Roman officer nodded his head apologetically towards the Dobunni rulers, his eyes seeming to reflect embarrassment at the rudeness of his superior officer. This centurion was handsome, in a masculine way, and something about his eyes both charmed and repelled Endellion.

'Do you wish me to stand the guard down for the night, my lord?' the adjutant asked in a carefully modulated voice. 'I've inspected the stables and the accommodation provided for our men will more than meet our expectations. Men and horses will be quite comfortable.'

'That would seem to be in order, Constantinus. You can stand them down immediately.'

Turning to Aeron, Marcus casually introduced his adjutant to the king and queen. 'May I present this young centurion to you? He is Constantinus, my adjutant and my second-in-command. He is one of Rome's best officers and has my total confidence. Any questions regarding the activities of my men can be referred directly to him. He has limited experience in the social graces, but he will carry out any tasks you may ask of him.'

The face of the young adjutant became flat and expressionless. Endellion felt a frisson of sympathy for him.

For his part, Marcus smiled vaguely and spoke directly to Aeron without any consideration for his lack of good manners. 'I'm rather tired after my long journey, King Aeron, so I'll feel more comfortable if I take some rest and meet with Lady Severa at a more convenient time.'

Aeron apologised tersely and turned to his queen. 'Endellion, send the maids to find the girl. She was here a moment ago, but she decided to brush her hair and refresh herself. Perhaps you might ask her to present herself immediately so our guest can recover from his long journey.'

Both Aeron and Endellion felt their hackles rise at Marcus's presumption. For a suitor who was petitioning for Severa's hand in marriage, he was acting as if he was conferring a meaningful gift on their household through his very presence.

'Not so, Highness! I'm very tired! As I said, I have undertaken a long journey and Mistress Severa will no doubt be grateful for some extra time to primp and pamper herself for the meeting with her suitor. Young girls like to be prepared for such meetings.' For reasons known only to himself, Marcus seemed eager to defer his first meeting with his prospective bride.

The young adjutant returned after ensuring that his legionnaires were satisfactorily billeted. Those who were part of Marcus's personal guard had been allocated better quarters within the palace itself.

Endellion had concluded that this Roman aristocrat who intended to court Severa was actually older than she had first thought because, although his ginger hair had a slight curl which even close shearing couldn't hide, one of his fine locks had escaped from his oiled hairline to roll over his ear, revealing traces of greyness. Endellion's lips curled scornfully, but she managed to suppress all signs of dislike and contempt by rising to her full height, staring directly into Marcus's eyes and launching into speech.

'If you'll follow me, sir, I will take you to your quarters where you may rest and refresh yourself. I will instruct your manservant as to the location of the baths and other facilities you will need for your personal comfort. Severa will be present at the evening feast, so you can meet her at a time when she's at her best.'

Marcus nodded and stalked away ahead of her. He was obviously unwilling to permit a woman to lead the way. So she skipped ahead of him with a wicked smile and led the small party into the domestic wings of the villa.

When he was ushered into his spacious apartment, Marcus could find no fault with the large, airy rooms. Endellion pointed out the small cubicle intended as quarters for his manservant and another, smaller anteroom that had been provided for his adjutant. Marcus nodded rather ungraciously before throwing himself across the fine bed and soiling the furs with the dirt from his sandals. Behind her, Endellion heard a slight indrawing of breath as the adjutant winced.

Endellion made her bows and pulled the door closed behind her, before sighing deeply. This Roman was a bore and his manners were execrable, but he had the power to deliver Severa from a life of barren uselessness. Would he make a suitable husband, or was his character too flawed?

Time will untangle this skein, the queen decided as she made her way back to the atrium. I'll not coerce her, regardless of the cost.

Oddly, Endellion was certain that the problems of this match would be solved. How this would happen, or why, eluded her gift. She must wait until in the fullness of time everything was revealed.

As Endellion reached the atrium, the adjutant caught up with her in the passageway, having ensured that his master's immediate requirements had been met. He bowed low as he drew level with her, his black curls catching the light with the colour of mulberries.

'Your Highness,' he greeted her as he paused, allowing Endellion to notice that his dark eyes were very intelligent and knowing. The hair on her arms rose in response.

'Yes?' she answered.

'My master is weary from his travels, so I'd ask that you excuse any failings in courtesy on his part.' As he spoke, Constantinus blushed; he was breaking the first maxim of the legions. Rome's soldiers must never apologise to the local aristocracy.

Endellion smiled and waved away any hint of an apology, for she realised that this centurion would not normally have made such an admission.

'I noticed a very young Briton among the cavalrymen and I could clearly see that he wasn't a Roman. Who is he?'

Grateful to the queen for ignoring his earlier gaffe in protocol, Constantinus was more than willing to satisfy Endellion's curiosity.

'The lad's name is Vortigern, Highness, and he is the son of the king of the Demetae tribe. He has been sent to Deva to learn the ways of the legions. He's a promising young man, so he absorbs knowledge like a sea sponge.'

Endellion nodded as if this trivial piece of information was of little account. However, the name echoed through her skull with the sound of storm winds. Vortigern! It had an ugly sound and her extra senses quivered with the recognition of danger.

With her feelings under control, she smiled distantly and escaped into the triclinium where the servants were preparing for the night's feast. Nor did Endellion depart from this room until she was certain that the adjutant had passed through the villa's entrance that took him out into the forecourt. His eyes saw too much.

THE TOWN OF CORINIUM
AND ITS ENVIRONS

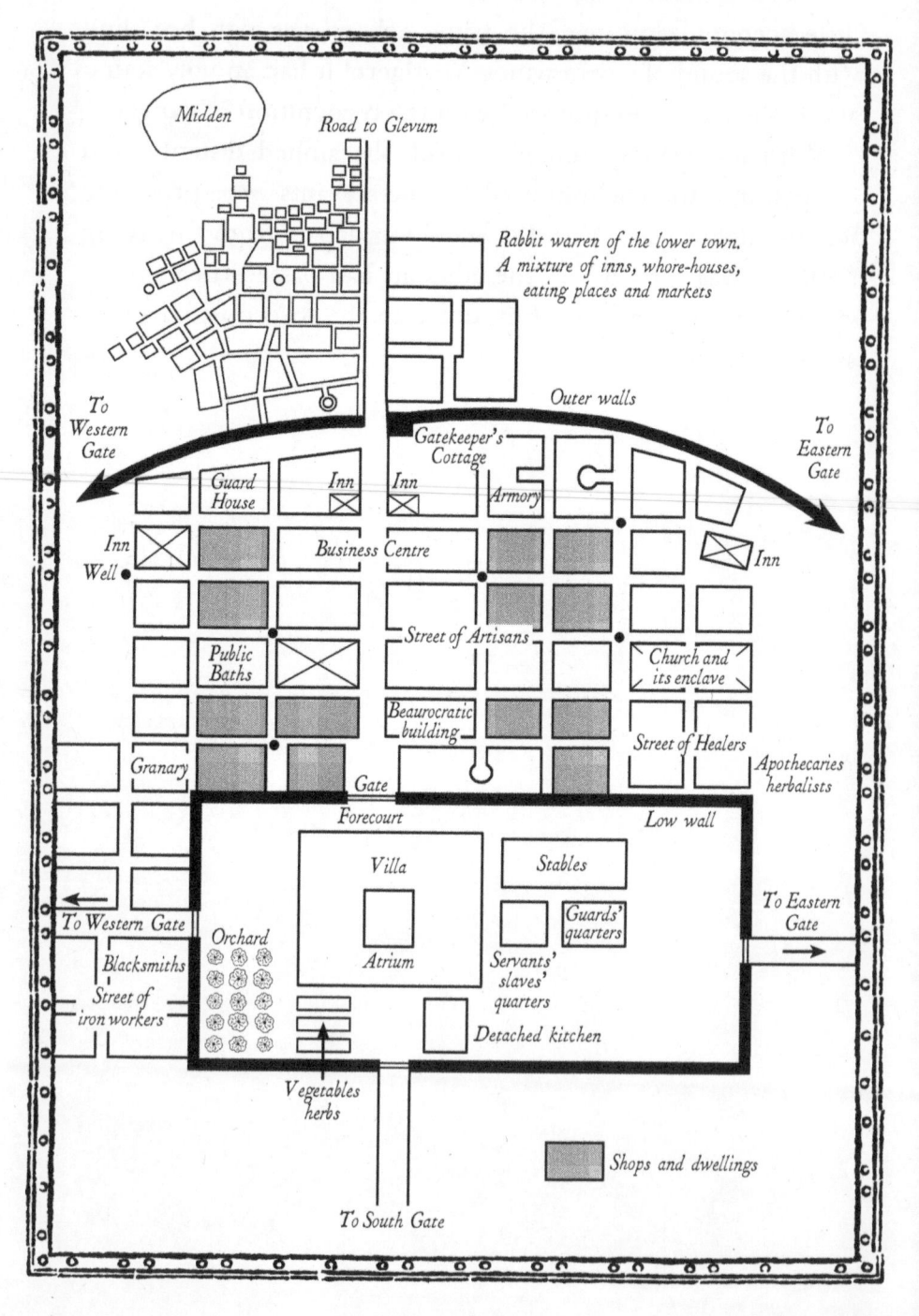

CHAPTER III

LOVE AND MARRIAGE

Wilt thou have this woman to thy wedded wife, to live together after God's ordinance in the holy estate of Matrimony? Wilt though love her, comfort her, honour, and keep her in sickness and in health; and, forsaking all other, keep thee only unto her, so long as ye both shall live?

Solemnisation of Matrimonial Exhortation,
Book of Common Prayer

The priests had come as representatives of several disparate groups of tribal kings, with assorted princes, to oversee the interests of their families and absorb every detail of Corinium, its defences and the efficiency of Aeron's agricultural and military expertise. As an afterthought, these aristocrats were also charged with the task of recording details of Severa's appearance, manners and opinions and to watch the performance of the Roman, Marcus Britannicus, who was expected to become the High King of the Britons.

The villa was filled to bursting and every Dobunni aristocrat was expected to do their duty and either find space for a visiting dignitary or provide billets for their attendants. Endellion, given no peace, was required to rush through every waiting hour ensuring that her guests were content and replete. Her facial muscles ached from hours spent smiling inanely while attempting to look sincere, a seemingly hopeless task since she was convinced that Severa could never find happiness with such a rude and pretentious Roman as Marcus Britannicus.

Aeron and she presided over the legal rites of the marriage agreement without any real enthusiasm, but they maintained brave faces out of respect for Severa. When Endellion's girl had finally met her Roman suitor, he had exerted himself to be charming and, because Severa was inexperienced for a woman of twenty summers, she was easily impressed by his suave boasting.

Endellion had sought out her ward on the third day of Marcus's visit.

'Well, my dear, what do you think of him?' Endellion asked in her most forthright manner. Severa blushed hotly at the question. 'Can I assume that you liked him?'

'I'm having difficulty making up my mind, Mother Endellion. I've had few opportunities to meet potential suitors, so I'm unable to make a reasoned assessment of his suitability. He's very free with his compliments and he does have a manly appearance.'

'I suppose you're right,' Endellion answered with an edge to her voice that Severa knew indicated her dislike for this particular young man.

'I know you worry about me, Mother Endellion, and you're concerned that the man I eventually marry will try to use me to win power and a throne. But I will have to marry someone at some point in my life. I yearn to give birth to babies of my own before I'm too old and too careworn to enjoy their creation.

Master Marcus might be a little pompous, but he's attractive enough and we know that he's a man of means.'

'A little pompous,' Endellion almost spat out the words. 'That young man's sense of his own importance reminds me of a bladder that has been filled to its full extension. He must be careful where he stands in case someone inadvertently pierces that self-importance. Have you ever considered another man in your search for a husband?'

Severa's cheeks paled with embarrassment, then two spots of colour gradually appeared on each cheek.

'So there is another young male who has caught your eye. You must tell me, Severa. Who is this man?'

'My feelings shouldn't be a matter of vulgar curiosity, Mother Endellion,' Severa retorted shortly, but she was quick to apologise. 'I have no reason to think that Marcus's adjutant even notices me ... but my heart has skipped a beat on the few occasions I have seen him. I've learned that he has a young son called Constans. He must be wed, but he is a fine young man and seems to have excellent manners. I'm told that his men hold him in high regard. Unfortunately, I must seem like a halfwit to the poor man, for I have been rude to him or stupid on those few occasions when I have been in his presence.'

Endellion carefully examined her ward's face as the girl began to blush even more under her foster-mother's close scrutiny. Severa may have been flattered by Marcus's compliments, but in the days that followed, Endellion had many opportunities to see the admiration in her ward's eyes whenever the handsome young adjutant came into view.

Endellion began to wonder about this young man and his prospects in Roman Britannia.

* * *

For his part, the adjutant also felt the same feather-like brush of attraction, but he was tortured by other, darker emotions less palatable to an honourable officer of the legion.

At first sight of the beautiful Severa, Constantinus had recalled the ravings of an old hermit and his promise of future greatness. Instinct, or the touch of Lady Fortuna, told him clearly that Severa was the woman who could hold his future in her aristocratic hands.

But this princess was so far above his station that any thought of the prophecy reaching fruition was nonsense. He told himself to put all thoughts of her out of his mind.

'You didn't know what you were talking about, old man,' Constantinus muttered to himself as he fled from Severa's tongue-tied presence after they accidently met in the atrium.

Both young people had been unable to look directly at the other.

Late at night, in the cubicle allotted to him in the villa, Constantinus wondered how Severa would fare as the wife of Marcus Britannicus. The Shit-head was known for his pretentiousness, his rudeness to inferiors and an all-consuming taste for low sex, so Constantinus feared that the girl would have reason to regret the match that had been made for her. But since the centurion had neither birth nor powerful friends to recommend him, Severa would soon become Marcus's wife. Fortuna had turned her ironic face away from this girl.

With some regret, Constantinus decided to dismiss the prophecy as the madness of a reclusive old hermit in an attempt to forget Severa's clear and trusting eyes.

With almost indecent haste, the clerics and contract-makers of the land were summoned to carry out the formalities of marriage from the moment that Severa gave a bland acceptance to Marcus Britannicus's final proposal. Neither the prospective bridegroom nor the bride seemed terribly excited about the prospect although, when Marcus placed what should have been a chaste kiss on the cheek of the bride, he took the opportunity to grip her firmly by the buttocks with one hand in a manner that embarrassed both Severa and her guardians.

He was already laying claim to his property.

Sharp-eyed Endellion saw Marcus's groping hand and noted that the Roman adjutant winced and turned his eyes away from the spectacle.

As the city began to fill with strangers and citizens with important and dignified names, both Aeron and Constantinus began to feel some concern. The king's young son, Pridenow, had caused some alarm during the previous night, when he woke screaming after a series of sleep-horrors in which he babbled of blood-splattered bodies and burned features. For her part, Endellion had also felt the presence of nameless terrors that rose in her imagination like a tide of filthy water.

Yet Marcus felt no inkling of this miasma of impending disaster. As arrogant as ever, and as patronising as any emperor who had already been crowned, the Roman wandered through his days in Corinium, signing the required documents with a flourish whenever he was asked to do so, while devouring the last pears from the trees in Endellion's orchard. He even dropped the cores indiscriminately and ignored most of the dignitaries with scant regard for diplomacy or tact. By the fourth occasion that she had been forced to pick up his fruit cores, Endellion would have happily killed the man herself.

The business aspects of the matrimonial contract were eventually completed and the last cleric departed from

Corinium. The princes, kinglets and witnesses were on their way, surrounded by their guards, and the Dobunni royal family sighed deeply, for their premonitions had told them that there was some risk of a political assassination. Despite the departure of their noble guests and the completion of the regal betrothal, Pridenow's eyes remained hollowed and bruised from his recollection of his bad dreams, while Endellion felt revolted by the sight and smell of food. Mercifully, Marcus did not insist on his conjugal rights with his betrothed, a demand which he could have exercised before the wedding, once the legal niceties had been met.

In fact, he was feeling in a celebratory mood. Aeron had insisted that Severa's dowry should be provided by the council of kings, so his betrothed came with a casket of river pearls, bars of Cymru gold, a cache of fine weapons from both ends of the province, many bolts of finely woven wool and exotic cloth. Like a large fat cat, Marcus purred in the sunshine and drank Aeron's best wines with the appreciation of an epicure.

But Marcus chafed under the dignified confines of family life. He was aware that the tribal queen, that long streak of opinionated and aging womanhood, considered his appearance and his manners to be inappropriate. His own stepmother in Italia had worn that same scornful look, as if she could smell something rank on his person. Meanwhile, Severa would suffice as a wife in these backward lands, but he had no intention of taking her back to Rome. His friends would laugh at him.

Inevitably, Marcus broke away from all strictures.

Corinium was far from the ports along Britannia's coasts, so the town lacked a discreet district where whores and houses of ill repute were in clear evidence. But no town will ever be entirely free from prostitution; outside the town gates, and free from the direct control of the city fathers, several grimy streets boasted houses with grandiose names like the House of Rose Petals and the Bower of Beauties. The actual structures were ramshackle and dun-coloured. Neither Endellion nor her husband considered for a moment that a guest of breeding, such as Marcus Britannicus, would contemplate a visit to the verminous streets of the Whore's Quarter.

But Marcus Britannicus was bored and he had always considered virginal young girls to be tedious and unexciting. Regardless of her beauty, Severa was too tall and far too robust for his taste. He had felt the strength in the muscles under her fine, golden skin and had been repulsed on the one occasion when he had taken her hand. He might have been flattered if she had been in awe of him, but the expression in her guileless blue eyes told him that she was trying to guess at his motives whenever he was in her presence. Marcus recoiled from such female curiosity and took pains to avoid her, except when he had little choice.

I will need to get her with child, so I'll be obliged to bed her eventually, Marcus thought casually after one unsatisfactory meeting. Afterwards, I can do as I please. With any luck at all, the bitch will die in childbirth like her mother, and I'll have the throne, my heirs and all that her dowry has brought to my marriage. I'll say one thing for these dirty Britons. They understand gold and have made sure that she has a significant dowry.

Then Marcus felt Endellion's gaze boring into the side of his head and he turned towards her with an obliging smile.

Damn the bitch, he thought acidly. Who does she think she is?

'I pray that you'll be happy with my Severa,' Endellion began bluntly, as she invaded his personal space in such a way that hinted she had no such expectation. 'I should tell you, my lord, that while I was sired by a famed and noble warrior, I am also the daughter of a seer. I always keep my promises and, because Severa is so very dear to me, I would be sorry if I found myself at odds with her newly wed husband. I have always admired our Roman friends and colleagues, because my father gave me a detailed understanding of your people.'

'How could any man wish harm on a sweet girl like Severa?' Marcus replied with a smooth, amiable expression that failed to reach his eyes.

'These things can happen, my lord. I'm sometimes surprised to discover that there are some ignorant Romans who still believe us to be superstitious savages, despite the fact that most of us worship the gentle Jesus and have come to reject the old religions.'

Marcus realised that her smile was as false as his own, yet he found himself enjoying the game he was playing. His mind drifted off to thoughts of his mother and his patrician wife who were safely domiciled in Rome. He shuddered delicately as he compared the women of Rome with those of the provinces. If this tribal female thought that she could win this exchange of banal hyperbole, Marcus was determined to prove her mistaken. His smile remained sweet as he countered her riposte.

'Come, Your Highness. I've seen a number of your native rulers parading themselves with their talismans and the crude images of long-gone deities. I would be the first to commend your husband for providing the niceties of life, such as your baths, but most of his peers are ignorant, illiterate and unclean. Indeed many of them have a bad smell that precedes them.'

Endellion flushed at his sneer of triumph. 'We all smell to some extent, Marcus, even if the more civilised among us have learned to conceal it with perfumes and precious oils. My father would have counselled you to watch what the British kings do, rather than be influenced by what they reveal to you in open discussion. He would also have advised you to be cautious among the women of Britannia, females who have demonstrated an ability to be more than mere decoration in bygone days.'

Marcus cleared his throat and paled a little. 'Are you threatening me, Lady Endellion, now that we can loosely be described as kin?'

Endellion widened her eyes as if his words had surprised her.

'Me, Marcus Britannicus? I would never do that! There would be no gain in threatening you because, as you say, we are almost linked by marriage. I believe we will come to know and understand each other very well in the years ahead.'

Not if I order you to be garrotted to stop your wagging tongue, Marcus thought.

Endellion understood him as clearly as if he had spoken aloud.

'I find myself a little weary after your kind hospitality,' he said. 'So I beg you to pardon my departure in advance. I plan to go to my bed early this evening, so I can be fresh for my bride and the blessing of the church on the morrow.'

You're a nasty worm and I'll wager you're up to something vile, Endellion thought, without a flicker of her feelings crossing her face.

Having said nothing that was openly offensive, the two aristocrats parted. Despite their diplomatic banter, each was hoping that the other would choke on their supper.

Aeron never thought to warn the guard that they should observe Marcus's movements, or to provide him with any form of security. Quite simply, it never occurred to the king that this

Roman nobleman would choose to frolic with the pimps, whores and bullyboys of the mean streets outside the city limits.

Marcus Britannicus had learned through experience that noblewomen and respectable servants recoiled from some of his more exotic and disgusting pleasures. Unwilling to give Aeron any power over him, Marcus decided to relieve his persistent itch by cavorting with the denizens of the Bower of Beauty where, if a girl died or was badly scarred, an exchange of coins would always put the matter to rights. On those occasions when he was in a mood to suffer personal punishment, he became particularly careful. While sadism was considered to be a manly pursuit, the desire to be debased and defiled was generally considered by Marcus's peers to be contemptible. He had no desire to be mocked by his troops over his personal pleasures.

So the Roman commander ordered his only fully trusted personal guardsman to make the necessary arrangements for a night of pleasure with a small group of tawdry women inside one of Corinium's whorehouses, a place where he had no need to maintain a pretence if he had sufficient coin to pay for the women's services.

Constantinus, in his commander's opinion, was far too naïve and prim to understand Marcus's preferences for exotic pleasures, so he informed his adjutant that he would be enjoying an evening alone.

Like any competent adjutant, Constantinus had heard tales of Marcus's more repulsive sexual escapades at first hand, so he was unable to school his face entirely, or to maintain his usual bland expression. Why any man would enjoy being disciplined by a naked woman was beyond the centurion's understanding.

'I would hate to think that you are sneering at me, Constantinus, for I won't tolerate insolence from my junior officers. You'd be well advised to understand that I'll soon become the High King of the Britons once I return to Deva with my bride. I will then have the authority of the Britons as well as the power of Rome to enforce my will.' Marcus smiled throughout this threat, his porcine face dripping with sweat as he savoured the discomfort of his adjutant. 'I'd suggest that you should ensure I lead a contented life, else you'll end up in some flea-bitten fort at the far reaches of the Roman provinces.'

'I am yours to command, Highness,' Constantinus replied, forcing himself to ignore his natural affront. A lifetime of self-control was serving him well.

'Find my personal guards! They will accompany me during my absence from the palace. I won't need your protection, and I wouldn't appreciate any curiosity on your part.'

'I wouldn't be doing my duty if I didn't warn you that there are enemies of Rome, Excellency, even in a peaceful place like Corinium. There are men in these lands who would pay much for a chance to be alone with you. I beg you not to leave the town limits unless you take six of your most trusted men with you and, in addition, send some of our legionnaires to reconnoitre any destination you intend to visit. I ask that you take basic precautions, sir, and accept my advice in the spirit in which it is offered.'

If Marcus had hoped to punish Constantinus by dismissing this advice, then he should have been happy. The adjutant could feel the palms of his callused hands begin to itch with a premonition of impending disaster as soon as the commander waved away his imprecations. Disguised by dark clothing, Marcus rode away at dusk. He was flanked by two of his most trusted guardsmen who were noted more for their sycophancy than for their fighting skills, leaving Constantinus to cool his heels in the royal villa.

The hours limped slowly by.

The watch was changed, and even in the stews of the outer town, the lights were slowly extinguished as the sounds of carousing in the inns died away. And yet there was no indication that Marcus and his guardsmen were making a belated return to the royal villa. Constantinus was becoming more and more concerned for the safety of his commander for he knew that Marcus would never sleep in the dirty beds of the Bower of Beauty, regardless of the deviant pleasure that had been enjoyed among the lice and bugs. So where was he?

Constantinus's nerves had stretched to breaking point by the time he lost all patience.

'Paulus! Crispus!' Constantinus bellowed, careless of who might be wakened if he decided to initiate a search. Fortunately the two officers were billeted in the villa, so they were immediately at hand. They appeared before him in an instant, an indication that they, too, had been awake.

'Rouse ten men immediately and order them to don full battle kit. Our commander hasn't returned and I'm concerned for his safety.'

The veterans shot concerned glances at Constantinus and hurried to carry out his bidding as quickly as possible. They knew that this adjutant had a nose for trouble and wielded a thoroughly wicked gladius, but Shit-head wouldn't thank them if they were to disturb the entire garrison while carrying out an unnecessary search.

But, because Constantinus was approachable with the men, they respected his rank and obeyed his commands without hesitation.

In contrast Paulus and Crispus had learned quickly that Marcus Britannicus was never wrong, even when proved to be so.

'I can still remember the Ides of March last year when the Picts attacked us after Shit-head led us into that river valley without sending scouts out to scour the countryside,' Crispus remarked in a low voice. 'Marcus had Rusticus beaten half to death when he failed to hold his place in the line. And he inflicted the punishment in front of Rusticus's troop. The poor bastard opened his wrists, and I still hold Shit-head responsible for his death. Rusticus was a good kid. He might have been a little green, but he was a good legionnaire, for all that.'

'I'd keep my mouth shut about Shit-head if I was you,' Crispus murmured, his eyes scanning the shadows of the stables in case they had been overheard. 'The walls have ears and we know that the bastard will pay for information about those he suspects might be disloyal to him. We'll suffer for our sins if we flap our gums carelessly. Besides, the adjutant wouldn't like it, and I do care what *he* thinks.'

The bunks of the sleeping legionnaires stretched along the full length of the long room above the stables. The facilities were cleaner and more comfortable than most billets provided for common soldiers, so the men who were wakened from their sleep seemed well rested and content with their lot. Normally, being roused in the middle of the night from a warm bed would elicit an angry and defiant response, but Corinium had seen to the full bellies and creature comforts of these Roman soldiers for several weeks, more than most of them had experienced during years of military service.

None of the legionnaires, or their officers, expected any real problems. Constantinus had no doubt that Marcus would be furious to be roused from between a whore's breasts by his inferiors, but the adjutant was adamant that his commander should sleep within the safe walls of the city. He tried to ignore the suspicion that Marcus was in any real danger, except from some of the unpleasant sexual diseases that were ever-present among the lower denizens of Romano-British society. Wisely, he had always kept his mouth shut on the subject.

The small troop marched out of Corinium under the pale light of a gelid moon. Constantinus briefly imagined that he was leading a troop of cadavers who had recently died and had turned livid at the lips and the fingers, but were still stiffly animated under the cold, unnatural glow. As if they shared his fancy, his men moved silently, without the usual clang of weapons or noisy footfalls on the cobblestones. Even their steaming breath in the cold air seemed part of a poisonous miasma.

The guard had passed through the gates of the town on foot as there seemed to be little advantage in rousing stable boys and preparing horses for such a short journey, even to carry an inebriated commander back to his quarters in the royal villa. The road was wide, as befitted a major thoroughfare leading to Glevum, so the men marched easily and maintained their gait without difficulty. As the hour was long past midnight, the laneways leading off from the main artery were dark and silent, and all open fires had been cold for some time. Then, once the troop reached a crossroad, complete with an empty gibbet, Constantinus led the patrol down dark alleyways and entered a maze of ramshackle, double-storey buildings that leaned drunkenly towards each other. Rickety, external stairs that hadn't been painted for many years led up into dark rooms under the eaves of steep decrepit roofs.

The two streets that had been given over to sexual licence were, superficially, the best tended in the outer village. But Constantinus knew that first impressions were deceiving, for some entrepreneurial pimp or madam had used whitewash to disguise the dirtier planks along the façades. Unfortunately, the stench of invisible latrines and accumulated filth in corners of the laneways was so rank that he almost gagged. Several mangy dogs lifted their wary heads out of the darkness, growled threateningly, and then melted away.

Surprisingly, the streets were utterly empty, and no comatose vagrants were sleeping drunkenly in the shadows. At this late hour, wastrels and carousers would usually be found in various stages of undress and inebriation along this trouble-some stretch which boasted several wine shops and alehouses, although they had already closed. Alert to unseen danger, Constantinus peered into the darkness and saw that there was no movement in the malodorous spaces between the buildings and the filthy gutters.

Paulus caught the adjutant's eye. 'Something's wrong here, master. There's not a slut in sight, and there's no pimps or drunks. I'm beginning to think that Shit-head might be in real trouble.'

'Two men to the front, two on each side and two behind us,' Constantinus ordered crisply. He felt the hairs on the nape of his neck rise.

'Keep your wits about you, boys,' Paulus said quietly.

Although his nerves were screaming that some disaster awaited them, Constantinus thanked his lucky stars that veterans had been sent to Corinium as Marcus's junior officers.

'Thanks be to Mithras that Tribune Maximo didn't trust Shit-head any further than he can throw him,' Paulus added, although the adjutant shot the decurion a warning glance before moving towards the guards at the head of the troop, who had slowed and were moving as silently as possible.

And then their destination came into view.

A battered, primitive sign depicting a naked woman loomed out of the darkness, lit by the two torches born by the leading guardsmen.

The name, Bower of Beauty, was obviously a joke on the part of the owners, considering that a skeletal moon obscured much of the brothel's dirty face. The crude painting and a crooked sign in struggling writing proclaimed its name, but the building itself was ugly and even more ramshackle than its immediate neighbours. None of the men could understand why any man of discernment would want to seek amusement in such a place.

'The girls here must be offering special favours,' Trufo, a legionnaire, hissed at Crispus, who simply grunted in reply.

Constantinus frowned at both men before advancing to a set of raw wooden stairs. Careful of loose boards, he pounded on the door with his bare fist. There was no sign of either a door knocker or a bell that could be used to waken the building's inhabitants.

Constantinus pounded again, but the house remained dark and uninviting.

Undismayed, he removed his dagger from its scabbard and rapped with the hilt, setting up such a racket that the noise should have woken the heaviest of sleepers. An oil lamp flickered to life in one of the adjacent buildings, but the Bower of Beauty remained silent and dark.

Eventually, a muffled female voice swore crudely from somewhere in the building's upper storey, while Constantinus eventually heard dragging footsteps. Untrusting, he stepped back from the door and kept his dagger at the ready in his left hand.

The creak of rusting hinges heralded the opening of the unprepossessing entryway. A woman holding an oil lamp that reeked of fish oil peered out at them.

'What do you want? This is no time to come looking for a girl. Come back tomorrow.'

The woman would have slammed the door shut in his face, but Constantinus thrust his shod foot into the space between the door and the doorframe. A blowsy face glared at him from out of the darkness.

Constantinus was immediately on his guard. Unless she was blind or drunk, the woman could hardly miss the polished armour and red cloaks worn by legionnaires. Even her affected language seemed false, as if she was trying desperately to sound and look as if everyone in this house was uneducated, stupid and harmless. He indicated that his torchbearer should illuminate the features of the woman who looked down on them.

The harridan had a wild, unbrushed tangle of red hair liberally streaked with white. Thick cosmetics had turned her wrinkled features into a parody of youth and her speech revealed that she had lost her two front teeth. The remainder of her mouth was filled with brown canines that jutted out from greyish gums. Her generous breasts were largely hidden by a dirty wrapper that had once been a beautiful silk shawl but was now stained with perspiration, food, wine and other nameless substances. Her feet were bare and dirty.

'Paulus! Bind this harlot! Trufo? Send in five of the men to rouse the girls and anyone else who might be sleeping inside the house. You can drag Marcus out as politely as you can!'

Then, in mid-sentence, Constantinus became very still, like a hunting dog that suddenly takes the scent and stiffens in every muscle.

Trufo followed the direction of the adjutant's pointing fingers and there, on the cracked interior wall of wattle and painted daub, the bloody handprint of a man could be seen in the torchlight. A small puddle of the same dark, viscous liquid seemed to be drying on the coarse flooring.

'That's blood!' Trufo hissed to Paulus, as the whole tenor of this mission changed.

These legionnaires' commander was now in grave danger.

The oil lamp was removed from the whore's shaking hands before she could throw it at Constantinus. Forced to restrain her, Paulus took great care to avoid her filthy, hooked claws in case they broke skin and infected him with disease. In the process of binding her and dragging her down the steps, the drab's grey bush and loins were exposed and Constantinus marvelled that any intelligent man could be so desperate that he would risk his life and his health to slake his desires inside her grimy flesh. Then, as she tripped over some large stones in a corner of the muddy roadway, she began to scream and curse, so Paulus cuffed her around the ears to shut her up.

With typical Roman efficiency, the legionnaires began to strip the house of all potential threats and arrest the occupants of the building.

Three more women were roused and dragged out of the building, as well as two large men who were obviously the house's bodyguards. One of them had the pegged teeth and blurred features of an unfortunate who had been born with few wits. Like a child, the huge man wailed and wept until the centurion ordered him to be gagged.

The other bodyguard was smaller, whipcord thin and dark-haired, although a large bald spot on the crown of his head marked him as middle-aged. Even though he had been sleeping in his filthy underwear, Crispus soon discovered that this man was heavily armed. With brutal efficiency, the legionnaire stripped him of two wicked throwing knives, one in a scabbard at the small of his back, the other strapped to his left calf.

Two more women, obviously worn-out old whores who were now working as slaves, were found in a tiny, locked room adjacent to the grimy kitchens. But there were no signs of Marcus Britannicus and his two guards, other than those ominous bloodstains.

'Crispus! Get yourself back to the stables and rouse the rest of our legionnaires,' Constantinus ordered briskly. 'They must don their armour and march here at speed. Once here, they will wait in the street until such time as I issue further orders. Then leave the men to their officers and go to King Aeron's apartments and inform him personally that Marcus Britannicus is missing. The king is to be woken without any demur from his servants. Tell him that I will speak with him as soon as I have clarified the situation with the vermin who inhabit this place. There's one final task! I'll need my horse, so have it saddled and brought to me.'

'Aye, sir! But is it a little late to be rousing the king and his household?'

Constantinus's glare would have frozen milk.

'Until such time as Marcus Britannicus is found, I'm in total command of this detachment. I don't countenance *anyone* questioning my orders. Ever! Is that understood?'

The adjutant had spoken in his normal conversational voice, so perhaps it was this total lack of emotion that chilled the legionnaire's blood. Suddenly, waking the king of the Dobunni seemed not only reasonable, but vitally important.

'Bring more torches!' Constantinus added. 'Marcus must be found before first light.'

Crispus took off in double time. By the time he had returned with reinforcements, horses and blazing torches, the brothel was being torn apart. But their best efforts were ineffectual.

'King Aeron will join us shortly. He was abed and asleep when my message concerning our commander's plight reached him,' Crispus informed the adjutant as the troops were ordered into small squads to begin a door-to-door search of the outskirts of the lower town. The noise of the searchers had already roused the citizenry, who huddled at their windows and listened to the complex orders being issued to the legionnaires while trying to appear unobtrusive. But Constantinus understood all too well that a leaf couldn't fall in this outer community without one of the civilians hearing or seeing it drop, so he had no hesitation in sending small, three-man squads from door to door with instructions to question, search or torture any citizen who might have borne witness to the fate of the luckless Marcus Britannicus.

The searching troops found little of interest, except for a ragged trail of blood-splashes that stood out blackly against the cobbles and mud of the roadway. When an innkeeper was questioned near to one of the small bloodstains, Trufo applied a minimal amount of persuasion to convince the pasty-skinned host that he should reveal all he knew.

'I looked out from behind the shutters when I heard a group of men dragging three Romans down the street. One of the Romans seemed to be bleeding and he wasn't able to stand without help from his friends. I thought he might have been unconscious or drunk. But he could have been dead. Who knows? The fat one was blubbering and he was trying to scream but they shoved a dirty neckcloth in his gob. He was gurgling and crying like a babe. He made a run for it, but his fat legs weren't suited for any kind of flight. They caught up with him real quick, so they cuffed him about to let him know who was boss. When I was younger, Romans were real men. They were a different breed than this coward.'

When the adjutant was called to the square, he eyed the thin innkeeper with scarcely concealed disgust.

'Didn't it occur to you to call for the watch to help these men?' he asked.

'The five men who took the Romans away were all bullyboys. I've seen them around Corinium for weeks and they've been ripping silver out of decent businessmen like me. But we don't get any protection from the watch or the king's men. Any one of those bastards could break me in two with one hand tied behind his back.'

'You could have made some sort of effort to help your fellow citizens, couldn't you?' Constantinus spat. 'If Marcus Britannicus should die because you kept your tongue firmly trapped between your teeth, I might be forced to remove it personally.'

The innkeeper blanched at the threat and the name of one of the men who had been unceremoniously dragged through the streets. The king arrived at that very moment, so the villain thanked his many gods, hoping that the Roman adjutant with the wintry eyes might just forget his existence during the course of the continuing hunt.

Left momentarily to his own devices, the innkeeper took the opportunity to dart back into his inn while the searchers were discussing the situation with King Aeron. He scooped up a bag containing gold and silver coins, a rusty sword and a rolled sleeping pallet, before darting out through one of the rear doors, having decided to make an instant departure from Corinium.

Every Roman legionnaire and an increasing number of native troops were soon being added to the search parties scouring the streets and lanes of Corinium for some sign of Marcus Britannicus and his two guards. Constantinus had already concluded that Marcus might never return to his own comfortable bed, a fate brought on by his own stupidity.

But if Shit-head had been murdered, the Romans must find the killers and make them pay. A blow against a Roman was always reciprocated by blows against the perpetrators . . . and their families. Rome was a cruel master when her rules were flouted.

Meanwhile, the search parties had been instructed to bring each and every citizen out into the street so that suspicious persons could be found and interrogated. But the adjutant was becoming increasingly frustrated as their search came to naught. The earth seemed to have opened up and swallowed Marcus Britannicus and his two guards. As a further hour passed by, Constantinus accepted that his superior might never be found, as capture for ransom seemed like an unlikely prospect.

'This abduction might be some political ploy if these British curs aren't holding Marcus for ransom. Any number of tribal kings would be smiling if a potential union between Marcus Britannicus and Severa should come to nothing. Damn and bugger! We're probably looking for his corpse!'

Although Constantinus had whispered the words to himself, he took pains to avoid being overheard by those troops who were in earshot. Yet, for all his care, he could feel the wise eyes of King Aeron boring into the side of his face with grim attention.

He knows! Oh, shite! Why did Marcus have to be such a stupid, lascivious sod?

The search parties had reached the edge of the old town by now and were investigating the areas that lay beyond the last of the town shanties. Banking fires were just visible under the piles of stinking rubbish in the town midden. Constantinus knew, as did King Aeron, that the midden would have to be searched from end to end, regardless of its vile contents. As Constantinus began preparations for the task, the white moon stared down enigmatically from small gaps in a bank of charcoal clouds.

THE MURDER SITE OUTSIDE THE WALLS OF CORINIUM

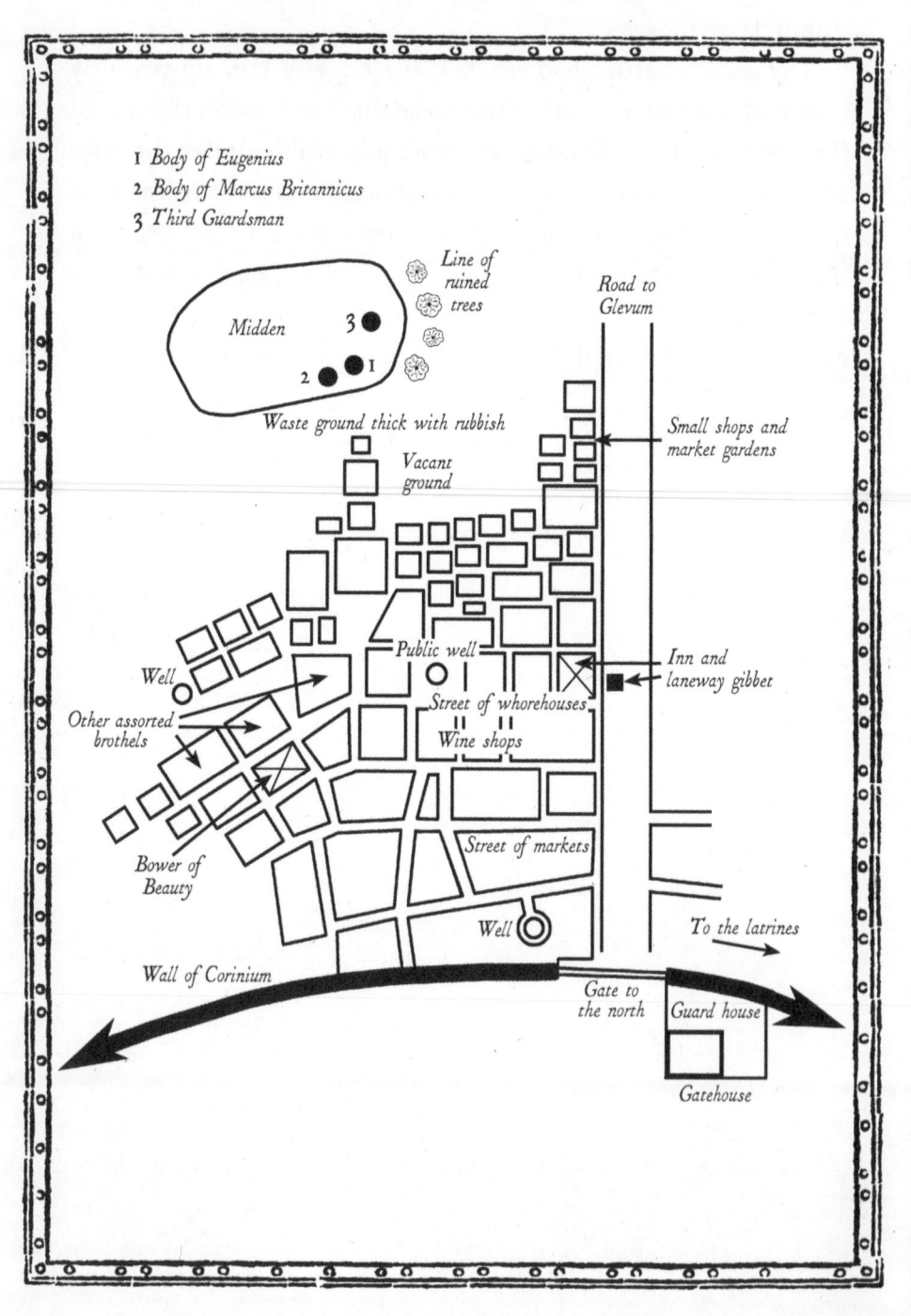

1 Body of Eugenius
2 Body of Marcus Britannicus
3 Third Guardsman

Line of ruined trees

Midden

Road to Glevum

Waste ground thick with rubbish

Small shops and market gardens

Vacant ground

Public well

Well

Inn and laneway gibbet

Street of whorehouses

Other assorted brothels

Wine shops

Bower of Beauty

Street of markets

Well

To the latrines

Wall of Corinium

Gate to the north

Guard house

Gatehouse

CHAPTER IV

OUT OF DEATH COMES LIFE

Each man is the smith of his own fortune.

Solem

Paulus saw the hand first. He had grown to manhood in Old Gallia and watched as Rome was driven back from the north, yard by bloody yard, until his eyes became as sharp as those of the eagles atop his standards. This hand was bloodless and very white against the blackness of rotting rubbish. A single scar, darker than the leached flesh, snaked across the knuckles.

'It's Eugenius! A Pict almost took his fingers off his hand with an axe some years ago, so I'd know that scar anywhere. What a place for a good legionnaire to meet his fate!'

Constantinus grunted in reply and ordered Paulus to retrieve the body from the midden. Reluctant, but prepared to show he could dirty his own hands, the officer waded into the foul mess.

And then he almost tripped as his boot soles slipped on Marcus's corpse.

The commander's body had been thrown by one arm and one leg as far into the putrid midden as possible, but Marcus was heavily fleshed and his assailants would have had some difficulty in casting the remains into the centre of the rubbish mound. Naked, and with gaping knife wounds to the belly, the groin and the throat, the corpse of the would-be High King was sprawled on top of a pile of broken furniture, food scraps and the carcass of a dead dog.

One by one, all three bodies were found.

The two guardsmen had been despatched with military precision, but Marcus must have screamed shrilly after each stroke of the killing blade from thrusts that were designed to wound rather than kill. Constantinus found some dour amusement at the manner of Marcus's end. Regardless of his status, Marcus had been a vile man who was unworthy of the advancements that came his way with such regularity. His patrician blood and family gold had eased his way into preferment.

Then Constantinus recalled the face of the young woman whose beautiful eyes and quiet demeanour had gained an unusual influence on his untrusting heart. The poor woman had been betrothed to Marcus for less than a day, but her intended spouse had been assassinated and his body was now lying among the city's trash. Who would be the next suitor to drag her to the altar – with or without her consent? He wondered if he had the gall to scorch his hands against her dangerous flesh.

Was it a traitor's voice that rang inside Constantinus's head? The adjutant knew he was attracted to Severa, but would he be prepared to risk his own life in an attempt to possess her? The dice had been cast by Fortuna, so Constantinus guessed that Marcus had died because he had offended someone important among his peers, or he was considered by the British kings to be a threat to their aristocracy. But, in spite of the adjutant's doubts, the words of the hermit refused to be silenced.

The old man's tremulous voice grew louder in Constantinus's memory.

'Constantine ... Emperor that will soon be!'

The hermit had been crazed by silence and by his many years of loneliness. The old man's unfocused eyes had seemed to contemplate some inner world which mere humans could never hope to see or understand.

'Take care who you wed,' he had chanted with his cracked voice. At the time, Constantinus had laughed at the ridiculous prophecy, for how could a common soldier who had been elevated from the ranks and possessed neither birth nor gold hope to rise through the hierarchy of the legions? Raw talent had taken the centurion as far as he could go. Common sense told him that there would be plenty of shit-heads like Marcus who would climb higher and faster than him on the ladder of promotion. To dream of the throne was grotesque delusion, and Constantinus had never been a fool.

The adjutant shook his head to clear it of all dangerous thoughts, for treason could get a man killed even faster than the stupidity and character weaknesses demonstrated by Marcus Britannicus. He turned his attention back to the murder of his senior officer.

Was this assassination initiated by Rome? Or did it come from Britannic sources? One of the hierarchy wanted Marcus dead, so would a centurion fare any better if he decided to pursue Severa? In Rome's estimation, Constantinus was lacking in breeding. The adjutant was aware that a previous Roman claimant, Magnus Maximus, had at least possessed whispered links with his namesake, the first and most glorious Constantine, a linkage that had proved a powerful asset. Few comparisons could be drawn between himself and Maximus, except for youth and desire. But his mind refused to obey him as he struggled to focus on the three corpses at hand.

As Constantinus pulled himself together and leaned against a discarded table that was missing one of its legs, Marcus seemed to be staring derisively at the centurion from a hastily constructed stretcher on which the bloodied corpse had been laid.

You'll join me soon enough, Pretender!

The blued lips seemed to writhe with life, and the imagined horror sent Constantinus staggering backwards with a curse. Then a small rat pushed its way out of the tender gullet where it had been feeding. As it scuttled away from the torchlight, its scaly tail looked, for one ghastly moment, like a length of grey string that was pulling Marcus's spirit from his body.

Constantinus swore colourfully before reaching out with one trembling finger and pushing up the lower lip to close the gap. The rodent had been gorging itself on the tongue.

'I hate fucking rats,' Constantinus swore again with a visible shudder. 'Get these damned bodies out of this quagmire as soon as possible. Find a cart and have them transported back into the city. You can take them to the guardhouse so they can be prepared for cremation or burial. Best do it now, before the rats decide to carry the corpses away of their own accord. They were Romans and we look after our own, so have them cleaned up by the priesthood as quickly as possible. I don't want our tribal hosts to see the indignities inflicted on the body of Marcus Britannicus. Everyone in this brothel, including the bitch that runs it and all of its regular patrons, must be rounded up and held for questioning.'

His men obeyed immediately.

Searching for a water skin to wash some of the filth from his person as he made his way back to the town gates, Constantinus struggled to prepare an explanation for Corinium's king and queen that would prepare them for the ugliness that had been precipitated by Marcus's stupidity. Although King Aeron had already seen enough to know the broad outlines of the assassination, the centurion was determined that no outsiders should learn the more shameful details of Marcus Britannicus's death. Why feed the citizens of the town with vile gossip? But even as he scrubbed his hands in a pail of brackish water brought by the gatekeeper, the wounded features of Severa intruded into the thread of the unadorned speech he intended to deliver to the young woman. What would she think of this latest demonstration of Lady Fortuna's fickleness?

As a serving officer in Rome's legions, he had no right to aspire to a woman from the household of a native ruler. Nor was her face an appropriate subject for his thoughts at a time when matters of loyalty and honour were at stake. He tried resolutely to put all thought of her doe-like eyes away.

Nursing a headache, tortured by new and dangerous desires, Constantinus was forced to massage his throbbing temples before he approached the royal apartments as the small troop of Britons and Roman legionnaires returned to the guardhouse with their grisly burdens. He carried difficult and unsettling tidings with him, for he was now the senior Roman officer.

'It's likely that I could have commenced the search for my commander a little earlier, Your Highness, so I must take some responsibility for our lack of immediate action. However, I was aware that Marcus Britannicus was in the habit of occasionally visiting such low houses, and I was reluctant to raise an alarm that would humiliate my superior officer. I am aware that he has made similar late returns to his quarters in the past, so his foolish risk-taking wasn't unusual.'

'How did you come to know that Marcus could be found at the Bower of Beauty?' Aeron asked sharply.

'Paulus, my decurion, had heard whispers from my commander's bodyguard, Eugenius, who had made the initial preparations for Marcus's visit to the brothel. Even so, we searched all the bawdy houses in the area in case Eugenius had made a mistake or was lying. It has been a long night, Highness.'

Aeron grimaced and the dangerous moment passed.

When Aeron remained silent, Constantinus was constrained to make a report to the king that detailed the progress of the initial investigation carried out at the premises of the Bower of Beauty. He described the questioning that had taken place in an even, disciplined voice.

'I've taken the liberty of sending men to arrest everyone associated with the Bower of Beauty, a name which is a misnomer if ever there was one. If their appearance at night is the best face they can offer to the world, then I'm prepared to be shocked at what I'll see in the harsh light of day. I've also given the bodies of our dead over to the priests so they can be prepared for the funeral pyre. I'm certain that Marcus Britannicus would have been deeply ashamed if his abused body had been seen by any other persons, especially his betrothed, after his corpse had been abandoned in the filth of the midden.'

Aeron nodded. 'Have you considered that the choice of the midden as a dumping site could have been a calculated insult, Constantine?'

'The name is Constantinus, Your Highness,' the adjutant corrected him carefully.

Aeron noticed the younger man frowning, so this Roman was

either very angry, or was hiding something that he was reluctant to discuss. The king was immediately on his guard.

'My apologies, Centurion, for no offence was intended.'

The adjutant showed surprise at the use of his given name for the king was merely reassuring the young officer that he was innocent of any dereliction of duty. It was as if Aeron had peered into his mind and gazed at his darkest thoughts.

'No offence was taken, Highness.' He smiled agreeably, although his mind was racing. 'The perpetrators of this murder carried out a calculated insult when they threw the bodies of their victims into the town's midden. I cannot decide whether this affront was aimed specifically at my commander or was an attack against all Romans. But the betrothal of your foster-daughter to Marcus cannot be a coincidence. I don't believe in chance.'

'Nor do I, Constantinus! Nor do I!'

Before Aeron could speak further, Queen Endellion, who had been listening quietly, broke confidently into the conversation.

'What perversions drove your master to take such frivolous chances, sir? If you'll excuse my forwardness, Marcus appeared to be a man with a healthy regard for his own skin.'

'Yes, he was,' Constantinus replied slowly once his sluggish brain recalled that this queen was the daughter of one of Emperor Maximus's most influential friends. Little wonder that she was forceful.

'My commander was unusually careful with his person, Highness, but unfortunately he was indiscriminate in his sexual liaisons with inferiors.'

Embarrassed at having to discuss these matters with a woman, and ashamed, Constantinus was standing rigidly and every muscle was at attention as he struggled to control his tongue.

Aeron, realising what was troubling the Roman, shot a glance at Endellion that suggested she should exercise tact and leave the men to their discussion.

Endellion took the hint and excused herself on the grounds of needing to inform Severa of the changed circumstances in her marital expectations. As she watched the Roman from the corner of her eye, she noticed that he visibly relaxed as she prepared to leave them. Aeron would discuss the juicier details with her at a later time.

Constantinus indicated that Marcus had a penchant for pain, and he gave the king an explanation of his master's sexual proclivities.

'He enjoyed having punishments inflicted on his person during intricate sexual games that would nauseate most men with normal tastes. I've heard tales that Marcus enjoyed crawling on his belly on the floor and fawned over disgusting whores who would whip him if he was slow to carry out their instructions. On other occasions, he gained sexual fulfilment after being tied and restrained so he couldn't protect himself, and the harridans would be encouraged to urinate on him or commit other disgusting perversions. I've heard that far more grotesque behaviour is permitted in the salons of Rome. My commander came from this world, but Britannia cannot be equated with Rome. Marcus had flaws that would sicken most military men and, without doubt, most of his fellows in the officer corps. When coupled with a lack of common morality and the hubris that came with his birthright, he was a Roman who had made a host of enemies.'

'So,' Aeron responded, for he was surprised at the young Roman's frankness. 'You believe that Marcus's assassination was caused by some unknown person or persons who became part of a sexual tryst, or his death was arranged by an assassin who had been suborned into killing him by a third party who would gain politically from his death?'

Aeron's expression was clear and his questions were sharp.

'Exactly! But personal vengeances must also be considered. Marcus made many enemies on all sides of Britannia's politics, as any competent observer would agree. At best, my commander has shown himself to be an arrogant and foolhardy man.'

Constantinus paused to consider his next words.

'The field of potential assassins is very wide and I have no doubt that the number will expand as we investigate our commander's last hours in Corinium. If you are agreeable, I intend to torture the whores and bodyguards who have been working in this particular brothel. We have a reputation for success in dealing with malcontents.'

Aeron had heard descriptions of Roman techniques, so he agreed that most villains would confess to their crimes rather than undergo a serious Roman interrogation. Many innocent men would also choose a clean death for crimes they hadn't committed rather than experiencing a lingering fate where they were tortured into submission.

The tribal king nodded slowly. 'You may do as you see fit, Centurion. I'm not in favour of inflicting unnecessary pain, so I'd prefer to remain ignorant of your methods to loosen the tongues of criminals. I'll confine myself to informing Severa of the changes to her circumstances.'

Constantinus breathed a sigh of relief. He had been dreading the task of informing Marcus's betrothed that her intended husband had been murdered. Still . . . !

* * *

In the small chapel in the centre of Corinium, the body of Marcus Britannicus was washed and oiled, his gaping wounds were hidden by a fine white robe that doubled as a shroud and his hair was carefully cleansed, combed and styled. Coins were placed over his eyelids. Once the corpse was prepared for the funeral pyre, Constantinus surreptitiously slipped two silver coins under his master's tongue in order that his soul could pay the ferryman whose vessel would carry Marcus's spirit across the River Styx. Although he was a Christian, Constantinus was a wise man who was prepared to pay lip service to the old gods.

He gave a silent apology to the native priests who were offering prayers for the soul of his commander. Marcus Britannicus had met his fate and the murderous deed had been carried out with considerable expertise and efficiency. The legitimate nominee for the throne of High King of the Britons had scarcely prepared himself to make his mark on the world when he was permanently removed. But Constantinus's heart hardened as he left the tiny wooden chapel and strode towards the guardhouse where the prisoners had been incarcerated to await their formal interrogation. To kill a Roman officer was a serious crime, especially in an environment where the British lands were under threat from without and within, so he was determined to extract every piece of information, real or imagined, from his suspects.

The whores and their bodyguards had to be involved in the conspiracy, because the assassins had gained entry to the Bower of Beauty with relative ease. Constantinus had carefully examined the brothel's front door and had found no sign of a forced entry. The commander had been dragged bodily from the ramshackle building, so his prisoners must have observed the assassins during their murderous rampage. With luck, Constantinus would quickly learn the identity of the villains and, if he gained some recognition from the process, then so much the better.

In the cellars of the guardhouse, which also served as the community jail, narrow storage rooms had been converted into cells that allowed prisoners to stand or sit with their chained limbs drawn up above their heads. Other detainees had their hands tied behind them, an agonising position whereby the miscreants were slowly strangled when their chest muscles were unable to expand or contract. Constantinus decided to show a soupcon of mercy by permitting the prisoners to have their hands re-tied in front of their bodies. However, such relief was only temporary, because few of them could expect to survive his ministrations.

As he entered the cellar, he noticed that the brazier in the corner of the normally frigid little room was heating a number of branding irons designed to inflict hideous damage on the flesh of the unfortunate prisoners. With a flicker of disgust, he saw that several of the links of chain near the brazier had been inadvertently heated to a cherry-red colour from their proximity to the hot coals. His unfortunate prisoners must have been experiencing some pain already, but needs must be, when an important personage such as the Roman commander was assassinated.

'We'll carry out our interrogation with the women prisoners first, Paulus,' the adjutant ordered crisply, his face showing nothing of his internal struggle with his conscience. Several soldiers obeyed the decurion's command and released one of the locked doors so that three of the dishevelled women, in various stages of bluster or terror, were yanked by their chains into the main body of the cellar.

The obese madam spat in Constantinus's direction and was cuffed for her insult by Paulus. Within moments, she was chained to the stone wall of the cellar with her arms above her head.

'Come, woman! Theatrics won't help at a time like this,' Constantinus warned as the three women were pulled up on their chains until only their straining toes could touch the ground.

Constantinus began to pace up and down the stone flagging in front of the prisoners, taking pains to stay just beyond the reach of the madam's spittle.

'Your name, woman?'

She spat again, but Paulus grimaced in disgust and yanked her considerable bulk off the ground.

'Shall we try again, woman? I can easily discover your names, but the knowledge I intend to extract from you should be learned, ideally, with a minimum of suffering. I advise you to be truthful!'

Constantinus's words were so reasonable that the grotesque woman, hanging painfully only inches from the ground and weighed down by her own gross folds of fat, tried to flinch away from his icy face. 'My name is Clidna,' the woman eventually slurred through her gasping and distorted mouth. 'I'm a businesswoman. I'm not a killer, *so fuck you*!'

Paulus had picked up a plaited leather whip with a surface studded with small metal barbs. With a gentle flick of his wrist, he lashed Clidna across her upper thigh. Her flesh parted to release an instant flow of blood and the excruciating pain robbed Clidna of her breath.

'Mind your manners, Clidna. My master asked you a perfectly reasonable question. He was very polite, so I suggest that you answer his questions in the same way.' If Paulus felt any reservations about torturing women, his face revealed nothing. With the calm discipline that he always demonstrated when carrying out his duties, he flicked the whip against his boots and small droplets of blood and shreds of flesh fell to the stone floor.

'I want you to tell me everything you know of Marcus Britannicus, your client, and your dealings with him during his last evening on this earth,' Constantinus demanded. 'I intend to interrogate every single person involved in this matter, so telling lies will be a waste of time. We are already aware that one of our comrades had bled inside your house, so you and your friends have earned your deaths. How you die will be entirely up to you.'

Constantinus prayed that Clidna would see sense and reveal all she knew of the assassination plot. A practised twist of the wrist by a strangler and this woman would have a quick and merciful death.

'Your master sent a messenger to arrange his entertainment. I don't remember his name but he had fair hair and blue eyes,' Clidna explained painfully. 'He was a pretty boy!'

'Eugenius,' Paulus stated.

The grotesque woman sobbed with agony. 'If you want to know what happened, you'll have to let me down a little so I can breathe.'

Constantinus felt a surge of respect for the gross brothel-owner. Her weight had probably dislocated both of her shoulder blades, to judge by the odd appearance of her upper torso.

'Lower her down a little so she can stand on her feet,' Constantinus ordered.

Paulus obeyed, but his face showed an edge of disapproval.

'I've made concessions for your comfort, woman, so answer me quickly.'

Constantinus ceased his pacing and stood directly in front of the madam so he could stare into her muddy eyes.

'Your Roman friend wanted some special arrangements,' Clidna explained. She spat out the mucus that had collected in her mouth, but she was careful to aim at the flagging near her swollen feet. 'We cater for all types at the Bower of Beauty.' She chuckled thickly at some distant memory until Paulus flicked his whip.

Constantinus shot an admonitory glance at his decurion.

'Continue, Clidna. Paulus won't hurt you if you're truthful.'

'Your Marcus liked to be dominated, as long as we didn't really hurt him or leave marks where they could be seen by others. Soft paddles . . . that sort of thing. He had a number of other little games that he wanted to experience and my girls were happy to service him with the pleasures he was seeking, as long as they weren't hurt for their trouble. Men like him are easy gold for girls like us. Late in the evening, your man came to the Bower of Beauty with his two guards, including the pretty lad with the blue eyes. He was a fine-looking boy, so I'll be sorry if he's dead. I'd have fucked him for free!'

Paulus tapped the whip against his leather-clad knees, so Clidna's eyes widened and she immediately lurched into another line of thought. The blood from her torn leg was dripping on to the stone flagging.

'Your Marcus was a cultured Roman gentleman on the surface, and he didn't allow us to forget it. He demanded wine when he arrived, but then referred to our vintage as swill. Still, he drank it! He guzzled some and then told me that my girls were to be brought before him. There are only two girls working at the moment. Clyte and Gwennan were there, so I brought them to him. Our other girl, Dorcas, was visiting an important friend inside the town. Master Marcus wasn't pleased at her absence, because he wanted all three girls to join him in his little games. He also demanded privacy while he was in my house, so his guards told me that my cook and the kitchen hand would not be required and could leave early. I'd already sent them home, which is why they weren't arrested when your soldiers arrived.'

'What are their names?' Constantinus asked quietly, although he swore inwardly that none of his soldiers had considered the possibility that some servants might already have left the brothel before they carried out their initial investigations.

'My cook is half-Roman and is called Selwyn, although we call him Little Grandfather. The kitchen hand is Lachie. He's a bit wanting in the head, just like his brother, Nudd, who works as one of my two guards. Lachie has probably been in hiding since he heard that his brother was arrested. We also have another guard, Lewis, but he seems to have disappeared.'

'Find them, Paulus,' Constantinus ordered tightly, although his voice remained calm. Inside, he was seething with temper at the carelessness of his decurion. The Romans had been stupid to discount the involvement of other workers who were absent from the household.

Two legionnaires were sent to carry out this urgent task. They swore to locate Little Grandfather and Lachie, and bring them back to the cells within the hour.

With a sudden change in manner, Clidna began to show an eagerness to provide Constantinus with the sordid details of the evening's entertainment. This sudden enthusiasm co-incided with the arrival in the cell of Clyte, a small dark girl who could lay claim to some prettiness under a rime of dirt and old cosmetics. This young woman was weeping and begging for mercy, so she was soon providing her Roman interrogators with more details of the demands that Marcus made on her.

But the most interesting details were provided by the third girl, Gwennan, who seemed an unlikely whore in a town such as Corinium.

Gwennan was very tall for a woman, with long, cleanly modelled limbs. To Constantinus's eyes she was graceful, even in the chains that constrained her. He could see that her face was almost beautiful under the cosmetics that encircled her eyes and coloured her pale cheeks. A sharp knife had sliced its way across her forehead at some time in her past, so her right eyebrow was puckered into a permanent expression of surprise.

Unfortunately, Gwennan was proud for a low-caste woman and her scornful expression showed that she held a loathing for all men. Constantinus had heard that some prostitutes shared similar hatreds, having received nothing but persecution and cruelty from the men they serviced.

'I can promise you, girl, that you won't be tortured if you speak the truth. I want to know if there is anything you can add to what your mistress has already told me?'

'Does it matter what we say, Roman? You're going to kill us anyway.'

The adjutant refused to be drawn into more senseless violence unless there were no other options available to him. He knew instinctively that torture would be pointless with this woman.

'Do you intend to punish me if I speak the truth as I know it?'

Constantinus remained silent.

Resigned to the probability of death, she sighed as the excruciating pain of her stretched arm and shoulder muscles continued to dominate her thoughts.

'Very well, Roman! I can tell you that your Marcus Britannicus was a cruel and heartless bastard when he was clothed, but he became a snivelling babe when he was naked in the presence of women. But he never fooled me from the moment he arrived. If we were too aggressive, or if we ridiculed his long-held image of himself, that animal would have changed from a fawning worm into a typical beast in the blinking of an eye. He'd have killed me without mercy.'

The adjutant eyed the tall woman with her dirty black hair and her vivid amber eyes, while admiring the way she met his stare and refused to blink or flinch.

'Were you the woman who was with my commander when he was taken?'

Now, she flinched visibly.

'Aye, but I had nothing to do with the attack on him. When the outsiders came into my room, your Roman was on his hands and knees in front of me. His hands were only loosely bound so that he was able to kiss my feet when ordered to do so, while I was beating him with a padded whip. It couldn't even break the skin, but he needed the thought of a little pain to . . . to get it up, you know?'

Gwennan paused and her embarrassment, usually foreign to whores, flooded her pale face and made her even more attractive.

'I understand, woman,' Constantinus replied gruffly. 'What happened next?'

'Three men burst into the room with drawn swords. I didn't know what to do, so I found a corner of the room and tried to hide there. They lifted the Roman, who kicked and spat like a madman as he tried to throw them off. He was punched several times and his nose started to bleed, so I'm sure you'll find lots of his blood in my room. I thought I'd be killed, but they ignored me as if I was invisible. Then they dragged your Marcus Britannicus away.'

Constantinus leaped on Gwennan's use of his commander's name.

'How did you know his full name? I've treated you fairly so far, Gwennan, but I'll strip the flesh from your bones if you are proven to have lied to me. Do you understand me?'

'You used his name yourself. I've heard everybody using that name, especially the mistress. He could have been the King of Londinium for all I knew, so I just used the same one that everyone else was using. I didn't know the men who burst into the room, or I don't think I did. Their faces were hidden by heavy woollen scarves. They were wearing black cloaks and they kept away from the oil lamps as if they didn't want to be seen. I swear, master! I had no notion of what was about to happen to my patron.'

'If your mistress gave you his name, how did she happen to know it? What else did she tell you?'

'Shut your stupid mouth or they'll kill us all,' Clidna howled at Gwennan and received a backhand blow across the face from Paulus for her trouble. Her smashed nose bled in a fountain of rich red that ran down her face and over her cursing mouth.

The tide of invective continued to flow and Paulus would have struck her again, but Constantinus gripped his hand tightly.

'Force the whore to explain herself,' Paulus complained. 'She doesn't want her girl to speak, so these bitches must know something else. I'll get it out of them if I have to roast them over a fire.'

'He told me his name,' Clidna mumbled triumphantly through the blood. 'You can't prove otherwise!'

'I can do whatever I want, bitch,' Constantinus retorted. 'I can kill you at any time of my choosing. I can also make it an easy death or a hard one. The only matter that concerns you is that you'll experience a great deal of pain while I'm extracting the information that I require from you.'

'Clidna knew his name and she told me he was very important,' Gwennan interrupted with a sneer of contempt. 'I'm the one who looks after the difficult pigs who have special needs . . . Clidna had to list his requirements, or I'd not have been able to please him. But she was very pleased with herself when she told me about your friend, because she told me he was worth a lot of coin to the house.'

'So she was well paid for her services?' Paulus interrupted. The whore cast a scornful glance at her mistress.

'I don't know! All I know for certain is that Clidna told me I might win my freedom from the house, if I performed well and behaved myself. I'd give my right arm to leave this shithole, even pander to a slug like your Roman friend. But I can't tell you how those men entered the house because Clidna always kept the doors locked after dark. All of our clients know that they have to knock in a certain way to be admitted. Nudd, our guard, isn't very clever, but he understands he has to protect the house from noisy or dangerous customers. As well, Nudd has been sweet on Clyte for a long time. He might be half-witted, but he's as strong as an ox and I've never known him to admit anyone who was armed. Why would he do so now?'

'I've been told that there were five men in the gang that came to the Bower of Beauty.' Constantinus examined his nails as if the question was unimportant, but just a recapitulation of previously agreed fact.

Gwennan shrugged as well as her bound hands would allow. 'I only saw three of them. They locked me in the room and, although I yelled and threw my weight against the door, I was forced to stay in my room until Clyte let me out.'

'Clidna swears you were accompanied by Clyte and herself during your ... er ... ministrations to Marcus. Yet you're suggesting now that you were alone. Who is lying?'

Gwennan's face became flat and unreadable. She had obviously been trying to save her own skin, but her owner's admissions were implicating her in the crime at every turn.

She sighed, and then continued. 'Every woman has a speciality in the world of the brothel. Mine is pain! I learned before I was ten that my speciality saved me from some disgusting contacts with many of my less likeable customers ... and the bastards pay very well for their humiliation. I've already decided that I've earned enough to get out of this cesspit and start a new life in the north. If your family is very poor or indebted to someone, they'll sell promising daughters to the local house for a few copper coins. That was my fate. I was only eight when I first came here, sir, but I'm not stupid.'

Constantinus nodded, feeling a frisson of guilt, as if he personally was at fault for whores' miserable lives.

'On this visit, both Clyte and Clidna joined me in my room from the very first. We were ordered to strip off our clothing, but I refused, because I knew that this patron would want me to act like a haughty lady. He smiled at me, but he still ordered Clyte to undress so he could inspect her body while he cavorted with me. Clyte is a nervous little thing. She's fourteen, older than most of the girls who enter our trade, but she has never been comfortable with life in a whorehouse. I felt sorry for her, because there have been nights when I've heard her crying for her mother in the darkness. I'd protect her from harm if I could ... but I can't even protect myself.'

She paused again to consider her next words.

'On the other hand, Clidna wasn't to the Roman's fancy. Too fat, I suppose! So he called her an ugly cow and ordered her to leave. The mistress wasn't pleased! After she left, I insisted that the client wouldn't need Clyte until I'd completed my ministrations and I would be the one who would tell him when the time was ripe for him to fuck her. He liked that! I tied his hands loosely and then struck him several times with the paddle to get him in the mood for what I wanted to do to him. Do I have to say?'

Constantinus shook his head.

He could easily imagine the scene she described, so her words had a ring of truth. Yes, Gwennan's story made a grim sense.

'I believe your Roman was happy when the masked men broke in,' the whore explained. 'I was about to call for Clyte to join us when the men entered the room through the door. I swear that I only saw three of them and I hadn't heard anything that concerned me except for the sound Clyte, who was crying in the next room. They said nothing and the silence that settled on the room was very frightening.'

'Did you notice anything about the men that would be useful to me? Anything at all?'

While the girl racked her brain for anything that might save her from the agony of torture, Constantinus considered his next step. It might be easier to glean some information from the half-wits, Nudd and Lachie, since they would find it difficult to hide what they knew.

'One of the men had an unusual-sounding voice that I couldn't recognise. He was speaking in an old-fashioned way, if you know what I mean,' Gwennan said slowly.

'Was he a tribesman? Or even a Briton from another tribe? Was he a Roman?'

'No! I think he was a Briton. I've heard some very old people use some of his expressions, but I don't really understand what they mean. But the man wasn't an ancient, and nor were the rest of the men. They looked like soldiers, although they had plaits under their disguises. They could have been Britons from some distant tribe. There's something about the way that Roman soldiers stand and walk. They come down hard on their heels as if they're marching off to battle. They always look as if they are disciplined, I guess. But these men weren't Romans. I'd have known if they were.'

'Thank you, Gwennan.'

Constantinus turned to his junior officer. 'Let her down, Paulus. Give her a couple of coins and set her free. Don't argue with me! She's told us all she knows as honestly as she can, so we'll send her on her way. However . . . not so the rest of them!'

Constantinus turned back to the shocked woman, who had been thoroughly convinced that she would be killed out of hand for her complicity in the crime. As Paulus released her chains, Gwennan almost fell the last few inches. She crawled shakily to her feet, careless of how her robe fell open to reveal a freckled breast. Then, as she felt the eyes of the soldiers on her, she pulled her clothing around her with protesting arm muscles.

'You will absent yourself from Corinium before tomorrow's dawn or I'll be forced to change my mind. And if anything else comes to your mind before you leave, I would suggest you send me a message. It would be best for you if you didn't see me again, Gwennan. Do you understand?'

Gwennan nodded. Still amazed at her good fortune, she was escorted out of the cellar by Paulus.

When Paulus returned, he leaned in close to his commander. 'That might be a mistake, sir. You should have tortured that bitch a little to make sure that she told us everything she knows *before* we let her go. It sets a bad example for the others if we don't use a little force.'

'I know what you're saying, Paulus. But I don't believe that torture would have made any difference to that woman. Clidna, however, is a totally different matter . . .'

Both pairs of Roman eyes turned towards the breathless woman who was hanging with her swollen feet barely reaching the ground.

'Our attention returns to you, Clidna, so we'll start all over again! But this time, we'll be telling the truth, won't we? Did you allow five men to enter the Bower of Beauty?'

Clidna was struggling against the chains that clattered from her efforts to free herself, but her face was a mixed study of fear and cunning. 'I allowed no one in but Marcus Britannicus and his two bodyguards,' she retorted triumphantly.

Constantinus sighed. 'Lift her up a little, Paulus, to convince her we mean business.'

Paulus complied, roughly jerking her off her feet while ignoring her shrieks of pain.

'We aren't hurting you yet, so don't try for sympathy. Did anyone else let the five strangers enter the house?'

'My boys might have let them in. I can't be held responsible for everything that happens in the Bower of Beauty.'

'You own this particular shithouse, so I'll hold you responsible.' Constantinus turned to his decurion.

'Bring in the two missing brothers, Paulus, if they've been found yet.'

'You'd better hope, woman, that I don't catch you out in a lie or I'll let Paulus convince you of the severity of your sins,' he added for Clidna's benefit. 'Paulus doesn't like parasites that prey on Roman legionnaires, do you, Paulus? Sooner or later, you'll beg him to listen to the truth, because no amount of coin is worth the pain we'll inflict on you. Your confederates are miles away by now and they won't return to save you, so you'll be suffering instead of them. Never mind, Clidna! It's your choice!'

Clidna swore and wept in equal measure while Paulus checked on the status of the search for the servant, Lachie, who was still missing. Meanwhile, Nudd was dragged out of his cell by two legionnaires and bound to a chair near the brazier. He whimpered in fear, an incongruous noise coming from such an enormous man.

Nudd was a veritable giant. He stood a head taller than Constantinus and weighed almost twice as much. His arms were very long and hung almost to his knees. Conversely, his legs were thick and short by comparison with his torso. Muscle mass ridged his whole body and fat veins wound like ropes along his powerful arms. His neck was so thick that his chin seemed to rise out of his chest.

By comparison, the fair-haired head that topped the huge body was small and delicate. His features seemed unformed; his small blue eyes were widely spaced and slanted upwards at the ends, with lashes and eyebrows so fair that they were virtually invisible.

'Do you know the difference between truth and lies, Nudd?' Constantinus smiled gently as he spoke in the careful, unthreatening patterns he would have used with a child.

Nudd nodded so vigorously that it almost seemed he might shake his entire head off his straining shoulders. 'Me mam taught me and me brother good so the priests wouldn't take us away to a dark place where we'd never see her again.'

His voice was a high-pitched squeak. Constantinus lifted up

Nudd's chin and discovered that he had never grown facial hair, a strange feature that added to his unfinished appearance.

'Do you know how old you are, Nudd?'

The huge bodyguard kept staring around the room and whimpered when he saw his mistress and Clyte hanging from their chains.

'Have they been very bad?' Nudd asked, with tears glistening in his eyes.

'Yes, Nudd. They've been lying to me.'

'Even Clyte? I like Clyte! She's my friend and she gives me sweetcakes if I help her. I don't like it when you hurt Clyte.'

The last sentence was spoken with more determination, as if Nudd had found a reason to offer resistance to Constantinus and his other torturers.

'If you tell me everything I want to know, perhaps I can make sure that Clyte won't be hurt any more. Is that what you want?'

The lad paused for a moment, and then nodded enthusiastically. Constantinus realised that violence against Nudd would be pointless.

'Now, Nudd. I'll ask you again. How old are you?'

Nudd's expression was painful to watch as he was afraid to fail this man who owned such a bright sword and such dark eyes. Distress caused him to fidget on his seat.

'No, sir! I can't remember things real good. Lachie might know, because he remembers things better than me.'

Nudd had some difficulty with the word *remember*, but after several false starts he was finally able to pronounce it.

This interrogation will take all day at this rate, Constantinus thought irritably, but he tried to quell his impatience.

'Do you remember the men who came to the Bower of Beauty?'

'Yes, I remember. One man in a fine cloak wasn't very nice, but my mistress took him upstairs so Gwennan could make him happy.'

'Listen carefully, Nudd. I want you to tell me what happened to the two men who were with him.' Constantinus spoke slowly and clearly.

'Selwyn took them to the kitchens for supper.'

'You're being very good, Nudd, and I think that Clyte is pleased with you as well. You are pleased, aren't you, Clyte?' Constantinus responded silkily.

'Yes, Nudd, I'm very pleased.' Clyte spoke clearly for the first time in her childish voice. Clidna opened her mouth to speak, but Constantinus knew that the brothel-keeper would terrify Nudd if she continued with her tirade. He had no hesitation in ordering the whore to be gagged, an instruction that both legionnaires obeyed with pleasure as they rammed a dirty cloth into her bleeding mouth.

'Why are you hurting Mistress Clidna? Did she also tell lies?'

'Yes, Nudd, she did. And she has been cursing too much. Did your mother tell you that it is wrong to use bad words?' Constantinus managed to sound both fatherly and censorious.

'Yes, but Lachie says that Clidna's the mistress, so she's allowed to say what she wants.'

'Did you go to the kitchens with Selwyn and the two men?'

'No! Mistress Clidna told me that I was to wait and open the door for some more visitors. She said someone would be coming soon.'

Constantinus held his breath while Clidna struggled to spit out the wad of cloth that had been jammed between her teeth.

'Yes, sir! I heard them when they knocked on the door, but

I was afraid because there were a lot of men on the doorstep. They had black cloths over their faces so I could only see their eyes. They pushed straight past me and didn't speak. Two of the men went into the kitchens and the other three went upstairs to Gwennan's room.'

'What did you do then, Nudd? Did you try to find your mistress?'

'She was already waiting for them at the top of the stairs. She told me to go to my room and stay there.' Nudd paused for a moment. 'So that's what I did. I stayed there until Lewis came and let me out. I went to bed then.'

'Now, Nudd, the question I'm about to ask is the most important one of all, so I want you to think very hard before you answer me. If you can tell me the truth, I will let you and Clyte go. Please don't bother to tell any stories, because I'll know. Just tell the truth! Are you ready?'

Nudd's changing facial expressions spoke eloquently of his understanding.

'Yes. I'm ready.' Nudd squared his shoulders.

'Did any of the men say anything that you can remember? Clyte is depending on you.'

Nudd burst into speech and repeated every word he had heard, reciting all of the various conversations in a flat voice as if reading from a script. As he spoke, Constantinus realised that Nudd was a true savant, a person with very little understanding, but with an uncanny ability to recall verbatim everything he heard, no matter how trivial or how meaningless it might be to him.

With a sudden flash of recognition, Constantinus stopped the recitation of a five-way conversation. 'Repeat that last part, Nudd. I want to hear the bit where the man mentions the name of his master.'

The whole room was silent except for the small explosions of sound that came from the brazier and the fire pit. Nudd seemed to be mentally running through the conversation from the beginning while the Romans held their breath.

'You agreed to keep the Roman occupied until we got here. We've paid you in gold coin for your troubles, so don't think you can increase your price now that Lord Conanus has decamped and is far away. You have no idea how long his reach is. He'll stop your tongue, you fat bitch, if you speak to a living soul about those things that are about to happen in your house.'

Then, like a small child, Nudd pursed his lips. 'He wasn't a nice man, was he? He frightened Mistress Clidna with his knife and he swore at her. He's a bad man!'

'Yes, Nudd. He's a very bad man,' Constantinus answered him seriously as Clyte started to cry in earnest and the half-wit looked around at his audience with wondering, confused eyes.

CHAPTER V

A DANGEROUS AFFECTION

Your great glory is not to be inferior to what God has made you, and the greatest glory of a woman is to be least talked about by men, whether they are praising you or criticising you.

Thucydides, *History of the Peloponnesian War*

While Constantinus continued the unsavoury task of interrogating the prisoners, Endellion tentatively entered the rooms of her foster-daughter to explain the fate of the girl's intended husband.

Severa was mending a torn under-skirt with determined patience. She had taken her new role to heart and was valiantly attempting to sew a neat, invisible hem with doubtful skill. Her small pink tongue was caught between her teeth as she concentrated fiercely on the task.

Endellion smiled and cleared her throat.

As soon as Severa noticed her, she put the under-skirt to one side with obvious relief.

'I'm afraid I bring sad news, my dear,' Endellion began in a conciliatory voice.

Severa paled visibly at her foster-mother's sombre expression.

'Has Father Aeron taken ill? I saw him when he broke his fast and he seemed perfectly well. Is it one of the boys? Are the children safe?'

Endellion reached out one sympathetic hand to smooth the girl's pale hair.

'Aeron and the children are safe, my dear, and are playing in the forecourt as if nothing has been happening. No, Severa, I'm afraid that your betrothed has been assassinated in the small village just outside the city walls, along with two of his body-guards. I cannot tell you much of what has happened because Aeron and the senior Roman officer are still interrogating the suspected perpetrators and witnesses to determine the identity of the culprits. It's a very sad time for you, my dear, because you will have to prepare yourself for an interment at a time when you have made your destiny known to the citizens of Britannia.'

Severa stared blankly in amazement.

'I don't understand. Marcus seemed perfectly well when I spoke with him yesterday, and he seemed eager to make his preparations for the wedding. How could an assassin breach the walls and guards of Corinium?'

'As I said, Severa, Marcus was killed outside the walls. The incident seems to have happened at some time around midnight.' Endellion was hoping to deflect any questions concerning the nature and place of the incident, although she had little hope that the vulgar gossip-mongers would spare Severa when discussing the unsavoury details of this crime.

Severa composed herself. Although she had no love for Marcus Britannicus, he had represented her salvation from a barren existence without the hope of love or children.

'The smallest and most unimportant urchin in the city will soon be aware of the grisly details of what happened to Marcus, Mother, so I will appear foolish if I allow myself to be kept in ignorance. I need to know the whole truth – regardless!'

With minimal hesitancy, Endellion began to explain the embarrassing nature of Marcus's foray into the Street of Whores where he had met his fate, how he was taken prisoner and the foul place where his lifeless body had been found.

Severa pondered the embarrassing situation in which she had been placed.

'Such a scandalous death of an important personage will be impossible to keep quiet, so his murder might have saved me from a life of future humiliation. Who found his remains?'

'Constantinus, his second-in-command, led the search that found the bodies. I know you had feelings for him when you first arrived in Corinium. Have you spoken to him at all?'

'Yes. I've spoken with him on a number of occasions. He has always been courteous and seems eager to please.'

Severa blushed and Endellion examined her face with interest.

'I agree with you. I rather like the man, but I've found him to be a little too formal. He sees women as fragile creatures that should be protected from the ills of the world.'

'Is my interest in the man so strange, Mother? Aren't I entitled to take pleasure in the attention of a handsome and upright man who treats me with respect and compassion? I allowed myself to become the intended of a man who died as a result of his disgusting habits. Oh, I'm aware that everybody will try to keep the details of Marcus's flaws from me, but I realised what he was like at our first meeting. The touch of his hand made me want to vomit, but you and Aeron have raised me to do my duty at all times, so I accepted my destiny. I also heard some gossip among the servants when they thought I wasn't listening. Marcus would have given me a lifetime of embarrassment and despair. I'm glad he's dead and I'm also pleased that honourable Romans such as Constantinus remain alive to protect our people. In fact, he is one Roman I'd be prepared to marry without hesitation. But, like you, I accept that he is a man of honour and dignity who might not have any use for the child of a traitor to Rome's interests such as Flavius Magnus Maximus, another soldier whose ultimate failure was to snatch at the crown of the Roman Empire.'

Endellion murmured further words of comfort before hugging her charge and leaving. Perhaps Aeron would know what she should do to allow life to return to its usual peace and tranquillity.

Constantinus questioned Lachie after the servant was eventually run to ground in his hiding place near the latrines that lay outside the city walls. Like his brother, he seemed to be slow in intelligence, with an ugly squint and a look of low cunning in his watery blue eyes. But Constantinus quickly decided that very little would escape Lachie's calculating mind, no matter how stupid he pretended to be. Tied firmly to the chains vacated by his brother an hour earlier, and with the madam, Clidna, returned to the cells, Lachie looked around the cellar with desperation.

Clidna lay in an untidy heap on the floor of her cell. Her greyish flesh was streaked with blood, serum and excreta. Her laboured breathing suggested that she was close to death from a number of burns, whip marks and broken bones. No matter how much pain she had endured, she refused to provide any detailed information on her master, Conanus, and why his name filled her with such terror. The Roman commander finally terminated her torture without learning anything of Conanus's likely hiding places.

Clidna's interrogation had only just drawn to a close when Lewis and Selwyn were dragged into the cellar and chained up in the positions so recently vacated by Clyte and Gwennan. Lachie's hunted eyes searched among the faces of the other captives in an effort to discover what he must say under questioning, but each man avoided his gaze.

'I'm tired, Lachie, and I'm irritated by the number of lies I've been told,' Constantinus said softly. The calmness of his voice was more disturbing to the prisoner than any ranting could ever be. 'Clidna made a grave error when she treated me like a fool, so you can see for yourself how she came to regret her decision.'

Lachie's pale eyes swivelled to the open cell where Clidna was lying. Every detail of her condition was engraved into his calculating brain.

'Is she dead?'

'Not yet!'

Terrified, the Briton lost all control of his bladder.

'You're a dirty fucker!' Paulus suddenly exclaimed. A small puddle of urine had run down Lachie's legs to pool on the floor below his chair. 'You'll lick up the mess next time you do that.'

'Do what you want with him, Paulus, but not yet!' Constantinus interrupted. 'Now, Lachie, your brother told me that you had far more to do with this matter than he did. Was Nudd telling the truth, do you think?'

'Where's my brother? What have you done with him?'

'Don't worry about Nudd. In point of fact, you could be joining him in a very short time,' Constantinus responded, a subtle hint that Nudd had been taken away for execution.

Lachie shook his head and tried to break his bonds, but only succeeded in bruising his flesh. The fat tears that leaked from his eyes began to run down his blunt features.

'I've been told you were still in the kitchens when Lewis brought in the two Roman guards who accompanied their officer. Is that correct?'

Lachie nodded, having decided to co-operate . . . at least, as far as he dared.

'Were you by yourself?'

'No! Selwyn was there. He was told to prepare food for the client and his men, so I helped him to serve up some stew and a jug of new beer.'

'And?' Paulus interrupted, expecting a long recitation of what they ate, how they cleaned the kitchens and how they had departed before the strangers arrived.

'Little Grandfather was the first person to leave. He was frightened, so he was determined to vanish as soon as possible. He told me that our mistress wanted me to leave, but I was curious about the Roman guards. I've never spoken to Roman soldiers before.'

Constantinus took up the questioning again.

'What did the Roman soldiers say to you, Lachie? What did they tell you?'

'Nothing much, I swear. They drank the beer and then they started to doze off. I was surprised. The mistress must have added one of her potions from the black bottle that she keeps in her room. I was frightened by then, so I left as well. I expected that the Romans would wait for their master to return, after he had played his games with the girls.'

'Why did your mistress add her potion to the beer, Lachie?'

Constantinus kept his voice unthreatening, remembering how well this tactic had worked with Nudd.

But Lachie had decided that he was more frightened of the assassins than he was of Constantinus. Closing his eyes, he refused to reveal any further information.

The adjutant turned back to his decurion. 'Paulus, show this fool that we can extract the truth from anyone. You can also convince Lewis here that he ought to consider his own skin, since Lachie is so careless with his life.'

'With pleasure, sir!'

Paulus selected one of the metal tools that had been placed among the hot coals in the brazier, lifted one out to examine its cherry-red tip and spat on the sharpened point. The spittle sizzled and disappeared in a hiss of steam. Then Paulus advanced towards Lachie, who was watching with wide and mesmerised eyes.

'I'm told that an eye cooks like an egg around the heated point if you use hot metal on the face. But we'll be kind, and we'll start on your chest. We'll work our way up, but I'm afraid that this might hurt a little,' Constantinus added in his most reasonable voice.

Lachie screamed as soon as the hot iron seared his flesh but after a while the agony took his voice away. He almost fainted, but when Constantinus asked the questions again, he learned that the servant had seen two masked strangers approaching the kitchens and had decided to make good his departure before he became aware of their intentions.

'I wanted to save myself,' he shrieked.

After this the interrogations went much faster. Aware that Lachie's evidence had damned him, Lewis admitted that Clidna had warned him that strangers would soon be coming to remove

Marcus Britannicus's guards. She had not been able to estimate
how many guards would be accompanying the Roman officer on
his visit to her establishment, so she had provided a soporific to
put the Roman guards to sleep and ensure that their capture
would be an easy task. Lewis admitted that he had seen the two
guards dragged to their feet and pushed, staggering and
stumbling, down the passageway and out into the street.

'You don't seem to have raised a hand to help them,'
Constantinus said, his voice thick with contempt. 'Was this
Conanus with them?'

'I knew there would be trouble,' Lewis said. 'No one said
anything about the murder of a highly born Roman officer. I'm
not an idiot! I'd never have taken part in killing a Roman, no
matter how much coin was offered. One thing was certain! There
was no Conanus in the group that I saw. They talked about him,
but I thought the five men among the assassins were all paid
killers and were following his orders.'

Lewis was quick to blame his mistress for the entire plot. He
pointed one quivering finger towards her prone body.

'She promised me that the patron wouldn't be harmed, but he
would be frightened into paying some outstanding debts. I knew
we were in trouble as soon as I saw their red cloaks, but what
could I say? I went along with her crazy plans and I hoped that
no one would notice the Romans were missing until morning. I
should have run as soon as the assassins were gone, but I was
afraid.'

'You're right! You should have taken to your heels while you
had the chance. Put him in the cells, Paulus, unless he has
something more to offer that might merit a faster death.'

'Stop! You must stop! One of the strangers in the kitchen
swore that he'd only be happy when the job was done and he

was back in his home again. He said he hated Britannia and its lousy weather. He also said that he hated the British people, although he'd been raised to believe that this island was his true homeland.'

Constantinus and Paulus glanced curiously at each other.

'And did he name this particular homeland?' Constantinus asked while he tried to hide his excitement.

'Yes! He did! What was it? I'd never heard the word before, so I could be wrong. I think it was Armorica! That's it! Armorica . . . wherever that is. They were from Armorica – all five of them.'

'Thank you, Lewis. You've provided the last part of the puzzle, so you will be rewarded for your good memory.' Constantinus turned away to leave the small cellar that still reeked of seared human flesh.

He paused at the door and looked back at Lewis, Lachie and Clidna. 'You, Lewis, will be strangled before you're crucified. The others can take their chances.'

'So, Your Highness, we have achieved our aims. We've managed to extract most of the details that these underlings know about the assassination that took place,' Constantinus explained to Aeron, after interrupting the king as the ruler was dispensing justice between two of his quarrelling citizens. Aeron had adjourned his court immediately and, as soon as the hall was cleared, Constantinus revealed what he had learned during the interrogations.

'I have no idea who this Conanus is,' he stated. 'Nor do I know much about the land of Armorica in Gallia. I've heard it referred to as Brittany, too. I've been told that there are a large number of Britons living there. I don't know what their presence has to do with my commander, but it's almost certain that these five men came from Armorica with the avowed intention of killing Marcus Britannicus while he was in Corinium. I understand that the assassination was carried out on the orders of this mysterious Conanus.'

To Constantinus's surprise, Aeron paled noticeably at the information provided. The king's eyes became wintry and his mien changed. Constantinus had considered that Aeron was a mild-mannered man, but now the warrior within the king's nature rose to the surface like a pike that hunts at the bottom of the deepest pools and rarely needs to venture into the light.

'Perhaps we should wait for a moment while I call for my wife. I knew a Conanus who served under the favour of Flavius Magnus Maximus in Gallia. Maximus was a close friend of King Caradoc of Tintagel, and she is Caradoc's daughter. I believe she has met Conanus, who is Severa's uncle. I'm aware that Endellion knew Maximus when she was a young girl, so it may be that old sins have come back to haunt us!'

Realising that King Aeron was serious, Constantinus took the stool that was offered to him and awaited the arrival of the queen, while he tried to keep his reservations under control. He wondered what use a woman could be when he was in pursuit of a pack of murderers. But this queen was a strange one, as reportedly were all the British rulers who originated in Tintagel.

Aeron quickly brought his wife up to date with the information that had been extracted from the prisoners during their torture. The queen grimaced at this, but Conanus's name and the reference to Armorica prompted her to sit down and stare fixedly into the middle distance.

'It isn't possible!' she breathed and her gaze moved from her husband to Constantinus as if she expected them to admit that the information was part of an elaborate jest. 'Conanus couldn't expect to be given the throne on the basis of his tenuous relationship with Severa, could he? Nor would he be likely to come to Corinium where one of us might recognise him. We'd still know him, even after all this time. The man isn't easily forgotten.'

But her voice wasn't convincing and Constantinus was certain that she knew exactly why Marcus Britannicus had been murdered. He could feel his temper beginning to fray. He had experienced a long and wearying day, during which he had been forced to extract information from a band of inept criminals. No matter how necessary his actions had been, he felt soiled by condoning the use of torture; angry and frustrated, he would have happily screamed at the two Britons till they told him everything he needed to know about Conanus and the assassins.

'Who is this Conanus, and what is his connection to Severa? Pardon my rudeness, but I have little time before the commander of the legion will be demanding answers from me.'

'I can understand how you feel,' Aeron answered soothingly before his wife had a chance to respond. But the Roman commander was certain that the king would continue to speak in riddles until such time as he had discussed the matter with the queen.

These fucking Britons! Even the best of them are determined to make us look like fools, Constantinus thought acidly. Some of his temper must have shown on his face, because Aeron called for wine and invited the adjutant to relax into a comfortable chair.

'I'm afraid that this story will take some time in the telling,' Aeron explained with a far-off expression on his face. 'It's a tangled tale that stretches back into the past, but I think I know what Conanus wants.'

'Be patient, Centurion! We've lived with the memory of Maximus, Conanus and Gratian for many years,' Endellion added. 'No one willingly remembers such men, nor wishes to recall the terrible years that blighted our youth. You must excuse us if we make the tale longer in the telling than you'd prefer. Aeron was Maximus's scribe, so he was privy to many secrets, discussions and violences that still bring night terrors to him.'

'I'd still recognise Conanus if I were to see him again,' Aeron said. 'He would have risked discovery if he had entered Corinium and, from my knowledge of the man, I'd say that Conanus has always been very careful. Without the information you succeeded in extracting, none of us would have guessed at his complicity in this crime.'

'Conanus would have hidden himself away in the lower town,' Endellion went on. 'He wouldn't have entered the city gates and would have frequented places where he could fit in with the poor and criminals. He was already a master of disguise when, with Andragathius, the officer who slew Emperor Gratian, he feigned the role of an androgynous harper and entertainer. It was Conanus who talked his way past the Praetorian Guards to kill Gratian. He would have feared my sharp eyes and Aeron's memory, so it's probable that he came to the Street of Whores some time ago to make his arrangements to use the Bower of Beauty as part of some nameless plot. Conanus is a man who knows how to wait.'

As Endellion spoke, Aeron formulated the tale of Conanus's life from that long-ago time.

'Conanus was Elen's brother. As Elen was the wife of Maximus and the birth-mother of Severa, Conanus is actually Severa's uncle. That makes him her closest male kinsman and the paterfamilias of her family. He was a prince of the Ordovice tribe, of which his father was one of their more competent rulers. Like many of our young men, including myself, Conanus was seduced by Maximus's promises of power and lands in Gallia if he was prepared to follow the High King in his pursuit of the throne of Rome.'

'But the rise and fall of Flavius Magnus Maximus happened years ago, so why now?' Constantinus protested. He vaguely understood the position of this Conanus within the political landscape and how such a man might wish to foment trouble and achieve some political prize by interfering with Severa's marriage arrangements. But he could see no reason for a complex plot involving the assassination of a senior Roman officer. Precipitate action could be expected to bring the full weight of Roman revenge down on those who participated in such treasonous activities.

'The events of which we speak all happened in recent history, both for Rome and Britannia,' Endellion added. 'Much bad feeling was generated when Maximus was killed at the hands of Theodosius and Valentinian, who were the emperors of the Eastern Empire and Western Empire respectively. As you might remember, Maximus was also the emperor of Gallia, Hispania and Britannia, all of which were won by right of conquest. He ruled ably until he attempted to take Rome by force of arms. Unfortunately, ambition drove him and he succumbed to hubris, knowing that he was a better man than the weakling, Valentinian. But he forgot that Theodosius, his kinsman, was also a soldier of renown. Chance cost him his moment of glory because the Scythians became the agents of his destruction.'

'Maximus was a foolish man in many ways,' Aeron continued

seamlessly. 'He could have ruled wisely and well in Britannia, but he hungered for the right to seat himself in the City of the Seven Hills. It is evident to me that the Emperor of Constantinople would never countenance the presence of an able general on the throne at the Palatine. Valentinian is the perfect co-emperor for Theodosius, because he's inept, lazy and easily led, just like his predecessor, Gratian.'

Constantinus was unable to keep the sneer from his lips, for he had heard many senior officers discussing the Battle of the Save in scathing terms. 'I have heard that Maximus over-reached himself by trying to defeat Theodosius in the field. My Roman peers believe that Maximus's foolishness cost him the battle.'

'I was there, Constantinus, and Maximus was anything but a fool. He had the numbers, the seasoned troops who were ready to die for him and a strategy that brought him close to success. But the Scythians were Lady Fortuna's practical joke that she used to temper his hubris. Their feats on horseback cut our legions to ribbons. What Roman cavalryman could compete with a horseman who uses both hands to draw his bow and loose an arrow at the height of a battle?'

'I've never seen Scythians fight, so until I do I'll probably hold the view that they wouldn't be a match for our seasoned Roman cavalry,' Constantinus answered haughtily.

'Then you would have died on the battlefield with the rest of Maximus's forces. Theodosius was beaten until the Scythians took to the field, and I remember my amazement when they began to pick off our commanders with a rain of arrows that were perfectly aimed to cause the maximum of carnage. Have you seen such small men, armoured in scales of iron, who can hold the reins of their horses in their teeth and control their horses better with their knees than a Roman can control his horse with two good hands?'

'Perhaps all that you have said about this battle is true, but none of this old history explains why Conanus has devised a plot to assassinate Marcus Britannicus.'

'Conanus served Maximus with distinction before the emperor's death so, out of the commander's gratitude, he was given lands in Armorica as payment for his loyalty. These were larger than any kingdom in our isle, and his wealth was greater than any reasonable man would desire. But Conanus was always a greedy man, so he was anxious to possess even more wealth and power. I'll wager that he'd lay claim to anything he thinks he can grab, by force or otherwise.'

'Are you saying that Conanus might be prepared to capture Maximus's daughter, set himself up as her regent and then force the British kings to declare a husband, chosen by him, as the High King of the Britons? I could understand this reasoning, but it wouldn't work unless he married Severa off to some person who could be kept under his total control.'

Constantinus paused. 'Is it possible that he has a son?'

The king and queen were so alike in their thinking that they both shrugged like twins.

'Why would Conanus assassinate Marcus, a stupid act that could bring the Roman legions down on his head? And why has it happened now?' Constantinus asked.

Endellion sighed, both from frustration and a growing presentiment of fear.

'I believe that Conanus planned this coup a long time ago, but he has only recently been forced to show his hand when the British kings chose a Roman to marry Severa. Such a betrothal would have been anathema to Conanus and he would go to any lengths to prevent the marriage from going ahead,' she explained. 'The man I met when I was only a slip of a girl was hungry and ruthless. I'd be surprised if he has changed.'

'Then your Severa is in grave danger. Conanus will want to have her wedded to a husband of his choice as quickly as possible in case Rome becomes aware of his plans and takes action to isolate him. According to an innkeeper I questioned, the five assassins had been in Corinium for some time, so I assume they were waiting for their master to unleash them on Marcus Britannicus or some other prospective husband. If you are right about his fear of exposure, he will have left your town long before the assassination was attempted. He would have been concerned about the possibility of being rounded up with other undesirables in the event of a full-scale search. He will have removed himself far enough to be safe while still being able to communicate with his men. I doubt he will have returned to Armorica, because he must know that you can easily find another suitor for Severa if you wish to.'

Endellion nodded. 'You've accurately expressed my worst fears. He can thwart all further betrothals if he captures Severa and imprisons her by force.'

'I agree! That is exactly how I would expect Conanus to proceed,' Aeron added.

Constantinus thought very carefully as he tried to reason like a Briton.

'Regardless of where he is hiding himself away, Conanus is suffering under the weight of several pressing disadvantages. Much of his time will be wasted as he waits for couriers and sends replies to his assassins, so you will have some time to move Severa out of harm's way. The only problem is finding a safe place of refuge.'

'Tintagel!' Endellion said firmly. 'Conanus couldn't hope to be successful against Tintagel because he couldn't gain entry to the fortress. It's the safest place in Britannia for our girl. My brother is king and our kinfolk have no love for those men who went to Armorica. It would be even better if you could take her, Constantinus, for Conanus would be reluctant to attack a century of Roman legionnaires without a large army at his back.'

The conversation was becoming alarming to Constantinus and his love of order. He was loath to act without express orders from his superiors and he was feeling the firm earth turning to quicksand under his feet. He had much to lose if he agreed to hastily constructed plans devised by a tribal king and his wife, if these ran counter to the wishes of his masters. On the other hand, he would certainly carry much of the blame if Severa should be taken and used as a pawn in a rebellion against Rome. He could find himself in the wrong, no matter how he acted.

'I'd like you to send a courier to Tribune Maximo to request his approval for this course of action,' he decided. 'Meanwhile, I'll make preparations for a departure from Corinium at short notice.'

'But we don't have the luxury of time,' Endellion protested. 'I believe you must leave for Tintagel immediately, Centurion, although I can understand your concerns. I will send my own courier to Tribune Maximo with a scroll explaining the gravity of our situation. Should your tribune require you to be recalled from this duty, I will send a further courier to inform you of the decision and release you from your commitment. I will then make alternative arrangements to spirit Severa to Tintagel. Would you accept such an arrangement?'

'I agree with Endellion. Tintagel would make a perfect haven until such time as your commanders make a firm decision on what is to be done with our girl,' Aeron added in his most reasonable voice. 'Meanwhile, it would be best to send several couriers to Deva by different routes, thereby ensuring that at least one of them will be successful in notifying your commanding tribune of your actions. When the couriers return I will send further couriers to Tintagel where you should be safely ensconced. Severa isn't safe here. Corinium is a trading town, and its walls and warriors are hardly adequate to protect a determined assault by an aggressor. But I do accept that the ultimate decision must be yours.'

Constantinus was painfully aware that he had been trapped, but Aeron's logic was sound. If they were wrong about the involvement of Conanus in this plot, then no harm would be done if his column escorted Severa to a place of safety. If Conanus was involved, and if he did plan to capture this girl, Constantinus would have demonstrated his initiative by spiriting her away. Whatever happened, his position was relatively secure.

'Very well, Highness! I will tidy up the last threads of my investigation into the death of my commander and will assume his role until such time as my superiors issue me with further orders. Those who played a dishonourable part in the assassination of Marcus Britannicus will be crucified tomorrow at the town gates so that all men can see Roman justice in action. At first light, several couriers will be sent into the north. I intend to depart for Tintagel at noon tomorrow with your foster-daughter. We will travel at the best speed that our charge can endure.'

The rulers of Corinium nodded in satisfaction.

'Severa is strong,' Endellion said with a tiny smile. 'She'll endure, and she won't complain. Meanwhile, I'll help her to pack for the journey and I'll write a short message to my brother,

Cadal, that will explain your needs. You'll need such a missive if you are to gain entry to the fortress.'

With an uncomfortable feeling that he was still being manipulated, Constantinus excused himself and left the hall. The light was already fading and long shadows barred the street in bands of charcoal. Although he tried to discover a flaw in the plan, every detail seemed reasonable, so why was such a weight pressing on his chest? Why did he long to flee from this place and pull the mountains down around him so he could hide himself from the view of all-seeing God?

Constantinus pushed his unwanted fears away and walked out into the early evening to do his duty.

THE JOURNEY FROM
CORINIUM TO TINTAGEL

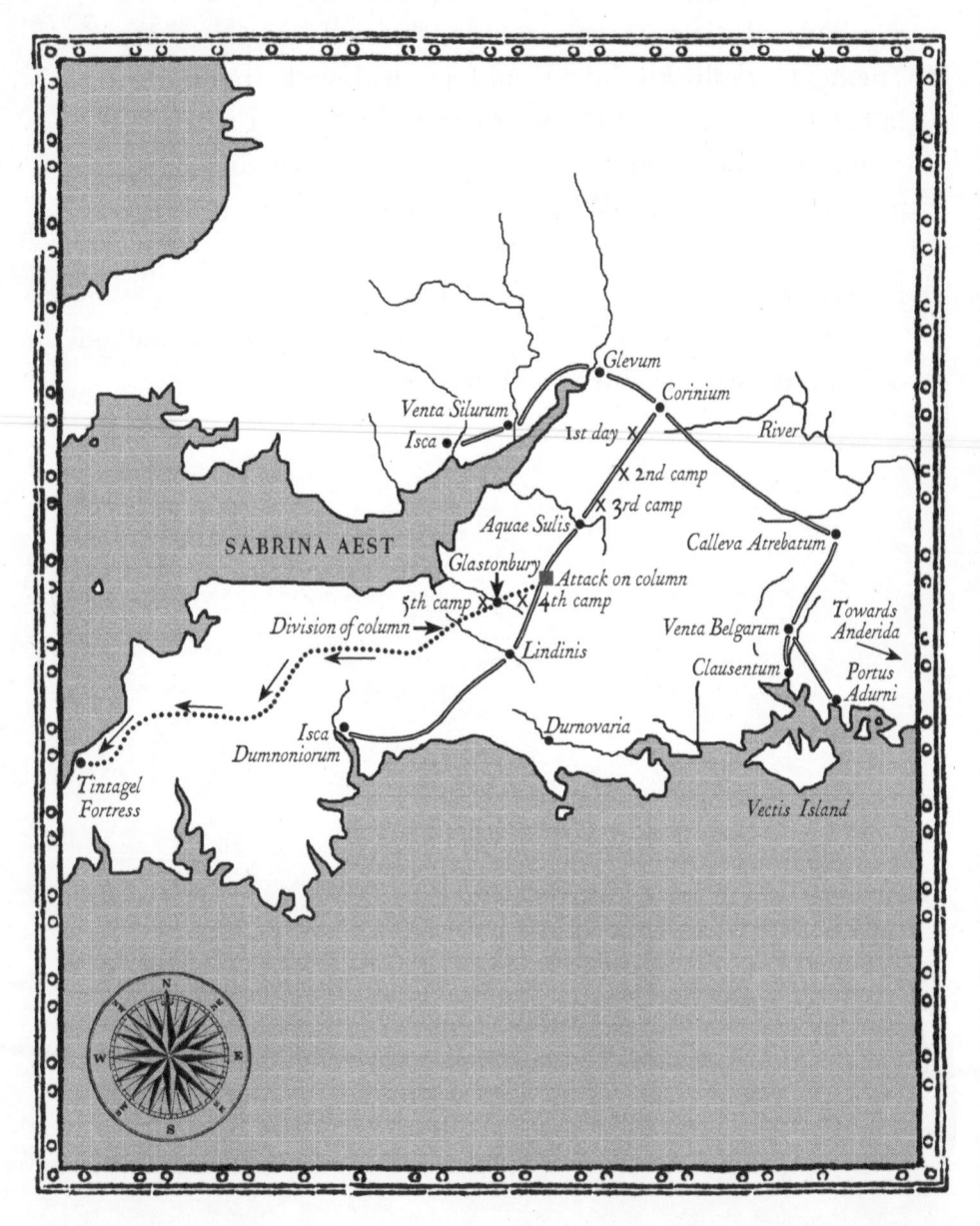

CHAPTER VI

A HURRIED JOURNEY

Never shall I say that marriage brings more joy than pain.

Euripides, *Alcestis*

Aeron demonstrated the value of his years of service in Maximus's legions by the speed with which he organised everything for his foster-daughter. Before the hour was out, two couriers were sent by differing routes to alert King Cadal of the imminent arrival of distinguished guests. Meanwhile, Severa was given an appraisal of her situation before being sent, protesting, to pack sufficient clothing for the journey.

'But why am I in danger?' she demanded of Endellion. In her youth, she had loved Tintagel, but to be packed off to such an isolated place with a solitary maid as company was not to her liking. Endellion merely shrugged and continued to sort out suitable clothes to combat the strong ocean winds that blew there.

'No one bothers to explain anything to me,' Severa pouted. 'My intended husband has just died and you've told me that I must leave Corinium immediately. I'm not even allowed to pay him the courtesy of attending his final rites. How will my absence appear to our people? Unseemly talk will smear my reputation and my early departure will make me seem heartless. What overriding need requires me to run off to a rock in the middle of the ocean?'

'We've been given information that convinced us that you are in grave danger, Severa. It's likely that a usurper has concocted a plot to capture you and hide you away until such time as he can use your bloodline to exert power over the British people. If these plans succeed, the scion of one of the kings involved in this treason could be elevated to the position of High King of the Britons. The other kings of Britannia would be forced to comply eventually because such a marriage has historically been the way in which some unscrupulous men have gained power ahead of the legitimate claims of their peers. If the plotters achieve their aims, your new bridegroom will be a Briton rather than a Roman. Think of the implications of such a match, Severa! Did you not wonder whether Marcus Britannicus was assassinated because he was courting you?'

'I thought Marcus was killed because his enemies wanted to punish him for his sexual activities.'

'I imagine that was what we were supposed to believe,' Endellion replied shortly. 'Hurry now, Severa. You don't want to be working all night and find yourself tired on the morrow. Whatever your feelings, we've decided that you'll be leaving for Tintagel at noon.'

But Endellion knew that the girl remained unconvinced of her danger. Severa's folded arms, tapping feet and set lips screamed irritation and rejection of the queen's argument. The queen rarely lost her temper with her foster-daughter, but now her anxiety and weariness meant she spoke more sharply than usual, taking Severa aback.

'You ungrateful girl! A number of people will be working through the night to prepare your baggage train for the journey to Tintagel. Some of our servants have opted to undertake the journey with you, despite our concerns for their safety. They will be risking their lives to keep you safe, yet you sit here and complain that you can't see the need to protect yourself.'

'But . . . I only . . .'

'I'm tired of hearing your childish objections, Severa. Go to bed now while I finish your packing for you. I'm sick of arguing with you!'

Severa, deeply hurt at the rebuke, was beginning to feel vulnerable, which was Endellion's precise intention. The girl's eyes filled with tears, but Endellion merely continued to pack Severa's travelling chest with a smooth, practised motion. Eventually, Severa wandered away with her shoulders slumped in misery.

As soon as her foster-daughter disappeared into her sleeping chamber, Endellion straightened her aching back and surveyed the almost-filled chest with satisfaction and a twinge of sadness. Were they making an error? Was it possible that Severa could be safer with her family in the heart of Corinium?

Endellion began to recall Conanus as she had first met him, all those years earlier at the little town on the wild northern coast of Cymru. His hawk-like face had been set and angry, while his black eyes had stared at her with a mixture of disdain and sly sexual interest. She had known from the moment she first laid eyes on him that he was dangerous, even though he was the very young heir to a small clan within the Ordovice tribe. What must he be like now, after serving with Maximus for six years and ruling a large swathe of Armorica for more than a decade? By her reckoning, Conanus must be close to fifty. Did those internal fires still burn hotly within his nature now that he was the ruler of a land that was far larger than his father's kingdom?

Yes! Conanus was a man to be feared. He would always want what he couldn't have.

If he was the perpetrator of this assassination, he must have decided to become the ultimate High King of the Britons and, if his men should capture Severa, he would have her married off to one of his sons. Later, he would ensure that there was an unfortunate accident so that he could assume the throne as the regent for the child who was a result of that union. Later still, he would have the child murdered and become the High King by right of blood. Who would stand against him? He would rule Britannia and Armorica, and his growing strength would make him a clear threat to the Romans, whose hold on Gallia was weakening daily.

Her silent thoughts spun inside her head like the portents from a seer. Severa was at great risk. Endellion had no hesitation in putting her feelings of loss and doubt to one side as she finalised the packing.

Pridenow surged out of a night horror, his eyes wide with fright and his screams echoing within his own ears. Fortunately, these vivid dreams faded quickly.

As if by magic, his mother suddenly appeared in his doorway.

'Hush, darling boy, there's nothing here to frighten you.' She took him in her arms and snuggled into his narrow pallet so she could hold him tightly. 'Can you remember what you were dreaming about, sweetling? Night terrors don't really mean anything and they rarely come true, so you have nothing to fear.'

'I feel sick,' the boy responded with what she knew was the residual horror of the dream.

'There's no need to worry, darling. I had many frightening

dreams when I was a child, but most of them never became true,'
Endellion lied. Better to avoid the truth while her son was so
young, rather than terrify him with this grotesque gift he had
inherited from her bloodline.

'Severa's in trouble, isn't she? I'm sure of it, because I saw three
men surrounding her. They were holding her tightly so that the
bad men couldn't take her away. Don't let her be hurt!'

'Hush, darling boy,' Endellion repeated, while she stroked his
hair.

'The first man is already here in Corinium, Mama. He's the
Roman who came to the villa with the dead man who was
supposed to marry Severa. You know the man I mean.'

'Is he the centurion?'

'I think that's the man,' the boy answered sleepily. His mother's
warmth was soothing his anxiety and he began to drift back into
sleep, even as he was speaking. 'I don't really know what a
centurion is, but the other Romans obey him.'

'His name is Constantinus,' Endellion answered.

'Yes. He was wearing a crown and a funny band of leaves around
his forehead, but I don't think he's a king. Is he a king, Mother?'

'No, he's not.' Endellion tried to school her voice to remain in
the soft croon of a mother.

How could Constantinus, as a Roman of no birth and damned
little prestige, become a king? Could it happen through Severa?
The laurel crown was reserved for those few men who attained
the position of emperor, so this was highly unlikely. The Romans
would never elevate a landless man of no gens to such heights;
Pridenow's dream was just as it seemed – the strange rambling
of a child's brain.

'I liked him, Mother. Did you know that he also has a son like
me! His son was also in my dream, but I can't remember his

name. He wore a crown too, but ...' The boy's voice faltered, for he suddenly remembered something else that terrified him. 'But someone had hurt him. Someone had cut his throat and he was still bleeding.'

'It was just a dream, sweet boy, so try to go back to sleep.'

'I remember the other men now,' Pridenow said suddenly. 'They were horrible, Mother, and they were trying to carry Severa away. One was an old man with white, curly hair. He was looking at me as if he hated me, and he told me I would become the Father of the She-Dragon. What did that mean?'

'No one hates you, Pridenow. If anyone did, your father would kill them as quick as can be, just to make sure we keep you safe.'

'Truly?' Pridenow asked in a childish treble.

'Truly!' Endellion replied with feigned confidence.

'The other man was a bad man! He was a Briton, and I could see that he had long black hair and a pointed beard that looked like the blade of a spear. He was wearing a crown.'

'Did the old man with the white hair wear a crown?' Endellion asked, hardly daring to breathe.

Pridenow thought hard.

'No! I could see all his hair, so he wasn't wearing a crown. He wasn't a king.'

Endellion sighed with relief. If the child's dream held truth, Conanus would never become High King and her beloved island might still be spared from his depredations.

'I don't want to think about the dream any more, Mother. I don't want to remember that poor boy with his cut throat.'

'You've been very brave, my darling boy, so it's time to go back to sleep now. You can wake early enough to say your goodbyes to Severa because she's going on a visit to see your uncle, King Cadal, at Tintagel Fortress.'

'Is she going with the centurion?' Pridenow asked, yawning.

'Yes, darling. The centurion will protect her during the journey to Tintagel.'

'That's good, then! Severa will be safe with him to guard her.'

Before Endellion could stir on the warm pallet, the boy had dozed off with both fists curled together under his chin.

The midday sun had come and gone while Constantinus and his troop waited impatiently for Severa to join them. The first wagon had been packed with the clothes, gifts and luxuries that Severa would need for this journey, while the second wagon had been laden with supplies for Constantinus's column of foot soldiers and cavalry. Eventually, the king and queen followed Severa into the courtyard where they could bid farewell to their departing guests.

Constantinus's horse was showing an obvious eagerness to be gone, and he had to maintain a tight grip on the straight bit.

He decided not to embarrass his royal hosts by forcing them to look upwards at a mere centurion, so he dismounted to make good his farewells. Aeron inclined his head respectfully to acknowledge the gesture.

'My foster-daughter has already made more than her share of farewells to her siblings, my wife and all the servants, so I believe she has no further excuses to delay her departure. Could I ask you to assist her into the wagon, sir?'

Endellion winced at Aeron's jest. She had yet to share her misgivings with her husband, but she was concerned at the thought of Severa and Constantinus thrown together during their trek to the coast and safety, a journey that could take as long as a week or more. She felt no surprise when Severa blushed as Constantinus offered her his hand.

'Mistress?' the centurion began. 'The roads will be a little rough along the route we're taking, so I'm afraid the journey will be less than comfortable in places. You'll have to make sure you wear a hat and a veil if the horses' hooves raise large clouds of dust.'

Constantinus realised he was babbling as soon as Severa's eyes met his. She accepted his assistance to climb up to the crude wooden seat beside the driver, who had constructed a light canopy over the seat to provide some shade.

Endellion felt her eyes prickle with tears as she waved up to her foster-daughter. 'Go with God, sweetheart. Give my love to my brothers.'

'I will, Mama Endellion. Goodbye, and don't forget to ensure that Pridenow takes care of my dog.'

All her sulks and complaints of the previous night had been completely forgotten in the excitement of this unexpected journey.

Constantinus remounted and nodded towards Paulus, who issued the command to march. As usual, each of the infantrymen carried his shield on his back with full packs containing every item of equipment that these fighting men might need to survive in wild country where danger could be waiting in every copse of trees. At Constantinus's instructions, Paulus had warned the men that this particular journey could be threatened by those same assassins who had murdered their erstwhile commander, so a wary force of forty infantry and twenty-eight cavalrymen marched out of Corinium with Constantinus at the head of the extended column.

As they marched through the cobbled streets of Corinium, the townsfolk came out into the streets to gawk, to cheer or to press flowers and small gifts upon the soldiers. The people of this trading centre knew all too well how much was owed to their Roman overlords.

The king and queen stood on the steps of their villa and waved until the cavalcade was finally out of sight. 'Well, that's done then,' Aeron said with finality. 'If Conanus plans to capture Severa, he'll baulk at making an attack on this force of Romans.'

'Perhaps! Unfortunately, the Conanus I remember would consider an armed century to be a challenge rather than a major obstacle. Oh, I do hope we're doing the right thing.'

A sudden wind caught at the aspens and stirred their leaves, tearing at the tender new growth and rattling the branches. Endellion watched as several ravens took wing and flew off into the south.

Then, as one particularly strong gust raised dust from the square, Endellion's veil was torn away and sailed off after them. Like a white bird, its corners flapped and twisted as it climbed in the gusting wind until it became tangled on one of the towers above the gate. It opened to the wind, a veritable flag of surrender to the exigencies of fate.

Endellion stared after it, as if it held some important message within its sheer folds.

'What else could we have done, woman? If Severa had stayed here, we'd be afraid of the assassin's knife during the night until such time as that bastard is caught and killed.'

Aeron was unusually curt with his wife, a sure indication of his concern.

'I know! I know! But I don't have to like this scheme, do I? Severa is far too fond of that young Roman for my liking.'

Her eyes returned to the flapping veil above the town gates.

'Don't worry, sweetheart. Even Caradoc would agree that you've done everything possible to protect Maximus's daughter, so everything that happens from now on must have been determined by her destiny. You've told me often enough that fate will confound all our hopes and dreams, regardless of what we humans do to protect ourselves.'

Endellion squeezed his hand to comfort him.

'You're right, beloved. Whatever will happen, will happen! Severa is now in the capable hands of Constantinus, so I'm hopeful that everything will work out for the best.'

Yet deep down Endellion was certain that Pridenow's dream was a message from Fortuna of some future disaster.

Then, as if an invisible hand had gripped it, the gusty wind swept her beautiful veil away forever.

The road that led into the south from the gates of Corinium, that Britons called Fosse Way, was well maintained and perpetually dry, for it had been built atop a ridge of low hills. Most of the going had a slight downhill grade, so the travellers could see the landscape of neat farms, bordered by dry walls of fieldstone that divided the countryside into green and golden rectangles dotted with the white and black of sheep. The adjacent hills were also thick with forest, providing swathes of shadowed coolness that beckoned the marchers towards places of rest as the sun sank lower in the sky.

Severa looked down from her high perch behind the sturdy horses harnessed in the traces. Well cared for, their coats shining in the afternoon sun, the animals seemed indefatigable as they easily pulled the heavy load behind them. Their hooves threw up small clouds of dust which managed to insert its way into every private place of her body. Yet even this small discomfort was new and exciting, because Severa had rarely travelled for any distance from her home.

She had feared that she would be very bored during the journey, but her worries had proved to be groundless. The unrolling scroll of the landscape passed by slowly enough for her to be captivated by the lives of the farmers that she observed at close quarters. She could tell that the livestock fared well within this kindly landscape, where the grass was lush and green and wildflowers grew among the weeds. Even the verges of the road were productive with blackberries growing wild among the walls and fences. Severa longed to dismount from the wagon so she could wander along those same verges.

'The youngest farm-girl knows more than I do about how to exist outside the four walls of a villa,' she said to herself.

'Begging your pardon, mistress? Do you have a question?' The driver was holding the reins loosely in his hands, but Severa could tell that those muscular fingers would be the equal of any emergency, while his ruddy face was weathered from many years on the road. His sky-blue eyes were bright and startling and she decided that this man would be kindly, so she smiled appealingly at him.

'I'm sorry for my ignorance, good driver, but I'd like to speak with you during our journey together. Are you permitted to tell me your name? How should I address you?'

The driver, taken aback by her frankness, realised how inappropriate her approach to him would be judged given the wide disparity in their social status. Even the presence of her maid might not save him from punishment. Yet he responded to the friendly approaches of this ingenious girl-woman.

'My name's Cael, mistress. Me old da said it means *slender*, though I'm not so much like me name any more.' He laughed deprecatingly.

'It's a lovely meaning, Cael, and a good British name that's far better than mine.'

'Still, Severa has a pretty sound, mistress. The Romans have been here for hundreds of years now, so I wouldn't be surprised if lots of good British people had a drop or two of Roman blood in them. I've heard that your da was a man of importance and great courage.'

'That's very kind of you, Cael.'

Severa continued to engage Cael in conversation during the afternoon. She learned many small details about farming life from her driver, for he had been raised on a small-holding near Caer Fyrddin.

When the evening began with its long twilight, Constantinus ordered the troop to halt for the night. His scouts had alerted him to the presence of a river that needed to be forded on the morrow, so he decided not to risk his wagons while the horses were weary after a day's work. Even after a long march, the troops were still required to dig a ditch around their encampment, and to prepare pits for makeshift latrines, and set up fire pits and tripods for cooking. Stiff in every joint, Severa eased her aching back and climbed down from the wagon, tearing off her protective veil as she reached firm earth.

'If you need to walk off any stiffness, Mistress Severa, you must stay within the perimeter of the campsite.'

The sudden instruction from Constantinus had come from behind her. The Roman was so cat-footed that she hadn't heard his approach. Recovering quickly and patting the dust off her skirts, she smiled up at the centurion and stamped her feet to recapture some feeling. 'The seat is very hard and the wagon becomes quite dusty.'

'And this is one of the better roads,' Constantinus riposted with a wry grin. 'The last part of the road that takes us to Tintagel is supposed to be little more than a goat track.'

Severa smiled in response and began to stroll through the

encampment, taking care to keep within the ditch dug by the legionnaires. At a loose end, and momentarily at a loss for words, Constantinus followed her.

'Do you still believe I'm in any danger, Centurion? My foster-mother sometimes overreacts when she's concerned for my safety.'

'My commanding officer would be the very first person to answer you with the well-known cliché that *it's better to be safe than sorry*, mistress. Is there any harm in visiting your kinfolk in Tintagel?'

As the centurion's voice carried a hint of censure, Severa felt herself begin to bridle.

'I wouldn't want you to end up in a midden with a dozen knife wounds in your body,' Constantinus added. 'Marcus's murderers were ugly, determined ruffians who will not hesitate to kill anyone who interferes with their plans. I carried out the interrogations of the whores and other workers who were at the brothel where he was captured, and I was eventually convinced that their final responses were truthful.'

Severa ignored a twinge of warning that told her to remain silent. But her curiosity overshadowed her cautious nature.

'How can you be sure that the servants didn't lie to you, Centurion?' Severa wanted to learn every grisly detail of Marcus's murder, not out of morbid curiosity, but to satisfy herself that this long journey was necessary. 'They would hardly wish to incriminate themselves.'

Constantinus grinned mirthlessly.

'No, the poor beggars never lied to me. At least, not at the end of the interrogation! Few people can resist torture. We all think we can withstand pain, but a red-hot shaft of iron driven into an eyeball will achieve the required compliance on every occasion it's used.'

Severa gasped with shock.

'But that's bestial!' she exclaimed. 'How could any civilised person inflict such pain?'

Constantinus halted, so she was forced to pause and then turn to face him.

'My duty was to discover why my master was murdered in such a vile manner. I consider myself to be a *civilised* person but, first and foremost, I'm a loyal Roman officer. I would never permit squeamishness to deter me from performing my duty.'

'I meant no offence, Centurion,' Severa gasped hurriedly. 'You surprised me.'

'I disagree, Severa. You meant exactly what you said,' Constantinus responded in a clipped voice.

'I did mean what I said, Centurion, so I apologise for my words. I don't know anything about torture or political matters at all . . . and I suppose I don't really want to know. I was irritated after I was sent away to a fortress far from my home against my wishes. I'm still not convinced that such a journey is necessary. But, if you believe that the servants at this brothel finally told the truth after they had been tortured, then I probably need to think again.'

'I accept your apologies, Severa. I've always believed that well-born women should be protected from distasteful matters, so it was wrong of me to be so blunt with you.'

Severa smiled. 'So we're both wrong. Perhaps we should begin again.'

The legionnaires in Constantinus's command were amused by the sight of their master, hands clasped firmly behind his back, as he escorted the young lady about the camp while talking genteelly of such topics as farming and blackberry picking. There was no spite or jealousy in the campfire banter that followed. These men knew that their commander was a very good officer whose roots were similar to their own, a leader who had been clever enough to rise to the highest echelons of the legion. With some pride, and no signs of resentment, the men gossiped about his son, Constans, and wondered who the boy's mother might have been, how Constantinus had arrived in Britannia and whether he'd manage to bed this noble princess from the British tribes.

Severa's first night under canvas came with a rush. Flushed from her first rambling stroll with a man, she scarcely noticed the bland stew that lacked salt and herbs to give it flavour. Sleeping on a thin pallet under the wagon was an amazing adventure and she could delight in the river of stars that were sailing through the night sky as she lay under her warm covers.

From across the camp, she could see that the centurion was staring out into the darkness as he stood beside the fire pit. No light spoke of farmsteads and even the folds in the earth were devoid of domestic animals. Somewhere out there, Constantinus knew that trouble was waiting to fall on his column at any time, especially if he became careless. Somewhere beyond this small fortress of order, a small group of six assassins, at the very least, was waiting to make an attempt to capture Severa. For Constantinus, his duty was clear: Severa would be taken to the safety of Cadal's fortress at Tintagel, and the Roman was prepared to give his life to ensure that this mission was successfully completed.

As for the girl herself, he was attracted to her, as any man with red blood in his veins would be. But, when all was said and done, his duty required him to consider her as just another pretty face. He recalled the words of the Wilde Man of the Woods and decided that he must take the sensible path of prudence unless circumstances indicated otherwise.

Perhaps, somewhere beyond the reach of time, Lady Fortuna was laughing at him.

The Attack on
the Wagon Train

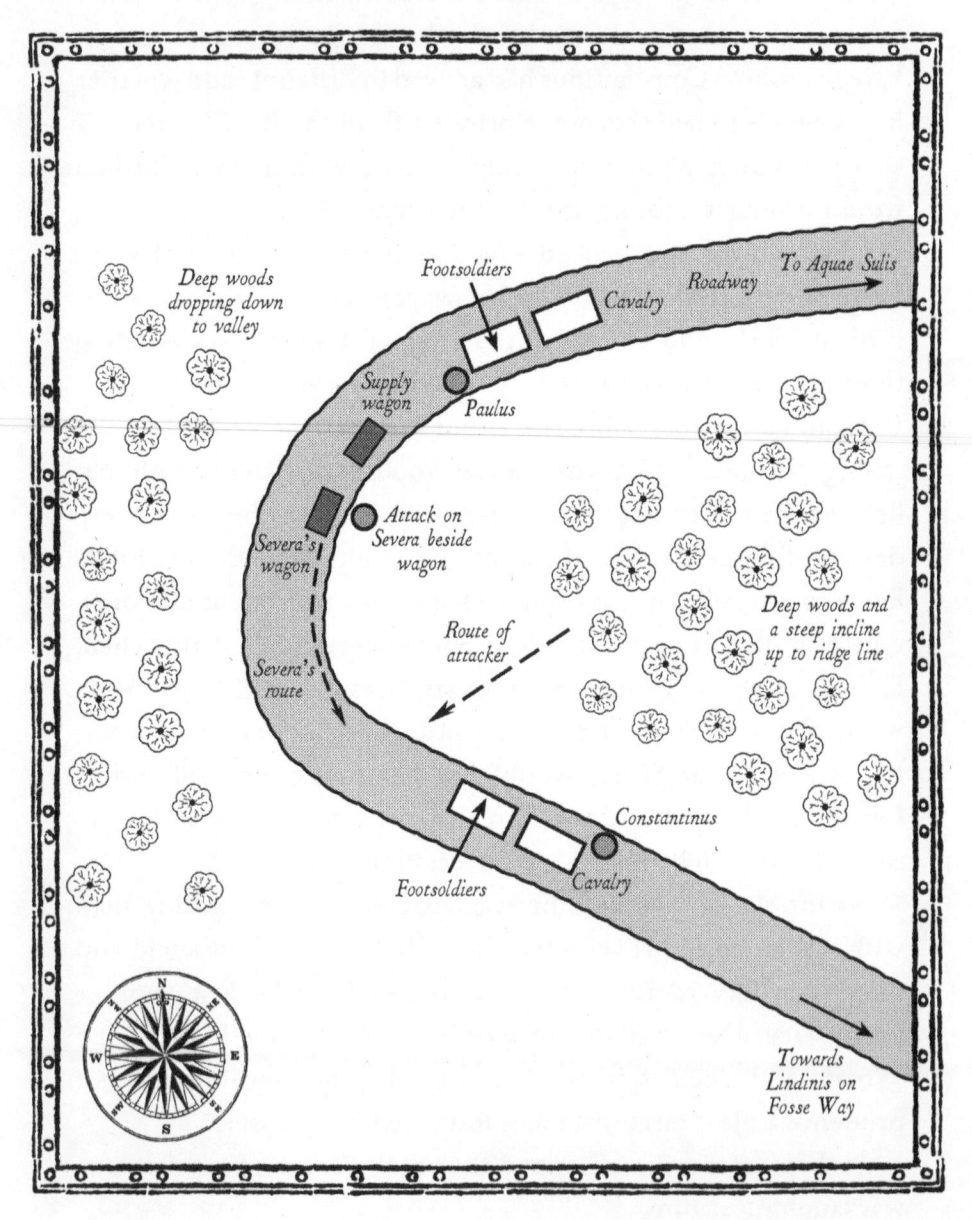

Deep woods
dropping down
to valley

Footsoldiers

Roadway

To Aquae Sulis

Cavalry

Supply
wagon

Paulus

Attack on
Severa beside
wagon

Severa's
wagon

Route of
attacker

Route of
attacker

Deep woods and
a steep incline
up to ridge line

Severa's
route

Constantinus

Footsoldiers

Cavalry

Towards
Lindinis on
Fosse Way

CHAPTER VII

AMBUSH

The road up and the road down are one and the same.

Heraclitus, *Die Fragmente der Vorsokratiker*

Two long and dusty days followed as, hour after hour and day after day, the horses raised white clouds of fine, powdery grit that covered every surface. Each evening, in an unvarying ritual, Severa and the centurion would walk the perimeter of the camp before eating the same tasteless stew. Later, she stared out at the countless stars that seemed much brighter than those that filled the skies of Corinium.

Her maid was always five steps behind her when she and Constantinus were alone, always silent and forever watchful. When Endellion had thrust one of her own women upon Severa, her foster-daughter had been irritated and complained angrily at the queen's lack of trust, but Endellion had no hesitation in explaining that this maid was more of a chaperone than a servant and was travelling with the girl to protect her reputation.

'The British kings will use the smallest excuse to blacken your name in days to come, my girl, so it's time for you to develop some common sense and start to act responsibly.'

Severa was therefore forced to accept a chaperone with very little grace, and responded by ignoring her newly appointed servant whenever possible.

Aquae Sulis was situated inside a swathe of rolling plain-land that was rich and densely populated, with expensive villas perched atop every raised hill or suitable building site within sight of the city walls. Constantinus studied the town from one of the few vantage points and quickly recognised the Roman flavour of its architecture. But the pleasures such a town could offer would present too many temptations for his legionnaires if his charge was permitted to dally there, so he decided his column would make an overnight bivouac outside the town limits before resuming their journey in the morning.

Severa was quick to express her dissatisfaction at his decision.

'Every person I have known who has been given an opportunity to pass through Aquae Sulis has spoken of the wonders of the goods in their markets. The food! The shoes! I've dreamed for years that I, too, would get to see those markets . . . and now you're telling me that it's too dangerous to pause and satisfy my curiosity.'

Constantinus was annoyed by the girl's indignant manner.

'I find it strange that you'd risk your own life and the safety of my legionnaires so you can indulge yourself with a little shopping in the markets, Severa.'

Severa continued to pout throughout the evening, but Constantinus stood firm and refused to discuss the matter. Eventually, he left the girl at the fire pit and disappeared, which plunged her into even greater gloom.

Inexperienced and vulnerable, Severa was falling in love with the handsome young centurion. Constantinus, however, was more discreet. During his career as a legionnaire, he had known many women on the Roman frontiers, but his heart had never been engaged in his sexual escapades. Even his first wife, a girl from his own village who chose to follow the legions to be close to him, had scarcely stirred any deep feelings or regard. Try as he might, Constantinus could no longer remember her face. She had vanished into the river of time.

Could he have fallen in love with Severa in three brief days? The Roman searched for an answer as he attempted to understand the sick nausea in his belly that came over him at the thought of her marriage to another man. He realised that he was attracted to this woman, who was an important political pawn from the heartland of Britannia where Roman and British cultures met, and part of his cold inner self realised that there could be advantages to his career if he formed a liaison with her. Yet he was also attracted to Severa's childlike womanliness, her ignorance of the arts of romantic love and the lustre of her physical features. But he was honest enough to admit that any attraction towards her would begin to vanish from the moment he finally possessed her.

'However, if her very presence is sufficient to raise my heartbeat, then my attraction towards her might add up to love of a sort,' he whispered doubtfully into the breeze. 'Perhaps the emotion I feel for this girl might truly be love, rather than lust.'

For all his external coolness and rigidity, the centurion was capable of sudden flashes of generosity and sweetness. And so, just on full dark, he found Severa as she stared into the dying fire as if it held the deepest secrets of her future.

'Mistress Severa!'

She half rose, spun to face him, and then seated herself once more. She drew her robe neatly over her knees.

'I realised you were disappointed by my decision to avoid the markets in Aquae Sulis and the many beautiful objects that are always on sale there. It's unfortunate, but it would have been foolish of me to allow anyone in this column to make an unnecessary visit to the town. However, as you are my guest and my charge, I thought I might atone for my misdeeds by presenting you with a special gift that I have purchased as a gesture of my good will.'

Constantinus held out a wrapped parcel of cloth. Unused to gifts from strangers, Severa flushed as she removed the string that held the wrapping cloth in place to expose a beautiful comb designed to hold back her hair.

Severa stroked the ivory bauble, heavily carved with depictions of flowers and fruit. At the very centre of this comb, a sea-pearl was set amid the glorious carving.

'This object is far too beautiful and too expensive to be given as a gift,' Severa protested. 'The pearl alone must have been costly. Considering my sulks and rudeness, I should have been punished for my sins rather than rewarded with this exquisite gift.'

'A person of worth should own such a fine object,' Constantinus replied. 'Why should it be someone other than you? When I purchased the bauble, I had a fancy to see this particular comb set into the amber locks of your hair which is extremely rare in the land of Britannia. The shop-keeper was happy to reduce the price to suit my purse, especially when he learned who the recipient of the gift would be. At any road, I have little to spend my pay on, so I'd like you to indulge my fancy to see you wearing it. Unworn, and beautiful as it is, it has little value for a man.'

Severa blushed, but she raised her arms and used the comb to hold her curling tresses away from her forehead. The creamy ivory and the gentle glow of the pearl glimmered there, just as he had imagined it.

'I love it, Constantinus. Does it look well?' she asked, as excited as a young child with a new toy.

He nodded, trying to hide his own pleasure and surprise. The embarrassment he felt was compounded when Severa suddenly threw her arms around his neck, careless of the hard edges of his armour. For one brief moment, he stood rigidly in her embrace. But then, his demeanour seemed to change and his arms lifted of their own accord to hold her tightly for an instant, so she could feel the long, lean lines of his body. He rested his chin on her shoulder for just a heartbeat and she could smell the combination of wood smoke, the oil he used on his weapons, the scent of pine cones and his masculine sweat. Then, abruptly, the centurion pulled away from her, cleared his throat, apologised for overstepping his authority and turned on his heel to march back to his own fire pit and the remnants of stew that he had almost missed by making a short visit to the traders of Aquae Sulis.

Severa watched him stalk away with regret. Yet, somewhere in the pit of her stomach, her nerves twitched and her heart sang with triumph. He must harbour *some* feeling for her.

As she settled herself down to sleep under the watchful eyes of her serving-woman, Severa sought out some of the familiar stars in the growing river of white light that crossed the broad expanse of sky.

'Is it true!' she breathed aloud. 'Can wanting and possession be the same thing, if we are determined to pursue those things in life that matter to us?'

Severa had come to a decision regarding the man she wanted

to wed. Whether this choice was sensible or not, she considered that the price paid for a loving marriage would be as nothing when compared to a loveless future.

She was still too young to understand that the power of love can make the most sensible of women blind to the realities and cruelties of life.

The fourth day of the trek resulted in greater difficulties, especially for the wagons that were forced to struggle up a long line of hills crossing the line of Constantinus's intended march. The Roman engineers who had originally built this road had done their best, but the gradients of the hills were such that the column's progress was slowed to a crawl. Severa and her woman were forced to walk up the steepest of the inclines in an attempt to spare the horses, but this allowed Severa to pluck wildflowers from the verges and seek out berries that grew wild beside the road. Cael cautioned her to beware of clusters of the lovely blueberries, citing the rural wisdom that poisons are regularly found in many blue-tinged growths.

The woods were quiet and deep here, while the mounted troops and infantry had disappeared behind a rocky outcropping. Strangely, the men in the rearguard had lagged some distance behind and were still out of sight. Severa was beginning to feel the first pangs of hunger when a strange whistling sound came out of nowhere and her maidservant grunted oddly and fell from the seat of the wagon. She seemed to have a long wooden stick sprouting from the side of her neck.

As the woman's body began to crumple, Cael shouted, 'Run, mistress! Run to the centurion!'

Still rooted to the spot, Severa heard the whistling sound again and another shaft appeared like magic from out of Cael's side as he called out his warning to her. With imploring eyes, he fell across his seat like a stone, awakening her from her trance-like state. Then she ran like a startled rabbit.

The woods had seemed empty at first, but she finally saw some movement across from her as a figure thudded down the hill in an attempt to cut her off before she could reach the forward column that had turned the corner ahead of her. She shrieked out the centurion's name, to warn him as she ran.

'Attack! Constantinus! We're under attack!'

The figure who was trying to intercept her was a faceless shape in the shadows of the trees as he leaped over obstacles in his attempt to catch up with her on the roadway, so she screamed again in terror as she heard the distinctive sound of loosened arrows behind her.

She could now hear the sound of shouted orders and galloping hooves that drifted towards her from the direction of the rearguard, but all her strength was focused on outpacing the thug who was determined to catch her before she could round the corner and reach the safety of the forward element of the column. The attacker launched himself into space from a rocky outcrop on to the cobbled surface of the roadway in an attempt to cut her off, but Severa had spent her whole childhood running with Endellion's children, and her strength was greater than that of most girls of her age and circumstances. She put on one last, desperate spurt of effort so that her pursuer could only grasp at a handful of her cloak. With a desperate shrug of her shoulders, she twisted out of her cloak, tearing away the pin in the process, but she did manage to catch a brief glance at the distorted face of her enemy before she eluded him once more.

He's wearing a knitted mask, she thought, as she forced her thigh muscles to make a final leap into open sunshine and found herself directly in the path of four galloping horsemen. She barely had time to throw herself bodily towards the forest verge as Constantinus and three gladius-wielding cavalrymen surged past her to capture the dark figure who was now trying to escape into the woods that climbed upwards from the roadway.

'Get after the bastard! Don't let him escape! Where the fuck are you, Paulus? There must be others in the woods, so get after them. Where's the lady? Find her, or I'll have your heads.'

Horsemen scattered in several directions into the woods, their shields employed as several arrows rained down on them from isolated hiding spots among the trees. The man on foot was just ahead of the three cavalrymen with Constantinus, but he was using the trees and his remarkable agility to evade them.

Meanwhile, Constantinus had ridden after the man on an angle designed to outflank the assassin. This strategy was risky, because he was trying to anticipate the direction that the failed killer would take. Unfortunately, the intruder tripped over a tree root and fell ignominiously to his knees. Inevitably, he was quickly surrounded.

'Surrender and you might yet live. Fight, and we'll cut you down like a dog,' Constantinus warned.

'You speak lies, Roman! You won't let us live, so don't bother with the blather.'

'You'll die more easily if you cause me no trouble. We know why you've attacked us, so we don't need to torture you,' Constantinus retorted evenly, gambling that the assassin would assume that they knew more than they actually did.

'We learned about Conanus and the plot to capture Maximus's daughter. Only a fool would hope to persevere and succeed with such a daft plot,' he added.

The assassin bared his teeth and sank into the defensive position used by all soldiers to repel an onslaught by armed men. This man was an experienced soldier and a competent warrior.

'Take him alive unless you have no other choice,' the centurion ordered the three cavalrymen who took up positions that could be used to probe at the assassin's defences.

Then, just when the capture of the intruder appeared to be certain, the characteristic whine of loosed arrows caused all four Romans to flinch. Three arrows struck the intruder in the chest in a neat pattern in the approximate position of his heart and he died on the leaf mould in the forest without uttering another sound.

Try as they might, the Roman cavalry found no one else during a systematic search of the woods. The surviving assassins had vanished like smoke on the breeze.

Severa's maidservant was dead and the girl regretted the casual manner with which she had treated the quiet, motherly woman. She had even failed to learn her name. As for Cael, the arrow had penetrated deeply into his armpit to wedge itself into the muscle of his upper chest.

'The arrow will have to be removed or he'll die,' Constantinus told her. 'I don't suppose you know anything about medicine or healing, do you?'

Severa shook her head. Her eyes registered her misery, for Cael had quickly become a favourite companion and any thought that he might suffer a slow and painful death made her feel sick with guilt.

'Are there any towns close by where we can find someone to help him?'

'One of the men who is familiar with this part of Britannia tells me that there's a religious community in a nearby valley that might be able to help,' Constantinus said. 'This sanctuary is at a place called Glastonbury. The priests might have the skills to save him, but I'm afraid we're a good day's journey from there.' The centurion looked genuinely regretful. 'One further complication is that the pathway might well be rough once we get off the formed road.'

'He could be laid out in the wagon, even if we leave the arrowhead still in his shoulder. I can drive the wagon. Please? I'd like to save him if we can.'

Despite his own misgivings over the success of the journey and the probability that the wound would become poisoned, Constantinus was unable to resist her appeal. At the very least, the proposed detour would throw any pursuers off the scent.

'Very well, Severa. We'll try, but you won't be driving the wagon. You lack the muscle to control a team of horses if we have to move at speed. No, I'll put one of my own men into the driver's seat. He'll also be a useful protection if the assassins try to mount another attack. Hopefully, they'll be expecting us to follow the Roman road. Damn it! I wish I had the time to track those bastards down.'

'We can't be sure that my uncle ordered the attack,' Severa replied doubtfully.

'They tried to kill your servants, but they could have killed you on quite a few occasions during the attack if they had a mind to do so. No! Their intention was to capture you and to drag you off from under my nose. They almost got away with it.'

Angry with himself and carrying the responsibility for the success of the mission on his shoulders, Constantinus stomped off to redirect their journey towards this Glastonbury and a religious community that might not even exist.

Necessity forced Constantinus to keep his command on that section of road leading down from the hills before he was able to enter an older section of road that would take them to Glastonbury. Mostly disused, this road proved to be little more than a goat track that took the column into the south-west. Meanwhile, the body of Severa's maid had been wrapped in her cloak and laid out in the bed of the wagon alongside Cael, who was trying to make light of his wound, despite the pain that was clearly visible in his grey face. The time taken to bury the maid would eat into any chance of throwing off the pursuit by the assassins, but Severa refused point-blank to leave the woman's corpse behind as a feast for the scavengers.

The roadway taking the column to Glastonbury had obviously been constructed for use by farmers to carry their produce to the markets in Aquae Sulis, the only town of any size in the district. Poorly maintained, this narrow track was mostly straight and true, and followed a section of lowlands that forced them to cross over a number of streamlets and rivulets. The surrounding countryside was very rich as the farms attested with their deep, viridian grass and contented animals.

A ridgeline ran parallel to the valley, so Constantinus imagined that a great sea might have covered the lowlands and lapped at the slopes leading up to the higher ground in days gone by. Then, when he saw something glittering in the mud, the Roman commander felt a shiver begin at the base of his spine. Obviously exposed by the hooves of a horse or a farm animal, the clay had been hiding the spiralled shape of a whitened seashell.

Constantinus dropped the clay with a curse of disgust. Like everything else in this weird landscape, the earth revealed strange inexplicable contradictions.

'Ride on,' the centurion snapped when he found the column had been dawdling along as they waited for their commander. Swearing under his breath, he remembered an undone task and rode back towards the wagon that held Severa.

When he reached the wagon, he found the girl was sitting with Cael, attempting to calm the frightened man by explaining that Constantinus intended to take him to Glastonbury where his wound would be treated by the religious healers. Like all the peasantry, he held little hope that even the best of healers could repair his wounded shoulder.

'I've never heard of this Glastonbury, Cael, but I'm aware of the medical knowledge held by the Christian priests and brothers. If anyone can save you, the little fathers can do it.'

'I don't want to die, mistress.' Cael coughed awkwardly. 'I suppose I might never get to see Tintagel now.'

When he inspected Cael's wound, Constantinus could see that the stump of the arrow was protruding from the bandage that covered his naked chest. Blood stained the bandaging and an occasional cough would bring threads of blood up in Cael's sputum, symptoms that Severa wiped away quickly before the wounded man could see this evidence of internal damage.

'How are you, Cael?' the centurion asked gruffly.

'I've been better, sir, but I thank you for asking. The mistress here has taken care of me real well and she told me that you're taking me to a place where I'll be able to get some help. Thank you, sir, because you didn't have to do that for a stranger. You could have just left me on the side of the road to fend for myself.'

The driver's eyes filled with tears and he grabbed at Constantinus's hand and kissed it.

Flushed with embarrassment, Constantinus would have

pulled away, but the genuine gratitude in the man's eyes caused him to pause.

'My legionnaires never abandon their companions,' Constantinus told him. 'We stay with our men or we carry them out with us, even if they are badly wounded. You're in my employ, Cael, so you're just as Roman as any of the British cavalrymen under my command.'

No one listening to his even words would have doubted his honesty. But the centurion could recall times when other legions had left their men behind to be slaughtered by barbarian hunting parties. In the old days of the Republic, during the times of Marius and Julius Caesar, his assertions of Roman honour might have been true, but Constantinus rather feared that the legions had become dominated by practical concerns that invariably overshadowed Rome's loyalty to the individual.

However, Cael's eyes reflected a growing feeling of hope, so Constantinus sighed with relief. Severa would remain calm if she thought that the Romans were doing something – anything at all – that might save the life of her driver. With renewed confidence, Constantinus explained his plan to them.

'I intend to be in Glastonbury by tomorrow morning, but I must warn you that it's a very strange place. If you're a Christian, you might be interested to learn that Joseph of Arimathea, kinsman to Jesus Christ, is supposed to have built a church there, so many men believe that Glastonbury is very sacred. If your wounds can be healed anywhere, surely the settlement where the kin of Jesus once walked in these lands would be such a spot.'

'It's kind of you to say so, sir,' Cael wheezed, so the centurion suspected that one of his lungs had been punctured by the arrowhead. The wagon driver would probably not survive his wounds, regardless of what the religious community could do.

Constantinus fell back to speak to Paulus.

'Keep your eyes sharp, Paulus. This place is giving me the creeps.' Constantinus wasn't alone in his nervousness. The other cavalrymen in the column had the finely honed instincts of self-preservation that had kept them alive through many battles. Something was in the air or blowing in on the wind! The more thoughtful Romans imagined themselves to be part of a long procession that was taking them to some secret, dangerous and unfathomable place where humans were never intended to tread.

The column would occasionally see neat pigsties and paddocks, or an occasional drift of smoke on the higher ground, but the landscape was mostly devoid of life for the whole day of travel. To add to this perplexing emptiness, the legionnaires sensed eyes that were following their every movement.

'The assassins haven't given up,' Paulus warned. 'I saw the reflected light of metal when we were passing between some of those hills in the earlier part of the afternoon.' The decurion pointed towards the hills that ran parallel to the long valley.

Constantinus nodded. 'I haven't seen them, but I've been sensing their presence all day. They're just watching us now, so they're waiting for us to make a mistake.'

'It's a strange situation,' Paulus replied. If the conspirators we interrogated at the Bower of Beauty were speaking the truth, there were only five assassins involved in the murder of Marcus, so that would mean that we are only facing a threat from four men now that one of them has been killed. Why is it that I feel we're at a disadvantage in this place?'

'We've got too little information to assume anything, Paulus. I'd never have sent a small group into alien territory without any reinforcements. I'd want extra bodies to be secreted away if I should need some support. Wouldn't you do the same?'

'It's quite possible, sir, because this Conanus is a very determined sod. And he's a watchful bastard as well. That ambush in the hills was an inspired piece of improvisation. Who'd have guessed that the rearguard could lag so far behind our little princess that she was out of their sight. I won't sleep easy now till we've ditched the maiden at this Tintagel place.'

'I agree, Paulus! I agree wholeheartedly!'

After a nervous night, the party set off before first light without even the warmth of a reheated stew in their bellies. Constantinus was eager to reach Glastonbury and its illusion of safety, so he had instructed his scouts to find the shortest and easiest route that would deliver Cael into the hands of the healers with minimal delay. As it turned out, the scouts soon returned to the column with the welcome news that the religious community was only a few hours of easy travelling to the south.

'You can't miss it, sir. We just follow the track that lies to the right of the big tor on the horizon. Many pilgrims come to Glastonbury every year, and they all take this path.'

The tor was clearly visible. As the sun continued to rise above the eastern horizon, the top of the hill seemed to float on a sea of mist so that its head, crowned with some kind of structure that appeared like a pointing finger, rose out of a sea of grey and pearl waves. Constantinus felt the hair on his arms rise with superstitious wonder that this soggy earth was considered to be a land where giants and creatures from Britannia's mythic past had proliferated, including ogres, hags with black eyes, great wolves, giant boars and other monsters who lay in wait to feast on human flesh. Then the centurion chided himself, replacing the sinister images with rational Roman explanations.

'There are no such things,' he reassured himself.

Before the sun was fully up and the mists began to shrink into the hollows, the cavalcade followed the slowly curving road that allowed the wondrous tor to become clearer.

He immediately recognised the thin spine of a religious construction at the apex of the tor. The tower held a signal fire that could be seen on the horizon. Constantinus swivelled in his saddle and looked back towards the range of hills where they had been ambushed. At another high point at the apex of the surrounding hills, he expected to see the ruins of another signal post, but his eyes weren't strong enough to pierce the prevailing mists.

These fires, once lit, could soon warn the populations of the isolated villages and those warriors who protected them of attacks.

He stared back towards the south again where he could barely make out another tor that lay several days' march to the south. A warning could leap over many days of travel, moving from signal fire to signal fire, all the way to Sabrina Aest – and to the population centres that lay in the west.

A feeling of respect for those ancient warriors who had devised these sentinel fires stole over him. He recalled the derision of Marcus Britannicus for all things British and then smiled with grim amusement. British ingenuity had put Marcus in the midden.

'I'll try my best to never underestimate any Britons who might become my enemies,' the centurion muttered to himself, a new habit now that he had assumed the role of commander. Surprised at the realisation, he shook his head briskly and called for one of his scouts.

'Drusus! Ride ahead and warn the good fathers that we're coming to them with a wounded man who is near to death. Go alone, so they aren't alarmed at the sight of armed men. You'll need to show good faith, so answer any of their questions with complete honesty.'

Drusus nodded his head and kicked his horse into a gallop. The column's protection was soon far behind him.

When he saw the hamlet of Glastonbury come into view, Constantinus was surprised by its size. Built along the base of a long slope that eventually led to the tor itself, the enclave was surrounded by low stone walls that served as boundaries rather than protective barriers. Behind these walls, a number of stone and timber buildings clustered on the flat earth at the base of the rise, where sheep and cows were cropping on knee-high grasses.

As the centurion drew the column to a halt a respectful distance from a set of low gates, a place where the pilgrims were given permission to enter the community, he saw evidence of good husbandry, discipline and hard labour in the surrounding fields. Men and women were working in the fields and Constantinus decided that they were either lay persons or members of the Aryan Church that controlled and administered this remote area of Britannia. Men in homespun robes were instantly recognisable among the workers toiling in the vegetable plots and herb gardens of Glastonbury.

'Good!' he said to himself. 'If they're growing herbs, they must have a healer.'

Within minutes, a small procession of robed men approached the gate with Drusus following at their heels. The Roman scout ran nimbly to join his commander, with his bronzed face impassive under his helmet.

Constantinus dismounted as the wagon carrying Cael drew up at the head of the column.

'Sir? This man is Father Gregory, the priest who is the leader of this community.'

Drusus gestured towards an unimpressive man whose only distinction seemed to be his wide, innocent smile.

'The good abbot bids you welcome and will offer our legionnaires the use of the quarters that are usually preserved for pilgrims who make the journey to see the church of Saint Joseph. Father Adolfus, a healer, will care for the wagon-master and I've been assured that he is very skilled in matters of health and medicine.'

One of the priests, a saturnine man with a blued shadow on his chin that gave him an unshaven appearance, approached the wagon like a fussy rooster that has been brought to service a difficult, bedraggled hen. The man's manner may have been unfortunate, but Constantinus spied a face that was alive with intelligence and eyes that were kind, so he turned his attention back to Father Gregory.

'I apologise for appearing at your gate without warning, Father Gregory, but Mistress Severa begged us to do what we could to save her driver after we were attacked by brigands yesterday. We must have seemed like a force of ignorant aggressors. I am Constantinus, a Roman centurion, and this lady is the Princess Severa who usually resides in Corinium. She has been placed in some danger by assassins, so we are escorting her to Tintagel where she will be well-protected.'

He continued with a brief and simplified explanation of the situation in which Severa had been placed, her status in the political landscape of Britannia and a sanitised version of the reasons for escorting her to the fortress at Tintagel.

The priest nodded affably. Both of his hands were hidden in his capacious sleeves and he smiled beatifically at the Roman officer as if he was accustomed to troops of soldiers arriving on his doorstep on a regular basis. Then, turning to the wagon, the priest bowed low to the young lady who was alighting with the assistance of Drusus.

'Be at peace, Lady Severa. Father Adolfus will do all that can be done to care for your servant. See? He is already arranging for your driver to be moved into our hospice. You will be able to sit with him after you have broken your fast.'

Severa could only curtsy awkwardly to this composed man who barely reached her shoulder, and yet seemed so much more powerful than men like her foster-father. His impervious facade of good humour left her with nothing to say.

'You are welcome to share the bounty of Glastonbury with my people, noble Constantinus. My brothers will show your men the way to the stables and the comforts of the pilgrims' quarters. We ate hours ago before the sun rose over the tor, but I'd like you and your officers to break your fast in a more congenial place than the gateway to our home.'

Constantinus glanced towards Severa, his mind already wondering how he could protect her in this strange place. Father Gregory followed his gaze and guessed at the problem.

'You need hold no fears for the lady,' Father Gregory responded smoothly, as if he read the centurion's mind. 'Our lay women will see that she is fed and housed in a suitable dwelling. All the necessary precautions have already been taken, so she can sleep soundly under the protection of Joseph the Trader of Blessed Memory while she dwells within Glastonbury's walls.'

Then, with Paulus in tow, Constantinus found he had been adroitly separated from his troops as they were led into the heart of Glastonbury and a wooden refectory building that was filled with soft golden light. Bemused, he followed Gregory's portly figure without hesitation, as if he was already trapped within the glamour of this remarkable place.

'Be seated, Constantinus of the Legions, for we have been waiting for you. Glastonbury offers sanctuary for as long as your need is great.'

CHAPTER VIII

A HOLY PLACE

Ah! Gentle, fleeting, wavering sprite,
Friend and associate of this clay!
To what unknown region borne,
Will thou now wing thy distant flight?
No more with a wonted humour gay,
But pallid, cheerless, and forlorn.

Hadrian, *Address to his soul when dying*

The refectory's furnishings were simple and spartan. A roughly hewn table, capable of seating at least twenty men, filled most of the rectangular space. Attracted by the age of the timber and its solid design, Constantinus stroked the surface of the table and felt its smoothness, polished by years of oil from elbows and palms.

In the centre of the table, a large jug was filled to the brim with water. The priest filled three beakers and offered them to Paulus and Constantinus, while he took the third for himself.

The two Romans had always obeyed the maxim that soldiers and native Britons alike should only drink clean water that had been collected and boiled by their own hands. As water purity varied from location to location, the two Romans stared at this water with obvious scepticism, for they would normally have preferred to drink beer when they were in strange surroundings.

Surprised, Father Gregory gazed at the faces of his two guests before realising their reservations.

'Oh! I see! There is no need to fear the quality of the waters that come to us from the holy earth of Glastonbury,' he explained with a deprecating smile. 'The water from a great underground river comes to the surface at this blessed spot. It is free of all ills and all corruptions, and some say it cleanses both the body and the spirit but, as educated men, you wouldn't believe such myths.'

Without taking his eyes away from the priest's face, Constantinus slowly raised the terracotta beaker to his lips and drank deeply. The water was sweet and clean, and had the faintest after-taste of iron beneath its refreshing coolness. Constantinus and Paulus both drank their beakers dry, after which Gregory refilled the drinking vessels with a cheerful smile.

Two of the brothers entered the refectory on silent, sandalled feet. The first carried a platter of plain wood which bore a loaf of newly baked bread and a knife. The second man juggled another platter with two bowls of the familiar terracotta, two spoons, another bowl containing sweet honey on the comb and a tiny wooden jar of salt. The eating bowls were filled with warm porridge and the Romans' mouths immediately began to slaver.

'Try a pinch of salt with your porridge,' Gregory advised his guests. 'It adds to the taste of the food, even when new honey is used to sweeten the meal. God has endowed our community with a precious gift of healthy and tasty food, whether we be rich or poor. I beg you to share the fruits of our toil and His generosity.'

Each man thanked Father Gregory once again and resumed eating with obvious pleasure. Paulus was well used to gritty porridge without the benefit of either salt or honey, so he was amazed at the difference these two precious luxuries made to the taste of the food.

Constantinus's food experiences were wider than those of Paulus but, once he had eaten and drunk his fill, he was hard-pressed to remember a meal that he had enjoyed more. Delighted, he said as much to Father Gregory, who flushed with pleasure.

'I thank you on behalf of my brothers who labour so willingly for the glory of God. As you can see, we live simple lives here. Our community accepts that Jesus of Nazareth travelled here with Joseph of Arimathea, before he began his ministry in those far-off days when the Romans first came to the shores of Britannia. My people are as one with these lands that bore the feet of Our Lord, Jesus, so Glastonbury has a special aura that tells us we live in a place that is truly blessed.'

'I agree with you that Glastonbury is certainly a special place that has no equal in my experience,' the centurion responded carefully. 'But there is one thing I don't understand. You said you had been expecting us, Father. Did Drusus not tell you about our journey during the short time he was here before our arrival?'

'Of course. But we had already received word of your journey.'

'But how? We left Corinium in secrecy and wouldn't have diverted to Glastonbury if our wagon driver had not been wounded. We would have taken a different road into the south, one that would take us directly to our destination.'

At that crucial point in the conversation, one of the brothers who had served the meal knocked gently on the door frame. The monk's face held a concerned expression, so Gregory rose to speak to him quietly. Then, when the brother took his leave, the priest returned to the table and seated himself carefully.

'Adolphus sends word that your man is gravely ill. If you wish to see him, perhaps you should do so now. My healer believes his life is in the balance.'

'Is Lady Severa aware of the situation?' the centurion asked crisply, all thoughts of his previous question driven out of his head by the urgency of this new difficulty.

'The lady is with him now. It appears she refused to leave him – even when Adolphus cut into Cael's chest to remove the arrowhead. She believes that your driver needs a familiar face to remind him that life is sweet and good. She is strong-willed, that little one, but she has no idea what she is facing.'

'Then I'll join her!' Constantinus said decisively before turning to speak to his decurion.

'See to the men in their billets, Paulus. They may have some rest while we remain here, but I'd like to make sure they're kept occupied while we are enjoying the good father's hospitality. Perhaps our men could provide some assistance to the brothers who work in the fields, if the abbot is agreeable. There's little else we can do until such time as Cael's fortunes are decided, one way or the other.'

Constantinus followed Father Gregory out of the refectory and along the neat paths that ran in a network connecting the community's buildings to each other. Tidy patches of vegetable gardens were laid out between the buildings, the produce so lush and well maintained that Constantinus was transported back to his childhood and the farming existence that had been his lot in life. Fruit trees, shrubs and climbing vines had been planted to act as windbreaks as well as providing a food source for the community.

The hospice was some little way from the refectory, but the site had been selected to take advantage of a grove of apple and pear trees that sweetened the air. The sick and the dying could rest in a quiet, sweet place where the only sounds were the breezes and the movement of foliage in the trees.

Constantinus felt the peace of this quiet place soak into his soul as soon as his feet crossed the simple stone threshold.

The space used to house those members of the community in need of medical treatment was small, sweet-smelling and consisted of one large room for the patients and two smaller annexes used to store supplies and provide an overnight sleeping space if nursing supervision was required. Two patients could be housed in the warm hospice with relative comfort and, unlike the spartan accommodation favoured by members of the religious community, ailing patients were provided with woollen pallets and a number of warm blankets to ease the pains of aching bones or the final hours of the dying. Every surface in the rooms was spare and clean, for the hospice's fittings were scrubbed regularly by several women who laboured with Father Adolphus to ensure that patients would survive, if such was God's intention. If the patient was dying, a woman's hand smoothed their brow and another woman sat by the pallet and offered the comfort of a mother until death came. In the good father's care, the ill were never alone.

In the annexe used as a storeroom, Adolphus kept powdered herbs, tinctures, various pain-killers, the tools of the surgeon's trade and the mortars and pestles used for grinding roots and other vegetable matter into pastes. Some of the dried objects stored on the healer's shelves caused Constantinus to repress a shudder when Father Gregory showed him the facilities available to the healer.

At this moment, however, all the attention of Father Adolphus and his women was focused on the pallet where Cael was lying in a profound sleep.

Severa was seated on a stool by the pallet, holding Cael's hand, although one glance at the driver's flushed face and his sweat-drenched flesh told Constantinus that Cael was oblivious to her presence.

'How is your patient, mistress?' he asked in his kindest voice to quash any residual irritation that might lie at their enforced delay. 'Has his condition changed since I last saw him?'

'Father Adolphus removed the arrowhead as soon as we arrived. He says that Cael is fortunate that the head wasn't barbed and poisoned, although I doubt that Cael would care much either way. The good father gave him a soporific to put him to sleep, so he is hoping that he might wake in a few hours. I've promised Father Adolphus that I'll bathe Cael regularly to keep him cool once his temperature begins to rise.'

Then Severa blushed at her innocent slip of the tongue. 'Of course, one of the women here washes his whole body. But the pair of them, Mara and Hisse, work so hard that I'm happy to ease their labours by washing poor Cael's face, neck and arms to lower his temperature.'

Severa glanced down at her shoes. When she raised her face again, Constantinus could see that her eyes had filled with tears.

'Cael thinks he's going to die, but I've sworn that I'd do everything in my power to save him if it is at all possible. And I will.'

The comatose man's skin was blotched with fever as he stirred and mumbled in a restless sleep. The top half of his chest was swathed in bandaging and Constantinus was surprised to discover that the driver had a strong musculature, but then realised that a wagon-driver would probably need upper-body strength to control a team of horses or oxen.

'He's a strong man, but I believe that his wound might have been untreated for too long. He still has some chance, Severa, but you must prepare yourself for the possibility that he'll die.'

'I've tried to, but someone among us should believe that the man will survive his wounds. Cael was wounded because of me, Centurion.'

'Don't be foolish. Those men who triggered the ambush are the guilty parties, not you.'

'True, but I can't convince myself in here.' She thumped her breast with her clenched fist.

Cael lay between them like a marble effigy. Constantinus wanted to comfort Severa, but he knew that there was a line that he wasn't permitted to cross.

'Send word to me if Cael's condition worsens, mistress. In the meantime, I must insist that you rest and eat. If you should become ill we'll have further delays inflicted on us. In the meantime, I must see to my command and make my preparations for the rest of our journey to Tintagel, so I'll bid you good day.'

Once outside the hospice, the centurion drew Father Adolphus aside and asked him to elaborate on Cael's condition and prognosis. 'I'd rather you didn't give me any comforting ambiguities, Father. I'm a fighting man, so I prefer accuracy to kindly lies and I must plan the movement of my column over the next few days. Can you make an educated guess as to Cael's chances? I assure you I won't discuss your prognosis with the lady.'

'I really don't know,' Adolphus replied. 'The fever might continue to rise and that would surely kill him, or it can break and the man will live. I will do all I can, but his fate will remain in God's lap. Certainly he has been fortunate so far in that he has had you and Lady Severa to care for him and bring him to our community.'

'Aye, he was fortunate that Lady Severa took a liking to him. I can't say I'd have gone to this trouble if it weren't for her insistence, because Roman legionnaires are usually assisted to enter the shades when they are as sorely wounded as this man.'

Father Adolphus nodded crisply and made his apologies before returning to his patient. At a loose end, Constantinus stared back towards the hospice where the priest and the girl were already soaking cloths in cold water to make compresses for Cael's feverish head.

Constantinus spent the rest of the day walking all over the grounds of the enclosure. Its agricultural wealth was significant, and he would happily have sworn that he had never seen a more efficiently run farming community, but he realised that, as he had first thought, the walls of the settlement would never repel attackers.

The hours passed pleasantly.

A bell rang from somewhere in the settlement, sweet and low, inviting the workers in the fields to pick up their baskets and their hoes and begin the walk back to their living quarters. Their day of labour was drawing to a close, although the light was still bright. The quiet patterns of country life had already begun to embrace many of the Romans, filling them with nostalgia. But Constantinus's thoughts and anxieties dwelt on the chances of his enemies regrouping or being reinforced, while his own column whiled away the hours in the peace and comfort of Glastonbury.

'Lord, make Your decision on how long we are bound to stay in this strange place in Your own good time but, please, if You care for the devout members of Your flock, make our stay here as brief as possible,' he prayed into the evening breeze.

Then, with a shrug of acceptance of the inevitability of fate, he joined Paulus to carry out a snap inspection of the horses and his legionnaires.

Cael lived through the night. Against all expectations, he lived through the next day too, although his temperature stubbornly refused to fall and he continued to rave during a troubled sleep that frightened Severa by its intensity.

'Don't be disheartened, my dear,' Father Adolphus urged with a bracing smile. 'The time when we must become truly concerned is if he falls into fits. If fitting does occur, we will know that his body is being attacked by fires that are present in his wound. At the moment, his spirit is fighting the poisons that lie at the heart of the infection, so I remain hopeful.'

Father Adolphus attempted to convince her to rest, but Severa laboured on, pitting all her womanly strength against the power of the infection.

Constantinus and Paulus chafed under the inactivity forced on men of action. They curried their horses and exercised them, cleaned their armour and sharpened their weapons, but the hours seemed to drag on and on without any respite.

The legionnaires spent their free time exploring the lands that lay in the vicinity of the religious community, including the villagers' cottages clustered around the margins of the church's enclave. Constantinus climbed the peak of the tor and discovered the ruins of the crude communication tower he had remarked on when they first approached Glastonbury.

The Romans also found the point at which an underground river came out of the ground, including a special chamber below it where deposits of minerals dripped down from the ceiling like the teeth of some gigantic carnivore. A pond filled most of this cavern, a stretch of water that was as red as drying blood. Yet, when Constantinus dipped his cupped hands into the cold fluid, the water that slid between his fingers was as clear as the finest Roman glass.

A short ride away, they discovered the last traces of an abandoned village that had been erected on high wooden stilts, as if the original houses had stood over large sheets of water. The waters must have receded, leaving marshy ground behind, along with the mute evidence of sea shells still trapped in the mud of ages.

Constantinus struck out with his sword at one of the uprights of timber that jutted out from the ground like a single fingerbone. Much to his surprise, it made a sound like metal striking stone. A close examination showed that the timber had been cut crudely and then driven deep into the mud that would have lain below the waters of the inland sea. Over the years, exposure to the elements had given these poles the consistency and hardness of granite, as if some gorgon had turned them to stone.

'Glastonbury is really very, very strange,' Paulus repeated.

On one of the hills close to the settlements, a feature that was shaped like the curved spine of a fish, Father Gregory had taken the two officers to a small tree that had grown crookedly on the site. Then he told his guests of a local legend that a remnant of the Crown of Thorns had been carried across the waters and planted here after the death of Jesus in Jerusalem.

Constantinus and Paulus stared at the small tree with varying degrees of incredulity.

'I won't accept that this scrawny specimen grew from a staff or a crown of thorns,' Constantinus muttered doubtfully. 'It sounds like so much wishful thinking to me.'

'But we've seen stranger things,' Paulus responded sardonically. 'I still remember the talking tree we saw when we were in Gallia? To this day, I still believe it was an old druid trying to frighten the villagers into giving him food and shelter. Yet, there's something about the tree that Father Gregory showed us that was familiar to those legionnaires who served in Jerusalem. It certainly has vicious thorns . . . and it doesn't look like any trees I've seen in Britannia.'

'When it comes to religion, we're all credulous fools,' Constantinus replied. 'I'll believe in the tree when it bears the staff of Joseph of Arimathea as fruit.'

Cael lived through the second day then, on the third day, surprised his nurse when he woke from his long and feverish dream.

At the same time, Constantinus, Paulus and three of the Roman cavalrymen were carrying out a reconnaissance along the long marshy valley that stretched into the south when they saw a plume of smoke rising from a low rise roughly parallel to their position.

'That looks like a signal fire, sir,' Paulus warned, as the small patrol came to a halt. 'What are your orders?'

'We'd best investigate,' Constantinus decided as he wheeled his horse.

'We could be riding into a trap, sir.' Paulus's eyes swivelled from the near side of the slope to the hills on their left.

'Without Severa in tow, we're just a difficulty that must be killed off when we are prepared to engage with them. With luck, they'll abandon their observation post rather than risk their troops in a minor engagement. Even if Conanus has received reinforcements, Armorica is far away and he'll have difficulty getting more men.'

Paulus chewed over Constantinus's answer as he followed his centurion towards the hilltop and the grey feathers of smoke that were dissipating on the breeze.

The riders found long grasses thick with buttercups and other wildflowers as they approached the top of the treeless hillock. With the horses' hooves sending clods of earth flying, the cavalrymen galloped to the site of the drifting smoke to find an abandoned fire pit that had been erected at the highest point. There was no indication of an enemy presence on the hill, which was bare of all cover.

As Paulus sent his three cavalrymen in separate directions to check on the possibility of ambush, Constantinus directed his horse towards the still-smouldering warning beacon.

The fire had been set in a simple circlet of stones prised out from the soil of the hill. He could see evidence of at least two riders who must have been watching the Glastonbury settlement from this vantage point, which overlooked the track leading to the south; the Romans must have been observed from the moment they left the settlement.

Constantinus looked southward, shading his eyes with his hand.

'I just saw a flash of sunlight on metal,' Paulus called from behind him. 'There are also signs of movement among those trees that line the hills to the west.'

'Aye! To the right of the road as it reaches the lowest point of the valley.'

Paulus nodded. 'The bastards have been watching us from the moment we left Glastonbury. They lit that warning fire when they realised we were advancing along the valley floor where the main force must be positioned.'

Constantinus examined the fire pit, the marks of heels and the tracks of hooves in the sod. He then checked every square foot of land around the signs left by the enemy scouts. Eventually, he barked in triumph and snatched up a small gold ring, designed for either a woman's hand or a man's little finger.

'Look at this! One of Conanus's warriors has dropped a bauble and it's been ground into the dirt when a horse's hoof stood on it.'

It was a small, simple plait of pure gold. A single word, *Elen*, had been crudely carved on to the inner band; Constantinus tucked the ring into a pouch attached to his belt.

'We ought to return to Glastonbury, sir. We're vulnerable here, and we might be caught in the open by whoever lit this beacon,' Paulus warned. 'The bastards could easily double around and outflank us during our return journey.'

'I concur! Conanus's main force must be close, so they're probably watching us even as we speak.'

On their return to Glastonbury, the scouting party was apprised of Cael's return to consciousness.

'Thank the Lord! It's about time we left this gilded little trap in which we've placed ourselves,' Paulus stated.

'Aye!' Constantinus agreed. 'But it's going to be a difficult proposition to escape unscathed.'

Constantinus spent a few hours in amicable discussion with Father Gregory, during which time the Roman commander asked for the services of a young woman who could act as a chaperone for Severa during the journey to Tintagel.

'In the eyes of the world, it's a little late to employ a chaperone if you've been alone with the young lady for at least one night,' Father Gregory pointed out.

'We were as alone as one can be when one is surrounded by a detachment of seventy legionnaires. Still, you could well say that we were alone, in a fashion,' Constantinus replied drily. 'However, I would still prefer that my charge has a chaperone for the remainder of the journey.'

'Then I'm sure a suitable woman from the village could be found who would be prepared to accompany the young lady to Tintagel. I won't force anyone to volunteer for such a dangerous task,' the abbot replied. 'Although there'll be a number of young girls who will leap at any offer that will bring them into close proximity with your young cavalrymen.'

The Roman centurion went on to discuss the escape plans he had devised to spirit Severa out of Glastonbury and, later, to Tintagel, while avoiding open conflict with an enemy of unknown size and efficiency. He was confident that Father Gregory understood his need for absolute discretion.

Then, once Father Gregory had offered his advice and provided the name of a suitable woman who could serve as a lady's maid, Constantinus strode to the hospice to speak with the newly conscious patient and Severa.

The largest room in the hospice was drenched in golden afternoon light as Constantinus entered the building. It gave Severa a halo around her unusual hair, as if God had conferred sainthood upon her. Constantinus shivered.

If Constantinus had committed a blasphemy through his errant thoughts, then his attraction for this British woman and his delight in her features combined to sweep away any guilt. The maturing young girl was taking on the trappings of a nun or a saint, someone who was pure of spirit and self-sacrificing in her motives.

Yet Constantinus could also remember the flirtatious girl who walked the perimeters of their night camps with him, her smile both knowing and innocent.

Would this complicated, albeit naïve young woman agree to his plan? Would she take such a huge risk with her reputation, one that might never be mended? And would she dare to place her life into the hands of a man who was still a relative stranger?

Then, before his resolution could fail him, Constantinus strode into the hospice. He congratulated Cael on his survival and then began to explain his plans for making good their escape from Glastonbury to the incredulous lady.

Nothing would be quite the same for either of them – ever again.

THE FLIGHT FROM
GLASTONBURY TO TINTAGEL

SABRINA AEST

The Tor

Glastonbury
enclave

Route of
the three
travellers

Paulus's route with
main column

Signal fire

Sighting of
smoke

Capture of
Cledwyn of
Conanus

Isca
Dumnoniorum

Cairn of
Roman
dead

Durnovaria

Tintagel

Column under attack

Wagons left

CHAPTER IX

UNION

Few famous men have the whole earth as their memorial.

Thucydides, *History of the Peloponnesian War*

Three riders trotted through the long grasses behind the tor on almost silent hooves. The darkness was complete, although a cloud-obscured moon permitted a faint glow occasionally to illuminate the three black-clad horsemen who hunched over their horses' necks. Even the metalwork on their harness had been dulled with mud to conceal its steely glitter.

The horsemen rode cross-country and avoided any tracks as they set their horses' heads towards a river that wound unseen from its source in the east where the small settlement of Lindinus nestled on the main Roman road. On reaching the river, the horsemen planned to cross the stream at a shallow ford before turning to the right to travel in a southerly direction.

Back in Glastonbury, the religious enclave was still and silent with sleep. Nothing moved, not even the dogs that protected the herds of sheep grazing along the slopes of the tor. Above the stables and inside the pilgrims' quarters, the Roman legionnaires slept lightly, as all fighting men do, always ready for attacks that might come under the cloak of darkness.

Perhaps those among the enemy who were watching from around a banked fire near the beacon on the hill were expecting little subterfuge from members of the *Equites Legionis*, the special century created to escort the late Marcus Britannicus to his betrothal. Perhaps they believed that Romans favoured physical might against skulduggery when devising their strategies. Perhaps, too, they might have been lazy.

One thing was certain: Conanus's force was unaware of the Roman scouts who had been observing their activities or else they were so arrogant and confident in their strength that they were unconcerned. In fact, the leader of the enemy force had forgotten that the more gifted commanders in the Roman legions always devised a number of alternative plans to use on those occasions when they were confronted by complex problems.

By early morning, before the sun had begun to rise from the thick blanket of white fog that shrouded the Glastonbury environs, the Roman column had begun its march into the south after bidding farewell to the small cluster of prelates, torches in hand, who watched their guests as they made an obviously carefree departure. As was his habit, the centurion rode at the head of the column. Meanwhile, Severa travelled on the seat at the front of the wagon with her replacement driver, a local villager. Wrapped in a heavy cloak to ward off the cold mist drifting towards them, Severa kept her wonderful hair dry inside its capacious hood.

The Roman column had covered several miles and Glastonbury had disappeared into the early morning like a dream by the time the rising sun burned off the ever-present night mist. Off to his left, Paulus saw a sudden thread of grey smoke rise from the highest point of a rounded hill. He watched with interest as the smoke plumed thickly at first and then began to thin when the light breeze in the upper air whipped it away. Paulus grinned with satisfaction and the cavalrymen closest to him noted the odd smile that curled his thin lips. Something in that smirk promised pain for someone.

'Send word back to the infantry that we will be attacked at some time in the next few days. It might be sooner, rather than later, but every legionnaire is to remain on constant alert. We can expect a shower of arrows to come at us when we enter the trap that will almost certainly be set for us. Open ground should be safe, but we must be careful when we are close to the forested sections of the route we will be following. When the enemy unleashes its arrows, the infantry will form a fighting square around the wagons to protect the woman. The cavalry will scatter to protect the horses at the first indication of bowmen mounting an attack. Once clear of the ambush site, the cavalrymen will re-form along the flanks and be prepared to mount a counterattack on the enemy.'

Alerted to the dangers that lay ahead of them, the cavalrymen rode gingerly through a soggy landscape of shallow swamps interspersed with small hillocks of dry earth. Mud clung to the horses' hooves and the wagons' wheels in thick black rinds so that the going was predictably heavy. Inevitably, the wagons were regularly bogged down; when these irritations occurred, the cavalrymen dismounted and used human muscle and the strength of their horses to force the wagons free from the sucking quagmire. Within a short period of time, every man in the column was carrying his fair share of mud on previously spotless red cloaks.

* * *

As they rode through the woodlands parallel to Fosse Way in an effort to avoid any signs of civilisation, the three horsemen found a copse of trees that provided shelter, so they took a long-awaited opportunity to dismount and stretch their limbs. Constantinus took off his cloak and laid it on to a bed of thick grass in a sun-dappled space between patches of dense under-brush.

'You'll need to rest for an hour or two, Severa. Once we're clear of the low-lying swamps, we'll be able to make better time. After that, we'll try to ride through the nights to outstrip any possible pursuit, so you'd best sleep while you can. You'll be stiff and sore before we can rest again, so make yourself comfortable. We'll eat as we ride!'

'How good this grass feels,' she sighed as she pulled off her sturdy boots and ran her toes through the ferns and ground cover. 'Thank you, Centurion.'

Constantinus had been worrying about the slow pace of their journey so far, but the girl's gratitude jerked him back to the present.

'What for? Surely you resent being dragged away from a warm bed in the middle of the night? Aren't you a little nervous at being separated from your bodyguard?'

'I think you are sufficiently capable of keeping me safe, Centurion. If my uncle Conanus is determined to capture me, then he'll be making his best efforts to find me. You've done your utmost to outfox him, so it's pointless for me to worry. I'd rather enjoy the adventure, especially the male clothes! I know that I'll be married off soon enough, after which I'll spend the rest of my days wearing women's gowns, raising children and doting on grandchildren – if I'm lucky.'

She thought of her mother's death in childbirth and was suddenly afraid for her own life. 'That's if I live long enough to become a mother.'

Constantinus found himself bowing his head, for he was aware of the presence of Drusus, the scout, who was hobbling the horses a few feet away. Severa's male dress was highly inappropriate; leather trews covered her legs and a tunic rendered her torso completely shapeless. Her hair was braided tightly around her head and covered by a knitted cap. With her freckles, she could easily be taken for a boy who was travelling with his kinfolk. However, if the ruse was discovered, her reputation would be lost forever.

'The only way you will fall into the hands of Conanus will be after my death, and I'll not perish in the immediate future. I have a destiny to fulfil, my lady, so you have my oath that you'll survive this journey and your life will go on for many, many years. I can swear to the truth of this statement.'

Severa smiled distractedly and lay back on the centurion's cloak. She closed her eyes, turned several times to find a comfortable position and then, like a healthy young animal, she fell asleep. Constantinus straightened and padded off with the water bottles and the hobbled horses to search for the streamlet that could be heard as it bubbled and gurgled its way over rocks inside the coppice.

Once the stream was found, the water bottles were filled and the horses permitted to stand, hock high, as they drank their fill, Constantinus allowed his thoughts to travel back over the previous day and his fears of an ambush.

Father Gregory had deplored the possibility that a violent confrontation was imminent, offering his opinion that consensus would always be a preferable response to most of the problems of the secular world. However, he was also a realist, and not so gullible as to believe that Conanus could be convinced to see reason.

'I agree that subterfuge is a more effective ploy than violence in this situation, Centurion. Would you consider splitting your command into two separate columns to convince this Conanus to chase after the wrong quarry?'

At the time of this discussion, Constantinus and Paulus had been breaking bread with the priests during the frugal evening meal; the centurion had been surprised by the cleric's grasp of an alternative means of denying Conanus's aspirations. Constantinus and Paulus had already considered that such a solution was the only viable means of keeping Severa safe.

'I'm reluctant to engage with Conanus's men in an ambush. I know we can defeat his forces if all factors are equal, but we don't know if Conanus has received reinforcements. It is possible that he has received support from one or more of the local British kings, rulers who could be colluding with him. If treason has been done, we will be putting Lady Severa's safety at risk. I know her death is the last thing that Conanus wants, but battles aren't predictable and stray arrows don't always choose their targets. I'd prefer to keep her away from danger.'

'But we can't stay here indefinitely,' Paulus replied. 'The longer we stay in Glastonbury, the more time we give to Conanus to amass an even larger force.'

'Father Gregory has a point, Paulus. What if Lady Severa and two trusted guards made a secret departure from Glastonbury by an unlikely route? The main column could make an obvious departure on the following day, despite the probability that they would be ambushed by Conanus's forces. We would need to convince Conanus that Severa was still travelling with the main column, but such a ploy will only be successful if the trio made good their departure during the hours of darkness.'

Paulus's mind raced ahead of his superior's explanation. 'Father Gregory has promised to provide us with a maid to accompany Lady Severa for propriety's sake. The spies at the signal fire to the south wouldn't be able to tell if a woman in the baggage wagon is Severa or not when the main column begins its journey.'

'True!' Constantinus replied eagerly as his own thoughts caught fire from Paulus's observations.

'I'll wager no one among Conanus's assassins has taken the trouble to do a detailed head count of the numbers in our column. They would have made a rough estimate of our strength from a distance, based on the size of our column while we've been on the march,' Paulus added. 'They won't really be able to tell if a small group of our cavalry are missing, so Father Gregory is right. Perhaps a little subterfuge might be better than the point of a gladius – at least on this occasion.'

During the next few minutes, the two officers devised a rough strategy between them. At first, Paulus was eager to accompany Constantinus and Lady Severa, but as a pragmatic officer he had to accept that the commander of the main column must be Constantinus's second-in-command. Paulus must assume the role of a centurion during the coming battle.

Father Gregory expressed his fears for the girl who would be taking Severa's place within the column, but Constantinus explained how their enemy had indicated their intention was to capture Severa alive. Still, any prospective maid must be warned of the dangers, and her family compensated for allowing the girl to put herself at risk.

With the worst of his own fears allayed, the abbot agreed to the plan and left the table to speak with his chosen woman and a member of her kin. He carried with him a purse of silver coins provided by Constantinus that would reward her for undertaking this task. The centurion felt a little like Judas Iscariot during the exchange, but he pushed all misgivings to one side.

'You'll bear the brunt of any attack, Paulus, even if I manage to escape cleanly with Lady Severa. My mission and my responsibility must be to ensure that she arrives safely in Tintagel, so I must be the one who takes her there. But I'll not sacrifice my men by stripping them of their most senior officers during the coming battle. As always, I have complete confidence in your abilities, Decurion, so I need you to take care of my men for me.'

'Aye!' Paulus answered with a sigh of resignation. 'I will obey!'

The Roman column moved along the road leading into the south-west with the heavy, arrogant movements that could be expected from the masters of the known world. In his borrowed helmet, Paulus looked out at the landscape around him, low-lying and sodden, so that only the track was raised above waterlogged meadows where dragonflies and butterflies danced in the morning sun. Too few trees provided the cover needed by an attacking force of considerable size. With a sigh of relief, Paulus decided that his men would be safe from attack for at least the remainder of the day.

But night would bring danger. Under the cover of darkness, their enemies could use stealth to infiltrate the Roman lines, unless the soldier on piquet duty remained alert. Ahead, perhaps a day's march away, Paulus could see the misty crowns of a line of heavily forested hills. Ambushes could be mounted from behind the cover of trees, so he sensed that the morrow would bring trouble.

The march remained uneventful during the remainder of the afternoon. The going was heavy with mud, but the day was pleasantly warm so the column was able to make good speed. Although the legionnaires knew that they would soon come under attack, they remained cautious but cheerful. For his part, Paulus accepted that every mile travelled was a mile closer to an inevitable ambush, but the joy he usually derived from battle was tempered by his sense of responsibility for his men.

As the long day drew to a close and the twilight softened the harsh glare of the sun, Paulus ordered camp to be made in a secure spot where a deep water hole would protect their backs and one of the flanks to ensure that their defensive perimeter was of minimal length. Meanwhile, he took pains to be as scrupulous in his demands as Constantinus would have been. Every legionnaire set to work to raise a low wall and a defensive trench around their section of the perimeter with good will, for all were aware that these small fortifications could save their lives. The horses were watered and tethering lines placed at the rear of the bivouac, while guards were ordered to act as rotating pickets to ensure that the beasts were protected. Then, once he was satisfied that his bivouac was as secure as he could make it, Paulus settled down beside his fire to snatch a few hours of precious sleep.

Despite following every detail of Constantinus's routines, as well as adding several of his own, he was unable to relax. He had debated with himself whether campfires should be allowed, but eventually came to the conclusion that his enemy already knew where the Romans had set up their camp, whether they had fires or not. In any event, he was reluctant to rob the men of the warmth of cooked food, while the loss of the companionship of firelight would be counterproductive, suggesting as it did that his men were afraid of an invisible enemy. As he ate a rabbit stew prepared by Severa's decoy maid, Paulus accepted that small luxuries such as this could give a warrior the heart to fight with more than his fair share of ferocity.

Meanwhile the small party of three riders continued to pick their way through challenging, hilly terrain almost completely devoid of farms and villages. The darkness was so thick under the forest trees that Constantinus ordered Drusus to make a torch out of dry wood, mosses, tree bark and a strip of torn cloth. Soon the riders were able to cover more ground with far less risk to life and limb.

'Could the enemy scouts see the torchlight and know where we are?' Severa asked nervously, her eyes darting from side to side as if her vision could penetrate the oppressive darkness.

'It's a risk we must take,' Constantinus explained patiently. 'Our plans will crumble away to nothing if one of our horses should break a leg, or if one of us were to fall and be injured. There've been few signs of habitation since we've been on the road, so I'm confident that we won't be seen.'

Severa understood the dangers of broken limbs, especially in remote areas of the countryside. Wisely, she decided to remain silent. The changeable nature of this centurion made it impossible for her to fully understand him. At one moment, he would be the personification of solicitude; then, for no reason that she could fathom, he would look at her as if he was harbouring thoughts of ravishing her, with or without her consent.

Do I love him? More to the point, do I want him? I have to marry someone, and the man I accept as my spouse will almost certainly become the next king of the Britons. Would Constantinus, who is as stiff-necked a Roman as I've ever met, give up his command in the legions for me? And would he consider a kingship to be a fair exchange for his freedom?

As Severa pondered his motives, the Roman was mulling over the same vexing problem.

Marrying her, considering the circumstances of their unchaperoned journey and their escape from Corinium, might not pose a particular problem. The king of the Dumnonii would probably demand some kind of union for the sake of Severa's reputation, even if she was opposed to marrying a Roman. But did he want her? She had many advantages that could be useful to an officer of lowly origins. Could he use this beautiful woman to advance his career in the service of Rome?

Perhaps it wasn't love that he felt for her, Constantinus thought grimly, with a flash of harsh self-knowledge. But was he prepared to leave the legions to pursue her and achieve the British crown?

The decision that finally sprang into his mind was so appalling that he jerked sharply on the reins of his horse, causing it to rear sharply in indignation. Unbidden, the face of the old hermit returned to haunt his thoughts like a cursed warning from Fortuna.

'I don't believe in magic,' he snarled, then realised he had spoken aloud when Severa turned in her saddle.

He grinned ruefully and apologised to his companion. 'I was thinking aloud, Lady Severa. I recalled that I had been warned long ago that I was to avoid taking unnecessary risks when I find myself in dangerous situations. However, the warnings have convinced me that I shouldn't allow myself to be frightened away from my desires . . . or my duty. I will always be, at heart, a true and loyal Roman.'

Surprised at his cryptic words, Severa blushed.

Does she know what I'm thinking? Constantinus wondered. No! It's impossible!

'I wish I could be as resolute as you, Centurion. I'm afraid that I've always done what was expected of me. If I'm to die on the morrow, I'll have robbed myself of my most ardent desires in order to satisfy the expectations of others. My life will have been half-lived and, therefore, scarcely lived at all.'

Before Constantinus could answer her, she turned in the saddle and kneed her horse gently to send it after Drusus's half-lit figure. Nor did the centurion speak to her again until long after the moon had begun to descend through the sky and he had called for the overnight halt to their journey.

Afternoon came and a further day in the saddle found Severa gritty-eyed and fretful. Drusus fetched the horses, while sulking under his facade of impassivity because his commanding officer had unaccountably taken his waking mood out on his underling. Unable to react, Drusus could only assuage his temper by yanking on the reins of the horses after they had been saddled and prepared for another day's work.

The three riders kept close to the tree line until Drusus stopped suddenly. There, ahead of them, they could see a flash of water through a gap in the thick trees and underbrush.

'The river!' Constantinus exclaimed, and his mood lightened as he realised that something was finally working out in accordance with his plans. 'We must be close to Lindinus.'

The small party had ridden for barely half an hour before Drusus drew their attention to a haze of smoke and industry in the distance.

'That's Lindinus, for certain,' Constantinus averred. 'All we need to do now is to find a convenient place to ford the river and we can continue our journey into the south. I believe we've outwitted your kinsman, my lady. God be praised!'

'Then I hope our good fortune continues,' Severa retorted emphatically. Embarrassed, the centurion's face coloured along his high cheekbones.

During their journey through the darkness of the night, the three riders had been oblivious to much of the landscape through which they were travelling. However, they could tell that the rough terrain had given way to lowlands that indicated a river valley. Also, the increasing evidence of domesticated animals in pastures and the grey cottages of some farmers attested to a land that had been tamed. Constantinus's mood improved with every new vista that spoke of provident and law-abiding populations.

They rode through the trees along the river bank, where Drusus began a search for a ford or a bridge that could carry them across to the far bank in safety. The steep, eroded banks spoke of the pressure of floods that arrived with the advent of the summer rains. The party rode on until the trees began to thin and water meads took their place, alive with long-legged birds, butterflies and bees.

In one likely spot, where the waters widened and an island butted out of the river like a neat, shaven skull, Drusus found a section of the bank that shelved gently to the water with the presence of some coarse-grained sand that would combat the river mud. He carefully rode his horse into the shallows, before forcing it into the deeper waters where the steed was required to swim briefly before emerging on the shingle on the far side of the stream.

Once the scout had successfully crossed, Constantinus led Severa into the river and remained alongside her in case she was washed out of the saddle. On the other side the going proved to be far easier, although the small party was turning back towards a line of low hills that raised their rounded heads towards a pale-blue sky.

Severa was numb with weariness by the time the centurion called a halt to their busy day, and she finally had an opportunity to dismount. Every muscle in her legs and lower torso was screaming in protest, so she wondered why she hadn't felt such pain and exhaustion during her first two days on the road.

'You're stiff from being on horseback for so long, Lady Severa. You need to soak in the river to lave away your aches and pains,' Constantinus advised her. He had spoken in a distant voice that indicated he didn't really care if she accepted this advice or not.

'It sometimes takes a day or two before I feel the full effects of a long journey on horseback, so I find that bathing in cool water often helps. I'll accompany you down to the river bank if you're nervous about walking to the river alone. I'll respect your privacy while you're bathing.'

Severa nodded, although her chief desire was to curl up on her saddle blanket and weep from exhaustion. Taking her silence for agreement, Constantinus picked up the pack containing her spare clothing and offered her his arm.

As he led her through a thicket of thorn trees lining the river, he pulled the branches aside to ease her descent to the water's edge but, unfortunately, she tripped over her own tired feet. Constantinus had to hold her upright with both hands to stop her from tumbling down the weed-choked bank. With a muttered apology, he felt his confusion return in a rush, for he had convinced himself during the previous night that he would take some precipitate action that would win Severa's hand.

'Thank you, good sir.' She gripped his forearm tightly to

maintain her balance. 'I'm really very tired today, or else I wouldn't presume on your time.'

As the silence deepened between them, Constantinus slid down the bank ahead of her and lifted her free from the last branches of the thicket of thorns. Depositing her on her feet beside a small pile of rocks on the very edge of the water, he backed away, dropping her pack on to a narrow strip of clean sward, before moving towards a small bend on the river bank.

'I'll wait for your call just over there. Just shout if you need me and I'll come immediately.'

Then the centurion moved out of sight. After a few moments, feeling awkward and at a loose end, Severa lowered herself gingerly on to the highest point of the largest sun-dried rock.

She began to remove her boots, throwing them behind her, then the long, knitted socks. Once her legs were bared, she could see the nasty chafing that had raised weeping blisters and swollen patches of flesh on her thighs and calves, injuries that looked almost as painful as they felt. Then she rose shakily to her feet.

Once she had lowered herself into the cold water, it gave immediate relief. Yet she was fearful of venturing too far because she had never learned to swim.

Even so this experience was thoroughly pleasurable.

Unwilling to put herself at further risk, the young woman waded deeper into the chill waters until she was immersed up to her waist. Slowly, she became conscious of the small details of life around her. She could even feel the attention of tiny minnows as they nibbled at her toes and hear the drone of bees searching for sustenance among the thistle flowers and the whirr of dragonfly wings buzzing along the banks.

Constantinus drew back from his position on the bank where

he was just out of Severa's view. Dishonourably, and against his better nature, he had watched her naked white thighs glimmer in the fading light and ached as he peered at the sweet, delicate line of her buttocks when she moved into the river. The familiar feelings of lust that he felt for this British witch returned to tease him, so that he was forced to turn away, red and embarrassed by his voyeurism. His yearning for her was wrong, but he still felt an uncomfortable urge to surrender to the attraction of rape. Then, once his lust had been slaked, he knew he could be free to complete the Corinium king's orders without further qualms.

But such desires were disgraceful. Spying on her private nakedness was just as treacherous as any other thoughts or actions, so he kept his back to the waters and steeled himself to resist any further temptation.

'Centurion,' she called suddenly in an alarmed voice. 'Could you please help me? The water is too deep. I'm having difficulty staying on my feet.'

He hastened to the water's edge, praying that the heightened colour in his cheeks was no longer obvious.

'Could you hold my hand so I don't fall? I don't know how to swim.'

'Of course, my lady. Take my arm and I'll help you to return to the bank.'

The centurion extended his right hand which she grabbed quickly. He had only taken a single step towards the bank when a moss-covered rock turned under his heel and, left arm windmilling wildly, he slipped backwards into the waters and dragged Severa down with him.

He rose out of the water spewing water from his open mouth and shaking his head like a dog. His right hand steadied Severa, whose hair covered her face in a tangled wave of dark honey. For reasons that she couldn't understand, he laughed.

Unaccountably, she also began to laugh. Despite her near-nakedness, she stood in river water in the embrace of a man who was not one of her kinsmen. In the circle of the arms that were steadying her, she felt no shame.

With a twinge of embarrassment, the two pulled themselves apart. Aware that their relationship had changed, the pair returned to their rudimentary camp after she had dressed. A long and frustrating night lay ahead of them.

CHAPTER X

TRAPPED

Deceive boys with toys, but men with oaths.

Lysander, *Proverbs*

Beyond the foul-smelling mud and clay tracks used by the lowland farmers, the Romans found a narrow valley heading into a more mountainous area, where some small homesteads were linked together by veritable goat tracks. On these uncertain paths, the column managed to find their way through the hills with the use of scouts to reconnoitre the land ahead of them. Paulus led his command in the general direction of the south-west coast. As he cursed this rarely travelled and mostly deserted landscape, the decurion guided his column through the valley, hemmed in with hills on either side.

'If I was going to attack a vulnerable column, this is the place that I'd select to carry it out,' Paulus said to himself. He imagined arrows trained on his back and stiffened his shoulders in response.

'Trufo! Send word back through the column. They must be on the alert for hostiles. This terrain is perfect for bowmen to hit us from the tree-line on either side of the track.'

Using his gladius, Paulus pointed towards the deep expanse of forest that covered the hills on both sides in two impenetrable, primeval walls. From the tree-line, narrow stretches of land swept down to a rushing stream.

'We're dangerously exposed here, so keep your shields close at hand.'

Suddenly, the column was forced to halt and retrace its steps when the river valley narrowed even more. The path had become so rough that the wagons could no longer move safely along the rutted track without disastrous consequences. The entire column was forced to retreat back to a point where the valley yielded up another pathway that had obviously been used in the past to carry market produce. Though overgrown, at least it was wide enough for the wagons to pass along it in reasonable safety.

At the apex of one ridge where Paulus had climbed to view the terrain that lay before the column, he found that the track was petering out once again, as if the farmers who had used it in bygone days had been stolen away by some terrible and pitiless foe and their farmsteads had been abandoned. He shrugged and considered divesting himself of the wagons that were proving to be such a liability in these wastelands.

After climbing a tree on the ridge, he could see the blue-grey curve of the coast beyond the rugged hills where a few protected crescents of beaches were barely visible. Segments of grey cliffs and stone ramparts seemed to mark the boundary between land and sea.

'Bugger me!' Paulus swore. 'There don't seem to be any trees or obvious places of ambush between us and the coast, but it's rough country, so there's no chance of taking the wagons over the ridge and through there,' he told Trufo. 'We'll ditch them and head into the south, hugging the coast as we go.'

Once he had made his decision, Paulus acted with typical Roman determination. The useful contents of the wagons were distributed between all the troops, so the rations and other stores were retained for consumption during the remainder of the journey. The horses became mounts for those persons who had travelled on the clumsy carts and the command was soon moving through the difficult terrain with greater speed.

Buoyed up by the possibility that his command might be able to reach the coast before they were attacked, Paulus faced the night with renewed confidence. He could finally admit to himself that he had been fearful of the Armorican and dreaded the responsibility for the men's safety that had fallen on his unwilling shoulders. His nerves had been stretched for days as he waited for an ambush that never came.

Perhaps the column could still reach Tintagel unscathed.

Shy when she was in the company of the centurion, Severa faced a new day with legs and feet that had much improved after their dousing in the river. Mindful of her mother's advice to always treat even the smallest break in the skin with medication, she rubbed a little unguent from her saddlebags into the chafing and blisters, while trusting to a good night's sleep that would speed the healing process.

Constantinus awoke before dawn and ordered camp to be broken. After days of travel, the three riders were accustomed to the patterns of the road. They had lived on cold rations for the large part, as the weather was still mild and a fire might attract unwelcome attention from their enemies. Severa's allotted task was to organise the camp and monitor their use of supplies and rations, as well as collecting any fresh water needed during their overnight bivouac. She would seek out places where springs reached the surface of the earth in the hope that these waters were safe for human and animal consumption.

Drusus cared for the horses and took more than his share of the night watches, as well as making frequent scouting forays to find suitable routes that would facilitate their passage through the countryside. Constantinus had determined that cross-country travel would be safer than trusting to the winding paths cut by farmers to move their supplies and animals. Each night, Drusus sharpened his weapons and maintained his equipment, although he managed to regale his travelling companions with tales of his youth and descriptions of the exotic places in which he had served his masters during twenty years in Rome's legions.

Constantinus was surprised to discover that Drusus had served in the far-off fortresses that dotted the eastern coast of the Middle Sea. He had been stationed in Jerusalem, a place of constant rebellion and religious strife, when he served in the legions of the Eastern Empire. The centurion was loath to ask why Drusus had left the service of the Emperor of Constantinople to once again serve the lords of Rome, because the Eastern Empire was far more stable and promised better career opportunities for a capable legionnaire. In fact, now that Drusus was travelling in such close company with Constantinus and Severa, his discipline, quick wit and experience seemed to indicate that he was more accustomed to giving orders than taking them. Constantinus filed these interesting observations away in his mind as a matter to investigate if he ever had the leisure to do so.

Then, as they reached the crest of one of the innumerable ridge lines, the travellers rested for a short time to spare the horses and drink some water. As the centurion dismounted and stretched his stiff muscles, Severa suddenly gave a small cry of surprise and pointed to where the vague outline of the coast could finally be seen.

'Look! Over there! There's smoke in the distance,' she called out excitedly.

He followed the line of her pointing hand.

'There seems to be a flock of birds circling near the smoke as well,' he said. 'They're a long way off, but they look like carrion birds to me. What say you, Drusus?'

Three pairs of eyes scanned across the distance towards the trail of smoke that pointed upwards in the still air. Then Severa's sharp eyes realised that the circling birds were certainly large enough to be eagles or other meat-eating birds, so she felt a hard stone of apprehension form in the pit of her stomach.

'Something must be dead over there if those birds are feeding,' Drusus agreed. 'But the fire could indicate some other event of little direct concern to us.'

'It would still be best to learn the worst while we have an opportunity to do so,' Constantinus replied. 'Even if it's the main column, I can't believe that your uncle could have found sufficient men to permit him to attack a column of Roman legionnaires.'

Severa bit her lower lip, already swollen from the persistent worrying of her teeth over the past few days. Given what Endellion had told her of Conanus's nature, Severa doubted that her uncle would be distracted by anything, so the small matter of numbers would only be an irritant to overcome. She sighed, because Constantinus's overt respect for a woman's reputation and safety did not extend to consideration of her mental abilities.

The small party set off, following a direct, difficult path that would take them to the source of both the smoke and the wheeling carrion birds. The route entailed steep climbs in those places where they were unable to find a simpler way of bypassing a line of hills. Several small streams pulsed out from narrow stone fissures that had been worn into the stone over millennia, and these proved to be dangerous impediments to fast travel. Unfortunately, the boulders in the creek beds were thick with slime and moss, so that even when on foot, the three members of the party found they were in danger of slipping into the water where the speed of the current could carry away the strongest of men, smashing bones against rocks.

Once, Severa slid on one precariously balanced stone and landed, fortuitously, on her backside. Her dragging cloak and her death grip on the reins of her horse helped to save her until Constantinus was able to grasp her shoulder with his strong right hand and haul her up again.

By the time they approached the last of the hills, all signs of the drifting smoke had vanished, but a spiral of black crows appeared out of a fold in the next escarpment and headed towards their roost.

Constantinus made an instant decision to camp at the top of the rise and learn what dangers lay before them with the coming of the new day. Only then, when she glanced upwards at the sky, did the exhausted Severa realise that they had ridden long past twilight; the first hours of the night had passed before she realised that they were still astride their horses.

Severa should have been both exhausted and ravenously hungry, but the heavy weight in the pit of her stomach was refusing to melt away. The darkness of this night had brought dread, rather than the welcome exhaustion experienced on previous nights on the road. Certain that something ugly and frightening lay ahead of them, she was fearful of closing her eyes in sleep, imagining nameless horrors. Instead, she begged to take her share of the night watches.

'Very well, Severa. Your offer is welcome! Drusus and I will need all the rest we can get if we should find trouble on the morrow. An hour or two would be fine, but no longer! And you must wake one of us if anything alarms you, even if you think your concerns are foolish. Understand? We're far too close to whatever happened in the fold in these hills for my liking.'

Severa bridled a little at his protective manner, but chose to keep her face compliant as she agreed to follow his instructions.

The ground in their camp was far too steep and dangerous to risk a beast falling while hobbled and trying to graze, so the animals were secured next to the rider's bedrolls for security. Severa realised too that the centurion wanted their mounts close by as an extra precaution if strangers should prowl around their campsite in the darkness. The excellent eyes and ears of the horses, coupled with their stolid presence, gave her an illusion of protection. When she rose to feed them the wilted tops of some carrots she had found beside a ruined farmhouse on the previous day, their velvety lips and gentle eyes proved companionable in this darkness where every shadow could be hiding a monster from her imagination.

Time passed slowly as the two men slept and Severa waited with nerves and ears acutely stretched for any inklings of danger. She sat in the shadows of the trees that protected the camp and listened to the night breeze that stirred the branches above her.

The moon had risen long before, but the clouds had begun to scud in with their promise of rain before morning. The increased cloud cover deepened the intensity of the darkness so that what light penetrated into the woods was only sufficient to provide a smudge of bluish highlights on the edges of the exposed tree roots. The few visible details of the camp and its surrounds were touched by this same blue light which should have been calming but, instead, was eerie and elemental. Severa shivered fearfully, despite the warmth of the night.

She slipped back to her pallet and slid down to sit cross-legged on it with her legs folded under her body. Constantinus was stirring from within his cocoon across the clearing where he was lying under the protection of a spreading oak tree. She recognised from the low groaning sounds that the centurion had been dreaming in his sleep.

A few body lengths further on, Drusus was sitting bolt upright against a wide tree trunk, his body surrounded by a stiff woollen blanket. He slept with both hands ready to grip his sword and shield at the slightest alarming sound. How he could sleep so soundly in this cramped position defied Severa's imagination, but she supposed that his long service in the legions had something to do with it.

Suddenly, from out of the darkness, she heard a sharp sound like the breaking of a tree branch. It was some distance away, perhaps at the bottom of the hill in the area where the woods retreated. Severa jerked upright, all her senses attuned to the direction from which the strange, penetrating sound had come.

The night was so silent that she heard the noise that followed as if it was quite near. A horse was forcing its way through thick underbrush. Controlling her fear, she moved to the edge of the sloping escarpment, a short distance from the trees where her two escorts were sleeping. Finally, she forced herself to wait on the shelf-like slope of land that fell away to the base of the hill. The underbrush was thinner here and trees were sparser, so her view of the lower slopes was somewhat clearer when the moon intermittently broke through the clouds.

A faint light appeared and disappeared as an intruder made his way through the underbrush. A torch, held by a person on horseback, would create that elevated light.

A stranger! Severa felt her heart leap into her mouth. He must be up to something wicked, for why else would anyone be riding in the woods at this time of night? Her companions must be warned that their small party was in danger of discovery.

She slithered away from the edge of the slope and moved as silently as she could through the undergrowth to the small clearing where her companions were sleeping. A cautious hand shook the centurion's shoulder and his eyes snapped open instantly. The small noises of movement he made as he climbed to his feet woke Drusus, who was immediately alert.

'What is it?' Constantinus hissed.

'There's a rider on horseback at the bottom of the hill,' Severa replied with admirable self-control. 'He's carrying a torch.'

'Stay here, Severa! Do you hear me? Stay here, and don't move,' the centurion repeated. Then he padded away into the darkness with Drusus close behind him.

Severa sat on Constantinus's pallet, clutching her knees up to her chin. Then she felt something hard under her feet and realised it was part of the centurion's leg armour. The rest of his armour was still in place beside the makeshift bed, including his chain mail shirt. Perhaps he didn't want the sound of metal on metal to alert their unknown visitor.

Fear clutched at her belly. Constantinus was unprotected against the stranger who was stalking them in the darkness. He could die without his mail shirt to protect him.

'Don't be a fool, Severa. No one has been stalking us,' she told herself. 'This rider could be anyone, so there's no reason to suppose that he means us any harm.'

As she waited in the darkness to learn what her companion had found, her ears strained to hear any tiny sound that was unusual. Filled with fear, she stayed within the circle of pallets, but part of her wanted to take to her heels and run.

The sudden sound of undergrowth snapping under a heavy weight was followed by a high, thin cry. Severa waited with her heart in her mouth. Nothing was worse than waiting in the darkness, even the constant fear of ambush and death.

Within seconds, she could clearly hear a number of bodies as if a small group of men was moving through the trees below the camp. The crackling noises of human movement came closer and the soft neighing of a frightened horse could now be heard as her companions were obviously returning to the security of their sleeping area. She sighed with relief. They must have captured the stranger, she thought.

Drusus, leading a horse, was the first to burst back into the clearing. Severa only had time to take in the roughly bound figure slung across its back before Drusus dumped the unmoving prisoner on to the earth with a nasty, bone-shattering thud before he attempted to quieten the frantic beast.

Constantinus followed his legionnaire into the clearing. He burst out of the leafy shrubbery at a trot, careless of a bleeding gash on his upper arm that was staining his tunic.

'Get that damned horse hobbled and silence him, Drusus. Our friend here might not be alone,' he ordered, with a level voice and darting, careful eyes.

'Severa? See if our visitor is alive. I was forced to hit him very hard with the hilt of my sword.'

Severa knew better than to argue, so she rose and approached the bound figure with some caution.

The prisoner lay on his stomach in the untidy sprawl where

he had fallen. Using all of her strength, Severa tugged at his bound hands, arms and torso until she managed to roll him on to his back. She could see from his face that he was surprisingly young, not even twenty, and his forehead was marked by a large lump that was already showing signs of bruising. The breath that passed through his gaping mouth was coarse and rough, but it was regular. Then, when Severa sought out the large, pulsing vein in his neck with her fingers, she knew that his life force was pumping strongly.

'He's alive, but he's unconscious,' she reported. 'He's very young . . . and he's very well dressed. He must be of some importance, because he has a large ring that looks like it's made of pure gold and his gloves are lined with quality fur.'

Tugging forcibly to remove the ring from his flaccid fingers, Severa eventually managed to remove the bauble and examine it in the moonlight that had finally broken through the clouds. She realised immediately that the ring had been made from a golden plait worked into a simple circular shape. When she turned it in her fingers, she discovered that letters had been engraved into the inner band.

She mentioned this to the centurion, who was visibly surprised. 'I've seen a ring like this before. Just a moment . . .'

With fingers that were still bloodied and slippery, Constantinus fumbled through the small leather pouch attached to his heavy belt until, with a cry of triumph, he snatched another plait of pure gold from its depths.

With a grimace of triumph, he handed his ring to Severa. 'This bauble is the same as the one in your hands. It's inscribed with the name *Elen.*'

Clasping the bloody baubles awkwardly in her hands, she examined both rings closely, although the dim light obscured the details of the inscriptions and she was forced to depend on touch to make her comparison. However she could feel that both rings had something engraved inside the rims and, in all other respects, they seemed identical.

'That's my mother's name – and it's spelled in exactly that way,' Severa breathed, hardly daring to reveal her discovery in a louder voice. 'These rings and the engravings inside them couldn't possibly be a coincidence.'

'Perhaps I should have made more of the first ring when I found it at the dead fire of those spies who were watching us at Glastonbury. But its discovery wasn't all that important at the time, because my first responsibility was to spirit you out of Glastonbury and escort you to a place of safety.'

'It's possible that Conanus sees the death of his sister, my mother, as some sort of justification for the plot he's devised. Perhaps the loss of his sister has somehow convinced him that taking me prisoner would be performing a service to his kinfolk. It's also possible that his attack on us represents his revenge against Rome, the rulers who were the indirect cause of his sister's death,' Severa said carefully. 'But he served Maximus for half a decade after Elen's death, so I'd have expected him to reveal his wounds at a far earlier time than the present, if he had any long-held animosity towards Maximus. I'm certain, however, that Aeron and his friends weren't aware of Conanus's conspiracy before you discovered it, for they'd have mentioned it before we left Corinium.'

'Aye! King Aeron would have heard some whisper of Conanus's activities and motives if a plot had been hatched over a long period of time,' the centurion replied.

Drusus had joined them by now and, when the bound captive groaned, Drusus kicked him casually in the stomach. 'This fellow will be able to tell us exactly what the rings mean when he returns to the land of the living,' he remarked.

As if on cue, the bound man moaned again and began to stir, while trying to turn onto his side. The centurion strode over to the struggling figure, gripped a handful of cloak and tunic below the lad's neckline and jerked him upwards until he was in a seated position.

'Get some water, Severa, and pour it over his head,' Constantinus demanded.

As Severa complied by fetching a pitch-sealed water bag, the seated figure raised its head and shook it vigorously. 'No! No! Can I drink? Please?'

Severa nodded when the approval was given. Filling a small tin cup with water, she held it carefully to the prisoner's lips.

He drank greedily.

'Enough of the niceties!' Constantinus ordered. 'Who are you and why are you abroad in the dead of night?'

The young man smiled amiably as if they were having a casual conversation at an inn, but Severa could see that his eyes were wary and anxious. He answered the centurion's curt questions in an open, cheerful manner which was meant to disarm.

'My name is Cledwyn and I'm simply a foolish traveller who has gotten himself lost.'

'That's a novel answer to my question,' Constantinus answered scornfully. 'You have a strange accent, so I'm forced to ask you where you were born. I'd warn you not to lie to me, because you won't enjoy my responses.'

'I'm a Briton, so I see no reason why I should justify myself to you or answer any of your impertinent questions,' the captive blustered.

Drusus responded to the prisoner's insolence by striking him with an open hand across the cheek. The handprint stood out in bright red across the youth's pale face.

'I'd answer the centurion properly if I was in your place, or we'll be forced to drag the answers out of you with pain and suffering,' Drusus added in an expressionless voice.

'We'll start again, Cledwyn,' Constantinus said as Drusus stepped back to stand directly behind the seated captive.

The lad sighed, but he seemed to be gaining fortitude from some internal decision.

'I'm from Armorica in Gallia where my family is the owner of a large estate, although I was born in Britannia in the north of Cymru. Perhaps my accent comes from my childhood, but I cannot tell. I have always believed that I sound like a true Briton, for we adhere to the old ways in Armorica. It's well known that we detest the influence of Rome on our people.'

'You're very brave for a man who has been taken by Roman legionnaires,' Constantinus said with no particular emphasis on his words. 'Perhaps you're one of those Britons who find Romans to be palatable during times of warfare, as long as we are on your side and your interests prevail.'

'I'll not be happy until all Romans have left our lands and my people are left in peace.'

Here speaks a fool, Severa thought. He can't possibly believe that Rome is to blame for all the ills of the world.

Drusus cuffed Cledwyn across the back of the neck once more, and the young man shook his head to clear his ringing ears.

'It's easy to be brave when your enemies are tied up and can't retaliate,' the young man muttered through his teeth. 'But your fellow Romans learned a little of our true mettle yesterday, praise be to the Lord of Hosts.'

Constantinus paled.

'You'd best pray that my men have suffered no lasting harm or you'll learn at first hand why Romans rule the world,' he replied, his eyes steely.

While this exchange and mutual chest-thumping was taking place, Severa watched both men closely, viewing their expressions, their gestures and their body language with more intensity than usual.

'Were you born in Caernarfon near the place that the Romans call Segontium?' she asked suddenly. She moved forward so that the moonlight lit her hair and bare face.

The young man turned towards her as if he had forgotten her existence, and the girl noted a sudden stiffening of his upper lip.

'Answer me,' she ordered.

'Aye! I was born in Caernarfon, some twenty-one years ago.'

'That's exactly what I would have imagined. You were already born when King Caradoc and my foster-mother, Endellion, came to your grandfather's court in those bygone days. My mother saw Magnus Maximus for the first time during that visit and she fell in love with him.'

She turned to face Constantinus when Cledwyn remained silent. 'This young man is my cousin. The family resemblance should be easy to see,' she added in a sad voice.

She paused to glare at the prisoner.

Constantinus responded by lifting up the captive's face and staring fixedly at him. Satisfied, he nodded in agreement.

'He knows who I am,' Severa insisted. 'You do know me, Cledwyn, don't you? And where you travel, your father will be close behind. He has already decided that you are to become my betrothed, hasn't he? You would have imprisoned me and begotten a child on me. And then you would have silenced me – permanently. You, sir, are little more than an animal.'

Severa's voice had risen with distress, so Constantinus raised his hand to cover her mouth in case she was correct, and Conanus and his assassins were close at hand.

Somehow, Severa worked her mouth free of the centurion's grip.

'Perhaps you can tell me what lies your father has foisted on your people, so that my mother's name should become a rallying cry for your cause? Has he said the position of High King of Britannia was stolen from him? If he has, he is a liar! My father earned that title by force of arms and risking his own life for the people of these isles in conflicts that he fought against the Picts, the Hibernians and the Saxons. But what has Conanus ever risked? He fought for lands and riches, and sought the spoils and prizes available to those who rode with Magnus Maximus. He is betraying the old oaths he swore to his master when he disturbs my peace and tries to steal my life and my destiny. I will never – ever – marry against my will, even if I have to cut my own wrists to defeat my uncle. If he wants a throne, he must look elsewhere.'

All three men stared at her openly, two with admiration and one with a dawning fear of failure.

'He didn't tell you that I would be an unwilling participant in his plans, did he? Were you led to believe that I needed to be rescued from a cruel oppressor?'

She paused for breath and her eyes flashed with the anger that surged through her.

'Was Marcus Britannicus painted as a wicked seducer who was determined to force his way on me? The gods knew that Marcus wasn't much of a man, but I would have been a willing participant in my marriage. King Aeron would never have forced me into a repugnant union, even if he had been disappointed at any decision I might have made. You must ask yourself why I'll have nothing to do with you and yours. If I have my way, you'll be freed so you can inform your father that I'll never yield to his demands.'

Constantinus cleared his throat and patted the girl's shoulders in admiration. But this caress was so brief that she could almost have imagined it.

'Unfortunately, Lady Severa doesn't have the power to free you. I don't intend to relinquish my hold on such a valuable prize as yourself, regardless of the fact that you are her cousin. We will be riding to the site of yesterday's confrontation at first light, so you should pray to your gods that I find nothing there that will earn you the harshness of a lingering death.'

The centurion paused and then smiled in a way that made the captive's blood run cold.

CHAPTER XI

AT DICE WITH DEVILS

And life is given to none freehold, but it is leasehold for all.

Lucretius, *De Rerum Natura*, Book 3

Four horsemen rested in the trees at the base of a tall row of hills. Although three of the horsemen crouched in their saddles, one was tied by his arms and ankles around the neck and flanks of his horse, a most uncomfortable position that meant he was staring at the earth below him rather than the landscape ahead. Without complaint, he had refused to speak further during the pre-dawn hours. The young man had given his captors his name and place of birth, but he had no intention of giving them any indication of his purpose as they rode through the uncompromising landscape in the early-morning light.

Frustrated, Constantinus had finally let Cledwyn ap Kynan be, but the captive took little pleasure from the cessation of the torture that had been inflicted on him.

'I'll find out your secrets sooner or later, boy, and you'll come to regret not being frank with me when you had the chance,' the centurion offered in a soft, controlled voice. Cledwyn had no doubt that the Roman meant exactly what he said.

Just before sunrise, Drusus forced Cledwyn to lie across his horse's saddle and then tied the prisoner's wrists to his ankles below the horse's belly. When he was immobilised over the horse's back, Drusus pulled the coarse ropes tight to ensure there was no chance of escape. Then, leading the horse by its reins, Drusus mounted his own stallion and the small party set off to investigate the smoke that had been observed on the previous day.

Almost immediately, they found the charred remains of deserted wagons. During the night, the three fugitives had been unable to see the dark shapes in the lee of the river. Now, at the scene, Constantinus saw evidence that the wagons had been deliberately abandoned by the legionnaires to increase the pace of the column, and he took heart from this small mercy.

They rode on, following the path of the river initially, but then moving away from the route followed by Paulus and his legionnaires, a dangerous place if Conanus was in pursuit of the column.

With scant respect for the comfort of their captive, the three travellers rode through a glorious late-summer morning. The sky was a soft-washed blue as the orange-red sun climbed above the cliffs. In the sunshine, the riders could feel its warmth but in those places where the hills were folded into ravines, they were plunged into pockets of deep shadow where a chilling breeze cut through them. In this wild landscape, Constantinus rode cautiously with a growing feeling of dread, although at least he could bask in the knowledge that possession of their prisoner, who was almost certainly Conanus's son, would be a strong bargaining tool if they were ambushed by the Armorican warriors.

The journey eventually came to an end when the small party rode cautiously around the base of a low hill and entered a larger valley carved into the hills as if a giant had taken a knife to the landscape and hacked out a river bed that could cope with a rushing stream. Across the waters, a tangle of dark rubbish still released an occasional twist of smoke that dissipated almost immediately in the breeze sweeping through the valley from the sea.

Constantinus rode up the slope, waving a warning hand to indicate that the others should await his instructions. As he reached his observation point, the scavenger birds saw him and took to the air in an untidy cacophony of curses and complaints, bloated from the gorged meat on which they had been dining. Constantinus shuddered at the sight.

The smell of burnt cloth, cooked meat and butchered offal struck him in a black wave. He knew that sweet, ugly aroma from bitter experience. As he peered into the mass of charred flesh he recognised the remains of bone and connective tissue that left the travesty of a hand clawing at the sky in a vain plea for mercy.

With the tip of Drusus's short stabbing spear, Constantinus carefully prodded at the pile of bodies in a vain search for the red cloaks of legionnaires or, perhaps, any face that might have been spared by the flames and remained recognisable. Meanwhile, Drusus had left Severa and the hog-tied captive, so both soldiers continued their grisly search until they were convinced that the ten bodies piled together in the unlovely sprawl of violent death were not Roman casualties.

Both legionnaires searched outside the perimeter of the pyre and discovered the eloquent signs of horses and men in combat, evidence that spoke of a sudden attack from a prepared ambush position. A troop of horsemen had thundered out of the east from a narrow fissure between two small hills in what must have been a surprise attack triggered by desperation. The centurion recognised the traces of Roman infantrymen who had formed into a defensive square to repel their assailants. Pools of dried blood, brown splashes on the dry grass and deeply churned earth had left a mute story of a vigorous defence.

After the skirmish, a troop of horsemen had ridden away in haste from the site of the battle. Another track, slightly larger, continued on in a south-westerly direction, so Constantinus reasoned that the troop of Roman defenders had let their attackers ride away while they cared for their injured and disposed of the enemy corpses.

'The only conclusion I can make from these remains is that some of our troop must have died and more would have been wounded, along with at least ten of the Armorican warriors,' he said as he paced around the battle site and evaluated the evidence. 'The Armorican force wasn't large enough to allow them the luxury of taking their dead with them, so they must have taken their wounded and ridden off to lick their wounds. Paulus would have carried out a mass burning of the enemy dead while he tended the Roman wounded from his own column. He would never burn the corpses of friends with an inadequate supply of lumber, so he will have taken his dead and burned them at a more suitable place along their line of march. I know Paulus! He'd never allow the scavengers to feast on the remains of his men. Never!'

'Then he can't be very far ahead of us,' Drusus added, his eyes scanning the landscape around them.

Constantinus began to walk briskly towards the top of the steeply eroded river bank. The erosion had left outcrops of loam and rocky areas where the roots of the undergrowth had well-established root systems.

'We'll scout among the higher points of the hills to see if there are any places where Paulus might have set up his camp,' he told Drusus as they surveyed the terrain around the field of death. They were quickly rewarded for their diligence.

At the top of a nearby hill, stones had been moved into place to erect a large cairn over a section of earth where recent rain had created a depression. The centurion realised immediately that this was the sort of burial site that Paulus would have selected, for his men could scrape away the loosened soil with their shields to create graves, where the physical remains of the legionnaires would be covered with the residual earth, and the entire site topped with local rocks and stones to ensure that the corpses couldn't be eaten by scavengers.

'Do you want me to expose the faces of our dead, Centurion?' Drusus asked.

'No! Let them rest. Given his situation, Paulus has done his best to give our men a good burial in a place that wasn't of their choosing. I'd like to know how many died, but I don't want to disturb them by interfering with the remains. I can wait till we meet up with Paulus to discover who perished ... and how.'

Severa prayed silently over the makeshift cairn, rather than ask questions about the centurion's plans for the future. She correctly assumed that he would inform her of his plans once they had been decided, so she forced herself to make no comment when Constantinus turned his horse in the direction of the track left by the Roman column.

'We'll follow Paulus at speed! Every moment separated from the column is dangerous now. Your uncle has exposed his determination to take you captive, regardless of the cost to the men who are part of his command.'

And so, regardless of the complaints from Cledwyn, the three rode at a brisk trot towards an uncertain meeting with Constantinus's own command.

* * *

When fugitives know that every tree might hide an archer and that every fold in the hills might harbour a force of assassins, each mile of travel becomes a contest between stretched nerves and the need to maintain a semblance of self-discipline. The horses caught a scent of fear from their masters and became fractious and inclined to bridle at any loud noises or changes in the breeze. As if in sympathy with the fates, a line of storm clouds began to gather as the day waned, and the members of the party could see that grey and sullen thunderheads were about to burst open in a torrential downpour.

Cledwyn complained that he had lost all the feeling in his hands and feet, but Drusus ignored him.

'Your father and his minions care little for the honour of warfare, so they prefer to attack from cover,' the scout responded succinctly. 'Ambushes are cowardly at best, but when so much death has resulted because an ambitious and greedy man is trying to imprison a woman who can be counted among his kin, none of his confederates have any right to comfort. Be grateful you're not dead!'

'Aye!' Constantinus added. 'Your only value is the fact of your birth, but you'd be dead already if I had any sense. Keep your fucking mouth shut!'

The threat silenced Cledwyn immediately. Severa was glad she was not an enemy in the centurion's power.

A long twilight was stretching out ahead of the travellers and, as their horses weren't overtired, Constantinus opted to continue their journey slowly until full darkness was upon them. But there was still some faint light to guide them on their way when they rounded a bend in the track and Conanus's true colours and ruthless savagery were finally revealed to the party.

No one in the small group had thought to wonder if the servant girl had escaped in the river valley. In fact, Severa had given no thought to the unfortunate girl at all, while Constantinus had presumed that she was still with Paulus and the column.

The fugitives found a message from Conanus that he had left for anyone who might be following.

Close to the path, the body of the servant girl had been laid out on a prominent rock which couldn't be missed by other travellers.

Severa was the first to see the discarded corpse. Her young eyes picked out a flash of white on the grey stone, the girl's body prominent in a landscape almost wholly composed of charcoal, dark-blue and dim greens.

Shel must have been captured on the previous day, because she was a novice rider and unable to control her mount.

Paulus was aware that the servant girl had taken the place of Severa in the column, so nothing was to be gained by carrying out a pursuit of her captors. Unfortunately, as the senior officer in the column, he couldn't take any action that might put his command at risk. But he would never abandon a women's corpse by the side of the road if he had been in the same position as Conanus. He would have ordered her corpse to be given a decent burial, even if such a decision had cost him valuable time.

No, this body had been dumped after the main Roman column had passed this way. Was the corpse a warning? Or was it just another demonstration of the Armorican's callousness?

When Conanus had begun his interrogation of the girl, he would have realised quickly that he'd been tricked and this girl had been substituted for Severa. He should have permitted the harmless creature to go free once he discovered that she was of no value to him, but he had been elevated to power in the service of Flavius Magnus Maximus, a pitiless man, and had fed on the Roman's power until it fitted him like a second skin. His own ruthless nature could be seen in the assassination of Gratian, the Roman emperor, in bygone years.

Conanus had maintained a hold on his lands in Armorica in the face of heavy opposition from his peers in Gallia and those emperors who succeeded Gratian in Rome. He had thrived because he was utterly ruthless and gave no quarter to anyone, be they kings, warriors or a harmless village girl.

With total disdain, Conanus had turned Severa's serving maid into a thing of no value. Her body bore the unmistakeable bruises, cuts and abrasions of pack rape, after which her throat had been cut. Then, as with the corpse of Marcus Britannicus, her remains had been dumped in a public place where her humiliation and shame could be seen by every bucolic passer-by.

Drusus swore, while Constantinus remained silent, although his lips tightened and his face paled. With unusual savagery, he dug his heels into the ribs of his horse and galloped along the track in uncontrolled temper.

Severa and Drusus took off in pursuit.

'Aren't we going to bury her?' Severa asked when she finally caught up with Constantinus. 'The woman deserves better than to be devoured by scavengers.'

Constantinus pulled back on the reins of his stallion with such force that the animal reared in protest. 'Do you want to join her? Your uncle is an animal and, once he's got you in his power and pulled a child from your body, you will not survive for a further day. Meanwhile, we would be exposed here if we were to waste time on a meaningless burial. I can feel eyes watching our every movement.'

'Why should that stop us from paying our respects to the poor lass?' Severa retorted angrily.

'Anything that slows us down before we reach Tintagel puts your safety at risk, Severa, so don't tell me what I should do.'

'I don't care about Conanus and what he intends to do, but I do care about that poor, innocent creature. She thought she had an opportunity to see the world that lies beyond the village of Glastonbury. She knew nothing . . . but we did. You must have known that the poor girl might be taken, regardless of your precautions. That was the whole purpose in taking me to Tintagel by this circuitous route. She deserves better of us than to have the crows eat the eyes from her corpse.'

Constantinus dragged his horse to a halt and turned to face the girl, his eyes burning.

'Yes, I did consider her situation. Yes, I decided she was expendable if that would save your life. I have no intention of risking you further by stopping to bury her. Did I think Conanus would give her to his men out of chagrin and spite? No, I didn't! I probably should have anticipated her fate, but I can't think of everything. Are you satisfied now, Severa?'

Severa knew that any argument was fruitless. The maid was dead, so there was nothing more that could be done.

As Drusus waited for her to proceed, Severa forced herself to sit upright in the saddle. Then, while wiping her eyes on her sleeve, she kneed her horse into movement. No one spoke a word until darkness shrouded the earth and the cloud-filled sky as light, drizzling rain began to fall.

Earth and sky; sky and earth. Hills that looked like their fellows; streams that hastened down river valleys in a rush to find a hidden sea; these details of the landscape were unchanging and interchangeable and they caused Severa to lose all sense of direction. Only the movement of the sun, with its dawning, its slow climb up the pale sky and then the equally dawdling descent gave the girl any clue as to the direction of the coast and the sea. But the scent of salt in the air, the wheeling gulls and the wide expanses of featureless grasses promised the travellers that the ocean was close by. It was just over the horizon, but still beyond reach.

Oh, that longed-for sea!

The coast and Tintagel waited for them in the darkness that enclosed them. By now, Severa had given up all hope of finding Paulus and the Roman column, despite Constantius's assurances that they were following the spoor of their comrades who must also be within a few days' march of Tintagel. But the hours of riding and the days of mixed boredom and terror had robbed her of any passion for the journey they had undertaken. She had night terrors about the girl on the reef of stone and felt herself in that stranger's body. The movement of insects and flies across her frozen face woke her on the first night. She was trying to scream, but Constantinus's hand was firmly across her mouth.

Then they rounded the hills and found themselves in a wide, undulating landscape, with the great sea to their right, far away but still visible, and with those same hills on their left. Still there was no sign of Paulus with the column. Perhaps the earth had swallowed them whole?

The centurion had never travelled to Tintagel or braved these alien lands before, so he had no means of knowing how difficult the terrain might prove to be. He had found that the distant ocean generated powerful winds that dragged at trees and travellers alike, gales that sometimes rendered the mildest of summer nights cold and unpleasant. The trees in this intermediate world close to the coast were twisted like old men huddling away from the strong winds. Coppices of straight-spined trees flourished in those valleys and ravines where the presence of windbreaks formed by the hills allowed them to grow naturally. Constantinus looked around at the arthritic and twisted trees in the open areas and shuddered inwardly at nature's brutality.

But he sensed that Tintagel was close. He had heard the defiant screams of sea birds and then, at the height of noon, he had seen two gulls squabbling on the wind like a portent.

The coast awaited and the pathway to Tintagel would soon appear.

'Lord protect us,' he murmured involuntarily, without considering Severa's closeness.

'Why? Are we under threat?' she asked, her eyes suddenly bright with concern.

'I'm sorry, Severa. There's no danger at present, but we are close to the coast now and we've travelled further south than I had bargained for. Tintagel must be nearby and I'm certain that we're hot on the heels of our column.'

'If the coast and the column are close, then Conanus must be nearby. He's running out of time if he's going to capture me. He must be desperate by now, especially if he's realised that we captured Cledwyn.'

Severa's voice was flat and unemotional. Never a fool, she was well aware that her uncle would do anything to gain control over her. He had risked his reputation, and his life, on succeeding with this desperate gamble. Fully committed, there was no going back for Conanus. He could not return to Armorica without her, so every mile travelled during this night brought the inevitable attack closer.

Constantinus must also have dwelled on Conanus, because he

suddenly halted Severa's horse by placing one strong hand on her bridle.

'If I tell you to ride, Severa, I want you to dig your heels into your horse's belly and kick him into a gallop. Immediately! Don't worry about Drusus and me, just dig in your heels and ride as if the Wilde Hunt was after you. If you should escape, you must head south-west towards the sea and then seek help from one of the crofters or a fishing village on the coast.' He pointed towards the west. 'The sea cliffs are in that direction . . . somewhere. And you must be prepared to kill anyone who tries to stop you – anyone at all! Do you have a weapon?'

Severa lowered her gaze to break the energy that seemed to be crackling between his black eyes and hers. She drew out a long, narrow blade from a scabbard she had secreted under her outer woollen tunic. The blade was slightly curved, like a butcher's knife, and was equally sharp, but its point was wicked and slightly hooked, so that any wound it inflicted would be cruelly torn when it was removed. Constantinus looked at the vicious weapon with surprise, for this weapon was a killing knife.

He raised one eyebrow.

'Cael gave it to me before we left Glastonbury. It was his personal knife and he told me he'd carried it for most of his life without ever having to use it on a human being. He believed it possesses good luck for whoever takes good care of it. He called it *Calindre*, which is a woman's name, a strange choice, but quite pretty for such a brutal weapon.'

Constantinus gestured wordlessly for the knife and examined its edge with great care when she handed it to him. The handle was covered with shagreen and the sharkskin made any slipping unlikely, even with palms that were bloodied and wet. The blade itself was very strong and unusually sharp.

'The swords of kings are given names because of their beauty, their workmanship and their rarity. A fair knife, wielded by an ordinary man, can be just as important and valuable to its owner. This blade deserves respect, so keep it close, clean and ready to leap into your hands.'

With that, Constantinus released his hold on her bridle and they continued on their way.

After the fugitives had settled down for the night, Cledwyn became feverish and had developed a cough, so Constantinus decided that their captive's bindings could be loosened while the man was incapacitated. He then ordered Drusus to start a fire in a small cavern the scout had found behind a number of large boulders nestling like sentries at the base of a steep hill. It was the perfect site for a camp, a place where they could warm themselves, sleep in relative comfort and protect themselves from the inclement weather. The cavern itself was reasonably discreet, although a trail ran past it that would permit horsemen to pass the cave in single file.

As she sat on the floor with her back against the rear wall and her blanket wrapped tightly around her, Severa felt safe for the first time in weeks.

Despite her exhaustion, she could guess at Constantinus's thoughts. A dead captive was of no use to the fugitives, so a fire was important if they were to prevent Cledwyn's condition from deteriorating into a severe illness. Moreover the flagging spirits and health of the three fugitives could be restored through the comfort of light and warmth in the Stygian darkness.

Severa used the fire lit by Drusus to boil some water and threw in the last of their dried rations. With a sigh of regret at having to use the last of their reserve supplies, she added the wilted greens, roots and wild-growing onions that she had scavenged from the long-overgrown gardens of a deserted farm passed during their earlier travels. Unfortunately, the vegetables were a little mouldy, so, with an apology to her knife for the prosaic use of its killing blade, she scraped away the worst of the rot and chopped the remains into bite-sized chunks.

'Needs must, Calindre! You'll get a special cleaning after we've eaten,' she promised.

The small party had full bellies by the time they settled down to sleep. Cledwyn's face had lost the worst of its pallor and he thanked Severa courteously when she fed him with her personal spoon made from a bullock's horn. Once fed and rested, the Armorican seemed to be marginally better. Then, with some surprise, she watched as Constantinus tossed a horse blanket to their prisoner so the man could keep his bones warm within its smelly folds.

The horses had been relegated to a picket line outside the cavern and to one side of its southern approach, successfully blocking off any unannounced approach to the cave from that direction. They were also protected from the worst of the weather by the overhang that created the cave, so they whinnied softly to each other contentedly. For their fodder, Constantinus and Drusus had used their knives to cut down a supply of long grasses from the plain adjacent to the slope. An illusion of safety settled over the campsite.

While Drusus remained on guard, the other travellers sank into a deep sleep.

Constantinus shook Severa into wakefulness as the first flags of light streaked through the darkness. The horses whickered companionably as Drusus brought them to the path outside the small cave before securing their reins to a sapling. He stamped his feet to ward off the early-morning chill and blew on to his cold fingers.

'I'll light the fire,' Severa volunteered and immediately set about her self-imposed task. 'All we'll have to eat is the last of the stew and some hot water, but even that should hearten us.'

She was surprised when Constantinus permitted this delay as, on previous mornings, he had urged them to be on their way, regardless of the weather or their weariness.

'Rain is on the way,' he said. 'It will come on us fast, so drink some of the hot water. It'll make us feel better if we're caught out by a storm. We'll lose all chance of tracking the column if there's a downpour but, on the positive side, Conanus couldn't follow us.'

With the dawning of this new day, the centurion had arrived at the conclusion that he was wasting his time by attempting to predict the actions of Conanus, who was an elusive and unconventional strategist. In future, he would merely take realistic precautions against possible attack.

Meanwhile, the iron cooking pot had been scraped thoroughly to remove the last of the stew, far more delicious than its unprepossessing ingredients suggested. Drusus was so hungry that he would have used his finger to steal the last traces of gravy from the pot if Constantinus had not been watching. And even hot water without flavouring ingredients warmed the belly and satisfied them as no plain draught should.

'If Endellion could see me now,' Severa murmured as she sipped at her water and cleaned Calindre until the blade was gleaming.

Once he had eaten, Constantinus was eager to be gone as usual so Drusus stamped out the fire and the legionnaire collected the horses from the track and walked them up to the cave mouth. As he bent to place the reins under a loose rock, the sound of a loosed arrow sent the companions diving for cover.

As Severa fell to the ground, she saw Constantinus lying prone near the mouth of the shallow cave. The black fletch of an arrow was protruding from his flesh near the left collarbone. Carefully, and with his teeth bared in a rictus of pain, he began to crawl into the centre of the cave as arrows whizzed around them at body height.

'Father? I'm in here! I'm alive, Father,' Cledwyn began to scream, but Drusus reacted by hitting him over the temple with the butt of his sword. The young man collapsed on to the ground like a poleaxed steer.

At the same time, the centurion reached the fireplace and lunged into the cavern. Raising himself carefully, he struggled to his feet.

'Let me look at the wound, Constantinus,' Severa demanded, careless of her use of his first name. 'Dear Lord,' she groaned as she tore away his tunic to expose his chain-mail shirt.

She couldn't decide whether fate had been kind to him or not. At the very edge of the shirt's wide neck, the arrow had entered the centurion's flesh with some force. Missing bone, the arrow had punched its way through his body, while missing his vital organs and driving its way through the skin of his back. The mail shirt had stopped the arrow from being driven right through his body.

'Can you cut away the arrow shaft at the front? I don't want to fall on it,' Constantinus asked Severa through white, bitten lips.

'Drusus? Can you do the same at the back? Shite, we don't have time for this. Conanus will be here within minutes.'

Then he groaned as Drusus cut around the shaft at the arrowhead before snapping it off.

Following his lead, Severa tried to do the same but her fingers lacked Drusus's strength. Without hesitation, the legionnaire pushed her out of the way and snapped off the fletch himself. Now, if he was to have a fall, he might avoid the crippling agony of collapsing on to either end of the arrow. The only real advantage was that the shaft prevented bleeding from both the entry and exit wounds. With a grimace, he tried to raise his shield.

Fortunately his left arm still worked, although blood seeped slowly from the wounds. Severa padded them with wads of cloth, then poured the last of the water over the hot coals that Drusus had failed to extinguish. The lingering traces of heat hissed as the fire unwillingly died.

'There's a bow and a sheaf of arrows on my horse, Drusus. Do you still have your spear? We'll need every weapon we have when Conanus arrives to reinforce his scout.'

When Drusus broke cover and crawled towards the horses, he raised his body to retrieve the bow and quiver from Constantinus's saddle. Suddenly, a fusillade of arrows whizzed by his head, forcing him to take cover with the bow and a full quiver of arrows firmly gripped in his hands. Then, after he had retrieved the stabbing spear, Drusus snaked his way back to Severa and the centurion.

'You'll need to use the bow, Severa. Have you used one before? Don't bother trying to string it because it's far too powerful. Drusus will do it for you. But do you know how to draw it and aim the weapon?'

The questions were rapid fire, but Severa took the strung bow and began to draw it experimentally.

'Of course I can use it. Mother Endellion insisted that I learn some means of self-protection and we held regular challenges at Corinium. I've never killed anything, not even a rabbit, but I'll cheerfully shoot at anyone who tries to touch me.'

For once, Severa felt gratitude to her long-dead father for the powerful physique and broad shoulders that he had bequeathed to her through his bloodline. She neatly notched an arrow to show that she was capable of releasing a barb when the need arose.

'Good! Now stand at the back of the cave in the shadows,' Constantinus ordered. 'Remember what I said about escaping if it proves to be possible, but you'll have to force yourself to kill one or more of Conanus's men to do it.'

His burning eyes were fixed on her face. 'Think of your maid and the corpse that Conanus left for the scavengers and you'll find you have the nerve to kill the bastards who committed that evil deed. Keep that picture firmly in your mind and don't hesitate. Hesitation means death, because Conanus won't give you a second chance.'

He coughed harshly, before wincing from the pain of his wound. 'And don't worry about us. Drusus and I can look after ourselves. We're partially exposed here, but they will have to mount an attack if they want to capture you. They won't use bows in the cave, because he knows that you and his son are here, and both of you are vulnerable to his arrows. But there are no such limitations on us. Shoot straight, Severa! Drusus and I will be depending on your firepower to slow the attackers down and stop at least two of them. We can take care of the rest of Conanus's men if God is with us.'

Severa nodded. She was so frightened that her fingers were beginning to tremble.

'Remember! You must think of what those animals did to your serving woman and how frightened she must have been if you begin to have any doubts. Remember her fate and avenge her!'

Severa went to her assigned station against the inside wall of the small cavern. Drusus used one of the outer walls for cover on the left side of the cave entrance, while Constantinus dragged Cledwyn to another irregularity in the cavern wall on the right side. Once again, Conanus's son found himself firmly bound and unable to move. Nor could he yell, for a length of dirty cloth had been shoved directly into his mouth.

Both Constantinus and Drusus were standing now with their shields at the ready, and each had his gladius poised and ready.

The silence became an agony of waiting.

'Why did you bring a bow on our little jaunt?' Severa asked in a shaky voice, shattering the tension and causing Constantine's concentration to waver. She knew the question was irrelevant, but her curiosity had been aroused. Besides, she mightn't survive to obtain an answer if she didn't ask.

'That's a foolish question, woman! Hunting has always been one of my favourite joys,' the centurion answered, his tone of voice somewhere between a snort of derision and a laugh. 'In fact, I had planned to get us a coney for the evening meal today. But as Fortuna would have it, I don't believe I need to worry about filling the cooking pot.'

'I'll carry out that duty if we survive today,' she said in a strained voice.

'You'll certainly survive if Conanus has his way, Severa. For our part, Drusus and I will prove difficult to kill. I have been told that I have a destiny to fulfil, one that includes you, so that will be another obstacle at the feet of our Armorican friend. Drusus is as tough as old boot leather, and he'll not be prepared to depart from this life without a great deal of encouragement.' Constantinus's words were whispered, because he had heard the unmistakeable sound of boots slipping on scree some little distance from their cave.

'They're coming,' Drusus hissed.

'Aye!'

Within the dim light that was beginning to penetrate the cave, Severa's ears strained to hear the slightest sound from outside the entrance. Her muscles were tensed with anticipation and she held the bowstring taut while sighting down the anticipated flight of the arrow. But she was far from comforted by Constantinus's observations about their safety. Capture would be another kind of death that might be worse than the cessation of breathing.

During the past month, she had tasted a free and untrammelled life, with the pleasures of self-determination that were enjoyed by men. She wasn't so foolish as to believe she could defy the rules of society and gain the total freedom she craved. Yet, if her birthright and her sex demanded that she must marry and bear children, she would rather die than become the wife of a traitor. Let the Armorican ruler come. Uncle or no, she would fight him to the death.

Short scurrying sounds of movement flickered past the horses' broad backs as if a body of men were inching their way towards the cave entrance but were wary of the hooves of skittish animals. The gloom within the cavern continued to defy the slowly brightening horizon where a red sun was beginning to rise. With her heart racing, Severa stilled her mind, forced her arms to remain steady – and waited.

She swore that the first person to enter the cavern would die, regardless of who he was. She drew in a deep breath to sharpen her mind as shapes coalesced on the periphery of her vision.

But she continued to wait for her first target.

CHAPTER XII

A BITTER LEGACY

Believe me, wise men don't say 'I shall live to do that,' tomorrow's life's too late; live today.

Martial, *Epigrammata*. Book 1:15

Severa's fingers strained on the bowstring and her nerves were as tense as the bent bow. With their backs lit by the rising sun, two figures bearing torches were approaching the cave entrance from behind the flanks of the horses. One pale hand rested briefly on Drusus's horse, partly for support and partly to calm the nervous beast.

She could hear someone breathing harshly within the relative quiet of the cavern. Then, from outside, some stones were dislodged as one of the men took an awkward step. He continued to move forward, and his blundering footsteps were shockingly loud within the confined space.

A third man also moved towards the opening. The noise of his movement told the defenders that this man was weary of lurking in the shadows and wanted to take the initiative. One stride and this warrior would be within reach of Constantinus's sword if the centurion could still wield the weapon.

Severa forced herself to avoid all further thought. With the bow at full extension, she released an arrow without bothering to follow its flight, for she had immediately reached into her quiver for another arrow to nock into the bowstring.

A sudden exhalation of breath was followed by the sound of a weapon clattering on to the hard stone floor. Then a sharp cry of warning was heard; four men appeared from out of the darkness as they tried to gain entrance to the back of the cavern where Severa was standing. Fear gave strength to her arms and she released another arrow into the broadest part of the leading shadow.

As the leading warrior fell, the edge of Constantinus's gladius caught a shaft of light from the rising sun as his weapon swept down on the arm of the man who had just thrown away his torch. His eerie scream shuddered through the confined space. Severa tried to release the next arrow, but the mouth of the cave was a tangled mass of limbs and straining bodies that were engaging in deadly combat. Her weapon had been rendered useless by the close in-fighting.

Bow raised and at the ready, she waited for an opportunity to fire at a suitable target.

But the mass of fighting men, who were probably no more than five or six in number, were encroaching into Severa's space by now.

She swore as she dropped the bow behind her where it would be safely at her feet. Then she drew her knife, comforted by its feel and texture. She tightened her fingers, lifted the blade to her lips and kissed Calindre's cold and beautiful surface.

'If you kill my son, you will take days to die,' a voice from outside the small cavern intruded over the grunts and curses of the struggling combatants.

'Make your retreat, Conanus!' Severa yelled, unable to control her emotions. 'Depart this place, Uncle, for I will not marry Cledwyn. I'd sooner die than serve your purposes and I refuse to bow before your threats.'

The sound of her voice seemed to give courage to her uncle's minions. Stupid! Stupid! Stupid! Calindre's silent voice upbraided her.

Fortunately, the Romans possessed an advantage in the narrow space leading into the cavern and several bodies lay sprawled near the defenders' feet. Blood had fouled the walls and floor of the shallow space, causing Drusus to slip on a slick rock on the cavern's floor, a fortunate fall that saved him from a slicing sword blade that would have eviscerated him if it had found its target. Severa watched in awe as Drusus, black with blood and with his face set into a grim snarl, despatched his opponent with a wicked stab into the upper abdomen. As he pulled his gladius free with a nasty twist of the blade, blood arced across his face.

Another warrior lurched towards her. This man's breast was a black bulk in the glowing light and she realised, in an instant, that this figure wasn't wearing body armour. Crouching as low as she could get, she brought Calindre up in a fast, stabbing motion that caught the man's foot when he tried to kick out at her. The point of the knife caught the warrior's ankle. He screamed and made an involuntary, backward jerk with the wounded foot as he fell. The knife was almost wrenched from Severa's hand, but she just managed to retain the weapon while slicing the palm of her own left hand in the process.

Without time to think, she slashed once again at the dimly seen belt buckle of the Armorican warrior as he regained his feet. She almost overbalanced from the full extension of her arms, but her assailant reeled backwards, keening thinly, while both hands were clasping at the middle of his body where her knife had made its entrance. A sudden spray of blood covered her face in a warm, sticky jet that tasted of metal. Sickened, she crawled back to the safety of her wall until her back was firmly pressed against its solid protection.

The attacking figures suddenly backed away and the half-light revealed the blood-spattered shapes of three mortally wounded Armorican warriors who were in their death throes at her feet. Two more men were lying at the entrance behind them with black-fletched arrows protruding from their bodies.

I've killed three men, Severa thought blankly. Strangely, she was still dry-eyed.

Meanwhile, the horses had fled from the carnage in panic, while ragged breathing and low, keening moans were the only sounds that could be heard.

'Do you still live, Conanus?' Constantinus asked softly. His ragged breath was a clear indication of the difficulty he was experiencing from his wound and the exertion of combat.

'Is my son alive?' an older voice replied from beyond the entrance to the cavern.

'I have no idea, Conanus. We've immobilised him, but I could cut his throat if such was your preference?'

Silence followed this threat.

Severa crawled through puddles of blood to reach the centurion, who was bleeding profusely from his shoulder wound and several other superficial sword cuts. His facial features were pale and Severa forced back a moment of panic before she found her cloak and used Calindre to cut the hem so she could tear it into long strips. Quickly and efficiently, she bound his wounds tightly. Her face flamed as she touched his cooling flesh with such intimacy, but she ordered herself to be sensible and complete her task.

Constantinus's eyes scanned Severa's body and the bloody knife that she had rammed into her belt for safety. One of his hands wiped away the streak of blood that covered half of her face, as if he sought to discover if she was carrying any injuries. She shivered as his thumbs wiped the gore away from her cheekbones.

Cledwyn moaned from his position on the floor of the cavern, so Constantinus shifted his focus and dragged the young man by the hair in front of his own body, almost as a shield.

'Can you hear me, Conanus?' He waited until he heard a muffled response.

'Good! If you want your son alive, you must allow us to pass. We intend to travel to Tintagel where Severa will be kept in safety until such time as the British kings determine her future. Her foster family has decided that Severa will be kept safe from you or, for that matter, any claimant who aspires to the throne of High King of Britannia. I have been charged with getting her safely to King Cadal, and I have made a blood oath that I will complete this task. Do you truly believe that you or your precious son is fit to sit on the throne where Magnus Maximus rested so easily? Such a sacrilege would never happen, Conanus, for the kings would never accept you. Nor would you be accepted by those Britons who are citizens of these isles. Never, Conanus!'

The silence dragged on.

Drusus finally stirred. A wounded man who had been eviscerated by the legionnaire's gladius was thrashing and moaning, and this distraction was drawing the attention of the two Romans away from Conanus's invisible warriors who were still unharmed and hiding beyond the entrance to the cavern.

Even Severa's inexperienced eyes could see that the wounded man had little chance of survival, but she still winced when Drusus drew his knife and crawled out into the opening of the cave. Using the corpses of the dead for protection, he cut the dying man's throat.

Mercifully, the man's death throes were brief.

Still Conanus remained silent and kept his opponents waiting.

Perhaps this form of torture was the worst punishment the Armorican chieftain could inflict on the three fugitives who were trapped inside the cavern. Waiting for an attack can be far worse than the actuality of a life and death struggle. Severa's imagination conjured greater horrors than her uncle could possibly create. Fortunately, the two Romans were experienced veterans who understood the emotional cost of a protracted battle, so they were grateful for any respite while Conanus determined his next move.

Then, as full daylight chased away the last of the shadows and, with it, any advantage that darkness gave to the enemy, Conanus decided to make one more throw of the dice and sent another four men into the cavern to mount another attack.

Somehow, Severa had retrieved her bow which, mercifully, had not suffered any damage during their earlier scuffle. Always vigilant, Constantinus had reminded her of its existence by miming the action of drawing back the bowstring.

Their situation had given strength to her muscles and she found she could draw the bow to its fullest extension with ease. Severa had seen cornered rats attack dogs that were many times their size with a ferocity and courage born out of desperation.

Her arrow punched its way into the leading warrior with maximum effect, the barb passing right through the man's body.

She could not have missed such an obvious target. The man screamed, but Severa forced herself to ignore him.

Just as she released her second arrow, a body almost collapsed on top of her when the Armorican was despatched by Constantinus, who was using Cledwyn as a convenient shield. Severa's arrow almost went astray, but it still struck the doomed warrior in the groin.

This second sharp engagement was almost identical to the first, but by the time Conanus's warriors were lying prone or attempting to drag their grievously wounded bodies out of the cavern, Severa noticed that Drusus had received a serious wound in his left leg. His opponent had fought with both sword and knife and, while Drusus had killed the man, this unusual combination of weapons had caught him by surprise. The Armorican's knife was now buried in Drusus's thigh, high up towards the groin, frighteningly close to the large femoral artery.

Severa leaped to her feet to assist the legionnaire.

'No! Stay where you are, Severa,' Constantinus ordered, but he was too late.

As she reached out to Drusus, an arrow plucked at her sleeve. She felt the heat of its passing along her arm, but she ignored the danger she was in and tore up the last remnants of her cloak to bind the wound and act as a tourniquet. With a broken piece of arrow, she used its leverage to make the bandage as tight as she could.

Then she felt a sudden shadow touch her. Constantinus roared out her name and she heard Cledwyn's body drop to the floor when the centurion tried to reach out to her.

But he was an eye-blink too late.

A dark, muffled figure lifted her off the ground from behind, and put a knife to her throat. Cursing herself for a fool, Severa forced her muscles to go limp in his arms and she felt his foetid breath on her jaw as she sagged against him, gathering together the last of her strength and resolve.

Calindre was still in her left hand, for she had used the knife to tear away at her cloak. The cold of the blade reminded her that she wasn't completely devoid of protection amidst the blood and the suffering surrounding her.

She struck out with the knife firmly gripped in her right hand, and felt the blade strike home as she stabbed at the man's body behind her with an upward movement that embedded the weapon to its hilt. He stiffened momentarily, and then his grip slowly loosened.

Then she was falling ... falling ... and a dead weight was dragging her down until her head struck the stone floor of the cavern with a resounding crack.

After that she knew nothing else.

Severa returned slowly to consciousness. It was only when she felt a sudden chill that she realised that someone was pouring water over her head.

'Severa! Wake up! Come on, Severa! You don't have time to rest, so wake up now!'

The hectoring voice dragged her out of the comforting warm nothingness and she spluttered and drew water up her nose. She coughed in a great spasm and then tried to open her eyes.

She thought she was blind at first, because her eyelids were gummed together. But once she forced them apart and investigated her face with trembling fingertips, she discovered that a long gash had split her forehead from her left eyebrow to the hairline and blood had seeped over her facial features in a thick, clotting shroud.

Her eyes began to close again of their own accord, but a sharp slap brought her back to her wits again, while a rough hand pressed a pad of cloth to her bleeding forehead.

'Hold this pad in place, Severa. You can't go to sleep, because I won't let you. Come on, girl! A little blow to the head won't kill you, but I do need your help.'

Constantinus's blood-spattered features swam slowly into focus.

'Wake up, Severa! Don't go back to sleep on me,' he repeated as he shook her again. 'You have to stay awake.'

'Yes! Yes! I'm awake, so stop shaking me.'

Severa dragged herself into a seated position with her back against the wall. Drusus was sitting beside her, half-slumped with weariness while he cautiously attended to his wounded leg. She noticed that he was still holding the fragment of arrow-shaft in the makeshift bandage to act as a tourniquet if the wound began to haemorrhage. A muffled shape lay partly over her legs with its back towards her. She stared at this figure incuriously as her eyes continued to digest the scene of carnage in the cavern.

Constantinus pushed the shrouded figure off her legs and the slack body rolled on to its back. Severa could see that the haft of Calindre was facing outwards from where it had entered the corpse's diaphragm; the man had been neatly disembowelled, although his dark clothing disguised the worst of the damage.

The man's hawk-nosed face was bone-white under what was left of a dark tan. White lines at the corners of his eyes and heavy, dissipated pouches beneath the eye-sockets indicated that he was older than she would have expected, middle-aged at best.

Severa had never seen her attacker before, but she recognised the similarities between Cledwyn ap Kynan and this particular

Armorican. She had killed her own uncle, Kynan ap Meriadoc, the ruler now known as Conanus.

A sob of guilt escaped from the depths of her body.

Then, as she gazed over the detritus of the battle, she realised that a half-score of men were lying in various positions of abandonment within the immediate confines of the cavern. Few parts of the floor were untouched by the blood or waste that these warriors had given for their Armorican master who had led them to their deaths in what, for them, was a foreign land.

A grieving Cledwyn was still lying at their feet, bound and weeping, his face purple-red with fury and misery. Severa wanted to apologise to her kinsman, but she lacked the words.

Constantinus saw that Severa was at a loss for words, so he made one more inspection of her head wound to save her from further embarrassment.

'She'll survive, Drusus, although I'm always wary of head wounds,' Constantinus informed his legionnaire. 'Both of you are in need of urgent attention from a healer and I must have this fucking arrow removed by someone who knows what he's doing. Do you have enough strength to round up the horses, provided they haven't strayed too far?'

Drusus shrugged and nodded.

'Needs must, sir, so I'll do my best to find the horses and we'll be on our way.'

'Be careful, Drusus. We don't know where the remainder of Conanus's Armoricans are hiding, so watch your back when you're blundering around in the woods.'

Constantinus's voice was crisp and alert, although his body was hunched into itself from pain and exhaustion.

'What happened?' Severa asked. Her voice sounded rusty; she

cleared her throat and spat into a scrap of fabric left over from her ruined cloak.

She looked down and saw that she had thrown up some partially clotted gouts of blood.

Constantinus saw the panic in her eyes, so he used his right hand to raise her chin.

'There's no need to be afraid, Severa. You've bled into your mouth from the wound on your forehead, but you haven't received any wounds inside your body.'

'But . . . I don't remember!' she began. Her words faded away as the centurion's eyes moved momentarily to the huddled body that lay on the ground.

'You killed him, you bitch,' Cledwyn howled. 'You've killed your own fucking kin!'

Constantinus moved the head and shoulders of Conanus with one foot so that the man's face was turned away from Severa. The action cost him dearly and he groaned painfully at the effort needed.

The distinctive, unadorned hilt of Calindre begged to be retrieved from its sheath of flesh, for the blade had ripped Conanus's abdomen open in such a manner that the torn and gaping flesh revealed loops of exposed bowel. The knife-point must have penetrated right up to the heart and his death would have been almost instantaneous.

'I killed him! I've killed my own kinsman,' Severa said flatly as the truth finally sank in. Constantinus had no inkling from her monotone whether she regretted her action, was appalled by it or gloried in the death of her nemesis.

'He was holding his blade against your throat, Severa,' Drusus added as he limped back into the mouth of the cave, leading their small string of horses behind him. His face was white, and

Severa saw that a snake of fresh blood was seeping from under the makeshift bandage to drip down his leg.

Constantinus also saw the bleeding. 'You'd best have a short rest, Drusus. We'll be in the saddle soon enough, but we might have to stay on the horses for the rest of the day. It's unsafe to remain here, so we'll have to secure our wounds after we've escaped from here and travelled a few miles down the track. I'm hoping we can still catch up with Paulus's column.'

Severa's hand rose unconsciously to her throat where a small wound made by Conanus's knife-point had narrowly missed the great artery in her throat. She shuddered as the memory of the blade came flooding back.

'My father wouldn't have harmed you, bitch,' Cledwyn shouted. 'He'd been planning a raid to capture you for more than six years. He thought he'd considered all the eventualities and puzzled over his plans until every detail was perfect, but the gods conspired to forsake him at the end – and you, bitch! He never imagined for one moment that you'd lift a hand against your tribal chief. You owed him your loyalty as kin.'

Constantinus's lips twisted in disgust. 'You were misled, Cledwyn. Severa is the daughter of an emperor and she isn't bound to the hubris of any man. Your father placed himself under sentence of death when he plotted the shameful death of Maximus Britannicus, so his fate was sealed from that point on. Fact is that Fortuna glared at him from the moment his hubris overcame his common sense.' Constantinus's face was cold beneath its mask of dried blood.

'Lady Severa has acted exactly as one would expect of the daughter of Flavius Magnus Maximus. The emperor would have been proud of his kinship to her and contemptuous of your father, a man who had sworn a blood oath to follow his master and protect the interests of Maximus's family for the remainder of his life. I've heard the soldiers' tales of your father and Andragathius, the men who killed Emperor Gratian when he was the ruler of the Western Empire. Andragathius was faithful to his vows and died in a state of honour and grace. Your father chose to live, and carved out a kingdom in lands that had been gifted to him by Magnus Maximus. This was a prize that should have been enough for any man, Cledwyn, so don't speak to me of kinship, or repeat your tales of woe. Conanus threw his oath away and trod his honour into the dust; even though he retained the name that Maximus gave him. Your father is no longer Conanus, but the Kynan of old . . . and is as nothing.'

After this ruthless assessment, Cledwyn lapsed into a miserable silence. He was convinced that Constantinus would kill him, now that his father's men had accepted their defeat and scattered to the winds. He also reasoned that the remnants of the force would make their way back to Armorica, and would carry the tale of their master's failure with them. Any dreams of a triumphant return to Britannia as masters of all the British tribes would be abandoned.

'What are we to do with you, Cledwyn ap Kynan, now that you're the king of the Ordovice people in Armorica? Should we kill you? You might be tempted to ignite the embers of your father's ambitions and return to plague us.'

'Just kill him and be done with it,' Drusus said blandly, for his distrust of the young man was clearly written on his pallid features. 'I doubt that any Ordovice could ever be trusted.'

Cledwyn remained silent for a moment.

'I won't follow you, Roman. Too much blood has been spilled already in this cursed quest,' he then began. 'My father was obsessed with dreams of kingship, for he had been poisoned by

245

the time he basked in the sun at the feet of Maximus. The terrible irony of this sorry mess is that my father had no great liking for the emperor.'

When all was considered, Cledwyn was little more than a boy, with his entire life before him. In his heart of hearts, he was reluctant to cast it away for abstract concepts like family honour. Yet the warrior in him refused to debase himself by begging for his life. He decided to control his emotions, and accept whatever fate this harsh, immovable centurion bestowed on him.

Constantinus recognised that the young man was making an effort to be honest, so he nodded decisively. Cledwyn could live.

'Take whatever possessions that you are likely to need for your return to Armorica, plus any horses that you can catch. I expect you to give me your oath that you will return there after disposing of the remains of your father and his men. What you do with their remains will be up to you, but I insist that you hold to any commitment you give to me. Your word will be your bond. All I require from you is your assistance to prepare Lady Severa's mount for the remainder of her journey. Then we'll take our leave of you. Our needs are small and we'll take some clean water and our horses. I'd prefer that we leave as amicably as possible, despite today's events. Now come closer, so I can remove your bonds.'

Within the hour, Constantinus's small party was ready to depart.

While trying to control his grief for his father and balancing this against his relief at Constantinus's generosity, Cledwyn carried out the Roman's instructions with barely controlled haste. He assisted Severa to collect her possessions and offered to help her climb into the saddle of her horse. But the young woman seemed to be in a daze and her body remained heavy and unresponsive.

'You must mount your horse, Severa, regardless of the pain you're feeling. Come now, girl!' Constantinus snapped. 'Cledwyn will help you to climb into the saddle, and your head will feel better once we are in the fresh air on our way. That's it!'

Between them, the two Romans and Cledwyn ensured that the girl was safely ensconced on her horse, then checked the bridle, reins and girths were correctly adjusted and safe for use, even for an almost-comatose rider. Meanwhile, Drusus mounted his own horse and Constantinus handed him the reins of Severa's so that her mount could be led.

Satisfied with his planning and fully prepared for a miserable day, Constantinus climbed gingerly into his own saddle.

He made a final farewell with Cledwyn, while assuring himself that the young man was suitably equipped for the long journey to his home in Gallia.

'Take your essentials and leave this sad place, Cledwyn ap Kynan. I hope that you can leave your father's memories behind you and make haste for the Litus Saxonicum. I should not have to remind you that there will be many in Britannia who won't approve of your being allowed to leave our lands without being punished for your father's misdeeds. My Roman comrades will be searching for anyone who is trying to reach Armorica, so ride hard and fast, and pray that we don't meet each other on this side of Hades.'

The centurion waved a quick farewell and led the horses of his two companions away from the cave.

Released at last, Cledwyn began the task of turning the cave into a tomb that would contain the remains of the Armorican warriors who had lost their lives during the battle. This would be the young man's final duty to his father and his king.

Once the corpses had been sealed for eternity and were safe from scavengers, he made good his own departure and rode into the north-east as fast as his weakened body would allow. Later, he would turn towards the south and head for the coastal ports. But, for now, his heart's desire was to leave this wretched cave, the lonely hills and the deserted valleys of the Dumnonii lands.

The three travellers let their horses pick the safest way through the terrain as they turned west and travelled towards the coastal cliffs. Constantinus could hear the cries of gulls and smell the sharp, clean scent of salt water and seaweed. That way lay safety and rest.

They rode through the long day that followed until they came to huge cliffs that nestled over lines of stony beaches. Beyond these grim and menacing headlands, the wild ocean churned and tossed its waves, while on the clifftops the ever-present winds and rain swept their way across the higher ground and twisted the trees into humanoid sentinels.

Through this inhospitable landscape they made their slow way towards the south-west and their destination. Somewhere along this isolated stretch of coast Tintagel awaited them and, somewhere in the growing darkness, the remains of Paulus's column would be searching for them. Another long twilight had begun.

CHAPTER XIII

DESTINY

It is convenient that there be gods, and, as it is
convenient, let us believe that there are.

Ovid, *Ars Amatoria*, Book 1

Severa surged into wakefulness like a drowning woman thrusting
upwards out of deep water. Then, as if she feared to know her
surroundings, she opened her eyes and slowly prised her gummed eyelids apart.

'You can rest. There's no need to be afraid now, Severa. You're
safe within Tintagel now.'

A wrinkled face swam into view and soft, hazel eyes smiled
down at the patient.

'Who are you? I can't remember arriving here.' Severa began
to search frantically at her waist as though she needed to locate
an invisible belt.

'If you're searching for your knife, it's in the shelf beside your
sleeping pallet,' the soft voice told her. 'Would you feel more
comfortable with it close to hand?'

Severa nodded faintly.

'You can have it. But the blade is very sharp, so I suggest you treat it carefully.'

Severa snatched at the handle and cradled the knife under the bedcovers where its cold blade gave her confidence. Embarrassed by her weakness, she shivered.

'Where is Constantinus? Is he alive?'

'Your centurion is well now. And he is fast returning to good health. However, he must rest for some weeks because poisons have been known to enter wounds after the shaft of an arrow has been removed. My husband, Cadal, has kept him amused since our healer has taken care of the wound. I am Ardunn, and I'm the queen of the Dumnonii, so I'll be your hostess during your stay in Tintagel. I'm happy that I've finally met you, Severa, for my father-by-marriage cared for you when you were a newly born infant.'

'Caradoc of great renown! Endellion, my foster-mother, has told me the whole tale of Caradoc and Magnus Maximus.'

'I believe that no one understood the relationship between Caradoc and the High King better than Endellion. Is she still as beautiful as ever?' Ardunn asked.

'Oh, yes,' Severa answered eagerly. 'Time barely touches her, although she has borne so many children. I often tease her by saying that she must be a witch like her mother.'

'Alas, we all age as the years pass by us. My children have all grown tall and they will all be married in the near future. Our children are babes for a very short time, but then they grow into adults and leave us.'

Severa examined her hands carefully and forced herself to keep her facial expression calm. The queen was working her way towards some pressing revelation, one that must be import- ant because the patient had yet to eat or drink after lying in a delirium for several days. Determined to get this strange discussion under way, she allowed an uncomfortable silence to drag on. Eventually, Ardunn was forced to launch into a short and rather embarrassing monologue to break the impasse.

'My husband and I will be responsible for your safety and reputation while you are visiting our home, and royal propriety dictates that we must ask a number of embarrassing questions of you, Severa, after which I'll see to your meal and a cup of warm broth. My husband, the king, insists that I ask these questions of you, so please forgive any perceived rudeness.'

'Of course! I'm your guest, so you may ask whatever you wish.' Severa smiled agreeably and waited for the Dumnonii queen to voice her disquiet over Severa's mannish dress and the free-and-easy banter with unmarried Romans that had developed during the journey from Corinium to Tintagel.

'I've been led to believe you've been alone with three men for many days, so we are forced to conclude that you haven't had the protection of a chaperone during that time.'

Severa nodded.

'Then I must ask whether your honour has been impugned during your travels? Has any of these men touched you in a manner that would force us to be concerned for your virtue?'

Severa gained some amusement from her hostess's embarrassment; she wondered how the queen would react if she knew that her valued guest had killed six men with her own hands. Would killing another human be less deplorable than sexual contact with a man?'

Probably, she thought sardonically.

'As you can see, I have been violently assaulted by enemies who wished me great harm and intended to capture me for their dastardly purposes. However, I will swear to you that no man has touched me intimately. My honour and virtue remain intact. Is that explanation satisfactory?'

'Oh, dear,' the queen murmured. 'This affair is so very awkward! The Roman centurion told us that your chaperone was used as a lure and rode in company with the larger Roman party, while you made good your escape by travelling unescorted with two men. He also informed the king that your chaperone perished when the ruse was discovered by your enemies after an ambush was sprung on the Roman column.'

'Aye! Her murder was a foul deed and the brutality of my enemies is beyond any understanding.' Severa crossed herself.

'Unfortunately, my husband believes that your reputation has been irretrievably besmirched, even if you remained chaste during your time on the road. The kings of Britannia aren't noted for their sense of justice and honour, so Cadal believes they will think the worst of you and the centurion.'

Severa began to feel the first stirrings of righteous anger.

'I don't care what the British kings think. The only persons whose opinions I value are those of my kinsmen and Queen Endellion. My word should be sufficient for all others.'

Severa raised her chin combatively as Queen Ardunn retreated before the icy expression in the girl's grey-green eyes. She patted the patient's hand comfortingly, although Severa wished that she could jerk her fingers away from the undesired contact.

'We'll have to agree to talk about this matter at a later time. You must rest now, Severa, while I fetch you some broth. You need to build up your strength.'

With a swirl of heavy woollen skirts, the queen rose to her feet and would have left the room had Severa not called her back to answer some questions of her own.

'Is Drusus recovering from his sword cuts? And have Paulus

and the rest of the column arrived at Tintagel? Please tell me, because a number of men and women have died to keep me safe. I've been very worried about them.'

'The other Roman in your party is recovering, while your larger column reached us a day before you arrived. Paulus is resting with his men in the barracks on the mainland. They are assisting with preparations to increase the defences of Tintagel Fortress, just in case the dregs of the Armorican party should be tempted to mount an attack on us. Cadal has assured me that any such action is unlikely, but the Roman officer has insisted on taking maximum precautions.'

Once she had responded to Severa's question, the queen swept out of the room with an audible sigh of relief.

Severa, disconcerted by this discussion, was alarmed by its implications.

Endellion had spoken lovingly of her half-brothers, Cadal and Cadoc, whom she described as worthy sons of the great Caradoc, but had also admitted that Cadal could be stubborn and con-servative when dealing with women. He had fought many battles against the barbarians and was a man of importance in Roman estimation, but he had little faith in the leadership of the legions and preferred to keep himself remote from the squabbles and enmities of the British kings.

'I'm just a lowly woman,' Severa said to herself with a distinct feeling of foreboding. 'What has Cadal got in mind for me if Ardunn is this nervous when she's in my presence?'

Before Severa had the chance to worry herself any further, a knock interrupted her rebellious thoughts as a serving maid entered the room. She presented a food tray on which a bowl of beef broth was steaming.

'My name is Dilic, mistress, and I'm to be your maid from

now on,' she explained, smiling. She was a pretty green-eyed girl with masses of coal-black, curling hair that hung down over her shoulders in a riot of ringlets.

'My queen has permitted the Roman centurion to pay you a visit after you have finished eating your broth, mistress.' Dilic smiled in a gesture of diplomacy, before pausing to cough delicately. 'However, she told me that I am required to stay in the room with you to preserve your modesty.'

Severa paused with the wooden spoon part-way to her mouth. She closed her lips over her teeth with a snap at Dilic's use of the word *modesty*.

Prior to her departure from Corinium, Severa would have accepted the presence of a chaperone as one of the tedious disadvantages of being a woman. Now, in a short space of time, she had cast off her conservative upbringing and had begun to question the foundations on which her life and culture was based. She had killed a kinsman and five other men, but couldn't be trusted to be alone with a man.

As she stared down at the bowl of broth, Severa realised that she had lost her appetite. Pushing the tray away, she placed her spoon carefully into the dish.

'I'm no longer hungry, Dilic, so you can take this slop away. You may usher in the centurion now. No, don't bother to argue that I need sustenance. I'll eat later, but I intend to speak with him before I do anything else.'

'Very well, mistress,' Dilic replied meekly and opened the door. 'You may enter, my lord,' she said to the centurion, who did so cautiously.

To Severa's relief, the Roman's face lit up from within as soon as their eyes met. She was surprised to see him looking so well, although she could see the white of a bandage under his tunic, a dressing that was stark against his tanned skin.

Clearing her throat to ensure that Constantinus was aware of her presence, Dilic drew up a stool close to Severa's bed on which the centurion could sit, before placing a low cushion in a corner of the room for herself. Conscious of the servant's proximity, the Roman officer seated himself on the proffered stool.

'You look very well, Centurion, so I suppose the shaft of the arrow was removed from your shoulder without difficulty.'

'Aye! Tintagel has an excellent healer and she uses some kind of paste made from seaweed to pack the wounds and keep them free of corruption. Drusus received the same treatment for his injuries, so I'm afraid our quarters smell like stale fish and sea salt. For all that, we have managed to survive and are still breathing, which is a certain sign of God's mercy.'

Severa bit her thumb reflectively and raised her eyes to meet his. There was a worrying gap in her memory, one that was causing her great concern. 'I still don't know how we reached Tintagel, Centurion. I can't remember anything of the journey, although I've tried and tried. I can remember being helped to mount my horse and I can also recall your voice when you told me to hold on to the mare's mane. I even have a vague memory of rain on my face and the wind in my hair, but that's all. The queen asked me what happened during our journey, but I didn't know what to say.'

'We rode all day and long into the twilight. But in all those hours, you wouldn't say a word. You seemed to be riding in a daze, as if you were asleep or unconscious, despite your wide-open eyes. We made you drink water and we made you rest whenever we could, but all we could do was search for Paulus and the column and hope to reach Tintagel as soon as possible.'

'My brain was addled,' Severa agreed with a rueful smile. 'So I'm lucky to be alive.'

'Aye! I've seen many men who have suffered wounds such as yours, and most of them never regained their memory – or their senses! To explain, we rode on into the evening and stumbled on to the track leading down to Tintagel. It was just after moonrise. I'm not a fanciful man, as you know, because the Roman legions aren't places for sentimental or superstitious fools. But I have to admit that I shivered with fear when I first saw the island, for it seemed to be crouching like a dragonlet on the edge of the ocean. Lights were burning at its crown as if the window openings were eyes or flaming nostrils. Then I realised that the crouching dragon was actually a fortress built on a rocky headland linked to the coast by a natural stone bridge. And then Paulus and Cadal's warriors appeared on the path leading down to the guardhouse, so we were soon whisked into the fortress.'

'I created a great deal of trouble for you and your legionnaires to cope with.' Severa was still hoping that Constantinus's recollections of their journey might restore her memory. If not, her involvement in that dreadful ride would be lost to her forever.

'My duty was to deliver you to Tintagel,' Constantinus continued. 'I succeeded by sheer luck. I was fortunate that you saved us from disaster when you played your part in the melee at the cave. Ultimately, Conanus's political plots were brought to nothing by your bravery. The man who played such a major part in the battle of the Save River and the assassination of Emperor Gratian in Gallia was killed by a slip of a girl in easy fashion, and I believe now that God must have been amused at the Armorican's presumption and hubris. Ultimately, your uncle was a foolish man who lost his last gamble with destiny.'

Severa shuddered as she recalled the incident in the cave. She had been holding the knife in her left hand, and hadn't made a conscious decision to use it when Conanus first grasped her from behind and lifted her off her feet. But her response had been instinctive and she could remember how easily the blade had slid into Conanus's belly, as if Calindre was actively seeking a scabbard of flesh. Her face paled and a line of sweat appeared along her hairline.

Constantinus reached out and gripped her left hand to comfort her. From her seat in the corner, Dilic stirred nervously and wondered what she should do to stop this unseemly gesture. Fortunately, Constantinus heard her faint gasp of concern and quickly released Severa's hand.

'You mustn't think of his death as a murderous act, Severa. You simply reacted like any person would do if they were forced to defend themselves against someone who proved himself to be a heartless assassin.'

'But it was my blade that killed him. I struck out at him without conscious thought, Centurion, but I deliberately pushed down on the haft of the weapon to ensure he was incapacitated enough to release me. The blade sliced into his insides and ripped his belly open when I tried to draw it out, so I killed him as surely as day follows night. I knew what I was doing. I was sick of running like a fugitive, eating hard rations and sleeping in the woods like a vagabond.

'Can you understand my concerns, Constantinus? I was tired of being harried and pursued like an animal, so I'm beginning to think I meant to kill him from the moment I had the opportunity. Perhaps I'm an incorrigible sinner who deserves to be punished, so the good Lord might still damn me for my selfish desires.'

Constantinus shook his head vigorously. 'Hogwash! You were

brave and your efforts saved all three of us from death, Severa, so you mustn't speak such nonsense. Besides, your memory of the events of that night is shaky at best.'

'I hadn't hit my head then, so I can remember most of the details. I can recall every smell and even the gasp that Conanus made when I stabbed him. He had his knife at my throat and he could have killed me if he chose to finish me off.'

'He tried, you little fool. Conanus had already realised that his plans had been thwarted and his whole scheme had no chance of success. He was prepared to cut your throat for the trouble you'd given him.'

Severa raised her hand to her neck and found the edge of a bandage that covered a shallow slice; someone had stitched the edges of the wound together.

'I'd forgotten that! He must have sliced at my throat just as I stabbed him. You're correct, I suppose. He'd already decided that I mustn't be allowed to live.'

Severa's thoughts were suddenly clearer, as if the accumulated clouds of doubt had been driven out of her head. Her uncle had tried to kill her after his ambitions were destroyed in the entrance of that paltry little cavern.

Constantinus understood that any residual guilt she felt had been greatly eased now she was aware of the wound on her throat. What a warrior she'd have made if Magnus Maximus had fathered a son instead of a daughter, he thought admiringly, while the lascivious part of his brain decided that she would be a particularly beautiful young woman with her amber hair loose on his pillow.

To his shame, Constantinus suddenly recalled the old soothsayer's prophecy and the confidences that he had related to Cadal during the king's earlier questioning. Could he really expect to marry this woman? He had been surprised when Cadal had queried his relationship with Maximus's daughter as soon as the centurion was well enough to hold a rational discussion. But both men had understood the implications of both Cadal's questions and the answers. Perhaps Constantinus's time had finally come.

As if she was reading the centurion's thoughts, Severa smiled and gazed directly into his eyes. 'The queen has questioned me about my behaviour with you during our journey from Corinium,' she explained. 'You know what the unkind persons around us will say about us. My name will be bandied about by the high and the low, for it seems that I'm not to be trusted.'

Surprised, the Roman realised that his thoughts had been so synchronised with hers that she seemed able to read his mind. Perhaps one of them might have spoken imprudently in the moments that followed, but at that moment Queen Ardunn swept into the chamber.

'Heavens, Centurion, our patient is scarcely well enough to receive visitors,' Ardunn admonished him while her quick eyes took in the untouched broth. 'Severa needs to eat if she is to become healthy. Off with you, Centurion! You can tell the others that Lady Severa is improving, but she is still confined to her pallet. As for you, Dilic, get yourself off to the kitchens and refresh that broth. I intend to watch this young lady as she swallows every mouthful.'

Severa opened her mouth to protest, but Constantinus raised one finger to his lips as he passed through the doorway, so Severa obediently lowered her mulish eyes and bit her tongue. Only Dilic saw the message that passed between them.

As the door closed behind the servant, Ardunn sighed with exasperation. 'Not only do you refuse to eat but you've welcomed that all-too-handsome legionnaire into the privacy of your room. I know what it's like to be young, but please be sensible, Severa. What would your father have thought?'

'My father is long dead, but from what I've heard, he had no patience with the opinions of other people, no matter how well-meaning they were,' Severa replied angrily. 'I want to know a number of details about the ambush in the hills that took place on the night before our arrival in Tintagel and Constantinus is the only person who can tell me the truth about what happened.'

Ardunn paled at such blunt speaking.

'Don't speak of such ugly matters, girl. Ladies don't bear arms! I thought you wanted your knife for protection, and I definitely haven't been made aware that you've used such a vicious weapon. I must insist that you remain careful, Severa, for people might decide that you're too forward for your own good.'

'If only . . .' Severa almost snapped out a sarcastic response. 'I've learned in recent months that I'm in the unhappy position of being the means whereby some utterly useless man will gain a throne if he can inveigle me into marriage, with or without my consent. It seems that I'd still make a suitable wife for men of ambition if I was in possession of two heads.'

This shocking statement left Ardunn speechless, and she began to wonder what kind of cuckoo had been thrust into Cadal's nest.

Dilic was holding court in the small stone building where all food was prepared in the fortress. By the light of a large fire, the girl sat on a stool and held the attention of a motley collection of servants, cooks and maids who rarely had anything of interest to amuse them.

'I'll not lie to you, Barrfind! That Roman is too pleasing by far and I swear the young lady is all too aware of every one of his many muscles. Oh, girls! He's something special and I'll not object if he plants his boots beside my pallet.'

Dilic's indelicate statement was met with ribald laughter and several vulgar comments were provided by the serving maid's male companions about what they would do to Severa if an opportunity should arise.

'I've been told she opened up her uncle's belly with a special knife that shares her pallet with her, Marcan, so I don't like your chances of survival with Lady Severa. If she was capable of slicing up her uncle, she'd make short work of a clod like you.'

Then Dilic made an exaggerated slicing gesture across her groin and the room was again alive with laughter.

She continued once the laughter subsided, but her manner was suddenly more serious.

'One thing I do know is that the Roman centurion is soft on her, although he doesn't seem to know what he wants. And she's as sweet on him as any sensible girl would be. The queen knows it too. The old witch came into the room with a face that would curdle milk, and I had a distinct feeling she was hoping to find them in a compromising situation.'

Dilic crossed herself with sincere gratitude for the gentility shown by her mistress and the Roman when the queen had entered the room without warning. She had never been flogged or dismissed for failing to carry out her duties so, with luck, she would be given the position as lady's maid during the interesting days that would lie ahead. Perhaps she might even be fortunate enough to be taken away from gloomy old Tintagel, where nothing interesting ever happened.

While Dilic waited for the flustered cook to refill the ceramic bowl with fresh broth, she was savouring her own secret dreams.

All that a clever girl ever needed was an opportunity and Dilic was determined not to let any fortuitous circumstances pass her by.

Meanwhile, as they waited for the evening meal, Constantinus was enduring a conversation with Cadal. The topic was pointed and awkward.

Initially, the king had insisted that his Roman guest should join him in the hall where his family members normally partook of their supper. However, he then decided that the complex discussion he wanted to pursue with Constantinus could best be carried out in the privacy of the high room of Tintagel, the same apartment where Magnus Maximus had been entertained by King Caradoc so many years earlier. Here, although the stout shutters kept out most of the prevailing winds that buffeted the window openings, its airiness meant that this vantage point would always be draughty and chilly.

Cadal cast his eye over the delicacies that had been prepared for his guest. Several trays of chicken, quail and chunks of beef were presented with roasted root vegetables. Fish in savoury sauce, roasted nuts, and mashed stone fruits in honeyed pastries were all laid out on small platters.

Constantinus entered the room under the watchful eyes of an accompanying Dumnonii warrior. The niceties had barely been completed before Cadal launched into a series of sharp questions on the Roman's intentions towards the daughter of Flavius Magnus Maximus.

'I understand that your actions have been shaped by your orders to deliver Lady Severa to our fortress . . . but . . .' Cadal paused delicately, as if to suggest that this line of questioning wasn't really as insulting as it sounded. But Constantinus was unmoved and remained silent. Finally, with a weary sigh, he tried to explain what had transpired in Corinium.

'That's correct! My instructions from King Aeron were clear and unequivocal. I was told that he required me to deliver Lady Severa to Tintagel at all costs, while he would notify my commanders in Deva of the task that had been delegated to me. He would also inform them of the fate of Marcus Britannicus. For my part, I was to employ all means at my disposal to ensure that Severa didn't fall into the clutches of her uncle, Conanus, an Armorican who was described as extraordinarily dangerous to Rome and Britannia, both in physical and political terms. There was no ambiguity attached to this task from my point of view as a senior officer of the legion. Severa must arrive at Tintagel unscathed, and I should use any resources at my disposal.'

Constantinus raised his chin pugnaciously, daring Cadal to find some fault with his statement. I am a Roman, he thought. Why do I need to justify my actions to a British king who matters nothing in the ebb and flow of the real world?

'I can understand your dilemma!' Cadal conceded. 'Unfortunately, the task given to you by Aeron has presented us with a vexing problem of morality that is not of your making. Aeron should have realised that we Britons have rules aplenty that are designed to protect our womenfolk from vulgar comment, especially since the advent of Christianity within our lands. Severa's honour might have been compromised when she was permitted to travel to Tintagel with you. She was unchaperoned during your journey, an oversight that could leave many of my peers to conclude that her worth has been soiled during the time she was travelling with adult males.'

Constantinus stared at Cadal with an unreadable expression.

'Your women's trustworthiness must be lacking, Highness, if

British men feel a need to watch their females constantly in case they fall into sin when they are absent from the seat of male domination,' he stated in a conversational tone, as if he viewed the customs as quaint and primitive.

'You insult me, Roman!' Cadal snapped.

'I might well ask what your conclusions say about my character,' the centurion retorted. 'You would rather that this girl should be dead, as long as she was chaperoned to the grave.'

'We Britons understand the lusts that live in the hearts of males,' the king replied hotly, as two spots of colour began to stain his high cheekbones.

'Cledwyn was bound, hand and foot, whenever he was in Severa's presence, so you can acquit *him* of taking advantage of her. Similarly, Drusus and I were always in each other's company throughout the time we were making good our escape from Conanus's minions. Finally, I hold no doubts that Severa's chaperone would have preferred to live, rather than being a victim of rape and murder at the hands of Conanus's warriors. Your social superstitions are nonsense, Highness, although I accept that you are entitled to hold concerns for the honour and reputation of Lady Severa.'

Cadal was unsure if he should strike this infuriating Roman down for daring to respond with such arrogance, or whether he should be swayed by the good common sense of the centurion's argument. Unfortunately, gossip had already swept through the south with Lady Severa the butt of this ugly, irresponsible chatter. Cadal was convinced that the girl's reputation had been compromised, whether the Roman accepted the challenge or not.

'The simple truth is that your attendance on Lady Severa is the source of any shame that will attach itself to her reputation. I know you didn't take advantage of her vulnerable position, but rumour-mongers will always prefer to believe the worst about their peers and their betters.'

Cadal paused and tried to recapture his earlier control of the conversation.

'The long and the short of the situation, my friend, is that I'm now of the opinion that you must marry the girl. Such a course of action will provide the rulers of the British tribes with a workable solution to a number of problems that are already troubling Britannia. I've discussed this matter with Cadoc, my brother, and we have agreed that a suitable ceremony between yourself and the Lady Severa would deflect any criticism from the British kings and the citizens of our lands.'

Constantinus had half expected such a practical solution would be proposed and, in all truth, he had been hoping for it.

What his Roman superiors would say about an unsanctioned marriage was a matter of conjecture. Many of Cadal's peers would consider a Roman centurion to be a fit husband, for their expectations of a ruler were more simplistic, or more honest, than the Roman hierarchical rules where social status was based on class and gens. Constantinus knew he would never be an acceptable husband to the Roman patrician class, but it had become evident in recent years that Britannia was losing its importance within the complex and constricting policies of Rome.

But the Council of Kings was a different matter.

A quick marriage to Constantinus would solve the political problems associated with Severa's long-term future. The Roman was also the answer to Endellion's plans for her girl, so he was less angry and antagonistic than he would normally have been if his honour had been questioned so openly. In fact, a secret part of his soul was dancing with glee, for he realised that the unsettling prophecy made by the Wilde Man of the Woods had finally come true. Still, personal probity demanded that he must make some kind of protest, even if only a token one.

'What if I don't want to be sacrificed on the altar of your British sensibilities? How could you possibly force me to wed this accursed girl, if I were to decide otherwise?'

Cadal had anticipated such a response.

'We can offer inducements that would encourage you to accept certain political realities if you agreed to wed her. Even a Roman cannot turn his nose up at the prospect of assuming the throne of the High King of the Britons if the opportunity should arise. Anyone who marries Severa will have his backside resting on the cushions of the throne of Britannia and that reward is no small thing. The palace at Venta Belgarum awaits such a man. I have no doubt that the British kings can be persuaded to accept your claim, especially as you are a Roman of exceptional talent who can be expected to protect our lands from foreign invaders.'

Cadal paused to give himself an opportunity to compound his argument.

'Beyond that, I can see no impediment to your success if you decided to carve out a kingdom of your own dimensions. After all, Conanus tried to steal the girl to achieve the same treasure that I'm presenting to you on a platter.'

'And how will you persuade my masters in Rome? I know that my superiors in Britannia won't cheerfully see a landless man of the legions given anything beyond his ordained station in life. Marcus Britannicus might have been a fool and a voluptuary, but his family was ancient and very wealthy, so marriage between him and Severa was more than acceptable to the Roman hierarchy.'

Cadal bit nervously on his thumb, a habit also practised by

Queen Endellion. It must be a family trait, the Roman thought irrelevantly. He knew that the Briton had caught a glimpse of his compromised heart and had seen the ambition clearly written in his eyes.

'I've noticed that Roman rulers are pragmatic men and, at bottom, they don't give a shite what we barbarians do. We are as nothing to them and they don't really care if the Scotti, the Hibernians or the Saxons invade us, as long as nothing is taken that belongs to Rome or the Romans. They'll see you as a useful adjunct to their power in the province, and a means of keeping the tribes under their collective thumb.'

The centurion raised one black eyebrow. Cadal was nobody's fool.

'True enough, but my masters will say that Severa should be wed to one of their own, and they will insist on one who is better connected than I am. Her compromised reputation, as you put it, might earn her some scorn and bad treatment from some candidates, but I can assure you that someone who is more suitable to the northern commanders will insist on making an offer for her hand, regardless of whether the girl's reputation is in tatters.'

'The Romans can want what they like, but Severa is one of Britannia's treasures. I have no intention of throwing her to the pigs! Queen Elen perished at the hands of her Roman husband, Magnus Maximus, and her blood still stains the Roman presence in Britannia. I'll not add to that guilt, so it will be *you* who weds her. Besides, any fool can recognise that Severa cares for you above all other men.'

To his credit, the centurion flushed hotly at the Briton's blunt argument.

For the next hour, Constantinus considered every conceivable problem that could confront this marriage, while Cadal knocked every obstacle down. The Roman had the sense to understand that he mustn't capitulate too quickly in case Cadal became suspicious of his true motivations.

Constantinus had often hated his tendency to blush hotly when he was embarrassed. On this occasion, his flushes of guilt were read by Cadal as affection for Severa of a lasting nature when, in truth, Constantinus had never known lasting love. He knew that he would survive and carry on with life if she were to be whisked away. At heart, he was a soldier; he knew that softness could be equated with weakness, and this flaw could easily be mastered.

'Very well, Highness! I know that I would be very foolish to reject a throne if I had the chance to achieve such an honour, but I don't want Severa to suffer a moment of shame because of my actions. I'll marry her, and do it gladly. I insist that she must be agreeable, for she's the one who has already been robbed of a suitable husband. If she agrees to the marriage, and if she is willing to be a mother to Constans, my young son, then you may draw up your articles of betrothal and I'll agree to whatever terms you should ask of me.'

He gave Cadal his hand to seal their bargain.

'You'll have to explain our decision to Queen Endellion, Highness. She'll want to crush both of us when she learns what has been done to her darling.'

Cadal allowed himself a brief, ironic smile.

'Leave my sister to me, my friend. You'll need to court your betrothed with pretty words and all the courtesies you can remember. She'll want all of the fine phrases and the oaths of eternal love that you can offer, because she knows her marriage will always be a matter of politics. Give her what her heart pines for, and I'll not complain. I can hope she'll forgive us both when she holds her first child in her arms.'

She will, Constantinus thought. She'll forgive me anything by then. For better or for worse, my fate has been decided.

Be careful whom you wed! The words rang through his head in time with a loose shutter that was thudding against the stone wall in the grip of the howling wind. Even after Cadal locked it in place, the sound continued to echo inside the Roman's head.

THE JOURNEY TO
VENTA BELGARUM

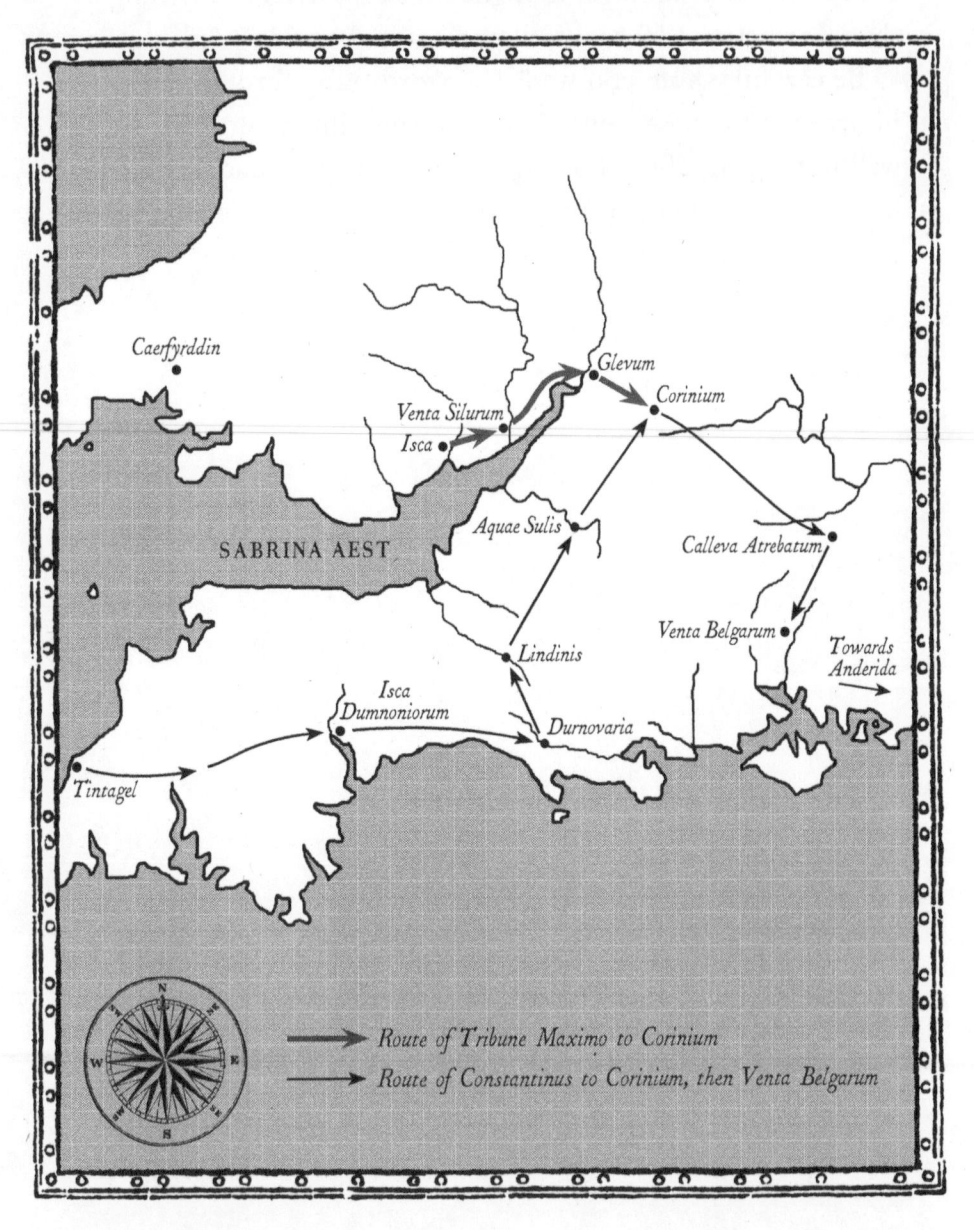

Caerfyrddin

Glevum

Corinium

Venta Silurum

Isca

Aquae Sulis

Calleva Atrebatum

SABRINA AEST

Venta Belgarum

Towards
Anderida

Lindinis

Isca
Dumnoniorum

Durnovaria

Tintagel

N

W   E

S

⟶ Route of Tribune Maximo to Corinium
⟶ Route of Constantinus to Corinium, then Venta Belgarum

CHAPTER XIV

BEGINNINGS

There's a snake hidden in the grass.

Virgil, *Eclogues*, No 3

Severa's body arched in pain as the contractions rippled through the muscles of her abdomen like rolling thunder in a violent storm. She had been in labour for over ten hours and she was weary.

Endellion fluttered around the birthing room with her usual grace, issuing orders to serving women and the midwife, while finding little luxuries to tempt Severa's appetite or add to her comfort.

'If you want to cry out, to curse your husband with the worst words you know, or rail against God for making you a woman, then be my guest and do it.'

Severa swore in all the colourful expletives of the legion, a tirade that raised Endellion's eyebrows in surprise.

'You appear to have learned some very colourful phrases that are anatomically impossible, my dear,' Endellion replied cheerfully, before repeating the curses in a studious voice so that she could use them at some time in the future when Aeron would undoubtedly upset her.

'Anyway, my girl, you were the one who chose to marry and bear children. You could have entered a nunnery if you chose, and you would have spent the rest of your life on your knees as you prayed with the merciful sisters. It's unlikely you would ever fall pregnant while you are doing God's work.'

Severa grinned wanly as the contractions began to ease.

'Don't tempt me, Mother. After this duty is done, a nunnery would seem like pure joy.'

'You'll change your mind once the birthing is over and the babe is safely in your arms,' Endellion answered carelessly, as she fluffed a pillow to place under Severa's head.

'No, I won't!' Severa panted. But Endellion only smiled indulgently.

Severa's wedding had been small, but the Roman Church had joined these two together with all the pomp of a Christian celebration. Severa had been surprised to discover that Constantinus was a devout Christian, because he had never revealed his faith to her prior to the ceremony. Then again, how much did she really know about her husband? In her crown of flowers and red dress, carrying a sheaf of wheat for fecundity, Severa had looked well, she knew, for Constantinus had stared at her with the approval associated with ownership. But what did a day's approval matter in a lifetime of dissatisfaction?

Severa stared at the heavy golden ring that rested so snugly on her right thumb. In the hours of congratulation after the brief vows were made, Constantinus had stolen a moment to give her the plain, undecorated circlet that a Tintagel artisan had made from the plaited golden rings taken from Conanus's minions. Severa smiled at the memory of her husband's thoughtful gift as they accepted congratulations from the limited number of guests who had been assembled in Corinium at such short notice. Yes, she loved Constantinus then, but his closed face and secretive habits sometimes rendered him a mystery to her and made him a source of constant anxiety.

Severa felt the beginnings of another contraction building in her body and groaned at the prospect of enduring further pain. Motherhood had better be remarkable if it was to compensate her for the indignities and suffering of labour, the new queen thought defiantly.

'Where is my idle husband?' Severa managed to ask.

'He'll be with the other men, who'll be drinking and congratulating themselves as if they invented the gift of procreation. If you bear your husband a son, he'll be transformed into the most manly and powerful of all the warriors in this land. At least in his eyes! But if your child is female, such an accident of birth will be your fault entirely.'

Severa recognised the sardonic humour in Endellion's face, coupled with a dry wit that understood the flaws in the natures of all males. Yes, her expression seemed to say, the men we love are foolish and boastful creatures, but they are *our* fools and we'll always honour them, despite their ignorance.

'How much longer before the child is born?' Severa panted as her body began to spasm again.

'You've barely started, girl,' Endellion told her. 'Be grateful that you're healthy, because you still have a few more hours of contractions ahead of you.'

After Endellion had given her a soothing back massage, Severa leaned back against her foster-mother's body.

'I pray my babe will be a girl, Mother. My father died in war and my uncle perished to win a crown with the point of a sword.

Men beyond counting have picked up spears and bows and swords, and they have all perished because of the violence that was ingrained in their blood. Better my child should be voiceless in a society of men and powerless, as all women are, but still remain free from the contamination of male violence. How could any mother live if her son should go off to war, only to perish on foreign soil?'

'Aye! It's true, petal! No mother should live longer than her children. But we know that God isn't always kind to us, so some children die before their parents go into the darkness. I've borne five living children, but two others died within the first week of life and my sweet Fionnuala died when she was barely three years old. And, yes, I'm aware that my boys might grow, merely to perish in a battle that will be of no importance to me. Such is the way of the world in which we live.'

'Then the world is unfair!' Severa protested.

'Would you rather your boy was a eunuch – or a nothing – someone who fears to raise a weapon to save you and yours? Would you have him fearful of all enemies who try to steal your lands? I'm certain that you'll learn to love and cherish whatever child God bestows on you.'

Then, before Severa had a chance to add to the discussion, the next contractions began.

Constantinus had chosen to take his bride to Venta Belgarum, where Magnus Maximus's palace had remained, empty, wasting and cursed, for nearly two decades. But, before he departed from the pleasant surroundings of Corinium, he was forced to endure the disapproval of his superiors, who had appeared in a cavalcade after his nuptials had been concluded.

At the head of the cavalcade, one of Rome's aristocratic

generals was riding in solitary splendour. The kinfolk of Tribune Maximo had served Roman interests as consuls and governors for many centuries. Having served with distinction, Maximo was offended that a nonentity from the ranks would outrank him when the pretender was accepted on the throne where Flavius Magnus Maximus had once enforced his rule.

'This whole marriage is preposterous,' the tribune stated without preamble, as soon as he was presented to Constantinus. 'Surely you accept that you are wholly unfit to become the High King of these fractious lands?'

'I had no intention of marrying Princess Severa, sir, until fairly recent times. I was ordered to accompany Marcus Britannicus as his adjutant, but Britannicus initiated this sorry mess of unhappy events when he chose to frequent a house of ill repute that was peopled by the lowliest and cheapest of whores. His actions precipitated a plot that caused his own death and those of the legionnaires who accompanied him. My sympathies lie wholly with those men who died to protect him. Britannicus placed the daughter of Flavius Magnus Maximus in danger and, as the situation developed, I was left with no choice other than to follow the instructions of King Aeron of the Dobunni tribe. I had no way of obtaining further orders from you at short notice, so I was almost forced to dance to Conanus's tune. Then, as now, I had to exercise my own initiative to make sure that Severa didn't fall into the hands of the usurper. One of the first questions I must ask of you is why this man, Conanus, hadn't come to the attention of the senior officers within the province's high command? The usurper's presence in Britannia without your knowledge, and without being recognised as a threat, is a blot on Roman security – and your leadership! If he had succeeded with his treachery, his lands would have been extended further into

Gallia and he could have threatened Rome itself.'

The general cleared his throat noisily to cover his acute embarrassment. Constantinus had heard a rumour that Marcus Britannicus hadn't been a universal choice as Severa's betrothed when the decision was made by the Roman command. The centurion had also been told that the tribune had received a number of complaints about Shit-head's morals, arrogance and lack of manners. Further, the presence of Conanus in Britannia had caught Rome's senior officers by surprise. Few of them had ever heard of the Ordovice prince, but those who were aware of him assessed Conanus as a British tribal leader who had settled in Gallia and gone to seed in that distant land. Few of the tribune's advisers would have considered Conanus a danger to Rome's governance of Britannia. Now, those same noble officers wanted the whole mess to go away before rumours were relayed to the emperor in Rome, especially as Magnus Maximus was still viewed as an evil influence whose reputation hadn't diminished with the passing of the years.

'You should have refused to wed the damned girl. You must have known how inappropriate this marriage is to the interests of Rome. You're not of noble birth, so your experience as a fighting man can only be that of a minor commander. You're incapable of carrying out the duties of a high king.'

'Am I?' Constantinus replied silkily, but his eyes were threatening and the tribune began to wonder if he might have underestimated the ability and motives of this importunate centurion.

The expression on Constantinus's face was wiped clean and Maximo was left to wonder if he had imagined the sudden flash of fury. The centurion leaned forward, as if eager to explain himself.

'I understand your reservations regarding this marriage, sir. I'll even agree that the Dumnonii king insisted that I'd compromised the girl when I'd actually tried to save her neck. But I can assure you that King Cadal wasn't interested in any candidate, other than me, for the post of High King of Britannia. The Britons consider that Rome's choice of Marcus Britannicus was such an insult to the tribes that they couldn't do worse if their next choice was made by a fool.'

The old tribune wore what was left of his hair in a silver circlet that surrounded his ears. Surprisingly, the fringe seemed more imposing than a laurel wreath. His pale brown eyes, much faded by time, snapped with irritation.

'The tribal leaders intend to control you. And, through you, they hope to manipulate Rome through your inexperience. I'll not have it! Do you hear me? I'll not have it!'

As the tribune's thin lips pursed in a narrow slit that seemed little more than a bloodless wound in his shaven face, Constantinus read the senior officer's response as an indication of his contempt for all things British. Another fool!

'You must be properly advised by my officers if you are to continue with this charade, Constantinus. You must understand that this throne only exists because of Rome's generosity, and we would have no hesitation in removing you from the position if the necessity arose.'

Constantinus accepted the naked threat with more apparent equanimity than he actually felt. But he was sufficiently wise to understand that Rome ruled these isles, although its power had diminished in recent times and most of its troops had been recalled to the continent. The token force left by Maximus after he departed had received few reinforcements in recent times. The tribune could bluster to his heart's content, but he had only been sent to Britannia because he was too old to serve in those lands where a strong military commander was required. Lack of finance would soon force Rome to move the last of her garrisons across the Litus Saxonicum to Gallia and the security of the isles would be left to those Britons and the few Romans who were prepared to spend the rest of their days defending themselves against the barbarian raiders. Constantinus had become a part of the landscape of Britannia, whether he liked it or not.

He forced himself to smile obligingly, while trying to cover a streak of rebelliousness that flashed momentarily in his dark eyes. Fortunately, the elderly tribune's sight was not good, nor was he in the habit of recognising insubordination in his junior officers. Even more tellingly, sarcasm was completely lost on him.

'I accept that I will need some advice, but I would prefer to have the assistance of men I can respect and trust, friends who will honour my wife and my position in these lands. Too many noble Romans have treated the tribesmen of Britannia as if they are barbarian fools or idiot children. The daughter of Caradoc, Queen Endellion, is clever and acute, much like her father who was a friend to Magnus Maximus. I will consider the advice of anyone you decide to send to me, as long as my conditions are met. Be it on their own heads, if they should fail to maintain my trust.'

Peeved at this ultimatum, the old man spat on the marble floor and the nearest servant hurried to clean up the spittle, appalled by the arrogance of this Roman overlord. Constantinus managed to control his facial expression, knowing that word of this lack of courtesy would soon be passed on to King Aeron.

'You're in no position to dictate to Rome what you want,' the tribune snapped dourly.

'But I'm in a dominant position, sir. Rome will be happy to accept a high king who is one of their own and, even if the legions finally leave these isles for good, I will still be the ruler of a province that is committed to trade and economic ties with the empire. I fill that description, whether you approve of my choice . . . or not! With all the faults you have ascribed to me, I am still a better candidate for the role of High King than Cadal of the Dumnonii, who is the best of the British kings and the one man who is most likely to be selected as the British ruler, if I was removed. Could you negotiate successfully with Cadal? I doubt it! For better or for worse, Tribune, you're stuck with me!'

'You're impertinent, Centurion, and you speak far above your station.'

'No, sir! You're the one who is wrong, for I'm about to become the High King of Britannia. I am no longer a centurion who is at your beck and call, so I expect you to speak to me with the correct measure of civility to which someone in my position is entitled.'

Constantinus's face was stiff and cold. Strangely, the tribune recognised the same cold anger that he remembered in the great ones, those men who used power like a blade to carve up the world for their pleasure. He shivered.

We may have misread this dangerous young man, Maximo thought. I will have to provide him with advisers who are young, but who are committed to the emperor, or else he will take these islands in directions that will lead to bloodshed. He's in love with power and death!

Henceforth, Constantinus accepted two Romans of note into his household. The first was a man from a minor branch of the Flavian gens, the royal house of Rome into which, ironically,

Cadal had suggested Constantinus should insert himself.

Flavius Constantine! The erstwhile centurion wanted to laugh at the pretentiousness of it all, but Cadal had a politician's understanding of symbolism, so Constantinus allowed his political aspirations to be guided by this clever British ruler.

The Flavian sent to Constantinus by Maximo had enjoyed all the benefits of his gens, although his branch of the family was relatively minor. The ambitious young man, Cassivellaunus, had been named as a sop to his British grandmother after a tribal king who fought against the great Caesar. This Cassivellaunus was a politician rather than a soldier, as was evidenced by his soft white hands and delicate frame. However, anyone who underestimated this beautifully dressed man would be making a serious error of judgement.

The other man was a centurion who bore the simple name of Gregorius, despite being referred to as the Watchman, a name bestowed on him by his peers and detractors. This Roman officer had a narrow, clever face marked by a scar along his jaw. His voice was soft and mellifluous, while his manner suggested gentle reason and was so persuasive that Constantinus found himself in constant agreement with the advice of his newly appointed assistant. This man might prove to be dangerous, Constantinus decided, once he had an opportunity to consider the undoubted talents of Maximo's appointee.

One other man had been sent to him from those dim mountains of Cymru which had been the birthplace of Conanus and his sister, Elen. Constantinus had yet to meet this young prince but the very name hinted at a dangerous streak.

Vortigern! Constantinus remembered the Briton far better than their brief meetings warranted. When Constantinus had led Marcus Britannicus's honour guard all those months ago as the column travelled to Corinium, Vortigern had been a member of the retinue. Their paths had not crossed during that journey, for Vortigern was a young prince of the northern tribes of Britannia, a leader of the future who was learning the ways of the world in which he would one day take part. Immensely proud, and raised by kin in Caer Fyrddin, this intense young Briton had no desire to cultivate an association with a mere centurion.

On the other hand, the late and unlamented Marcus Britannicus had been determined to keep his distance from Vortigern and all of his fellow Britons, for they were men that he deemed to be below his standing in the world of Rome. In the status-obsessed world of Britannia, too, men of means tended to stand apart from each other, and relied on their positions within their own hierarchies, determined by race, social standing and wealth.

Nor had Vortigern travelled with Constantinus and Severa into the south, choosing instead to carry messages between Tribune Maximo and King Aeron as a courier. The events of the past seemed as if they belonged to a long-gone era, but Constantinus hadn't forgotten Vortigern's hunger for knowledge . . . and something else that he hadn't yet been able to gauge.

But the unspoken rules of precedence had been set out of kilter when Constantinus had become the High King of the Britons through an advantageous marriage with a British princess. Vortigern would now be forced to bend the knee to a Roman and Constantinus could see some of the ripples of concealed emotions swimming in his dark eyes.

Careful of the threat he recognised in the young man, Constantinus was determined to regularly check his fingers and toes whenever Vortigern was in his presence.

Well, who *can* I trust? Constantinus wondered. At least he could take pleasure from the presence of Paulus, who had opted to remain a loyal retainer to his erstwhile commander. Given a grudging release from the legion by Tribune Maximo, the decurion had become something between a body-servant and aide de camp to his commander. Although he would never have stated it openly, Constantinus looked forward to navigating the difficult waters ahead of him, with Paulus standing at his back like a comforting rock wall.

The whole panoply that surrounded the prestige of the High King took Constantinus by surprise, especially the barbaric splendour of the court and the unfamiliar trappings of power that were showered over him. There were so many decisions to be made, and so many areas of contention that must be considered – or left untouched. As he and his wife undertook the journey to Venta Belgarum, in company with a coterie of British kings, Constantinus was reluctant to express any personal opinion on the choice of this old administrative centre as his capital. The British kings had simply informed him that Venta Belgarum had always been the seat of the High King of the Britons, having omitted to mention that Maximus had been capricious when accepting the site for his royal palace.

'But why choose Venta Belgarum?' Constantinus had asked Aeron and Cadal in the midst of their discussions. 'Surely your advice must serve some purpose, if you've selected this southern city over other centres that are much more suitable. Travel to Venta Belgarum will be difficult for many of the other kings, especially those whose lands lie near the Wall. Their journey would be difficult, costly and occasionally dangerous.'

Aeron glanced at Cadal, who shrugged carelessly.

'My father was Maximus's greatest friend in these isles and, according to his recollections, Maximus insisted on a capital that was close to the Litus Saxonicum,' Cadal stated in his usual forthright fashion. 'Even in the early days of his reign, he must have recognised a need to travel to the continent at some future time. My father also explained that the palace at Venta Belgarum was spacious and could be easily remodelled to suit the taste of a Roman ruler. Maximus particularly desired a palace with his own bathhouse. Besides, Maximus disliked the king of the Atrebates tribe and wanted his proximity to frighten the man into submission.'

'How odd!' Constantinus said drily. 'I've been offered a capital that was chosen by a previous Roman ruler who found the town to be conveniently sited for his future expansionary plans. While I accept that the presence of a working hypocaust meets with my approval, I would hope that I don't have to become involved in another personal feud with its rightful owner if I am to gain control of this palatial estate.'

'Aye! That's the description in a nutshell,' Aeron answered. 'It's our way of controlling one's opponents. But the palace has been renovated and it's waiting for you to grace it with your presence. As well, the church at Venta Belgarum is the site of Maximus's coronation and your wife was born in the main apartments of the palace. Elen, Maximus's wife, is buried somewhere in the graveyard attached to the church. Venta Belgarum may have had a chequered history as a royal residence, but the lives of your wife's kinfolk are intertwined with the history of this city. These matters will be of great importance if we are to create a lineage that will last into the future.'

Cadal paused and collected his thoughts before continuing.

He might not find this newly anointed king in such an expansive mood again.

'You must understand that Maximus was Britannia's first High King for hundreds of years so my people had no recent history on which they could fashion the role of overlord,' Cadal explained. 'Caradoc told me that Maximus considered himself to be the Dux Bellorum of Britannia, or its war chief, so that concept might be worth your consideration when you evaluate the task that lies ahead of you. Primarily, Maximus perceived his role as the ruler who must unite the tribes against a common enemy, halt the barbarian attacks and lead my people in the protection of the isles. My father agreed with Maximus, and he would have been the first to insist that Maximus needed a firm hand if he was to successfully control the ever-squabbling British kings. You'll have the same problems that plagued Maximus; I suggest that you raise a force of warriors who are loyal to you alone, ostensibly to repel an attack from an unknown quarter. You can't afford to depend on the kings to assist you at those times when you have a need of them, so levy the bastards in advance for enough men to satisfy your needs.'

This advice was wise. Constantinus's thoughts dwelled on the suitability of Venta Belgarum as *his* town while the two men were riding companionably at the head of the cavalcade. He had never visited this centre, although he knew that the surrounding district had a strong industrial and agricultural base. Significantly, the town lay close to the coastal centres of Magnus Portus and Portus Adurni that provided direct trading links with the Roman world. Cadal's assumptions were correct. The tribal kings were wealthy and could afford the expense of supplying him with a standing army.

Winter was finally loosening its hold on the south when

Constantinus and his new bride, accompanied by Roman and British notables, arrived in Venta Belgarum. Impressed from the moment of arrival, the new High King was surprised by the venerable age, vigour and wealth of the large town. As their horses climbed the heavily populated road leading to the forecourt of the palace, Constantinus felt a frisson of excitement. His success as a ruler would depend on his ability to turn this centre and its hall of justice into a capital city, both for himself and his heirs.

The thorny matter of succession was already beginning to trouble him. He was determined to leave his son Constans as a lordling or minor king once he had passed into the shades. To this end, he had sent for Constans, who had been living in Isca fortress where the remnants of the legion were quartered. The wife of a fellow centurion had seen to his care and education for a small stipend that was far more certain than the infrequent payments sent to the legion by their tight-fisted masters in Rome. By diverse ways, some of which were not exactly legal, Constantinus had always been able to ensure that sufficient coin was on hand to care for his first-born son.

As the cavalcade entered the cobbled forecourt adjacent to the King's Hall, Constantinus noted that the palace doors were twice the size of a tall man and were sheeted with panels of brass, copper, and gold, decorated with scarlet pigment. Behind them, the timber palace was rendered unusual by the addition of several windows made from real glass. Constantinus dismounted and, in company with a wide-eyed Severa, entered the palace through the great, creaking doors.

Constantinus experienced a moment of primeval panic. How can I expect to rule over these difficult and fractious islands, he wondered, as the darkness of the long-deserted hall pressed down on him. I don't have the faintest idea how to control the population and cater to their needs at the same time, as all my skills lie in the age-old arts of killing.

A huge, spacious hall appeared out of the gloom, while servants hurried to open the dusty banks of shutters that would allow narrow shafts of sunlight and fresh air to enter the long room. At the very end of the hall, a small dais had been erected above the stone floor, a place of distinction from which the High King would dispense justice to his vassals. In the centre of this dais, a sheeted chair was sitting in solitary splendour. It had remained untouched since Magnus Maximus had last risen from this seat of honour, so one of the servants whipped away the dusty covering.

Surprised, Constantinus drew in a sudden breath of air. This throne had begun its life as a stool modelled on the curule chairs of ancient Rome, but its structure had been modified on so many occasions that it bore little resemblance to that spartan, august seating. Elaborate carving on a tall back had been added to the original design, where depictions of imaginary beasts were struggling now for dominance. Although these carvings were crude, they possessed a strong visual power. A luxurious series of cushions had been added to the seat and its arms for extra comfort, their rich scarlet cloth covered with fine stitchery in silver and gold thread. Neglect had allowed moths and mice to feast on the fabric. In the centre of the dais, a sinuous dragon from the northern legends was crouching below the seat, its outline highlighted by huge wings and flashing, gold-painted claws.

'The chair is magnificent,' Cadal observed. 'I'd forgotten how Maximus enjoyed sitting in state when he was holding court.'

'And very colourful,' Gregorius added in his neutral voice.

Cassivellaunus whistled between his teeth. 'Maximus certainly knew how to keep the peasants impressed.'

'Perhaps the artist was showing us the power that a High King can wield if he so chooses,' Severa suggested amicably, although her husband recognised a certain steely disapproval on her face at the obvious scorn of the Roman advisers. 'Maximus understood the importance of the visual trappings of a king as much as the justice he dispensed to his subjects. To me, this throne shouts out a warning that the High King is the master of everything that happens in his kingdom. He is all-powerful, he is violent and he even commands the wild beasts.'

Severa realised that five pairs of male eyes were riveted on her face with varying degrees of disapproval, so she flushed under their scrutiny. 'Queen Endellion had her own opinions on the importance of pomp and ceremony,' she added hastily. 'But she could have been wrong.'

Constantinus winced at her capitulation to the opinions of these men. He knew in his heart that his wife's opinions were worth as much to him as those of his advisers but, to his personal chagrin, he failed to defend her because she was a woman who was speaking out of turn. Instead, he concentrated on smoothing over the awkwardness.

'No, Severa! Queen Endellion wasn't precisely wrong, but I agree with your opinion for the most part. Maximus chose this throne as a symbolic object and it shouts out to any person who looks at it that the man who sits upon its cushions is the ruler of all he surveys. However, the symbolism here is aimed at British tribesmen, rather than outsiders like his Roman allies. He knew such imagery would cut no ice with the pragmatic rulers who were experienced in the ways of the City of the Seven Hills, for we Romans are not easily impressed.'

The Romans schooled their faces to look complacently at nothing in particular, while Severa seethed at her husband's suggestion that Britons were superstitious and easily fooled. Perhaps, in the privacy of her rooms, she might be able to speak her mind.

Constantinus decided to carry out an inspection of the remainder of the palace. The baths, cold and unused for many years, promised sybaritic delights for those with Roman standards of cleanliness, while the apartments proved to be snug and warm with well-fitted shutters to keep out the weather. Even the quarters allotted to the guards and servants seemed to be larger and more congenial than usual.

He soon found he was looking forward to life in Venta Belgarum so, once he had viewed the royal apartments, he immediately made plans to levy the kings for the warriors who would form the nucleus of a future army. As he calculated his future requirement for men and supplies, he gloried in the fact that he would be living better than Tribune Maximo in the cold north of Britannia. For her part, Severa was captivated by the courtyards where the sun warmed the stone-clad floors and large pots of flowers, herbs and vegetables rendered the air sweet and clean. The haphazardly built structure seemed to incorporate Roman practicality with British love of luxury.

I can bear my child here in perfect safety, she thought immediately, as her hand strayed to her belly, which was still empty of anything but promise.

The rooms had been quickly furnished and decorated, while the courtyards were soon heavy with the smell of full-blown roses. Now, Severa was lying on her couch of pain and waited for the birthing stool to be needed.

The months had flown by as her husband learned the basic

requirements of kingship. Constantinus and Severa had been crowned in the city's church and Severa had been surprised at the weight of the crown that had been set upon her head. River pearls and carnelian added colour and lustre to the diadem of gold that encircled her forehead and she still wore it on those days that celebrated the festivals of Britannia and Rome.

As the offspring of a tribal ruler, she wore her crown with pride, for she understood that only the circumstances of her birth entitled her to any symbols of rank, and a wife was usually without importance in the world of men. But this young woman, Elen's daughter and Maximus's girl-child, was of value. As her foster-mother had trained her, she sallied into the town with simples for the sick, bread for the poor and help for the needy until the time came when her growing belly confined her to her courtyards. Her days had been full in ways that she had never imagined during her immature youth and, although a small voice told her that Constantinus had less love for her than her own depth of passion for him, she still blessed the day that she had first seen him.

Then, when her labour pains were fierce and endless and the child came from her body in a welter of blood and water, she had suddenly become fearful. Darkness had come and the sun had fled, so she prayed to the Virgin that her child should belong to the light.

'You've carried a boy, mistress,' Dilic cried joyfully. 'He's a fair beauty, with the strength and size of his father.'

Endellion held the child up and Severa felt her fears begin to fade. The child was full-term and his features were golden, from his cap of thin hair to the rosy tinge of his skin. She looked deeply into his infant face and saw that his eyes were a hazel-green shade that was quite different to her own.

'My babe will be his own self,' Severa murmured. 'He's a true child of the light.'

'I agree! You've done very well, my girl,' Queen Endellion added joyfully. 'Your father would have been pleased. Another fine young lad! And you'll be well and healthy too, so take the small babe in your arms. My, but he's nuzzling for your breast already.'

As the child attempted to suck at the proffered sustenance, her indifference was swept away in a great tide of love.

With a sudden pang, she realised she would probably die for this mindless, blind creature who would now hold her in thrall until one of them perished.

CONSTANTINUS IN THE CANTII LANDS

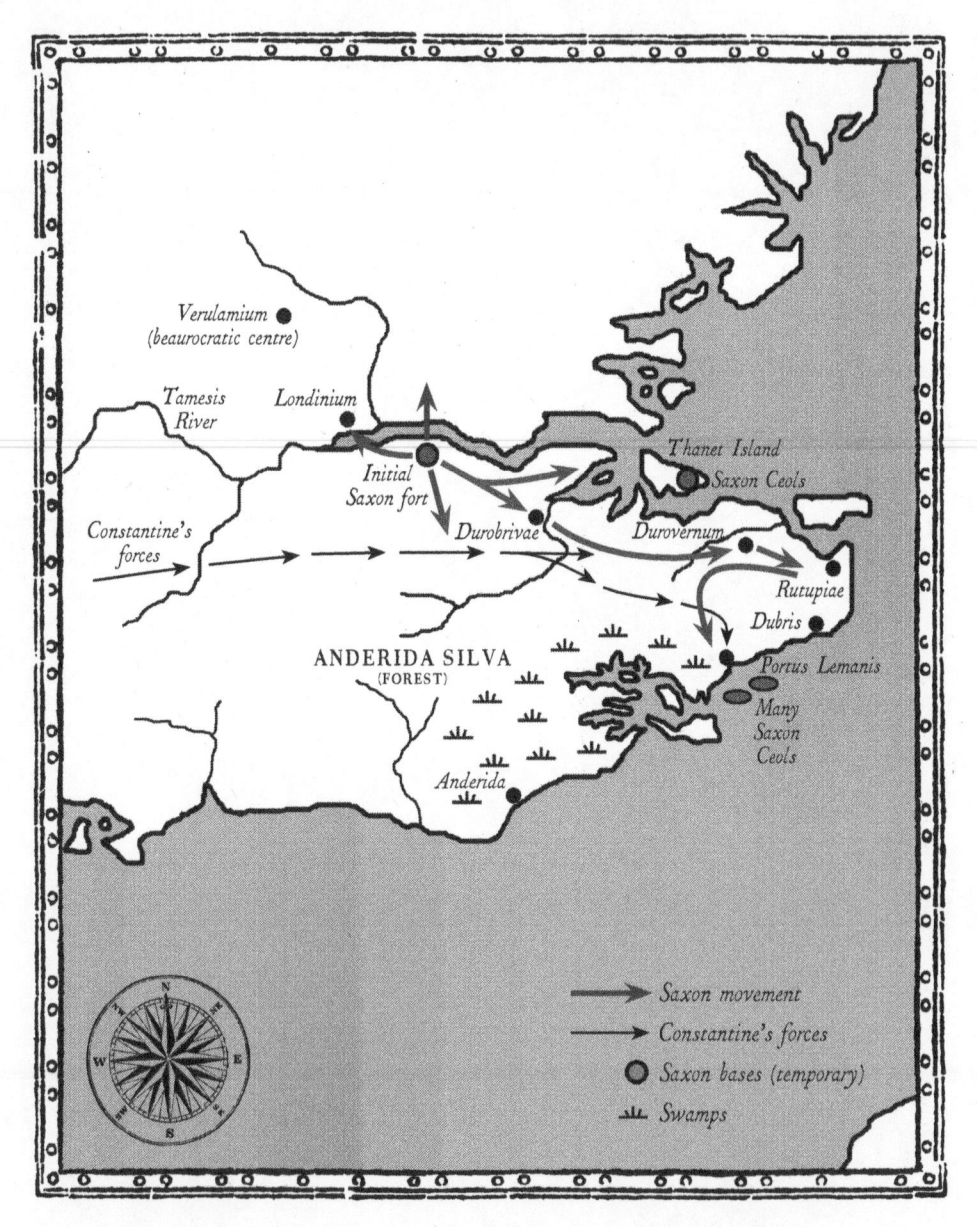

Verulamium
(beaurocratic centre)

Tamesis River

Londinium

Initial Saxon fort

Constantine's forces

Durobrivae

Thanet Island
Saxon Ceols

Durovernum

Rutupiae

Dubris

ANDERIDA SILVA
(FOREST)

Portus Lemanis

Many Saxon Ceols

Anderida

→ Saxon movement

→ Constantine's forces

◉ Saxon bases (temporary)

⚔ Swamps

CHAPTER XV

A SAXON SUMMER

To what do you not drive human hearts, cursed craving for gold.

Virgil, *Aeneid*, Book 3

During the first two years of Constantinus's marriage, sweeping changes were introduced to the household of the High King, but not all those new manifestations of love, family life and rule were good ones.

The late-summer wind tore at the leaves from the queen's favourite hazel tree and sent them swirling through the warm courtyard in scarlet spirals. Severa lazed in her sun-drenched garden and dreamed of happier times as one babe nuzzled at her breast and the other child played with dandelions on the cushion that lay at her feet. God had blessed her, because both of her close pregnancies had resulted in healthy sons. Meanwhile, at her wooden workbench, the enterprising Dilic worked on her distaff while the other servants hovered nearby to offer sweetened juices and tiny delicacies.

Dilic enjoyed the queen's confidence and friendship, so she

was always well treated and deferred to within the royal household. Quick-witted as always, the girl from Tintagel had made herself indispensable through her ready tongue, her cheeky and irreverent viewpoints and her absolute loyalty to Severa and the queen's brood. Had Constantinus been at home, he would not have been pleased to see that Dilic was playing the part of a woman of substance, rather than the kitchenmaid she had been until recent years. But Constantinus was mounting a campaign along Britannia's east coast where infiltrating Saxons and other barbarians were casting avaricious eyes on the affluence of the local population.

More than a year had passed since the birth of Ambrosius, Severa's first son. The little boy was pale-skinned and beautiful, and possessed a focused concentration that was quite unexpected in such a young child. In the tranquillity of the garden, the little boy stared fixedly at the puff-ball of a dandelion, while occasionally twisting its stem so that the tiny, whiskery seeds floated away on gentle currents of air.

By contrast, the baby at the queen's breast was far from contemplative.

Severa's arms were fully occupied with the squirming infant who suckled so fiercely on his mother's breasts that he often drew blood. His red gums had been broken by four milk-teeth at birth, and to make matters worse, the babe's size was such that his birth had drained Severa's dwindling store of strength, so that she was struggling to regain her good health.

Yet without her husband's presence in Venta Belgarum at the birthing, the bond between mother and son became stronger than she would have expected. The new-born child, Uther, was *her* babe rather than the offspring of Constantinus, because the king had yet to acknowledge the child. Not that there was any doubt of his parentage. But Severa used little Uther to ease the emptiness in her heart caused by her husband's absence.

She looked across at Ambrosius, the golden child, who was the source of Constantinus's pride. While her first-born was a lovely boy, the wild and ever-hungry Uther was the son who needed her most. Constantinus had his Constans and, to a lesser extent, Ambrosius, but Uther was *hers*.

As Severa recovered from her ordeal during the weeks and months that followed the birthing, she took every opportunity to doze in the sunshine and gaze at the *little demon*, as she called him. But such reflections were moot, for her husband had left her and her sons behind, along with Constans, his own offspring.

To compound Severa's misery, Constantinus had departed eagerly, as if he was running full-tilt towards an unknown lover. Some months earlier Constantinus had been called away to douse the flames of a relatively minor incursion into British lands by an itinerant band of Saxons, for such was the wording of the request for assistance made by the kings of the Regni and Cantii tribes. Strangely, she had given no thought to the possibility that her husband might be killed at the hands of this band of heathens who had travelled in their ceols to threaten Londinium itself. She still had no inkling when her husband would return from this campaign that had taken far longer than could have been anticipated.

Severa's pregnancy had been well advanced by the time that rumours filtered throughout Britannia that a force of barbarians had sailed up the Tamesis River and were erecting an encampment near the fringes of Londinium. These raiders had met no resistance, because the Roman garrison had been deserted for many years. This omission ensured the vast naval port, its dusty workshops and the stone fortress remained unmanned and silent. But, like all great cities, Londinium and her multi-racial citizens had continued to trade as they had done during the centuries of Roman occupation, for the great water cisterns remained undamaged, the public hypocausts still gave an illusion of Roman civilisation, and British trade with the continent continued to thrive. The legions had departed, but Rome was still in power.

Uncontested, this band of Saxon raiders spent the next few weeks plundering whatever valuables and supplies they could pillage from the small communities that had flourished around Londinium.

Now, in the wake of the slow Roman withdrawal from the remote areas of the province, the High King of the Britons was all that stood against the barbarian hordes who threatened Britannia during the spring. The barbarian raiders from the north had laid waste to the British coastline since the days of Maximus but, in recent years, they had demonstrated an ability to mount attacks from the north, south, east and west. Striking with lightning speed, they gathered their spoils, manacled their captives as slaves and then retreated to their temporary palisades.

But Londinium had always seemed so well defended by Roman-trained troops that this important trading hub was considered to be safe from seasonal raiders.

These bands of Saxons came because they could smell the rich pickings that could be culled from vigorous trade. The raiders became overconfident when there were no attempts to root them out of their encampment, so they elected to stay longer and extend their raids into the rich Cantii lands to the south of Londinium. Later, with winter storms making the sea crossings hazardous, they decided to rendezvous with their ceols in the safe anchorages to the south of the island.

Uncontested, the Saxons spent the next few weeks filling their ceols with plunder so that the vessels could return to their homelands with the spoils of their violence. The earth of the Cantii lands ran red with British blood.

The Regni king had been the first to bleat that his lands were under threat and his profits were imperilled by this nest of barbarians who were so assured of their military superiority that they had built timber fortifications along the Tamesis River.

Once he was aware of the problem and chafing after two years of inactivity, Constantinus was eager to smash some Saxon heads. But first, he must convince his wife that he would be obliged to remove himself from her presence for the duration of a military campaign. Perhaps, if he could defeat these barbarians, he might even be able to cast off his dependence on his wife and her sage advice. It might be easier said than done, for, while Severa was only a woman, she had been the device by which he gained Britannia's throne. Besides, he still hungered for her body.

To reign unfettered! To watch the Britons bow to their master out of legitimate respect, and not because he had married so very well! These thoughts chased through the tunnels of Constantinus's brain.

Like all sensible husbands, he waited until his wife was happy and comfortable. He held his tongue until they had completed a pleasant evening meal and the babe, Ambrosius, had been taken to his sleeping pallet by Dilic.

'Word has come to the court that Londinium is under attack from a force of northern barbarians. I'm obliged to take a column of my warriors and root out these fools before they can cause more ructions in Britannia by disturbing the sleep of my Cantii and Regni friends. They've beached their ceols at Tanatus Island and I'm told they are already sailing to and from Friesia and Saxony with the wealth they've stolen from the British people.' Constantinus's words sounded casual as he nibbled on a concoction of sweet honey and pastry, but he kept his eyes lowered so his wife was unable to read his thoughts. The bluntness of his statement was a stupid error, he realised, as soon as she began to digest his words.

Severa sat up a little straighter, a difficult proposition given the size of her belly. Constantinus could see that her eyes were shining with either tears or anger, but he was unable to judge which.

'Is this situation so grave that you must leave me when I'm so close to my time?' she asked evenly. Any sensible man should have been warned by her flat, unemotional voice.

'Londinium is a ripe peach that is ready for plucking, Severa. These Saxons are being overbold if they are prepared to hold my greatest city to ransom while I'm only a few days' ride away. They've obviously compared me to the Cantii king and found me negligible, a man who is unable to protect what is mine.'

'Yours?'

That single word fell into the silence like a stone cast into a pool of water, spreading ripples of possibility.

Constantinus felt a traitorous blush rise up his neck. Damn! His eyes hardened, although he tried belatedly to adopt an expression of surprised hurt.

Severa was unapologetic. 'I believe you mean *our city*, husband.' Her biting sarcasm showed her weariness and impatience with the world of men. 'I doubt that these raiders think of you at all. All they really care about are the rich pickings to be had from the villages outside the city itself and the wealth of those travellers who are making their way into Londinium. I suppose they must care for their families across the sea, but I doubt they consider the welfare of the citizens of Britannia for a moment.'

Constantinus swallowed a biting retort. He knew she was weary after two years of almost-continual pregnancy and his own lack of intimacy with her, as they struggled to learn the new roles that had come with the throne. But Severa was a woman, for fuck's sake! She had no business doubting or undermining her husband and king.

'You insult me, Severa, but I'll put your slurs down to weariness and the weight of your child. Though I'd prefer to be with you at the next birth, I have a duty to my fellow kings. I have sworn to defend Britannia, so I must travel to Londinium and remove these barbarians from our lands. I've already issued instructions to Paulus and my officers that they must be prepared to depart by first light tomorrow morning. Venta Belgarum will remain peaceful during our absence, but I've issued orders that a detachment of warriors will remain here to ensure your safety and the security of our town. I intend to return before our child is born, but I can't promise that my mission will be completed before the birthing.'

Constantinus threw off all pretence of consulting his queen before he left Venta Belgarum on this campaign. He was finding her to be increasingly bothersome and argumentative.

Severa knew that Constantinus was eager to escape from her presence for a short period of time. She told herself that he would return to her with renewed love and gratitude, if she withdrew her objections to his departure. Her foster-mother would have told her that she was being a gullible and sentimental fool.

As Constantinus rode away towards Londinium, he was

accompanied by his Roman advisers, a mixed force of fifty personally trained *cataphractii*, Maximus's beloved heavy cavalry, eighty light cavalry provided by Cadal and Aeron, plus sixty foot soldiers trained by Paulus. Vortigern was the sole representative of the British tribal kings. When couriers had been sent to the kings of the various tribes in south-eastern Britannia, as well as representatives from several settlements close to Londinium, the only positive responses had come from the Regni, Cantii and Durotriges rulers who agreed to provide some light cavalry and supplies to assist Constantinus's campaign when he passed through their lands. And so, with a small force of some two hundred and fifty men, Constantinus was forced to be content, for this number would be swelled by an unknown number of native levies.

The hour was still early and the sun had only begun to stain the sky with the approach of first light, although the horizon was clear of cloud and the last of the night stars were still visible. Torches flared and illuminated the mounted cavalry and foot soldiers, all eager to be gone before full sunrise.

Severa had kissed her husband in front of his troops to demonstrate her love for him, but Constantinus's tightly closed lips had been as cold as the grave. Somewhere, a thought had come unbidden to Severa that, sooner or later, Constantinus would ride away and she would never see her maddening, beautiful and fate-chosen man again.

Severa watched the lines of troops pass through the gates with a painful sense of loss.

Above the gates, she recognised the contemplative form of Constans, who was watching the departing warriors from a high vantage point on the parapet used by soldiers to guard the King's Hall. Constans had come to his father's town after the birth of

Ambrosius and Severa had been nervous about meeting this immature boy.

At some fifteen years of age, he should by rights have accompanied his father on this campaign, so that he could be blooded into the cruel world of warriors, but Constantinus was unusually protective of his eldest son and had refused to allow the boy to accompany him.

'Better he should learn the tedium and importance of rule,' her husband had told her.

But Severa knew that Constans was reluctant to bide his time in the palace while his father was riding off into peril.

'The boy is troubled,' Severa explained to Dilic, who screwed up her nose with scorn.

'He's just a silly child, regardless of his height,' Dilic responded. 'He does little, apart from whining and complaining that the people of Venta Belgarum are primitive.'

'You are unnecessarily harsh on him, Dilic. My lord wishes him to learn what it is to be a king, so I am prepared to instruct him. He hasn't had the benefits of a mother to guide him in the ways of good manners. To the best of my knowledge, he's never known a permanent home other than the Roman garrisons, despite growing up with the knowledge that his father cares for him above all other things. He's confused . . . and that doesn't surprise me at all.'

Dilic had disliked the boy from their first meeting. She resented him even more after her mistress had chosen to leap to his defence.

'He can't be trusted, mistress, and he'll see you dead if he has his way. I've noticed the way he looks at you when he thinks no one is watching.'

But Severa had stopped listening. She picked her way back to the ramparts and climbed the crude ladder to the vantage point where Constans was standing and staring after the dwindling column. The climb proved difficult because she was impeded by her heavy skirts and her swollen belly. Still, Constans was the apple of his father's eye and there was nothing that Constantinus would refuse her if such a choice involved the welfare of his eldest son. Somehow, she must make her peace with this difficult young man.

Ignoring the concerned pleas of her maidservant to return to ground level and safety, Severa hoisted herself over the last rung of the ladder to find that she now had a panoramic view of Venta Belgarum and the column of warriors winding its sinuous way through the town's eastern gate.

She straightened her skirts and gathered her wits together.

The boy was leaning against the parapet in order to follow the last traces of his father's red cloak as the rear of the column passed through the town gates. Constans was oblivious of her presence so she could use this opportunity to examine him without causing offence.

He's beautiful, she thought with surprise. His face was usually screwed up with strong emotion but, as he watched the departure of his father, his features were still and passive.

Severa had been nervous in the boy's presence, so she had difficulty in acknowledging his astonishing good looks and manly presence. The shock of black hair that fell over his eyes; the generous, mobile mouth; the muscles developed from his daily arms' practice; and the dark, penetrating eyes came together to describe a youth hovering on the brink of a remarkable manhood.

Severa cleared her throat, so the boy swung around to face her, his eyes flashing with an emotion that she only half understood.

'Your father is a gifted warrior, Constans, and I'm certain that God will care for him during the weeks to come. Would you like to come down now and break your fast with me? We do have a number of important matters to discuss regarding your future duties.'

Severa managed to keep her voice friendly and natural, although the very thought of climbing down the primitive ladder was making her feel sick. She held out her right hand in an encouraging gesture, but Constans ignored her small token of friendship.

The boy stared slowly and insolently at his stepmother. Severa was struck by the brilliance of his dark-brown eyes that were as bright and as hard as the stones in the lovely necklace that Constantinus had given her as a birth-gift. They pinned her in place as surely as if she was an annoying insect impaled by a long skewer for intense study. Cowed by his manner, she dropped her offered hand as it began to tremble.

'My father has gone off to battles and consigned me into the hands of incompetent strangers on so many occasions that I hold no fears for him. He says he'll return, and he will – when he's good and ready. Still, there are few Romans to guard his back on this punitive mission, so he'll be forced to depend on the courage and determination of native warriors.'

'The Britons under your father's command have been trained to meet the standards that apply to Roman legionnaires. I might add that these men are fighting for their own lands,' Severa added tartly. Irritated by the boy's arrogance, she longed to wipe the smirk from his handsome face. 'They have much more to lose than you do – or any other Roman legionnaire.'

'Clamber down to the ground then, Severa, and I'll join you in a few moments. Father has instructed me to obey you in all things, and I always abide by his wishes. Do you need my assistance to lower yourself down the ladder?'

Constans sounded sympathetic, but Severa was watching his eyes closely. His facial expression was flat and uninterested, expressing no empathy for the queen and her condition. Of course, the boy had also shown a distinct lack of respect by freely using her first name without paying her the courtesy of using her title. She was acutely aware that Constans knew better, but she resisted an urge to slap his bland face hard.

Now that the sunrise revealed his body in full, Severa could see that Constans's colouring was similar to that of his father. Nature had given his short hair that brilliant gloss and good hygiene had made his teeth very white and clean. The boy had dressed in his best clothes to honour his father. Such a handsome specimen as Constans would always attract the admiration of commoners and the queen had heard that he was seen by these citizens as a young emperor. This comment alluded to his abnormal beauty and lofty manner as much as his paternity. The wags in Venta Belgarum had summed up the lad's pretensions with cruel accuracy. Yet the boy's eyes were vulnerable and they touched her womanly heart.

'Very well, lad,' she answered casually, choosing a diminutive to demonstrate to Constans that she considered him to be less than a man. He flushed with affront, so she smiled beatifically.

'I can assure you that I'm quite well and strong, so I'll manage to climb down the ladder without any assistance. After all, I travelled with your father over very rough terrain when we made our escape from Corinium to Tintagel in those days before you came to join us. I will take great pleasure in introducing you to my friend, Calindre, after we have eaten. I've no doubt you have heard that Calindre was the knife that killed Conanus of Armorica. Yes?'

Constans nodded and Severa saw a brief flicker of interest flash through his eyes.

That's how I'll conquer your resistance, she thought jubilantly. You're still a young man with a boy's love of excitement, so I'll start working on you through your desire for adventure.

As it transpired, Constans rejected many of her efforts to forge a friendship and he was almost impossible to fool, so Severa spent the weeks before the birth of her second son by encouraging the ever-present longing for glory and adventure that existed in Constantinus's overprotected son. Constans had been banned from partaking in those ordinary pastimes that were dear to boys' hearts, such as fishing or hunting, in case he should drown or be attacked by wild animals. Severa introduced him to fishing and the boy quickly became obsessed with this harmless contest between man and fish. By the time she took to her bed with the first pangs of childbirth, Constans was fast becoming an able and dedicated huntsman.

She told him of her experiences during their flight from Conanus's assassins and the dangers of the journey, while making sure that the boy's father was shown in the best possible light. But for all her revelations, she carefully avoided being seen as a sycophant. Slowly and surely, Constans began to warm to Severa's approaches.

'Severa! Severa! A courier has arrived from Londinium,' Constans shouted eagerly as he charged through the doorway of the courtyard. 'Father has sent word of his campaign along the east coast.'

Uther was asleep on her breast and, for once, seemed

mercifully contented. Sighing, Severa handed the sleeping baby
to the wet nurse. With his eyes tightly closed, he opened his
mouth to wail out his anger.

'Oh, do hurry, Severa! The courier is waiting for us.'

Constans was bouncing from one foot to the other.

'Now, Constans, where is this courier?'

The young man led her towards the King's Hall at a trot. Like
an enthusiastic puppy, he tried his best to urge her to hurry.
Then, as they entered the majestic hall of Venta Belgarum,
stepmother and son found a young warrior waiting impatiently
to greet them. He was clearly anxious to complete his duty so he
could remove himself from the palace, either to attend the
nearest tavern or to return to his fellow warriors on the
battlefields of Londinium.

'My queen! Lord Constans! I bring a missive from my master,
Constantinus, High King of the Britons. He is resting with his
command in the marshes of Portus Lemanis. My lord has been
engaged with a large band of Saxons who have taken to the
swamps and sucking sands near the coast. Our enemy hopes to
be evacuated by their ceols if they can escape our retribution for
their depredations. The king has sent me with this missive to
ensure you aren't fearful if you hear news of the battles that have
been fought. He's asked that you should read his missive well,
Lord Constans, so you may learn what must be done if you
should one day become a king. I have been ordered to return to
the king's bivouac after you have arranged a suitable response.'

He discharged his memorised message with aplomb and then
handed a piece of vellum to Constans with a deep bow of respect.
Its red wax seal had been stamped with Constantinus's ring, an
intaglio stone with a dragon coiled within it – the insignia of the
Dracos Legion.

As the warrior backed away, the queen thanked him serenely and ordered one of her scribes to bring scrolls and writing implement so she could pen a suitable missive that would be taken to Constantinus by the courier. Once the niceties were completed, she moved swiftly to the prince's side so she could read Constantinus's spidery Latin script over the young man's shoulder. Severa had no difficulty in imagining the unspoken details implied by his words as the struggles of the last few months were brought vividly to life.

From the time that the High King and his column, supplemented by a further fifty warriors provided by the Regni king, moved into the lands ruled by the Cantii tribe, they found evidence that the Saxons had sought richer pickings than were available in Londinium and its surrounds. Burned crofts, where only the circular stone walls remained, were still smoking and exposed the pitiful remains of their British owners. Whole families had been hacked to death, a senseless waste as the younger crofters would have been worth a significant value in gold if sold as slaves in the markets of the continent.

The Saxons had chosen to kill their victims rather than impede their own mobility by having to place guards on long lines of manacled prisoners. Constantinus nodded in understanding of this strategic concept once he accepted that this pattern had been established by the enemy thane. He could now devise a suitable response to the no-prisoners strategy adopted by the Saxon force. For the invaders, the need for provisions was immaterial, for the thane intended to live off the land as far as possible. Once filled with loot, his ceols would sail away with skeleton crews and return to meet the raiders at a prearranged location, one where the troops could embark in the vessels with more accumulated treasure for the return journey to the Saxon homelands.

The route followed by the barbarians was clearly defined by a series of blood trails. Like clouds of locusts, the Saxon warriors had descended on the Cantii lands to burn, murder and loot against minimal opposition. At times, small groups would break away from the main column to attack isolated targets of opportunity before rejoining their comrades on the meandering journey that would eventually bring them back to the coast. Durobrivae was one such centre, a town where the area's agricultural wealth was brought to market and traded. Here, Roman support and industry had provided the building materials, metalware and pottery for a strong community where the population was hard-working, good-natured and peaceful.

Constantinus and his warriors soon grew tired of following the trail of burned bodies, slaughtered livestock and charred fields that the barbarians left behind them. The desire to strike out at this band of Saxons was so intense that he ordered his column to begin a forced march as soon as smoke was sighted in the direction of Durobrivae.

The lands around the town were flat and ideal for agriculture. The landscape seemed to roll on forever, for the terrain was covered by a warm green and gold blanket that rose in the south and climbed slowly towards a series of low plateaux that were gently sloped and richly forested. If the Saxons were unaware of their presence, then they would be easily crushed by Constantinus's well-trained warriors, since this landscape offered few hiding places.

Or so Constantinus hoped. He had made an initial plan to bludgeon the northerners by unleashing his British cavalry at the throats of his enemy. His available intelligence indicated that the Saxon thane held command over a detachment roughly the same size as the British column. Although this group wasn't the hard core of the Saxon invasion force, the column was far too well armed and dangerous to be allowed freedom of movement.

Yet, with typical Roman arrogance, Constantinus anticipated that his column would have little difficulty in dealing with a band of poorly disciplined barbarians who had been laying siege to the town gates. The Saxons were using felled trees as battering rams to gain entrance, and Constantinus could hear the regular thud as the improvised rams hit the wooden gates, obstacles that shuddered and splintered with every blow.

The officers at the head of the cavalry column paused as Constantinus drew his horse to a sudden halt and turned in the saddle.

'Paulus! Command the left cavalry column! Vortigern! Oblige me by leading the right! At my order, each of your columns will advance and position yourselves so that you reach the enemy immediately before the centre column, which will be under my command. Gregorius! Stay with the foot soldiers and join us as soon as possible. With luck, the Saxons will all be dead before you have to engage with them. With the walls of Durobrivae at the Saxons' backs, our cavalry on each flank and my *cataphractii* attacking them from the front, there will be no escape for this band of northerners.'

Vortigern nodded. His dark eyes were both expressive and secretive, a mix that caused Constantinus to wonder what the Briton was thinking.

'Cassivellaunus? With me!' Cassivellaunus wondered, from behind his watchful eyes, whether his master was adhering to the maxim of holding his Roman minders close to him where he could watch their every movement.

Constantinus raised his arm high into the air and then, as the noonday sun caught his armlet, he lowered his hand with a fast, sweeping motion. Paulus and Vortigern pointed their swords towards the enemy, still a mile distant, and their horses moved forward at a brisk trot.

As the outer columns spread across the flat landscape, Constantinus dug his heels into the ribs of his own stallion. Like Flavius Magnus Maximus before him, he had taken to riding a white horse, large and showy, but so powerful that its massive hooves could crush a man's skull with ease. As his horse sprang forward, Cassivellaunus gave the signal to the cavalrymen behind and the British force moved to their front in three deadly and determined columns at a steady, mile-devouring pace. To the right and the left, the cavalrymen broke into a gallop and moved away from the centre column.

And then the Saxon thane looked up and saw the red cloaks and brazen helmets moving inexorably towards his warriors outside the walls of Durobrivae. Like a nest of disturbed ants, he began to organise his warriors into a defensive line of sorts, with the walls of Durobrivae behind them.

'For God and the High King,' Paulus roared, and his warriors repeated his war cry.

Then the right wing followed suit until their voices thundered from one hundred throats as the centre hailed their leader. At a gesture from Constantinus, the troop's horn sounded out its brazen note and the cavalry swept onward to send green swards flying in great clods of earth.

Constantinus's men hit the enemy at the centre of the Saxon line like a falling hammer. The Saxon warriors must have thought that Thor had frowned on them, for the trained horses of the Britons used their bulk and their hooves to smash the flimsy wood and oxhide shields to worthless shards. Their rapidly mounted defensive line bent inward until, falling back from the flying hooves, the entire Saxon defence began to give way. But there was nowhere that the northerners could retreat to, so the reserves behind the defensive line were forced to use their shields to cover their bleeding comrades and take their places in the front line. Like a grim dance of death, the British cavalrymen manoeuvred their mounts in deadly patterns until the wings hit simultaneously and crushed the Saxon defence with the momentum of their charge.

Lesser men than these ferocious warriors from the north would have fallen and surrendered under the brutal force of swords, metal shields and maddened horseflesh, but these Saxons were huge men who were all hair, muscle and raw courage – and they had no rational word for the concept of defeat. Surrender was unthinkable, even as the line gave way and the warriors felt the stone walls of Durobrivae at their backs. When the foot soldiers arrived at the dwindling Saxon line and the cavalry pulled back, the legionnaires set to work their way through a bloody slaughter that left the Saxons with no chance of survival. If any of their number had survived the rout that followed, they would have sung of the courage of Ranald Ox-killer and the red death that had befallen them at Durobrivae. But no warrior would live to tell the tale.

The aftermath to any battle, even a skirmish such as this confrontation proved to be, takes many hours to clean up and set the victor's house in order. The Roman legions had developed systems of discipline for dealing with the remains of enemies and friends, so Constantinus's force set to work with few orders and minimal supervision. The Saxons were quickly stripped of anything of any value and their corpses were dragged by un-willing horses into a large pile of naked flesh. Still other troops collected flammable materials from the shanties and huts clustered around the outer walls of Durobrivae. Meanwhile, the wounded and injured among the Britons were taken into the town where the local healers would do their best to hold back the onset of death. Here, too, Constantinus would accept the gratitude of the townsfolk, whose wealth was manifested in the golden chains slung around the necks of those merchants who came to bend their knee to the High King of the Britons.

By nightfall, funeral pyres had been lit to consume the remains of friend and foe for disease would grow at a prodigious rate if dead bodies were allowed to rot without burial or cremation. Black, oily smoke rose into a pall, dimming the sky.

The British and Roman dead went to their funeral pyres with their weapons and belongings intact, but this sign of respect wasn't extended to the Saxon warriors. Prayers were soon rising around the funeral pyre as a hastily found Christian priest offered Constantinus's dead their own bulwark against the darkness of death.

The foot soldiers set up a bivouac that would supplement the temporary encampment ordered by Constantinus to ensure the cavalry's security during the coming night. The king sighed with satisfaction as he settled himself into a simple hide tent that was no better than the facilities provided for his men. His acceptance of their living conditions surprised some of his warriors, because rumours quickly spread that he had been invited to rest for the night in any number of fine homes within the walls of the town.

'Why should our officers stay in camp, sir?' Paulus asked curiously, after he discovered that his master had refused an offer of hospitality from one of the town's wealthiest traders. 'As for the men, there are a number of stables within the walls where they could sleep for the night. I'm assured that the shopkeeper has a hypocaust, buxom slave girls and some of Hispania's best wines at his disposal. A night's fleecing by the locals would put smiles on the faces of our men.'

Paulus's contempt for the merchant class was obvious from his scathing description.

Constantinus allowed himself a grin. Men of the legions had little time for civilians, regardless of their status or wealth.

'I've slept under roofs for too long while I hungered to see the stars or enjoy the smell of wood smoke and the leather of my sleeping tent. Life as a king can be very pleasant for a time, but a soldier's bones turn to rust if he can't raise a sword or feel a good horse under him. I thought you'd understand what I mean, friend Paulus.'

'Aye! A fighting man lives best when he's in a good bivouac or on a battlefield.'

Constantinus slept soundly the night and, for once, no night terrors troubled his rest.

The morning sun came with rain in its teeth, so he wondered if he had been hasty when he had refused the pleasures of a warm, dry billet. Still, wet tunics and sodden boots were pleasures that tame husbands never knew; he was certain he would never miss the luxury of a bland existence.

Unfortunately, this rain could quickly obliterate the tracks of the main Saxon column. Constantinus struggled into his armour, while ignoring Paulus's advice that they might consider waiting until the downpour had passed.

'According to our scouts, the main force of our Saxon friends is on the move and they seem to be heading in a southerly direction. It's probable that they are ensconced in those hills by now, and they'll be reluctant to fight a battle if we give them too much of a start. But our pursuit will be far more difficult if all trace of their passage is lost in the rain and we have to find them again? No, Paulus! That's not acceptable, so we'll prepare ourselves for an immediate departure. I want to reach those hills before we camp again, regardless of the weather.'

'One of the local crofters told me that there's a confluence of rivers that rise in those hills, master. Beyond them are the forests of Anderida Silva and, beyond those, there are dangerous marshes that stretch along the coast. If the Saxons plan to rejoin their ceols with the plunder they've stolen, they will be forced to head for a suitable embarkation area. My crofter assured me that there is an area near Portus Lemanis where the Saxon ceols could be hidden, places where the raiders could load their pillaged wealth in their own time. It seems like good advice.'

Constantinus collapsed his tent with a few quick actions, while ignoring one of the grateful servants from the town who had offered to help with such mundane tasks.

'Your guesses have proved to be better than the certainties of my other officers, Paulus, so I thank you for them.'

The decurion strode away to see to Constantinus's horse with a satisfied smile on his lips. His superior officer was changing and had transformed himself from a centurion into a superb leader who could command an entire legion like the tribunes of old. Best of all, his master understood that the men he was leading were flesh and blood, rather than simply numbers who could be wasted without care or regard. If the God of Hosts, Mithras and the old gods in the dead temples remained true to Constantinus, then his master would grow in the coming years until even the wide plains of Gallia became a part of his fiefdom.

CHAPTER XVI

AMBITION AND LIES

Pecunia non olet.
Money has no smell.

Vespasian, Suetonius: *Lives of the Caesars*

'Report, Vortigern!' the king snapped, his face furrowed in frustration at the pursuit of an elusive Saxon enemy.

An obviously weary Vortigern climbed down from his mare, wiped his sweating forehead and removed his helmet with a muffled curse. With a flash of resentment, he wished his master would at least permit him to dismount before making his demands.

Constantinus noticed immediately that a small blood-trail was trickling from a scab on the warrior's forehead.

He ignored the trivial wound, although he could see that Vortigern's arms were also spattered with blood, up to the elbows, despite the attempts that the Briton had made to wash and tidy his person before making his report to his master.

'I've damn little intelligence that will please you, sire,' Vortigern responded, although he wasn't so foolish as to show signs of anger before his liege lord. Even so, Constantinus's forehead furrowed further at this young man's clipped tone. His fingers began to drum on the folding table top inside the command tent as if they had a separate life to that of his arms or his body.

Vortigern was immediately on his guard. He was aware that the king's temper had grown shorter as the campaign against the Saxons had dragged on ... and on.

'The main Saxon force of about three hundred men had been divided into a number of smaller groups before we were in sight of Durovernum, and these columns headed into the south, the east and the west in such a manner that we could never have predicted their movements. I decided to follow the largest group of men, some ninety or more, who were heading into the south. Unfortunately, the bastards vanished into a forested wilderness in the only high ground between the town and the ocean. It took us a day and a half before we picked up their tracks again and decided they were heading towards Rutupiae. At that point, I began to wonder whether they were travelling towards some prearranged rendezvous with their ceols or, alternatively, they might have been trying to lure us into an ambush that would stop us from harassing their main column.

'But I was wrong, damn them! During the night, they divided again with such speed and dash that we totally missed the ruse until it was too late. We managed to redeem our error when we cornered one small band of ten men who had laid waste to a small village that didn't even have a name. We put those warriors to the sword.'

Vortigern's voice was tinged with regret as he described the tiny farming hamlet that had held some half-dozen structures.

316

Every woman, child and old man in the small stone crofts had been slaughtered and their bodies left to rot where they fell. The absence of able-bodied farmers had told Vortigern that the Cantii king must have stripped this tiny hamlet of all protection by conscripting every male over fifteen years to serve in the defence of his lands. The pitchforks and hoes used by the old men and young boys in the village had been no match when pitted against the abilities of experienced Saxon warriors.

Vortigern's voice remained flat and unemotional. The kinglet usually displayed a sense of drama that tended to turn the most prosaic engagements into a tale of intrigue, heroism and adventure. Unfortunately for Vortigern, Constantinus sensed that the unspoken details of this encounter and the chase of the last two weeks were a source of shame for him.

'What do you mean? Ten men? Ten fucking men? How did the other eighty manage to escape? They were afoot, and you were in command of fifty cavalrymen, weren't you? Explain yourself, Vortigern! You seem to have lost track of a sizeable war party.'

Vortigern flushed an ugly plum shade across his sharp cheekbones and the colour extended down his face and neck to disappear beneath his body armour. This Demetae chieftain was a patient and calculating leader, a young man who controlled his emotions in order to achieve greater prizes than the spoils won through displays of hot temper or vanity. But Constantinus's biting scorn had struck at his manhood, so his eyes narrowed to muddy green slits.

'They are afoot, sire, but I know that you're as aware of the abilities of these barbarians as I am. They have incredible reserves of strength and stamina, so they can run the whole day through while only resting briefly to piss and drink. They're masters of the art of travelling far and fast, and then fighting with demonic skill at the end of their journey.'

Vortigern paused to consider his next words.

'Their reserves of strength are amazing, sir, as we've all discovered during the past month. They use the terrain to their advantage and they disappear whenever they encounter stone, shale or any other terrain where they can't be tracked. They forgo cooking fires, so there's little sign of them until they destroy a village or put some isolated farm to the torch. We'd have missed the ten men we *did* kill, but the hay barn at the croft caught fire and the smoke alerted us to their presence. Even then, they would have eluded us, but one of the farmers had five sons who were almost fully grown. The boys were determined to protect their mother, and they resisted their murderers until just before we happened upon them. It was serendipity!'

'Serendipity, Vortigern? Did Fortuna spin her wheel and bless the Saxons again?'

'At least we killed this group of Saxons, although they won the sort of deaths that the bastards seem to crave. For them, a good death is one where they enter the shades with a sword in their hands. Well, we acceded to their wishes, but their demise was far too fast for my liking.' Vortigern tried to disguise the petulance in his voice, but Constantinus missed nothing.

The High King scratched at a week's growth of black stubble on his chin with the irritation of a man who prefers to be clean-shaven.

'We may have lopped the odd leg from the main body of barbarians, sire, but they grow another limb quickly enough . . . or they seem to. But we're still no closer to finding the bastards and their encampment.'

Constantinus rose to his feet and began to pace impatiently within the confines of his tent.

'Call Gregorius, Cassivellaunus and Paulus to me. Then find Drusus! I'm sick of stumbling around in the dark in search of an enemy that I can't see. We need to develop a strategic plan so we can regain the initiative. Durobrivae was easily won ... too easily, in fact, and I'd forgotten the chief lesson of any successful battle.'

'What's that, sire?' Vortigern couldn't resist asking.

'A commander is only as good as his last victory! We should never take our enemies for granted.'

While trying to appear untroubled, Vortigern saluted his master, picked up his discarded helmet and trotted off to find the Roman advisers. He was grateful for the respite, even if it was only temporary.

You almost got caught out then, you idiot, Vortigern upbraided himself mentally as he explained the king's demands to Paulus. He nearly had me today ... and he was right! I've wasted two weeks hunting for those Saxon bastards – and I've got shite to show for it.

Paulus gazed at Vortigern's feral eyes and wondered why he spent so much time in the company of his master. Obviously, Vortigern was a cautious leader who was still learning his craft, but Paulus could see no liking for Constantinus in those jade-green eyes. At this point, the decurion forced the demands of his duty to brush away the qualms that he always felt when he spent time with this cunning and self-serving Briton.

After scrubbing his arms, torso and head in a water bucket intended for the horses on the picket line, Vortigern harassed his body-servant until the hapless man found him a clean tunic, undershirt and fresh leather trews to replace his ragged and travel-stained clothing that had been worn for so many weeks. His mail was spattered with clotted blood, but any cleansing of this essential armour would have to wait. Attending Constantinus's conference took precedence over all else if Vortigern was to further his own ambitions and enhance the prospects of the Demetae people. His recent failings must be mitigated if he was to consolidate his position as one of Constantinus's favourites.

Fate had given an unusual facial feature to the Demetae ruler. The corners of his upper lip turned upwards, even in repose, so he seemed to have a smile permanently affixed to his face. When he was very angry, his unintentional smile could freeze the blood of the strongest man. The king had marked Vortigern down as one who was prepared to play the part of a sycophant to achieve his own secret ambitions.

Constantinus understood and approved of these ambitions, but trusting the young man was another matter altogether. And so it was that the two rulers plotted and counter-plotted in a game of personal and political intrigue that was fundamental to their natures.

Now, as Vortigern entered the High King's war tent, he saw that the two Roman advisers were already seated on folding stools as they drank wine. Constantinus's legionnaires had captured a wagon laden with the best Hispanic wines during the battle outside the gates of Durobrivae where Ranald Ox-killer, the Saxon war chief, had perished with many of his subordinates. This engagement, which cost the Saxons an entire column from their fighting force, near enough to a hundred and fifty men, had proved to be the only battle of significance between the Romano-British troops and the northern invaders during the long, two-month campaign.

The High King was seething with frustration. He gazed intently at the officers in the tent until their eyes dropped before his uncompromising expression.

'Vortigern has been led on a merry chase through the eastern fields beyond Durovernum by these Saxons who melt away like shadows in the night. We should be grateful that he managed to catch ten of the Saxons who were too slow to elude him. Meanwhile, the abbey near Durovernum was attacked after nightfall and the brothers were slaughtered at the altar of their church. The entire store of holy relics, as well as the gold plate, silver ingots and the treasure of the Cantii tribe that had been stored in the church's crypts, was hauled away by our enemies in stolen wagons.'

He paused. His advisers were attempting, and failing, to face him with equanimity.

'I await your report on anything of substance that your scouts have discovered, Paulus.'

Paulus placed the wine jug on one of the small tables and positioned himself so he could deliver his report. He cleared his throat noisily, aware that the advisers provided by Tribune Maximo considered him to be their inferior in every way.

'Lord, I would have informed you earlier of the news I am about to convey to you, but I wanted to await the arrival of Drusus who has only just returned from our scouting mission. It is important that the intelligence he has gleaned from his mission should be included in this report.'

Paulus cleared his throat again, while the advisers fiddled with their tunics or their armour to suggest their lack of respect for this relatively junior officer.

'At any road, my lord, you instructed me to carry out a short scouting mission with a small force of twenty cavalrymen. It was a mixed group of Britons and Roman-trained men that included Drusus as our scout. We were instructed to follow in the footsteps of an earlier patrol carried out by Lord Vortigern. I was happy to carry out this mission because the lads I took with me are superior to twice that number of Saxons.'

As the decurion spoke, Vortigern bridled at Constantinus's lack of trust and stole a brief glance at the High King before realising that the commander's face was hiding a sense of satisfaction behind his clenched hands.

So that's the way the land lies, does it? Vortigern thought. Interesting! I would have thought that all Romans would stick together. Well! Well!

'As with Vortigern's experience, I soon discovered that the Saxons divided their war party again and again in an obvious ploy that was designed to confuse us. It's clear to me that they are a large raiding party whose prime purpose is to pillage and plunder, but they are also keen to hide their actual numbers from us. Their commander is also trying to confuse those of us who want him to commit to making a stand in a set-piece battle. Sending his warriors in diverse directions at the same time served all his purposes. He has no intention of fighting a decisive battle with our force. Several of my lads are excellent scouts, so I stayed put and sent Drusus and my own men out to determine the exact location of the Saxon patrols. When the bulk of the warriors eventually re-formed into their original units, my men realised that their quarry was following a semi-circular route that would bring them back towards Durobrivae.'

Paulus paused before making his final comments.

'Drusus is an excellent scout who is hard to fool, my lord, as you will be aware from personal experience. I have complete faith in his observations.'

Constantinus nodded, but the advisers refused to accept Paulus's professional summary of the Saxon's intentions.

'They've fooled you as well,' Cassivellaunus sneered, while Vortigern felt the palm of his right hand itch to strike at the Roman's smooth, scornful face. As always, he was suggesting that the warrior class of Britannia couldn't be relied upon to make rational assessments on strategic matters. Vortigern had heard rumours of Cassivellaunus's antipathy for those men, especially Britons, whom the patrician considered to be his inferiors.

Fortunately, Paulus ignored Cassivellaunus's bad manners and continued. 'It is true that the Saxons caught us napping for a time ... but men afoot can't mislead good horsemen forever. I've been a Roman officer for too long, gentlemen, to put my trust in what the enemy *appears* to be doing. Anyone who trusts to luck when making assessments of their enemies is bound to fail.'

'Good man!' Constantinus murmured. His voice was soft but, nonetheless, Paulus flushed with pleasure at this compliment from his master.

'We followed the pack of men that was led by a tall bear of a man, who stood half a head taller than his fellows and outweighed them by the weight of a ten-year-old child. But he moved as fast as any of his warriors and was always at the forefront of each column. I took him to be the thane, even when the columns divided again and the larger group left him behind.'

Cassivellaunus clicked his tongue in dismissal but, true to his name, Gregorius the Watcher fixed his gaze on Paulus as the scout went on.

'Eventually, except for one of the token forces that Vortigern had pursued by accident, the different bands combined once again, turned in a new direction, and set off towards

Durovernum as if Satan was pursuing them. We couldn't be certain whether this change of direction wasn't another ruse, but we kept to whatever cover we could find and followed them as closely as possible. I hazarded a guess that their ultimate destination was an abbey situated some distance beyond the walls of the town.'

'Did you warn the abbot that his flock was in danger?' Cassivellaunus demanded.

'When I became certain that Durovernum was their target, I sent a courier directly to the abbot to warn him that an attack was imminent. My man, a sturdy young Briton who is an excellent horseman, barely got away before the commencement of the attack. The abbot refused to budge and averred that his duty was to guard his church. According to my lad, the abbot had called the whole community together to discuss the matter within the confines of the church. They were wasting valuable time, but he gave his people the option of staying with him when he attempted to reason with the Saxons . . . or they could travel to safety! Several of the laymen chose to escape, but fifty men chose to protect their church with their prayers.'

Cassivellaunus spat on the bare sod in disgust, although the king raised an eyebrow at the crudity.

'So you left those brave men to perish without attempting to stop the Saxons,' Cassivellaunus snapped. 'For shame, Paulus! Although I can't fathom whether more can be expected from men whose origins are so deeply rooted in the lower ranks.'

The temperature in the tent seemed to drop at this; Vortigern was surprised that the adviser's breath didn't freeze in the resultant chill.

'My own origins lie in the lower ranks of the Roman legions,' Constantinus stated with a mere hint of anger in his voice.

'Just like those of Paulus, Drusus and their forebears. Are you suggesting that we are lacking in courage and loyalty?'

Constantinus spoke with such silky and careful courtesy that only the most foolish of men could mistake his dulcet tones for a genuine inquiry. Cassivellaunus began to stammer out an apology, but the king waved it away.

'Continue, Paulus.'

'I was heavily outnumbered, my king, and the deaths of my lads would have been of no material advantage to you or to the brothers who were determined to remain inside the abbey. Some of my men had already been despatched on scouting duties, for we were still trying to locate our elusive enemies. I decided to wait and follow the Saxons once they left the religious community. The abbey was situated outside the walls of Durovernum and was some small distance into the countryside, so I hoped that the people of the town might go to the defence of the abbot and his flock, but this hope was doomed to disappointment. The fire at the abbey was very fierce and the flames lit the sky throughout the night, so none of the town's citizens could ever state that they had no knowledge of the fate inflicted on the good brothers. They knew what was happening, but they had no wish to join the priests in death. After all, they are civilians.

'Along with my two remaining scouts, I spent the night on a wooded rise beyond the abbey's boundaries. Shortly after dawn, we saw four wagons travelling along the track that led away from the abbey. These were so heavily laden with plunder that the carthorses struggled to haul the weight. I reasoned that our best chance to find the Saxon's temporary base would be to follow the wagons. We gave them a few hours' start and then followed the wheel ruts.'

'So you know where the Saxons are camped?' Constantinus breathed.

'The Saxons' baggage train has grown in size, sir. They've thrown together stolen wagons and enough horses to transport all the precious objects and they've begun to move, slowly but steadily, towards the coast.'

Constantinus's black eyes burned and, despite his fierce courage, Vortigern felt the palms of his hands grow damp as the High King turned towards him.

'Where are they headed, Vortigern? Only madmen would dare to sail through the Litus Saxonicum and the oceans beyond it in the gales of winter, and the Saxons have proved they aren't fools. What say you?'

Cassivellaunus muttered something in a strangled exhalation of annoyance. Constantinus's eyes flared for a moment in response to the rudeness of the interruption, but he chose to ignore it

Meanwhile, Vortigern licked his lips in an unattractive way that reminded Constantinus of a snake or a lizard tasting the air for danger. With some reluctance, the Briton began to explain.

'I'm prepared to hazard an opinion, sir. Portus Lemanis is a likely township that lies in a direct line with the general route that the Saxons have been following. But the thanes would have to be crazed if they tried to load their ceols with plunder at a functioning British port. I'd be prepared to guess that they've found a suitable isolated cove within the difficult terrain that lies to the west of Portus Lemanis where they could beach their ceols. Once established there, they could load their plunder without harassment or threat.'

'I agree with your assessment, Vortigern. You've salvaged some useful intelligence out of the chaos, mainly through the efforts of Drusus. Still, I'm indebted to you for your advice . . . and I don't forget my friends.'

The unspoken phrase, *and my enemies*, was as clear as if he had uttered it aloud.

'If we are going to filch their supplies, we'll have to attack the wagon train while we can,' Cassivellaunus stated decisively, as if no other option was available for consideration.

'Is that your recommendation, Cassivellaunus?' Constantinus asked quietly.

'Absolutely!' the adviser exclaimed. His patrician nose was raised into the air as if something putrid had fouled the space around him.

'And you, Gregorius. Do you agree?'

Gregorius felt the firm sod beginning to open up under the heels of his sandals, so his voice sounded hollow and indecisive when he finally cleared his throat to speak.

'I'd need to know the location of the main body of Saxons before I committed myself to capturing and protecting a slow-moving baggage train. If our intelligence indicates that we can overpower and capture those wagons without any real difficulty, logic suggests that the Saxons can just as easily take them back again when our own escape had been slowed by the weight of so much silver and treasure. There's no point in risking our warriors for the gains are minimal.'

Cassivellaunus was furious at this assessment.

'I hadn't thought to hear such cowardly caution from you, Gregorius. When did you trade your balls for a grand-dam's bonnet or an old man's slippers? You're suggesting that our troop of Roman-trained legionnaires and warriors can't protect a baggage train from a few Saxon guards and wagon-drivers. For shame, Gregorius!'

Gregorius flushed, but he refused to be cowed.

'The baggage train is so slow that they can't *possibly* escape us. Why should we have the speed of our cavalry impeded by lugging such an unwieldy burden behind us? As I've already explained, we'd almost certainly lose it again as fast as we capture it.'

Cassivellaunus stuck out his bottom lip and jaw aggressively.

'We must take it because that wealth is ours. Those wagons contain *our* spoils! And these Saxon bastards must be taught that they can't pillage Roman possessions with impunity.' Gregorius flinched, but refused to back down.

'You're wrong, Cassivellaunus,' Constantinus interrupted. 'Those spoils are *ours*. They are the property of the good people of Britannia who were robbed, killed and enslaved by these particular Saxons, rather than yourself or the Roman legion. Rome and her last British legion that sits in bivouac in the north have nothing whatsoever to do with the carnage that these invaders have inflicted on Londinium and the Cantii lands. Nor is that stolen wealth the prize of Rome or the tribune who governs my lands from his sanctuary in Isca. Perhaps I will send a share to our Roman governor from the people of Britannia as a gesture of good faith, but I'm not obligated to give Rome a cracked copper. I am the High King of Britannia and I'll decide when my force attacks this baggage train. Meanwhile, I can assure you that I have no intention of riding blindly into strange hills and areas of dense forest without intelligence obtained by my scouts, warriors who are already seeking out the enemy while we sit here in relative safety.'

He stared directly at Cassivellaunus until the adviser dropped his eyes; Constantinus permitted himself a brief smile.

'Do *you* accept my decision, Cassivellaunus?'

Vortigern recognised the danger immediately and lowered his own head in total acquiescence.

Constantinus's tone was friendly and reasonable, but the most junior officer present knew whose authority was paramount within this campaign tent.

An unlovely shade of purple began to stain Cassivellaunus's neck and his pale eyes flashed with anger. Even as Gregorius tried to catch his compatriot's eyes to urge caution, Cassivellaunus launched himself into a provocative speech.

'You forget yourself, Constantinus. You have no gens that will render you superior to your tribune, the Roman who is the legally appointed governor of this province. You've been permitted to exercise the privileges of your current position because of your superior officer's generosity. Had I been the man to choose Maximus's successor, I wouldn't have chosen a landless, nameless man who can't even be sure of his parentage. Your pater probably tilled the fields of Italia or Hispania?'

The silence inside the tent was gelid with danger as Constantinus carefully and quietly rose to his feet.

Gregorius could see that disaster was imminent, and knew he should keep his mouth firmly shut but, for once, the Watcher inside him chose to act out of character.

'Cassivellaunus is speaking without thought, sire,' Gregorius stuttered, his heart pounding as he searched for some way to save the skin of his fellow Roman.

'I spoke the truth, and I'll not resile from anything that I've said,' Cassivellaunus repeated, unaware of the sudden space around him as every officer in the room moved away from possible contamination.

'Sire,' Gregorius began again. 'Forgive him if he has caused offence, because he doesn't really understand the true political situation, either in Britannia or in Gallia. His opinions are those of a bone-headed patrician, sire, and he'll cease to offer threats or insults if you should accept his apologies ...'

'I don't apologise to anyone, least of all to the bastard Roman king of a backward province like Britannia.'

'Enough!' Constantinus's voice would have broken stone. The single word cracked like a heavy blow of an axe.

For the first time, Cassivellaunus really looked at the king and, all too late, realised he'd gone too far.

'Paulus! Oblige me by taking my adviser into custody and chaining him carefully. This man speaks open treason and has insulted my person, my throne and the kings of this land. I'll pronounce judgement on him when I have the leisure to bother with this trivial matter.'

'You can't ...!' Cassivellaunus began, while his face whitened around the gills.

'As the High King of the Britons and Dux Bellorum of these lands, I think you'll find that I can do anything, and everything, that I wish,' Constantinus answered dismissively.

Paulus attempted to lead the adviser out of the tent by his elbow. Then, as Cassivellaunus tore his arm from the grip of the decurion, two more legionnaires entered the flap of the tent, moved forward and pinioned him by both arms. Cassivellaunus's rage was so intemperate that he tried to kick out at his captors.

'What shall I do with him, my lord?' Paulus asked.

'Send him back to Durobrivae under guard. You won't need more than a couple of men if they ensure that the prisoner's arms and legs are manacled. He has the manners of a pig and the fighting skills of my old mother, so he's likely to hurt himself if he is given any freedom. The magistrate at Durobrivae, who owes me the freedom of his city, will oblige me in this matter. When I have time, Cassivellaunus, you'll be judged, found guilty and executed. I have no doubt that everything I have done in past months has been reported back to Isca, and thence to Rome, from the first day you were inflicted upon me. I detest traitors at the best of times and you are one of the vilest traitors that I've seen. You've also proved to be one of the most arrogant and stupid men to serve under my command. You should be executed for your incompetence as an adviser, but I'll stay with the greater charges of treason. I don't need a hammer to crush an ant.'

Cassivellaunus snivelled and tried to offer an explanation as he realised the danger of his situation. He scanned the room as he sought a means of escape or some ally who might be prepared to save him from the wrath of the king, but found neither.

'You won't execute me, Constantinus! Tribune Maximo would march against you if you harmed me in any way. He knows that I have an uncle in the senate and my family has served the empire for generations. Rome would never tolerate the murder of one of her sons.'

'Rome isn't Britannia, Cassivellaunus. Your tongue became the death of you, so I'll bid you good riddance. Remove him, Paulus, before I lose patience and cut his throat immediately.'

Arguing, struggling and crying out for rescue, Cassivellaunus was dragged away, leaving a nasty silence in his wake. For his part, Gregorius tried to look insignificant. He knew that something important had occurred before his eyes but, as yet, was unable to arrive at a rational analysis of the events that had taken place.

In truth, he was terrified. Meanwhile, Constantinus sat back in his folding camp-chair and examined the surviving Roman adviser through his dark, basilisk eyes.

'I have no argument with you, Gregorius, as long as you understand that I am the High King of Britannia and I intend to be treated with respect. The pleas you made in defence of Cassivellaunus have done you no harm in my eyes. In fact, you showed unusual courage when you tried to provide the fool with an opportunity to back down without too much shame. But you would be unwise to push your supposed superiority at me. And you should avoid lecturing me on decisions I might contemplate when you are speaking on behalf of your Roman masters.'

Gregorius wondered what had happened to the capable and reasoned centurion who had been elevated to the throne of High King in the teeth of his tribune's objections. At first he had considered Constantinus to be a harmless, easily guided choice, a man who would follow the orders of his Roman masters to the letter.

The advisor's thoughts were interrupted when Constantinus cleared his throat impatiently. The other officers were staring at Gregorius, waiting for a response from him. He gulped.

'I cannot justify my compatriot's actions, my lord. We both know that he has spoken imprudently on a number of occasions and he cherishes many of the prejudices that are common to his class. Unfortunately, Cassivellaunus has little understanding of the politics that he espouses. He's a babe in the game of diplomacy, so I'd be failing in my duty to my Roman masters if I hadn't asked you to show a little clemency towards him.'

'Would you have me show weakness to a man who speaks treason? Too many legionnaires and warriors have heard Cassivellaunus's insolent comments about the way I've conducted this campaign, but tonight's insults finally sealed his fate. He chose his own pathway to the shades, and so will you if you demonstrate that you can't be trusted. The question I am now asking is whether your allegiance is to me as the High King of the Britons, or to Tribune Maximo and the patricians of Rome?'

Knowing that Gregorius was an honourable man who took any oath seriously, Constantinus had manoeuvred him into a position where he could either swear his allegiance to the High King or risk execution by revealing his true loyalty to Rome. Constantinus was prepared to accept that Gregorius would consider his oath as binding if he swore to serve as Constantinus's vassal.

Finally, because he was an optimist, Gregorius made his choice. Better to be a live mouse than a dead lion!

I was foolish when I lauded Maximo's decision to support Constantinus's elevation, Gregorius thought regretfully, but I was convinced at the time that his choice was wise and considered. Ultimately, the centurion had trapped the tribune and, by God, he's also trapped me.

'My allegiance is to *you*, sire, for you are the protector of these isles. When I was given the task of coming to your court as one of your advisers, I came with the knowledge that I was expected to serve the newly crowned High King of the Britons in order to save this Roman province from the barbarians. As a Roman, I love and honour my ancestry, so I pray that I'll never find my loyalties are divided in such a way that I am forced to make an unwanted choice.'

Tribune Maximo had instructed him to remain close to the High King and influence his policy-making. Gregorius, a politician by nature, must entertain the hope that he could live by this oath.

The tribune had intended that Constantinus would never be more than a figurehead, saddled with the doubtful glory of spending his days repelling the increasingly insistent waves of barbarians who invaded Britannia's shores during the spring and summer months. But he had proved to be a true High King, a ruler who desired to bring peace and prosperity to these troubled lands.

Why did this British pimple on the backside of the world continue to produce so many political difficulties for Rome and its emperors? Gregorius thought back to the Iceni bitch who almost defeated the legions in bygone days. And, in recent times, Magnus Maximus had miraculously won the approval of the British kings and eventually attacked Rome herself. Maximus had damned near beaten the power of Rome. Against all logic, the isles had produced an emperor, no matter how briefly. Could it do so again? Just as the ancient kingdom of Judea had produced so many God-crazed challengers to Roman authority, so the populace of Britannia had given birth to their own line of successful rebels. Was another emperor rising to power before the advisor's terrified eyes?

'Please, God! Not again,' he whispered softly, then immediately began to wonder whether he could have been overheard. One of the servants was filling the goblets from a flagon; Gregorius accepted the fine red wine and gulped it down in one long swallow. The smooth, Hispanic liquor warmed his belly, but it had done nothing to wash away his fear.

'You spoke, Gregorius?' Constantinus demanded.

'Me?' The single word left Gregorius's mouth in a foolish squeak that forced Constantinus to hide a smile behind his hand. 'No, sire! I was reflecting on whether Britannia might yet avoid a costly campaign with the attendant loss of life.'

'Then you must devise more effective plans, Gregorius, and create better strategies that will kill the barbarians while protecting our own warriors.' Constantinus was perfectly relaxed as he sat at his ease, but his eyes were drilling through Gregorius's skull.

In a lucid moment, Gregorius sensed that there had been a certain rehearsed quality to the rage inflicted on Cassivellaunus, as if Constantinus had been considering this action for some time and had waited for an excuse to put his secret plans into action. Was Cassivellaunus, dead or alive, just another pawn in one of the High King's plots?

The flesh on Gregorius's forearms began to pimple with an imagined chill. His mouth was dry and he tried to remove the gravel from his throat before he answered.

Please, God, don't let this Constantinus be another Maximus. The West couldn't endure another protracted war . . . and Rome would have difficulty in defending herself if she had to throw off a determined attack by a pretender, especially one with the legions at his back.

But that day won't dawn if I can help it, Gregorius thought. Rising to his feet, he bowed to make his departure and recognised a glint of satisfaction in Constantinus's eyes.

Two weeks later, after entering an unforgiving expanse of swampy water, sucking mud and shifting sands, interspersed with isolated areas of firm earth filled with stunted trees and tracts of spiky ground cover, the Saxon thane discovered that Constantinus's mixed force of Britons and Romans had moved into an almost unassailable defensive position that blocked the Saxon advance towards the ceols awaiting them in a secret cove to the west of Portus Lemanis. He'd been given no choice. He couldn't outflank his enemy, so he must fight his way through their ranks if he was to make good his escape.

There was a single narrow track through the swamps. Overgrown, and almost impassable, it was the only route that could be followed by warriors through the dangerous terrain. But these Saxons were also burdened by wagons filled with heavy treasure.

The thane had despatched scouts who discovered that the Britons had straddled this route through the swamps that could take them to their ceols. But, along the track, intermittent patches of firm earth would permit some slow movement of the wagons as long as the warriors were prepared to dig out the huge wooden wheels whenever the wagons became bogged down in mud. What was originally determined to be a laborious, albeit passable, route to the coast had committed the thane to a pitched battle against a large force of Roman-trained infantry and cavalrymen.

Beached on the shingles of the cove, some of the boats were already awaiting the returning raiders, while others remained afloat and waited their turn to beach themselves. But the main force of Saxon warriors and their baggage train was trapped inland.

The thane met with his subordinates to consider the options available to them. The treasure in the wagons mustn't be risked, so a decision was made to hide the heavy carts among a small stand of forest on the last sizeable strip of dry ground before the Saxons entered the swamps. Guarded by a few reluctant warriors who could be spared from the battle soon to come, the treasure could still be moved to the beaches by hand if the swamps proved impassable to wagons after the hated Romans had been vanquished.

Then, once the treasure was secured, the thane sent scouts to the ceols in the cove by a circuitous route, carrying orders that the seamen must wait, under pain of death and accusations of cowardice, until after the battle was fought to its conclusion. The thane could imagine no worse fate for his warriors than being marooned in Britannia for another winter.

The scene was set, and the time for a final confrontation had arrived.

As soon as Constantinus's scouts had informed him that the Saxon ships had appeared in the small cove and some of the ceols had been beached on the shingle above the high-water mark, he sprang into action.

The Saxon force must be outflanked, so Constantinus must march his columns around it until he reached Portus Lemanis, then travel along the coast for a short distance before selecting a suitable stretch of coastal land where he could carry out an ambush that would halt the raiders as they attempted to make good their escape.

A forced march had brought the legionnaires to a small strip of dry land a little over a hundred feet wide and surrounded by many miles of treacherous swamplands. Even if the Saxons tried to outflank their enemy, their efforts would be doomed to failure for control of the cove and the embarkation beaches was the sole objective for the Saxon thane. His only option was a direct assault on the defensive positions selected by Constantinus.

From this strip of firm earth, Constantinus's men could hack their enemies to pieces before they reached the sands.

There was no other way that the Saxons could return to their ships.

Unfortunately for the Romano-British defenders, the terrain

was so treacherous that their cavalry were at a distinct disadvantage. Constantinus must relinquish his greatest tactical resource and confront the taller and heavier Saxons, face to face, without the benefit of his *cataphractii*. In a swamp or in scrubby terrain, his men would be forced to fight, mired in mud or entangled in heavy brush, so only the most determined and ruthless leader could hope to prevail.

The tired legionnaires were set to work with axes, clearing the chosen field of combat and erecting obstacles that would slow the attacking Saxons.

Constantinus had the advantage of choosing the battleground and had seized the initiative by selecting the best defensive position. Here his legionnaires waited for the Saxons to make their attack.

Once his men had bedded themselves down in sand and mud, Constantinus was grateful for the battles he had fought throughout Britannia where the landscape had been as fierce an enemy as his redoubtable barbarian opponents. Those experiences would save many lives.

Around the two forces lay a morass of swamps, a network of salt water, sharp grasses, stinging insects, mud and quicksand that might cause wary men to make mistakes. But would the Saxons remain wary? So far, Constantinus's force had remained invisible to the skeleton crews on the ceols although it was likely that some of the Saxon scouts knew of its presence. With his usual care, he ordered his own scouts to keep the boats and their crews under observation, and to inform him if there was activity behind his rear.

'Could the Saxons drive us into the swamps if they were able to hit us in a concerted rush?' Gregorius asked, while sharpening his blunt gladius. He'd been spared from the dangers of combat throughout his years of diplomatic service, so his weapon had never been used in anger.

'Of course! I'll speak to the men before first light, so I'll explain the likely course of events then,' Constantinus replied, his face alive with excitement at the prospect of battle. Gregorius shook his head in surprise at this love of combat. For his part, he was terrified of being seen as a coward or incompetent, so the anticipation on Constantinus's face was both inexplicable and vaguely comforting.

'There's no chance that the thanes will order an attack at night,' Constantinus added. 'Only a suicidal fool would try to find their way through the swamps in the dark, so the men can get some sleep and waken before first light.'

In a corner of Constantinus's tent that had been erected at the highest point of the perimeter, Paulus was working with a whetstone and polishing cloths to clean and sharpen his master's weapons. The High King's armour was waiting, glowing and burnished and ready for use. He preferred clean lines for any protective plate iron, so no embellishments had been used. Paulus partly regretted this, because the armour failed to celebrate his master's power and importance. Yet, practical soldier that he was, Paulus recognised that the unadorned metal offered no flourishes that could guide a blade into unprotected flesh. In his understanding of the tools of war, Constantinus was still a centurion at heart.

As the night dragged on, the sentries along the perimeter crept between the defensive positions like ghosts. Meanwhile, men tried to sleep, knowing that the dawn might bring the last light that their eyes would ever see. Those who managed to doze were restless and, occasionally, a man would call out in his sleep, only to be hushed by his fellow warriors. For his part, Paulus missed the soft noses of the horses on the picket lines and the sounds of harness jingling as scouts moved beyond the camp in the seamless, ceaseless patterns of patrol.

But his master was sleepless and hunched over a smoking lamp, writing on an old scroll that had been scraped clean again and again so that the hide was worn and thin to the touch. Constantinus wrote to his son, Constans, for he realised that a long-held dream was now within his reach. Constans must be made aware of his plans; his grown son would become the proof of his mastery in the days to come, if God or the Devil permitted Constantinus to survive the coming battle.

'I'll have my way or perish, by God,' Constantinus swore, as he signed his name with a flourish at the bottom of the scroll. Then he carefully rolled the parchment and slipped it into its hide and brass sheath before sealing the container with a gobbet of wax. Before the wax had cooled, he placed his dragon intaglio ring into it to sign his name so that even the illiterate would know it was a message from their High King.

This scroll belongs to Constantinus, the High King of the Britons.

Then, as his summoned courier came to the tent flap, Constantinus gave the man his orders. The young Briton's face dropped.

'But I won't be here for the battle, sire,' he complained.

'You'll be serving me in a task that is far more important than using your sword. Be careful to avoid the Saxons when you make your way to our picket lines, and then you must ride hard and fast. Much depends on your swiftness and courage.'

'May I return as soon as I have completed your task, Highness?' the young warrior begged.

'Of course! In any event, I expect that there will be a reply to my message,' Constantinus answered and clapped the Dumnonii youth on the shoulder with easy familiarity. The lad flushed with pleasure and pride.

In the semi-darkness of his tent, Constantinus eventually slept, while Paulus watched over him. The night wore away with infinite slowness until the first rays of scarlet blood streaked their way across the black horizon in the east.

The time for testing, for Constantinus and Britannia, had finally come.

The Battle at
Portus Lemanis

Saxon wagons on
high, firm ground

2 The second wave
attacks when the first
wave reaches dry earth

Small mound
where the last of the
Saxons were killed

1 The first wave
blunted by cast spears

Vortigern's
counter attack
from the west

Constantinus's
counter attack

Arrow attack

Arrow
attack

Archers

Archers

Supply
wagon

Flags and
banners

King's tent
and the eagles

British defence

Firm earth in swamp

To picket line

nb. Roman legionnaires
are placed in the
front lines

Swampy land

Low cliffs

Small band of Saxons

Cove

Pebbled and sandy beach

Saxon ceols drawn up to be loaded

Other ceols anchored offshore

CHAPTER XVII

TO GAIN AN EMPIRE

I hate and I love: Why I do so you may well ask.
I do not know, but I felt it happen and am in agony.

Catullus, *Carmina*, No 85

To my eldest, well-loved son, Constans.
Hail and all happiness to you. I trust you are healthy and content
with your stepmother in Venta Belgarum? Assure her of my continued
love and gratitude for the care she gives to all my children.

Severa peered over her stepson's shoulder so she could read the
spidery writing on the well-scraped hide. Her hands were
clenching at a fold in her skirts so strongly that her knuckles
were shining like polished ivory. Oblivious to her discomfort,
Constans read to himself while mouthing the words silently and
opening the scroll so slowly that Severa longed to snatch the
missive from his hands.

We are currently camped in the swamps, waiting for dawn and a
Saxon attack. They must come to us through dangerous terrain, so I

hope the force of their charge will be blunted. As this battle will decide the success or failure of the whole campaign, I am a little nervous. Be assured that I will win, for all my plans hang upon victory. Pray for my success, my son.

You must never believe that these Saxons are easy to kill, Constans. They stand half a head taller than I do and, as you know, I am taller than most of our legionnaires.

A man with a height advantage has a longer reach than a shorter man, so he can kill from a greater distance. But I don't need to explain this to you, for your tutors will have instructed you in these matters of single combat.

As I have told you, the barbarians are very hairy and wear thick and foul-smelling skins to ward off the cold. Their hair is lighter than ours, although it is hard to tell the true colour, for they use bear-fat to grease their locks. The rancid smell is distinctive.

'The battle will have been fought already,' Severa whimpered, her eyes wide with dread. 'Even as we speak, your father might be dead!' Frightened by his mother's distress, little Ambrosius began to wail in his nurse's arms.

Severa ignored her son as she contemplated a lonely future with horror. The life of a widow was precarious at best, regardless of her wealth or standing in the British homelands.

'Don't be foolish, Mother Severa. Father has been killing barbarians for near enough to twenty years. I can't recall half of the barbarian tribes he has fought during his postings to the more dangerous frontiers of the empire, but he has always come through without hurt. I always refer to him as Fortuna's Favourite, although he tells me I'm tempting fate by taking her name in vain. I swear that he's more than equal to the task, so see to your babe and make him stop his caterwauling.'

Paulus has often joked that the men can smell barbarians before they see them, but tomorrow their personal reek will compete with the foul-smelling swamps.

If I am still favoured by God, I will prevail tomorrow. Then, with the Cantii silver in our treasure chest, I can begin my plans in earnest. For years, I have thought on the life of Magnus Maximus and how close he came to wresting the empire from the ineffectual hands of effete and disreputable rulers and the proud old men of the Senate.

I fear that if Britannia does not take the power of Rome unto herself, then the barbarians will take these isles and will lay them to waste. Regardless of whether I, or another, rise against Rome, the empire is finished. The body rots already, although the heart and brain believe it is still alive.

I will look to you, my son, to hold my British kingdom for me if I should win the acclaim of my warriors and the permission of the tribal kings to seek the throne of the Western Empire, like Flavius Magnus Maximus before me.

May the gods of our fathers preserve and protect you.

Ave, my son,

Flavius Constantine Claudius

Severa gasped.

Her husband had taken his new nomen, Constantine, from that great emperor who had ruled both the Eastern and Western Empire in Rome's glorious past, so it seemed incongruous to her that he would inform her of the name change by scrawling it on a worn piece of vellum. A long-suppressed conviction, buried deeply into her memories of childhood, whispered to Severa that her husband was guilty of a primal crime against the fates and God.

Superstition had never plagued Severa overmuch, but only a

few short years had passed since her uncle Conanus had perished dishonourably at her hands.

She stared down at her right hand as if she could still see and smell her uncle's blood.

Her father had been beheaded and his corpse had been fed to the dogs in a distant town beside a barbarian river, far from his home and his kin. Flavius Magnus Maximus had met his fate after being overtaken by the same weakness of hubris. Would her husband also suffer because he dared to reach too high?

A disjointed sentence from the ancient Greek past invaded her thoughts. She had heard King Caradoc use it once when referring to Maximus.

Those whom the gods would destroy, they first make mad.

Had hubris driven her own practical and pragmatic husband into lunacy?

Severa, afraid, ran to the scriptorium to fetch writing materials, then made her way back to the hall and the two young men who were impatiently awaiting her return.

'I must send a message to my husband, so you must wait,' she ordered the courier. He ignored the sight of a woman wielding a pen to write on a scroll, a rarity in those isles where women were rarely educated.

On the other hand, Constans twitched at her brusque tone, for he considered that the letter was intended for his eyes only – so any reply should be his prerogative.

Severa set up her writing tools and seated herself on a convenient bench, then began to write with such swiftness and passion that she marked the pristine hide from which the scroll had been made.

Pointedly, Severa decided to use the High King's birthname, while ignoring the *praenomen* that he had stolen. Perhaps, she thought, this small gesture might bring her husband back to earth and force him to reconsider his future course of action.

Husband and Father.
High King of the Britons.
Constantinus, my love,

My heart is heavy with fear, although I know that you will defeat your barbarian enemies with consummate ease. You must forgive a woman's anxiety when she is forced to contemplate the possibility that her heart's love might come to some harm. Please forgive me.

I have borne another son and have named him Uther for his fierce cries and his great strength. He is as tempestuous as Ambrosius is placid, and I am sure he will make a fearsome warrior in the years to come.

Please return at your earliest, my husband, for your subjects have need of your cleverness and planning. I long for my husband, while Constans and my sons look for the guiding hands of a father. As a person who has seen such abominations as the murder of Marcus Britannicus, the perfidy of Conanus and so many other tragedies, I beg you to return to Venta Belgarum at your earliest opportunity. I will only be content when you take up the sceptre of power and rule these islands with strength and ability.

Constans asks me to assure you that he will do anything that you require of him, but he eagerly awaits your return to the home that is yours by right of reign.

Be assured of my desire to see you again before the onset of winter.

Ave.

From Severa, your wife and Queen.

Constans read the scroll over her shoulder, angered at her choice of words.

'I would never ask Father to rush back to Venta Belgarum if his heart dictates otherwise,' the youth snapped.

Severa glanced at the vacant face of the courier who was trying to display a total lack of interest in the dangerous, albeit interesting, conversation that was taking place.

'I'd never use love to tie my father to me, and neither should you,' Constans hissed in a voice that was barely discreet and controlled.

Ignoring her stepson completely, Severa rolled up the scroll and sealed it. She deliberately refrained from using the family seal. Then, satisfied, she called the courier to her and placed the scroll into his hands.

'Ride back to your master and give him my reply. I pray your journey is safe and swift, and that the cause of Britannia has prospered under the hand of God during your absence.'

The courier bowed, assuring her that he would carry out his duty to the letter.

The Saxons began their attack at first light and made their first forays as soon as sunrise made the terrain visible, a tactic that spared them from the dangers of blundering into man-traps or deep water during periods of darkness. The Britons were alert and ready, because they knew that this battle hung in the balance. While Constantinus's forces had superior numbers, the Saxons were compensated by their greater height and strength. Stripped of their cavalry, the Britons faced their barbarian enemy on foot, so they were forced to depend on the Roman battlecraft of old veterans like Paulus. Unfortunately for the Roman commander, the grim tactics needed to win this battle would favour the barbarians, warriors accustomed to the physical slog needed to snatch victory from an unfriendly landscape.

Constantinus had chosen to create a forward perimeter of defenders on the very lip of the swamp, a tactical decision that forced the barbarians to plough their way through muddy obstacles if they were to join battle with the British front line. Because the leading edge of the solid ground was too wide to man his defences in depth, and because he had no intention of being outflanked, Constantinus directed his archers, a mere thirty men, to take up positions at each end of the front line which was aligned to the east and the west. Here, the archers could discourage any flanking action taken by the barbarians. As the side press of foot soldiers was positioned obliquely to the east and the west, they would be able to defend themselves if the Saxons broke through the archers' firepower. The dice had been cast and few further precautions could be taken.

Ever so slowly, the British supply wagons had been manoeuvred around the swamp at impossibly slow speed, but they were resting now on the protected side of this reef of firm earth. For all practical purposes, the Roman line was safe from encirclement from the swamps, but the spoils in his baggage train would be lost to Constantinus if the barbarian warriors should eliminate the Roman archers and the foot soldiers defending the eastern and western flanks. Constantinus was determined to maximise the strength of his defensive lines on all three sides for, if the Saxons could break through to the beaches behind him, the Roman camp followers, supplies and wagons would become further booty for the acquisitive raiders.

Fortunately for the Britons, many of the Saxon warriors were inclined to fight as individuals and tended to think and attack with a fixed purpose. They preferred to charge directly at their enemy and batter their opponents until they defeated their opposition by brute force, or lost their own lives.

From the slight rise where his banner flapped in the wind above his tent, Constantinus watched as Paulus ordered his men to assume the positions necessary to repel a charge by massed infantry. Many of these soldiers were veterans from Gallia, so they were accomplished tacticians who braced their spear-shafts with one foot while ensuring that their shields protected them from frontal attack. Many too had fought with Constantinus in eastern Britannia, so he trusted their martial skills. Meanwhile, the line of legionnaires behind them used their shields to protect the heads of the warriors in the front rank, while the same strategy was employed on each flank.

So practised were the legionnaires in these tactical manoeuvres that a seamless face of overlapping iron, like fish scales, was presented to the Saxon warriors. Once settled into their places in the defensive line, Constantinus's men could face the vicious axes and the great height of the barbarians as they attempted to rain death down on to their heads. A roof of iron covered the defenders like the hide of a small dragon that Constantinus had seen in Egypt that the local population called a crocodile. Its scales repelled the sharpest iron weapons unless a hunter knew exactly where the hide was weakest and used his blade to stab under the throat or the foreleg. So too was this wall of iron vulnerable to clever penetration, but not before spears and swords took a terrible toll on the Saxon enemy. Ultimately, Constantinus hoped that frustration would goad the Saxons into taking foolish risks.

As well as having the tactical advantage of first choice of terrain, and sufficient time to prepare for the coming onslaught, the legionnaires would be able to deliver tactical surprises. Their short spears fitted with large, leaf-shaped blades would bristle toward their enemies like the spines of a hedgehog. And when the spears had been cast away or buried deep into the flesh of a dead enemy, the gladius would take its place. Breast to breast with an enemy, this short sword and the tactical expertise of the legionnaires made them almost invincible.

Now, as the Saxons ran, screamed their war cries and splashed their way through the mud and shallow waters, the Roman force settled into that dour, defensive stratagem that had won an empire for the legions. Constantinus could see that the forward momentum of the Saxons had already been blunted as their tree-trunk-sized legs became mired in the stinking black mud and sinking sands. The wiser barbarians attempted to use spear butts to check the nature of the land below the deceptive skin of shallow water, but such caution significantly slowed their advance.

With typical Saxon bravery, most of the warriors threw caution to the winds and hoped they would miss the quicksand and strike at the centre of the enemy line.

Most of them did.

'Hold your nerve, Paulus. Wait until the first wave is within four paces.'

Constantinus ordered his decurion, who would lead the defence from the centre of the front line, to instruct every second legionnaire to cast his spear at the enemy when the invaders were at close range. The risk of opening the wall of iron for a few seconds, in order to accomplish this strategy, was considerable, as was the tactical risk of wasting some of the spears allocated to the front line. But the advantage, if the manoeuvre worked, would ensure that the advance of the first wave was blunted and only half of its number would survive to engage the first line of defenders.

The risk was worth taking.

The slog of enemy warriors making their way through the bog seemed interminable although, from the perspective of the front line of Roman warriors, the advancing Saxons seemed awesomely tall, threatening and invincible. The rows of crouching legionnaires seemed like children playing at a mock battle with adults, men who filled the sky with their height and made the air tremble with their battle cries. Lesser troops would have turned tail and fled; throughout the spring and summer, the Cantii tribesmen had run from the invaders' aura of ferocity.

But the fifty legionnaires who manned Constantinus's front line had served in dozens of vile provinces and faced many fierce enemies. They had fought some of the most terrifying warriors in the known world and were proud of their reputation for never admitting defeat and never retreating. They were prepared to die rather than lose their eagles, and more than one of the men sought courage from these proud standards rising above them on the hill beside Constantinus's personal banner. Every legionnaire was duty-bound to protect these simple strips of cloth and gilded metal with their lifeblood.

For the Romans, retreat meant shame for eternity.

In a move that happened so quickly that Constantinus almost missed it, the forward line suddenly opened and a hail of spears filled the air between the combatants like a blanket of black, horizontal sleet. Behind the thrown weapons, the line closed again as fifty iron shields slammed together as one with an orderly clang of metal against metal.

Few of the thrown spears missed their marks, so the Saxon charge faltered momentarily as many of its warriors were impaled on the leaves of iron. Only the shafts, many of which were still trembling, were visible above the shallow mounds of men as they died in the brown waters or the stinking mud. Many of the Saxons drowned in just a few inches of brackish water.

But the Saxons knew, from long practice, that there was always a cost in being a combatant in the first wave of a frontal attack. Those men still standing upright had been among those warriors selected personally by their thane to receive the glory accorded to heroes who take part in the first wave, for every Saxon had been raised from infancy to believe in the honour of a good death at the forefront of a battle. For those men who died so gloriously for the common cause, the Valkyrie would come, armoured and winged, to bear their souls away to the drinking halls of Valhalla. Dragging their limbs through the mud that made every movement sluggish, they redoubled their efforts and howled to Odin and Thor to guide their weapons. Then, filled with dreams of glory, they crashed their considerable weight against the defending line of legionnaires with the brutal force of a giant hammer.

The shock of sixty huge warriors throwing their bodies against the interlocked shields of the defenders was audible as Constantinus watched from his knoll. He saw the Roman line bow inward under the strain until, slowly and inexorably, the combined muscle of the men behind forced the front line to straighten once again.

Swords appeared in the wall of iron, striking and stabbing upward at any unprotected body parts and spattering the mud with sprays of arterial blood. Meanwhile, axes shivered in the early-morning light as the weapons were pounded down on the protective shields held aloft by the defenders. Some of the wounded legionnaires in the front line were trampled into the mud as the second line of defenders climbed over them to reinforce the first rank. And so, inch by painful inch, the defenders were driven backwards until the Saxon warriors had achieved a small toehold on firm earth.

The battle seemed to change perceptibly as the Saxon thane unleashed a second wave of attackers. The commander sensed that there was a major weakness in the centre of the Roman line, so he was anxious to capitalise on this at the earliest opportunity.

But Constantinus had anticipated this and, as a naturally gifted strategist, he had made a brave decision to prepare two small forces that would mount counterattacks if required. Along with a small group of infantrymen, he had kept himself and Vortigern on the knoll for this eventuality. It was time to risk everything.

As the second wave of Saxons made their laborious charge through the corpse-littered mud, Constantinus unleashed these small squads of men. Hopefully, the warriors on the extremes of the Saxon line would be marshalled towards the centre of the attack where they would find themselves in harm's way. Protected to some extent by the bowmen, Constantinus's small reserve would attack from the east, while Vortigern would lead the detachment that attacked the Saxon line from the west.

Firstly, the archers exposed themselves by firing their supply of arrows into the front ranks of the charging Saxons. Tumbling from the momentum of their charge, wounded and dead Saxons fell, never to reach the weakened front line that Paulus was trying to hold with those inexperienced British cavalrymen who had replaced slain legionnaires. Faced with the enormity of their task, the Britons howled ancient war cries, half-maddened by the infectious wildness in the blood that hand-to-hand combat can bring to the surface in any warrior.

But the Saxons still held the whip hand and they were now in possession of a small strip of firm earth that had been won with the corpses of their own dead who were driven, ever-deeper, into the foul mud of the swamp by the feet of their fellow warriors as they struggled to throw themselves at the front line of Roman defenders.

Then Constantinus, Vortigern and their reinforcements, a mere twenty men in each group, slammed their way into the Saxon flanks at a time when the huge warriors were only a few scant yards from their prize.

Some twenty years earlier, when Constantinus had been a raw recruit and little more than a boy, his old commander had clipped his left ear painfully when the lad had voiced an opinion that a small force could achieve nothing against a larger group of heavily armed men.

'Don't be a fool – or a child,' the grizzled veteran had ordered with a snarl. 'Ask yourself what possible advantages a smaller group might have? Think, boy! Use your brains and not your pecker.'

Constantinus had been indignant. As he nursed his head and swollen ear with one hand, he recalled that his eyes had flashed with resentment. Then, to compound his embarrassment, he earned a further buffet to his right ear.

'A smaller group has room to move, boy, so don't you ever forget it. If the space in the battlefield is limited, your manoeuvrability will be lost. We Romans invented the Tortoise to capitalise on combat situations where space is limited, and we need to concentrate our force in difficult terrain. But tactics such as the Tortoise can work against us if we are so outnumbered that we are forced to retreat, or if we are driven backwards by the overwhelming weight of numbers. An enemy, no matter how large, will be forced to batter at us in similar tight formations. They won't have any other choice.'

'So? How can a small attacking force develop an efficient battle plan? The larger force can turn and spread out, taking all advantage away from the smaller group.'

Constantinus had responded with the resentment of youth.

The veteran decurion had sighed and started to scrawl in the dust with a pointed stick. Constantinus had followed his plan, at first with scorn and, later, with wonder. Even now, as he ran at the forefront of his reinforcements, he could still smell the dust, the male sweat and the greasy heat of that long-past day of training in elementary tactics that were instilled into all Roman infantrymen in their preparation for service in the legions of Rome.

The small groups of Britons hit the eastern and western flanks of the barbarian force like arrows and their momentum drove the Saxon flank towards the centre of the British front line where most of the northern warriors were already concentrated. The Britons had the advantage of speed because the Saxon dead provided a solid base where the defenders' feet could be placed, although they still needed to exercise some care. Their heaving adversaries had established themselves on small clumps of firm soil, so Constantinus's men headed straight for these islands and forced the Saxons back into the mud and brackish water.

Constantinus's swinging sword struck out at enemy flesh as he scythed his gladius through the air. His skill with the weapon was such that he scarcely needed the protection of his shield, which he used as an additional weapon to strike out at the Saxons. Then, whenever a Saxon faltered or reeled back from the attack, the Romano-British front line would open to swallow the man whole. Later, all that would remain of such unfortunate

Saxons was a battered and trodden corpse and smears of bloody mud.

Saxons, Romans and Britons alike were falling around him, but Constantinus seemed to be fighting inside a bubble of invincibility. The Saxon leader, a huge thane with an unpronounceable name, emerged from the steaming mists of early morning, his axe swinging high to cleave the man who was standing beside Constantinus. Then, with a courage which he never knew he possessed, Gregorius struck the thane across the knees to cleave away the warrior's kneecap, a blow that brought the giant to his knees in the mud. Surprised at receiving such an opportunity, Gregorius struck off the monster's head.

Bemused, he crouched among the press of struggling men with his face freshly sprayed by the arcing blood that escaped from the thane's severed neck arteries. Constantinus grabbed him by his tunic and lifted him upright.

'Now is not the time to dwell on the permanence of death, Gregorius. You can fight, or you will soon join your Saxon friend.'

Constantinus neatly evaded a wild swing from a Saxon axe and eviscerated the warrior from under his arm. Still grinning, Constantinus thumped Gregorius on the shoulder until the adviser finally responded to his ministrations.

I've killed a man, Gregorius thought as he parried a wildly swinging sword in the hands of a wounded behemoth with bright, carrot-red hair.

'I've killed a man,' he repeated aloud, as he lunged at the Saxon's wounded side. He buried his sword deep into the giant's vitals and then twisted the blade before removing it in response to some half-forgotten memory of past training.

'Hades! You've killed two of the bastards now!' Constantinus panted absently while making a mental estimate of his tactical position on the battlefield. Vortigern's men had cut a swathe into the western flank but their momentum had also slowed.

Constantinus came to a decision.

'Back! Back! Back! Return to your lines,' he shouted. 'Back to your own lines and repel any stragglers who try to outflank us.'

Halved in number, Constantinus's men fought their way back behind the British-Romano lines, leaving the concealed archers to pepper anyone who tried to follow them with their dwindling supply of arrows. Vortigern's men smoothly repeated the same manoeuvre. Then, once the Demetae had resumed his position at the top of the knoll, Constantinus forced his way through the decreasing number of defenders to the very front of the defensive line. The Saxons still possessed a slight advantage, but defenders and attackers had both fought fiercely and were weakening, especially the Saxons who had been forced to waste so much of their strength on combating the swampy terrain. Meanwhile, the loss of their thane also disorganised the Saxon force, so Constantinus knew that the battle could be won if he took decisive action. Now was the time to mount a counterattack.

Would his men have the will and the ability to make a desperate charge at their Saxon enemies?

The High King roared out a challenge in the British language, as well as in Latin, to the weary men who continued to fight among the press of bodies around him. Their faces were streaked with blood, mud and the detritus of battle, but their eyes brightened at the knowledge that he would personally lead the charge. Constantinus's head swelled with pride and gratification as he heard the voices of his surviving warriors rise in volume.

'Are we men who hide behind our shields? Now is the time to face our enemy, my brothers. It is time to be breast to breast, and sword to sword. Who will follow me? Who will follow Constantinus into the abyss?'

Many of the men were carrying minor wounds and the High King could feel their physical aches, so he was uplifted by the manner in which they unhesitatingly roared out their defiance.

'Then crush these animals and make them fear to ever set foot on our soil. *For God and Britannia,*' he roared. And then he repeated the war cry once more until he thought his voice would fray away to nothing.

'*For God and Constantinus,*' the warriors answered as one.

The front line opened and the men began to move forward, step by step and with shields still overlapping. The remaining Saxons were suddenly faced with a wall of iron that was firmly set on driving them back into the murderous swamps. Desperately, the Saxons redoubled their efforts, but the Tortoise was on the move now and the great size and weight advantage of individual Saxons was as nothing when compared with the combined weight of one hundred men who were moving ponderously against them as a single unit.

Gladiuses caught the sunlight as they sought out Saxon weaknesses. Roman sandals and boots struggled to find purchase on the bloody earth and slurry that was littered with the dead and the dying. The Britons raised their voices in fierce battle songs that were as old as the isles themselves, while the Romans countered with their own songs of victory. And so the morning rang with the triumphant sounds of fighting men as they pressed at their enemy, until the remnants of the Saxon force was driven into a final defensive position.

For the Saxons would retreat no more.

Constantinus stood upright and lowered his shield.

The surviving Saxons had found a small hillock of dry ground in the expanse of swamp. It was now the turn of the Romano-British legionnaires to stand, knee-deep, in mud and filth. But the small, dry space was holding the last of the Saxon force. There could be no escape for the seventy warriors, the survivors of a two-hundred-strong force.

No quarter was asked. None was offered – and none would be given.

Yet, as the sun burned off the last of the morning mist, the Saxons took heart from its warmth and screamed their own defiance at the Britons. They must have known that their tactical position was untenable, but they were determined to die at the greatest possible cost to Constantinus's legionnaires. There would be no surrender.

Constantinus ordered his men to surround the small island of earth, while he sent the archers to recover whatever arrows they could on the recently vacated battlefield. His veterans were also recovering the short spears that had been used to such effect at the commencement of the battle. As the remaining Saxons screamed out to their enemies to come forward and fight, Constantinus ordered his men to ignore their pointed insults. The High King was determined that there would be no further risk to his men, no matter how much the Saxons howled for hand-to-hand combat.

'Let them die like the dumb beasts in the fields, or the priests who were slaughtered at their prayers,' he snapped to his officers. 'None of them will be turned into Saxon heroes.'

'Is this the way to treat a courageous enemy?' Paulus asked at Constantinus's shoulder as his veterans surrounded the hillock, armed with their throwing spears. Even as he spoke, the archers were finding appropriate vantage points from which to unleash their fresh supply of retrieved arrows.

'When these bastards burned our abbeys and killed the churchmen, were the Saxons honourable and courageous? Were they brave and noble when they killed simple farmers and their families? Just because they have met us on the field of battle with valour changes nothing.' Constantinus's voice grated with his promise of retribution. 'I refuse to permit one more legionnaire to be wasted in killing these glory-hunting savages. I shall let them die with the same respect and nobility as the manner in which they killed the abbot and the priests of the religious community of Durovernum.'

Then he gave the order to the legionnaires to throw their spears into the packed Saxon force. And the archers nocked their arrows and began to fire their barbs at the remaining warriors.

A howl rose up from the hillock. This primal scream was a cry of rage and despair that they were being slaughtered like pigs rather than true men. No warrior woman would fly on the storm winds to carry the souls of these Saxon dead to the Land of the Gods. No glory would come to these men, and no songs of valour would be sung to celebrate their deaths. The swamps would devour their bodies and the mud would choke their mouths.

Some of the warriors attempted to force their way out of the killing circle as they struggled to find a better death than the ignominy of being cut down like beasts. But they were given no opportunity of escape. Their bodies lay in swathes and their blood ran in rivulets into the shallow waters of the bog to stain the feet of their enemies, who set about the grisly task of killing the last of the wounded.

By noon, the bloody battle was finally completed to Constantinus's satisfaction. As the scavenging birds circled and squawked out their impatience to eat their fill of the corpses on the battlefield, the High King of the Britons smiled a tight little grin of satisfaction and ordered that the arduous task of burial and incineration should begin.

He gave no thought to the old hermit and his ridiculous, terrifying prophecies. The old messages failed to disturb his pleasure. He imagined his path was now open and, with joy and anticipation, he could begin the long journey that would take him to the pinnacle of his secret desires.

He thought little of Severa, or Constans, or the two new babes who were safe behind the walls of Venta Belgarum, other than to imagine their pride when they heard of his victory. As for Severa's warning, when it finally arrived in the hands of his young courier, her words were forgotten within moments, now that his journey into history had finally begun.

As the black birds settled down to feast their fill on the dead Saxons before the battlefield was cleansed, Constantinus returned to his tent and, safe under the watchful eyes of his faithful decurion, slept the peace of the innocent.

But the gods were laughing.

CHAPTER XVIII

TO SERVE IN HEAVEN?
OR REIGN IN HELL?

Romanus orbit ruit et tamen cervix nostra erecta non flectitur.
The Roman world is falling, yet we hold our
heads erect instead of bowing our necks.

St Jerome, *To Heliodorus*, Letter 60, AD 396

'When will our king return? Where is Lord Constantine?'

The refrain ran throughout Britannia's south. The war with the invading Saxons was fading into the stuff of memory and winter was coming fast on icy feet. But Constantine's palace in Venta Belgarum seemed empty and unloved without his quick, impatient footsteps.

The guards at the gate must watch in vain for the return of their comrades and the High King, who would be mounted on his showy white horse in the vanguard of the victorious column. Word had reached the citizens of Venta Belgarum that he was crushing a minor tribal skirmish near Causennae, or riding towards the Antonini Wall to punish a Pictish raiding party that had left Blatobulgium in ruins. Couriers came rarely, so the queen must weep into her finely embroidered pillows, or sit in the High King's Hall of Justice in her lord's place when she was instructing the master's eldest son in the finer aspects of ruling a kingdom. She, alone, continued to refer to her husband by his birthname: to all others, he was now known as Constantine.

The winter city of Venta Belgarum might look in vain for its master, although her citizens muttered that they had been abandoned. But in all other parts of the isles, the common people were happily singing his praises. Like the unpredictable wind, Constantine seemed to arrive with his troops, so peace seemed to follow in his bloody footsteps. Meanwhile, the local kings complied if the High King required men, although there were times when their smiles of welcome and compliance were forced. Then, after the demands for men were met, Constantine made further demands for supplies, gold or coin.

Few souls among the wealthy were inclined to voice their disapproval at the higher taxes. Peace was a scarce and highly-valued commodity and was the lifeblood of trade within the British lands, so Constantine was hailed as a saviour, albeit an expensive one. If the price of doing business was a contribution of gold, grain and men, then he earned it.

The church also paid its share of the expenses because their gold ensured that the abbeys and churches were protected from pillage. The word of the Lord could not nourish the converted if pagans destroyed God's priests and turned His houses to ash. As the freezing winter gripped Venta Belgarum, Constantine rode into the fortress at Isca, in Caerleon, where the nucleus of Rome's last legion in Britannia had made its home. The remainder of the Dracos Legion had been spread thin as its commander attempted to keep some sort of order throughout Britannia.

Like a born emperor, Constantine arrived with a column of two battle-hardened centuries and British cavalry to demand the time of Tribune Maximo, the Roman commander. Maximo was roused from the arms of his Brigante woman to answer the High King's impatient request for an audience.

The tribune considered staying in the arms of his mistress while the presumptuous ex-centurion was allowed to cool his heels in the cold. Then, belatedly, Maximo reconsidered his position. Most of his forces were detached to Deva and Ratae, where they were mopping up the human detritus that remained from a vicious barbarian summer. Would his small force of garrison troops have the competence to defeat this upstart if they were ordered to throw him out of the gates of Caerleon?

Probably!

Would his men obey his order to lay hands on the High King and his officers, most of whom were ex-members of this Roman legion?

Possibly!

The tribune reluctantly decided not to push his luck by initiating a confrontation that could strip him of his post as governor of Britannia, as well as military commander of the province. Unfortunately, he was aware that the legionnaires in the ranks loved Constantine, not only those who had served with him, but also those who loved the *idea* of such a vigorous, victorious commander. How often did a centurion manage to rise so high in the service of Rome? And how frequently were senior commanders and patricians forced to bow their heads to a man of no birth and little influence, a true warrior whose sheer ability had made him the most important man in this benighted Roman possession?

Of course, marriage to Maximus's whelp had helped the

centurion to achieve a meteoric rise in status, but not all of his subsequent successes could be attributed to his choice of a marriage partner. The tribune reluctantly accepted that this new Constantine must be an able-enough fellow.

Resentfully, Tribune Maximo wished that some of the plump, supercilious politicians in Rome were here to solve the problems associated with the rise of Constantine. The senators were solicitous in their advice given from a distance, but the governor doubted they would be equal to the task of controlling this particular High King.

Maximo joined his visitor in the central, open-air garden that had been built into his quarters. A particularly fine aspen raised its naked branches and silvery trunk towards a grey, winter sky. A carved marble seat faced the central pool where water vegetation grew and occasional ripples hinted at domesticated fish that lived within the roots of the vigorous water plants. The occasional water insects were making nonsense of winter's chill by skimming over the water's surface. Constantine realised they were alive and healthy because of the comforting warmth generated by heated floors and the hypocaust, the outward signs of the tribune's wealth and influence.

One of Maximo's junior officers had ordered wine and sweet cakes for the visitor and had arranged for these delicacies to be placed in the triclinium that opened onto the courtyard. As the tribune shivered in his fur-lined cloak, he was surprised to see that the High King was wearing a sleeveless tunic over his mail shirt and his cloak was cast carelessly over a couch. Was this man inhuman, if this cold left him unmoved?

'Aren't you freezing, man?' Maximo grimaced as he sat down and wrapped his cloak around him so that most of his head was covered, except for the reddened tip of his nose. Maximo had a head cold, an affliction which added to his discomfort.

'A man would have to be moon-mad to go riding around the countryside on such an inclement day,' he added in response to Constantine's sardonic smile.

'I don't care about weather when there's work to be done,' Constantine replied crisply.

The tribune noticed that none of the centurion's previous diffidence could be detected in the High King's response. The man had the gall to speak to his erstwhile commander like an equal, damn it, or even as a superior.

'The weather to the north of the Antonini Wall is truly cold. It would freeze the tits off the empress and I've heard she's fairly frigid already. But those Picts who dared to attack one of my tribal towns are very, very dead now, so the ravens and crows are dining on their corpses. Their bodies will endure, frozen, until the spring, so their widows can wail in vain for their return. Their king can collect the bodies of their kin when the spring thaw arrives and he has paid a ransom for them.'

The governor knew that commanders occasionally demanded payment from vanquished armies to release the bodies of dead combatants, but the practice was unsanitary and, to Maximo's mind, not the action of a true gentleman. However, he decided to keep his opinions to himself.

Instead, he opted to discuss the matter of jurisdiction, for peace within the isles was still the business of the Roman occupiers. As governor, Maximo felt he should be involved in the decision-making processes if war was to be declared against the Pict tribes in the north.

'Why were you so far distant from your normal sphere of influence, Constantine? Venta Belgarum is in the south and any marauding Picts should, by rights, be my problem. Why am I only hearing about your expedition and the activities of this war band after their incursions have been fought off?'

The tribune was trying to present a facsimile of anger, but Constantine saw through his bluster with ease.

'Perhaps our northern tribe, the Novantae, believed that I would move with speed if I already have a seasoned force in the field? I don't consider the *ifs and buts* when my subjects ask for help, Tribune. I consider myself morally bound to crush barbarians if they threaten any of the villages or towns within the British tribal lands. Perhaps the Novantae king has been made aware of my determination to serve my people. Regardless of their reasoning, the deed has been done! The war party was destroyed and every Pict who crossed the Vellum Antonini is dead. Like it or not, the Picts will learn to stay in their pestilential mountains while I rule Britain. If they refuse, they will die.'

A small songbird broke into the conversation at this point with a sudden carol of twittering, so the happy sounds defused the hot words on the tip of the tribune's tongue. Both men turned to watch the bird as it perched on the upper branches of the aspen.

A readiness in Constantine's stance, something like the play of jaw muscles before a battle, warned the tribune that he must swallow all of the High King's insults until he knew what the upstart expected of him. With admirable self-control, Maximo decided to use this small diversion of the bird to obtain what information he could glean.

'I'll never understand what that bird has to sing about, unless it's pleased to be out of the weather,' the tribune complained as he clutched his cloak around him and sneezed explosively. 'It's freezing out here, so I suggest we go indoors where the floors are warmer.'

Alerted by the tribune's paroxysms of coughing, Constantine rose to his feet, his face radiating mock concern.

'Of course, Tribune. I should have realised that you weren't well. By all means, let's go inside where your servants can see to your welfare.'

'I'm not ill: I'm damned cold,' Maximo protested.

'Would some heated wine warm our innards? Our business can wait if you'd enjoy some warm gruel to put some colour back in your cheeks. I've been inconsiderate, sir, so I beg your pardon. Please ignore me.'

I'll ignore you, you bastard! Maximo thought, hoping his face concealed his fury. Everything that this man had said was either a threat or an oblique insult. Nevertheless he controlled the words he would have liked to use in response to Constantine's false concern.

'I'm not an old man to be cossetted and fed gruel, Constantine. I have most of my own teeth and I still have my wits about me.'

'Of course you have, Maximo. I meant no offence,' Constantine added with a smile both indulgent and vulpine. The tribune wanted to spit at him, or smash his smiling and complacent face in.

Once he reclined on his couch with his cloak and a rug wrapped comfortably around him, Maximo sipped at a large goblet of mulled and spiced wine. He was beginning to feel more optimistic, and could almost imagine that he was the master of his house again, for Constantine had managed to puncture his image of himself as the supreme ruler of this remote province.

However the wine turned to vinegar in the tribune's mouth as he considered Constantine and his damned delusions of grandeur. He snapped out an inquiry: why had Constantine made this unexpected visit to Isca?

'I need the services of the remnants of the Dracos Legion,' Constantine explained bluntly.

'What in Hades do you mean?' Maximo stuttered.

'I've been made aware that the men of the legions, both in Britannia and in Gallia, are discontented beyond reclamation. The legionnaires are tired of persistent failures in policy and administration by their masters in Rome. The fighting men and those who support them in the field haven't been paid for years and their conditions and rations would be laughable, if they weren't so insulting. Meanwhile, their masters live in the lap of luxury while the men struggle to find the coin to feed their families and keep their kit in good working order. The patience of Rome's legionnaires has come to an end.'

As the tribune opened his mouth to protest, Constantine raised a finger to order the older man's silence. Somehow, Maximo forced himself to remain seated and obey, when every instinct urged him to strike out at the insolent cur.

'To add insult to their injuries, any incursions by the barbarian hordes into the north is blamed on the ineptitude of the fighting soldiers, rather than the inexperience of junior officers, the incompetence of senior commanders, the lack of suitable reinforcements, or the poor quality of equipment issued to troops in the field. How can men fight when they are fed with rotten meat, spoiled grain and sour beer? The best warriors in the known world have been taken for granted by Rome's greed and laziness. Perhaps the patricians are simply avaricious and palm off the worthless rations to the provinces in order to make huge profits. Who knows? Perhaps the senate is happy to begrudge their legionnaires the rightful payments and rewards to which the fighting men are entitled. Whatever their reasons, the legionnaires have decided to demand their rights.'

The tribune leaned back on his couch and pretended a lack of concern.

'I've heard these arguments for years, Constantinus . . .'

'Constantine!' the High King snapped.

'If you insist! The malcontents within the legions are often dissatisfied with the conditions of their service. If it weren't for the legions, these self-same men would be starving in some filthy, diseased village in Hispania or Illyricum or Gallia. The legions are their father! Rome is their mother! We put food into the mouths of these ingrates and expect them to give loyalty in return. As a centurion in your recent past, you should know how certain traitorous individuals have always bitten the hand that feeds them and curse their betters who protect their worthless hides.'

'A noble defence, Tribune, but I know how thin your argument is. You are blaming the victims of Rome's incompetence. Rome would pull out of Britannia tomorrow, were it not for the trade in lead, wool, grain and meats that feeds the mob in the suburas of Rome and keeps the wheels of empire greased. And, for their service, our men are not recognised as worthy participants in the order of empire until such time as they're needed to bleed on the frontiers to keep those same wheels of empire turning. You can't even hope to justify the treatment that has been meted out to these loyal troops. Three years without pay? It's a disgrace, Tribune! How many more years will it be before the legions see a copper coin from the bounty that is transported to Rome?'

'It's not their place, or yours, to question the decisions of the emperor, or the senate.' Maximo's lips had thinned to ugly slashes in his florid, angry face.

'I could be swayed by your loyalty to Rome if you weren't so snug and warm, fed on the best bounty of these lands and surrounded by the expensive art objects in your palace,' Constantine snarled. Dismissively, the High King flicked a careless finger at the fine alabaster goblet he was holding in his hand.

'You hardly live the same life as your men, so you're in no position to make judgement on them or their motivation,' he added. '*You* are paid for your services!'

Maximo spluttered with fury, upending his precious goblet in his anger.

'The plight of my legionnaires has become my business, Maximo,' Constantine continued. 'Flavius Magnus Maximus was presented with the Grass Crown by Rome's legionnaires when he attempted to force the senate to treat his troops with honour. Likewise, the kings of Britannia flocked to his standard in a concerted effort to win respect from the emperor and a place in the empire, an action that demonstrated their loyalty. Maximus won a crown but his ambitions pushed him too far and, like all men who become convinced of their own godhead, he failed at the very last. But his defeat doesn't mean that he was wrong.'

Even a mention of Maximus's name and his quest for the purple caused a bout of queasiness in the tribune's belly. Maximus had assumed the gens of the Flavians to bolster his claims, just as this upstart, Constantinus, had insisted on being called by the *praenomen* of the great emperor, Constantine. But at least Maximus had been a scion of the patrician class. Constantine Minor was a plebeian and not even a Roman-born plebe at that.

'You have no right to take this action, so you will ultimately come to ruination, just as Maximus met a dishonourable end. The fact that you married well and became the High King of a sad collection of pathetic and argumentative tribal kings doesn't make you worthy of high command, least of all any elevation to the Palatine. I suggest you forget these ridiculous plans and go back to your comfortable dung-heap, where you belong. I will forget the treason that you have uttered today, for I have always admired your courage and your service to the legion.'

Constantine's smile would have curdled milk.

'I should be grateful for the concessions you have offered to me, Tribune, but I choose to be offended at your description of my birth. My religion, and yours, preaches that all men are equal in the eyes of God, yet you persist with the old dictates of class warfare that have brought Rome to her knees. Competent men are overlooked in favour of fools, fakers and thieves whose only talent is that they were born into the patrician class. I'll be taking your legion, although I'll leave you with your personal guard as protection. The troops in the north have already sworn to follow me and they are marching into the south as we speak. You'd best say nothing more, Maximo, lest I be tempted to cut out your tongue. I might add that your man, Cassivellaunus, learned of my mettle when he eventually exceeded the limits of my patience. If you are still looking to him for reports on my kingdom, no further missives will be forthcoming.'

'What do you mean?' Maximo asked fearfully, for this explained the adviser's long silence. 'You haven't . . .' His words died away in his fright.

'Yes, Tribune. Cassivellaunus believed that your patronage gave him carte blanche to speak treason against the person of the High King of the Britons. He has gone to his noble ancestors because, in his stupidity and total arrogance, he left me with little choice.'

Tribune Maximo had looked into the stern, uncompromising face of his own nemesis and felt the beginnings of a gut-wrenching terror.

Constantine's eyes were black holes behind which flames seemed to be burning, although the tribune told himself they were merely reflections from the small brazier that warmed the triclinium. Constantine's mouth was smiling, but only a fool would consider that respect or compliance lay behind that grimace. Gloating, disgust and an acute understanding of the tribune's powerlessness added a cold dimension to the High King's eyes, as if the man's disciplined mind was the only leash preventing the mad beast within from breaking loose.

Where had this man been hiding? Or had he always been alive, but disguised beneath the centurion's self-discipline and easy nature? What horrors had been released on Britannia when Constantine was given so much power?

'I'm imagining things,' Maximo gasped aloud, a statement that caused the High King's eyebrows to rise. Finally, Constantine chuckled and the tribune's blood ran cold.

'I'm a reasonable man, Tribune, so I'll not allow my men to take their revenge on those officers who have treated them badly in the past. We will wait here in Isca to reorganise our force, once the troops have arrived at the fort. Meanwhile, I will ascertain what supplies are available to us and what wealth is contained in your war chest. I have called for the tribes to levy their young men, for I mean to trade blows with Rome and her army in Gallia, much as Maximus did before me. Armorica will rise, as will the Frankish lands and the Hispanics, for Rome has been heavy-handed of late. The provinces will answer my call and cast off the yoke of their Roman masters. I'm certain that this plan will happen exactly as I have described it. As the Lord of Hosts is my witness, I will not stop until I become the Emperor of the West and the future of Britannia and my legions is secured.'

For one short moment, the tribune could imagine the wreath upon Constantine's forehead. Then, like smoke, the phantasm vanished and the High King seemed to wear a diadem of blood. The tribune blanched and lowered his frightened eyes.

'Whatever you desire, Constantine,' he mumbled.

'Now, Tribune, what delicacies can be found in your kitchens that can tempt our palates?'

The scroll came by courier at the start of the thaw, just as the fallow fields were thickening with spring flowers and new-born lambs. Venta Belgarum had experienced a vicious winter and, at times, the snows piled up around the houses so that families couldn't open their doors and were forced to remain within their abodes until shovels could be used to dig them out again.

As was her habit, now that Uther was past the immediate dangers of the new-born and as Ambrosius had been weaned, Severa resumed her visits to comfort the poor within the township. Cold was the great enemy of the poor, while widows were often forced to risk freezing conditions as they sought firewood to warm their little ones.

Severa kept several warriors busy every day, hauling fallen trees from a nearby wood for grateful family groups to cut into kindling and logs for burning. She preferred to use trees that had collapsed under the weight of the unusually heavy snowfalls but, on occasion, she was forced to take timber from the palace supplies. Constantine had ensured that they stored sufficient firewood for four winters, as if he had wished to provide for his family during a prolonged personal absence.

The morning of the courier's arrival was beautiful and balmy, after several days of rain. The sky had been washed clean in the laundries of heaven and even the bare trees responded to the unfamiliar warmth and light with a faint fuzz of bright green, yellow and russet shoots at the tips of every branch.

With an empty basket over her arm and her skirts raised decorously above the mud, Severa was returning to the palace when her maid, Dilic, came running towards her. The queen's guardsman immediately lowered his hand to the pommel of his sword in case some danger threatened the queen.

'Mistress! Mistress! The master will be coming by the end of spring. A courier has arrived with news of him,' Dilic panted.

'A courier, you say? When did he arrive?' Severa asked in a calm voice, but her heart skipped several beats.

'It was near enough to an hour ago, mistress. Your steward has seen to his comfort and his horse is resting in the stables. He's a cavalryman, very fine and handsome in his red cloak.'

Dilic dimpled prettily and Severa sighed for her maid's diminished reputation. Few attractive young men came to the palace at Venta Belgarum without falling into the girl's soft embrace. Amoral as a cat in the town's midden, Dilic saw no point in waiting for good men to offer their love, so she took up new men like gowns. However, once the novelty had worn off, she happily discarded them to search for another prospect.

As to the dangers of pregnancy, Dilic appeared immune, or at the very least knowledgeable as to which herbs would keep her waist slender and her belly flat. When Severa asked her how she managed this, Dilic merely winked and told the queen that her old grannie had taught her everything she knew.

'Do give the poor man a chance to resist your charms, Dilic. He could have already been wedded to another fair young maiden, you know.'

'I don't believe so, mistress. He blushed like a boy when I asked if he was very strong. A married man would know women a little better, don't you think?' Severa noted that Dilic already had that sharp cat's gaze of curiosity; it seemed that the fate of this young Roman cavalryman was sealed.

'He won't be staying in Venta Belgarum for long, Dilic, so I wouldn't want your heart to be broken. Or his, for that matter,' Severa gently reminded her.

'Why! I'd never hurt anyone, Mistress. At least, not deliberately!'

'Very well, Dilic. Take me to your handsome young paragon of virtue.'

The courier was a Briton with a jaundiced eye, a partially healed scar that bisected his eyebrow and ran down to his jaw, and a youthful, muscular body. His face exuded his irritation, for he felt that he had been kept waiting unnecessarily. When Severa entered the room, dressed in the old robes she often wore on her forays into the town, the courier's eyes flickered over her dismissively.

He obviously thinks I'm one of the servants, Severa thought with a grimace that contained little humour. Her moods had become darker as the months dragged on into a dreary winter, with no word of her errant husband except that he was rampaging throughout the north near Hadrian's Wall and, later, in the mountains of Cymru.

'Where have you journeyed from?' she asked in an imperious voice.

The courier was startled and looked puzzled until Dilic hissed a warning at him.

'The queen has asked you a question, dolt! Don't keep her waiting!'

I can't see how Dilic is attracted to this sullen-faced man, although I'll grant that he must have been handsome at some time in his misbegotten life, Severa thought, as she watched shock and horror play out across the courier's face.

The courier blushed and sank down on to one knee in an impressive obeisance.

'I meant no offence, Highness. I hadn't expected you to be so young and beautiful.'

'You're a quick-witted lad, of that I'm certain. But I would still like to know where you left my husband, the man who happens to be your king?'

The courier apologised profusely, while Dilic looked skyward in exasperation. Severa waited patiently, but she permitted an encouraging smile to enliven her face. This young man, wounded and scarred so recently, was not at fault for her husband's sins.

'I left my master at Isca, which we call Caerleon. He is the guest of Tribune Maximo while he awaits the return of the Roman contingents that have been about the empire's business in the north. The High King's forces have swollen our numbers and they will have to bivouac outside Isca's walls soon, for there will be a lack of space.'

Severa longed to scream out a long list of questions at the poor lad concerning her husband's plans, but experience told her that Constantine kept his intentions close to his chest and a humble cavalryman would never be privy to his master's thoughts. However, it seemed obvious that his future plans involved the movement of a large body of men, supplies and equipment.

What madness had her husband embarked upon? Would she ever see him again? Did he intend to visit Venta Belgarum before he set off on this grand adventure?

The courier drew a long scroll cylinder out of his saddlebag and presented it to Severa with a low bow. Only the sternest self-discipline prevented the queen from snatching it from his hands, but she managed to behave with some aplomb and thanked the young man.

'Dilic? Please accompany this gentleman to the guard's quarters so he can eat and drink his fill. I have no doubts that hard riding and vigilance has earned him a well-deserved rest, so our house shall be his home while he sojourns beneath our roof.'

With a self-satisfied smile, Dilic dragged the courier away, no doubt to discover every detail of his background, as well as seducing him.

Severa drew up a bench seat and sat at one of the long tables. With trembling fingers, she opened the case and pulled out the sealed scroll marked with her husband's intaglio ring. As the sharp nail on her forefinger broke the seal, she drew in a deep, shuddering breath as if she expected unwelcome news. Her instincts were correct.

To Severa, Queen of the Britons.
My wife

I, Constantine, salute you and thank you for your labours in my absence. But the needs of the British lands and its peoples are more important than the felicity of married life, so we must all be content with what God allows.

My troops have honoured me with the title of Imperator and I have sworn to take their complaints to the very centre of the empire – to Rome itself! The legion languishes with no pay, minimal supplies and inadequate reinforcements, so the legionnaires have lost patience with their absentee masters. Instead they have turned to me.

Cognisant of the great honour conferred on me, I have determined to take ship for Gesoriacum. From there, I will march into Gallia where I will engage the legions of the emperor. I shall not be deflected until I have won better conditions for my men and a promise of protection and safety for these isles. You and I have spoken often about the likelihood that the emperor will recall Rome's troops at the first signs of trouble, leaving Britannia at the mercy of the invading barbarians who visit our shores every summer. If I am successful, the emperor will agree to protect Britannia's interests and I will have fulfilled my purpose as High King and earned the trust that has been placed in me by the kings and the common people of our lands.

'Oh, Constantine, or whatever you've come to call yourself. You're beginning to believe in your own immortality. Where has my handsome, painfully honest protector disappeared to, for I hardly know you?'

For some reason beyond her understanding, the implied thoughts in her husband's letter seemed quite real when compared with the farrago of nonsense that he had written so easily. Surely, her husband couldn't believe that he was another Constantine, the great man who ruled the Eastern and Western Empires and founded the great city of Constantinople. Could he?

Severa read on.

I have levied the kings from north of the wall to the Litus Saxonicum and I await these reinforcements at Isca. As well, I have convinced the governor to part with the last legion, men who will accompany me to the continent. If Lady Fortuna is with us, the local troops in Gallia will flock to my standard, as they did for Maximus, for I doubt that the emperor treats his native troops any better than he treats the rest of us. I also expect to be joined by a contingent of Armorican Britons, warriors who will not forget the debt they owe to their homeland.

'You're a fool, Constantine,' she said aloud. 'Why should the kin and friends of Conanus lift a finger to further your ambitions? You will die! You'll be far from home, and I'll be widowed with two young babes.' Tears filled Severa's eyes and fell on to the vellum, blurring the writing; then with a very unqueenly blasphemy she continued to read.

> *Once the army is assembled, I intend to march to Dubris and take ship for the continent. The one gift I can give you is that Venta Belgarum lies in the south so, with a short detour, I look forward to the pleasure of seeing you again. I also yearn to be reunited with my son, Constans, who will assume the role of High King in my absence. I know he is very young and moreover is no kin of yours, but he is wholly Roman by birth. He is a good lad who will obey me in all things and hold my palace safe for me, when I am far away.*
>
> *I trust him with my most precious possessions – my wife and my infant sons.*
>
> *You can look for me at the end of spring. I will come. And I will be eager to see you again, although our time together will be short.*
>
> *Farewell.*
>
> *Written at Isca, by the hand of Constantine of Britannia*

Severa stared at the open scroll as if some secret cypher was buried within it. With Britannia stripped bare of her best warriors, both the British land and the queen were in deadly peril from the Picts in the north and the Hibernians from across the Oceanus Hibernicus. As soon as those fierce enemies learned that the strong arm of the Britons and the men of the legion had left her shores, Britannia would be put to the sword.

How could her husband do this terrible wrong to her and to his people? He was supposed to love her, but hubris had overridden his common sense. At the best, she would become the prize for any ambitious man who hungered for a throne. Once she had been taken, that man need only father a child on her and kill her sons to become the rightful claimant. Who would protect her? Not Constantine! And Constans, only fifteen, could not be trusted to carry out the tasks that would be asked of him, although he was a good and kindly boy.

Outside, the afternoon sun had disappeared and a chill rain was falling.

Leaving the scroll on the table for Constans, Severa made her way to her small bower in the courtyard, when a sudden squall rose and the cold began to cut into her bones. Although winter was nearly over, Severa imagined that she could smell a harsh change in the weather. If so, the young animals born with the onset of warmer weather would be doomed, freezing to death in the fields. Perhaps the young men of Britannia would be doomed too, because of her husband's hubris.

With a shiver of superstitious dread, Severa saw the first snowflakes begin to fall. Soon, more would come, until Venta Belgarum was encased in a shell of bitter cold.

And the young and the innocent would begin to die.

CHAPTER XIX

BEWARE THE MAN WHO
SMILES AND SMILES

I will have this done, so I order it done; let my will replace reasoned judgement.

Juvenal, *Latines*, Book II, Satire 6

Spring eventually shuffled late into Britannia, dead lambs and calves in its wake. The snow was deep. Many children froze beside dead fires in cottages where the banks of snow blocked the doors, while every piece of furniture had been burned by desperate parents. Again and again Severa heard tales of loss, courage and the fears that fill human hearts when faced with nature's extremes. In conjunction with Constans, who was rapidly learning the skills that would make him an able king, she presided over the sentences meted out to a grasping opportunist; to another man who had stolen firewood and left whole families to die of exposure; one further miscreant who had killed his neighbour over a flask of wine and an incorrigible poacher who repeatedly stole braces of chickens from widows. The queen was saddened to learn how easily desperation could turn humans into monsters.

Yet she had no hesitation in giving a death sentence to every miscreant, thief and opportunist who appeared before her.

But eventually the winter winds abated and the sunshine began to warm the land once more. The loam was so rich and moist from melted snow that crops seemed to grow in vigorous spurts.

Meanwhile, Ambrosius was learning to run on his sturdy legs and Uther discovered that smiles transformed his frowning face into that of a well-fed, well-loved infant. Severa would have been ecstatic if her husband had been by her side, but the road from the north remained stubbornly empty.

Severa despaired. No one, not even the cheerful Dilic, could make her smile.

She feared that he would share the fate of those other fools who had sought the throne of Rome under the guise of healing Britannia's historic resentments towards the conquerors. Marcus Britannicus and the bland patrician, Gratianus, had both died at the hands of assassins, and both had been born into families of wealth and patronage. But Constantine had come from nothing and nowhere. He would always be Constantinus of the legions to the masters of the Western Empire.

Now, a brief missive that scarcely acknowledged Severa as his wife revealed that he had added another gens to his name by adopting the title of Flavius. In doing so, he was claiming kinship to the family of the emperors. Flavius Claudius Constantine! Did her husband truly believe that the patricians of Rome would consider such blatant lies, if he repeated them often enough? Severa sighed for his naivety and ambition. Had he ever loved her at all, or was she merely the means to an end?

The queen feared she might never see Constantine again but simultaneously she held a more pressing fear that he would simply land, unannounced, on her doorstep. She had learned to think of him by this strange new version of his name, but had also begun to dread his arrival at her door and his entrance to her bed. Strangely, she found that she was unable to relinquish her fond memories of the man she had known during their long trek from Corinium to Tintagel. Would this new, ambitious Constantine still hold any love for her? He was certainly able to live without her at his side; his long absence was proof of that.

Each day she climbed up to the narrow ramparts that overlooked the main gates of Venta Belgarum to stare out along the cobbled road into the north. For the queen, the poorer sections of the shanty-town that lay beyond the city walls seemed refreshed by the spring rains, but she knew that this comparison was deceptive. Every week, she forced herself to enter the fringe village of bawdy houses, shops that sold second-hand or stolen goods and filthy eating-places. Most of the town's poor lived in these muddy lanes as they struggled to find enough food and firewood to survive. Here she dispensed bread, herbal cures and a pinch of hope. For their part, the inhabitants of the lower town became used to her daily visits to the ramparts at sunrise, so they were happy to wave friendly greetings towards her.

'She's pining for her husband,' one cheerful-faced whore gossiped with a farmer. 'It's a pity he should have been away for so long, but that's the way of things, isn't it? Men can't help leaving the women to do the suffering. For all her wealth and power, the poor woman gets little pleasure from her life.'

The farmer snorted with scorn. 'The queen doesn't know what it's like to be poor like us common folk. She's always had a fine bed and a full belly.'

'Shut your gob, Colwyn. She's good to those folk who need her, so keep your opinions to yourself.'

For all her charitable works, there was no one who could share Severa's daily fears or comfort the disquiet that lay in her heart. Loneliness gripped her.

So, on the morning when she saw a rising drift of dust in the distance, she assumed that a cavalcade of merchants bearing trade goods from Calleva Atrebatum was about to pass through Venta Belgarum while travelling to Britannia's southern ports, noting idly that this particular train was uncommonly large.

Severa was working on her stitchery when news of Constantine's arrival finally reached her. She was surprised when her steward entered the room at a run. 'You must come quickly, Highness! The master is here, and he's entering the lower town as we speak with a huge army behind him.'

'What is this nonsense, Jerome?' Severa replied in a stern voice. 'How can you tell that the master is here?'

The servant was virtually dancing on the spot with excitement as he tried to convince the queen that the High King had indeed finally returned.

'I speak truthfully, Highness! The master rides under the banner of the Roman dragon and he is astride his favourite white horse. He was too far distant to see his face, but I couldn't miss that showy steed.'

Seveta felt her heart lurch. 'You say that he's entering the lower town? Hurry then, Dilic, for I must change my gown and you must ensure that the children are sweet and clean.'

She turned back to face Jerome. 'Has Constans been told?'

'Aye, mistress,' Jerome replied breathlessly.

'It's near enough to noon so the master will be hungry. Warn the cooks that they will be expected to prepare food for a large number of guests and fetch the best Spanish wines from the cellars. And arrange for a large supply of beer too.'

Jerome bowed and ran off at a pace not normally expected from an ancient and stately steward.

In a quiet panic, Severa hurried to her apartment where she snapped out orders to her ladies. Once she was safely behind closed doors, she started to put her appearance to rights. A little of the precious nard that had come from the far side of the Middle Sea was rubbed into her hair and her arms as she settled into a robe of yellow silk which she knew looked well, and hastily pushed felt slippers on to her feet as one of the ladies attempted to neaten her plaits, but Jerome had already reappeared at the door of the apartment.

'My hair will have to do as it is. Dilic, where are the children?'

'Both here, mistress,' Dilic answered with a breathless gasp. They had red, freshly-scrubbed faces, and were dressed now in their best clothing. Both were mulish and in fact, a little frightened.

'Your father has come home, darling boy,' Severa told Ambrosius. 'The king has arrived to see his little princes.'

Ambrosius had no memory of his father; his lips trembled at the prospect of a strange man entering his world. Uther seemed aware of her emotions, as if he was desperate to discover what had upset her. Something protective and fierce lurked behind those pale-amber eyes, making her heart lurch. She pushed her fears away.

'Come, my darlings, your da will be waiting impatiently to see you.'

The homely words steadied Ambrosius's nervousness, but he still gripped her hand with all his strength. Matching her steps to his, Severa sailed down the corridor with a serenity that was wholly feigned.

The hall was already a heaving mass of humanity.

The most prominent half-dozen of Venta Belgarum's citizenry,

Constantine's officers and several massive fighting hounds from Cymru had assembled on the forecourt of the High King's palace and, from there, had been admitted to the hall in a milling, noisy tide. These notables had been joined by a cluster of Roman and British officers who had remained in Venta Belgarum to assist Severa and Constans with the day-to-day business of administering the kingdom during the king's absence. Dozens of servants attempted to keep them supplied with food and mugs of alcohol.

A tall figure was standing on the small dais at the centre of this chaos, apart from the joviality that swirled below him. He was holding the king's gold cup in one slender hand. The man's face was turned away from her, but Severa knew that the owner of that midnight-black hair was her husband. She had run her fingers through those short locks in the darkest hours of the night and had worshipped that lean, hard body with her own. Her fingers knew every muscle and remembered every blemish and scar. Constantine had returned.

Drawing a deep breath, she entered the hall in company with the two princes, as Jerome beat his staff on the wooden floor to bring the throng to silence.

'Gentlemen, the queen,' he announced in his loudest voice.

The hubbub from the gathering stopped almost immediately. Some of the men turned and stared, but most bowed their heads respectfully as she passed.

Many of the audience had never met Severa, so they stared avidly at the slight, upright figure that was a picture of elegance in the silk dress that showed off her porcelain skin and her remarkable golden hair.

Constantine's allies gazed on his wife and considered him to be a fortunate man.

Yet Severa would have loved to turn on her heels and run

from those many judging eyes; she felt like a swan traversing dangerous stretches of water where the frantic actions of her webbed feet below the surface contrasted with the serene appearance of her head and body. With supreme composure, she strolled to the dais and the man who turned to face her.

Without looking directly at Constantine, she sank into a deep obeisance. Her greeting was accompanied by deep bows from Ambrosius, her maid and the babe's wet-nurse. The only discord came from little Uther, who stared at his father with cold animal eyes. The king stared back at his son and a strange recognition of kinship passed between man and infant.

Then Severa lifted her head.

'Constantine!'

She said his new name with finality as she forced a sweet smile on to her face. This man who stood before her and leaned over to kiss her hand wasn't her Constantinus, although both men had similarities. Where was the humour that usually lurked behind his quirky black brows? Where was the longing in the full lower lip? And where was the need in those dark eyes?

No, this would never again be her Constantinus. She loved him still, but her passion was a habit of long standing and she knew her affection was fragile.

Attentively, he took Severa's hand and helped her to mount the dais so that she could be seated on the elaborate chair she was accustomed to using as queen during his absences. The babe's wet-nurse handed Uther to her mistress and Ambrosius wrapped himself protectively around her legs. The little boy's eyes were full of shadows.

'I've missed you, sire,' Severa lied, before dropping her traitor's eyes to her youngest son. 'Here is your third son, Uther, who has been waiting to meet with you.'

Pale eyes and dark eyes duelled again and the king lifted the infant into the air to present him to the crowd. Unafraid, the child gazed at the throng as if they were hardly human.

'This babe is Uther. He is my third-born, and is a fine young son.'

The crowd applauded eagerly, raising goblets and drinking vessels in their hands. A man with one living son was considered fortunate: a man with three was blessed by God.

'And this fine lad is Ambrosius, who is my first-born in Britannia.'

Ambrosius stood and faced the crowd with all the courage he possessed. As his mother had taught him, he bowed his head low to acknowledge the crowd, until the warriors stamped their feet and shouted their approval.

Constantine put Uther back in Severa's lap. 'You've done well, Severa,' he said quietly. 'You have given me two more sons that will make me proud.'

Then he faced the crowd and raised his voice. 'Where is my eldest son? Where is Constans?'

Constans, who had been waiting for this summons, pushed his way through the throng to reach his father, his face alive with joy.

The lad must have been practising his martial skills with the men-at-arms when his father arrived in the town, for he was still dressed in his practice armour. Once he arrived at the dais, the High King recognised his old, discarded sword swinging from the young man's waist in an old, ragged scabbard. He grinned with delight.

Then Constans knelt at his father's feet.

'Rise, my son, for your diligence pleases me. You will soon be ready to do battle.'

The crowd cheered enthusiastically, making the lad blush scarlet, but Severa noticed that the cries of approval from the Britons in the audience were more circumspect.

Constans isn't one with these people, Severa thought suddenly. He's an outlander, so the Britons won't tolerate him as their High King. Is Constantine aware of this small problem?

If Constantine noticed any British ambivalence, he gave no indication of it when he helped his son on to the dais. His steward hastily placed a stool between the two thrones.

When Constantine seated himself, the whole room erupted in cheers and barbaric war cries.

Then a single cry went up.

'Imperator! Augustus!'

The crowd grasped eagerly at the title and raised their voices higher and higher, until the rafters began to shake with the sound.

Eventually, Constantine raised both hands and indicated silence. In totally manufactured humility, he rose to his feet. Raggedly, the crowd obeyed and Severa turned her eyes away from their obvious devotion to concentrate on her husband, his bowed head and the stern lips that still refused to smile. She knew him so well that she could feel his excitement and gratification rising like a tidal wave whose power was expressed in his voice as soon as he began to speak.

'I haven't earned the title of emperor yet, my loyal men. However, we will succeed in our endeavours if God continues to smile on us. And *yours* shall be the hands that lift us all to the heights. *Yours* shall be the voices that will shake the old senators of Rome and wake them from their long sleep. The patricians will be forced to accept that they have forgotten *you* and their ilk must understand that they have insulted their legionnaires for far too long.'

When did Constantine learn to manipulate fighting men so well? Severa wondered.

The assembled crowd adored Constantine and he bathed in the glow of their regard. But Severa, aware that two other men had sought this same crown in recent times, felt the prospect of widowhood staring her in the face.

'With the legionnaires and the warriors of Britannia at my back, *we'll* win an empire and make these isles safe forever,' Constantine roared as he raised one fist towards the soot-stained rafters. The crowd stamped and then cheered, swearing that their loyalty would remain true until death overtook them. Then, drunk on the audience's worship and bloated with their love, Constantine spread his arms wide to embrace all of his legionnaires.

Severa felt her gorge rise and slipped away from the dais with her children. In the privacy of her room, she vomited into a bowl until her stomach and throat were raw.

Later, the queen gently raised the sword-callused hand that was still clutching at her breast and, when he murmured and rolled over in his sleep, she sighed with relief when she was finally freed of his weight.

The king had come to her bed after a night of carousing, so she had hoped that so much wine would render him incapable of making sexual demands on her. Faint hope! He all but raped her, twisting her tender breasts and biting her neck until he drew blood like an animal. Constantinus had never needed aggression to arouse his lust, but Constantine felt a need to inflict pain and subdue her. Now, bruised and aching, she listened to his steady breathing and wished she could smother him as he slept. These sudden, murderous thoughts sickened her.

'You've made monsters of us all, my darling,' she breathed into the darkness.

The rational part of Severa knew that she lacked the physical strength to hurt this man. But, alarmed, she had felt a sadistic desire rising within her own flesh, so she bit down on her swollen lips until the moment passed.

Constantine's drunken garrulousness had permitted his secretive mind to reveal his plans to her. He intended to emulate Magnus Maximus, her father, by forcing Rome to accept a system of joint rule over the Western Empire. Gallia and Hispania still remembered Maximus's able reign, so they would welcome a man who was recognised as the High King of the Britons and was following in his footsteps. He knew that the Gallic tribes would rise to serve him, because his enemy was their enemy. They, too, hungered to destroy the rotting cesspit that was Rome.

As for Constans, Constantine's heir, the lad would require a regent for a number of years if he was to be given the task of acting as High King during his father's absence.

'Constans is so very young, my lord. He's learning fast, but he needs an adviser with ability,' Severa offered carefully. 'Your choice must be someone, other than me, who can guide him in the niceties of kingship,' she added, for she was frightened of Constantine's temper. Great power had made him autocratic.

'I've already considered the matters that concern you, sweet girl, and I've made arrangements that I'm sure will please you. The young king of the Demetae tribe has served with my forces for some years now, and he's capable of following our directions. In fact, Vortigern is everything I need in a regent. Unfortunately, he's an ambitious man and that may become a problem one day. But not yet, so he's ripe for use. I can trust him to obey me as long as I remain alive. But I don't intend to die, so he's the perfect choice to protect my family and assist my eldest son to control the tribal kings who rule the British dominions.'

Severa could clearly see glaring weaknesses in Constantine's plans and she blenched at the dangers that might soon threaten the futures of her own children.

Vortigern is more acceptable to the people of Britannia than Constans could ever be, she thought, as her breath sighed to the beat of her husband's snores. The ordinary folk of these isles would elevate a British ruler to the High King's throne in preference to a Roman, especially if Constantine was killed while undertaking a foreign adventure. There would be no loyalty or gratitude in the hearts of the British kings, only self-interest.

Careful not to touch him, Severa slid away from Constantine's prone form and stood beside the single window. Air blew into the room, heavy with the smell of the coming summer and the promise of rain before morning.

Vortigern will kill my children as well as Constans if Constantine should fail in his grand plan, her thoughts continued. Any ambitious young king would be unable to resist taking such a prize if it was dangled under his nose. And would Vortigern permit me to remain alive once he'd achieved his ambition?

The moon slid behind the lowering clouds as Severa racked her brains and considered the ways that future events might unfold. She wished, for a moment, that Endellion's strange gift was hers so that she could part the heavy curtains of the future.

Yes! I am the daughter of Flavius Magnus Maximus and I remain fecund. I can bear the sons of Vortigern just as easily as I bore the children of Flavius Claudius Constantine. I will be permitted to remain alive, if such a fate is living.

Severa wept then and she wished she had the courage to open

her veins if that dreary day should arrive. But she was also certain that she could never leave her sons without the protection of a mother. Unprotected, they would face certain death.

But you, Constantine, aren't the only person in this world who can devise a plan. Given time, I will find a way to make my boys safe into the future. And I will bring about an outcome that has escaped your consideration.

The night wind had no answers, but Severa felt the first raindrops from the low, scudding clouds strike her face, as if the skies were also weeping.

A week elapsed. Then ten days, and the army continued to feast on Venta Belgarum's supplies like a hungry cloud of locusts. The town elders were already talking of the shortages that would plague them during the next winter, while Severa shook her head reflectively whenever she saw signs of rapine and pillage in the peaceful town.

On the second day of the bivouac at Venta Belgarum, Constantine had presented Vortigern to Severa and Constans. The queen was forced to admit to herself that the young kinglet had surprised her. She had imagined him to be in his thirties like her husband, but his age was similar to her own. Vortigern's curling mane of blond-red hair was very striking, as were his upturned lips, but his perpetual smile unnerved her because it never quite reached his cold eyes. Still, he was strong and gracious, and seemed to seek her favour. She felt a reluctant liking for this vigorous young man, despite the chill in his heavy-lidded eyes.

Vortigern was always kind to young Constans, even when no one was watching. He treated the youth as if he was his younger brother and displayed a companionable camaraderie, teaching Constans a number of tactical swordcraft ploys that might in future serve to save the young man's life. Unsurprisingly, Constans quickly became Vortigern's slave and Severa saw an occasional twist of jealousy on Constantine's face when he watched his eldest son trailing after the young Demetae king.

Severa wanted to warn Vortigern, but she lacked the courage. Her husband would resent an alternative hero-figure presenting himself to the boy, but the Demetae was careful to insist that Constans should dance attendance on his father at every opportunity. Severa understood from the Briton's machinations that he was manipulating Constans, but was unable to decide whether to be fearful, or to admire his diplomatic skills.

She concluded that Constantine was not as clever as he believed himself to be and, at times, an impulse to laugh at her husband's ignorance was almost irresistible. But then she recalled that Vortigern would be in control of *her* destiny, if her husband were to perish.

At the end of each long and desolate day, she knelt beside her bed and prayed that Constantine would succeed in his quest. When he saw her dedication to the teachings of the Church he was touched, so he treated her with more gentleness than before.

Although he remained a contained husband, Constantine warmed to his boys until Ambrosius forgot his fear of this stern man and Uther bestowed his charming smiles on the man who was both his father and his king.

For a month, a brief period of healing, Constantine and his army rested in their bivouac at Venta Belgarum. And then, as quickly as they had arrived and with as little fanfare, they were gone.

At the door of the palace, Constantine had paused to kiss each of his sons. Then, as his persona of a good and kindly king dictated, he embraced Severa as he would have done in days of old, an action that almost caused her to weep. Earlier he had made his farewells in private and kissed her with a brotherly chasteness quite different from his public display of passion. He would beget children on her as often as he could, but the change in his circumstances had fed something calculating and cold in his nature, so she knew he would never love her as she desired.

All in all her life would be better after his departure, she decided.

Like a long and slender serpent, Constantine's army marched through the fertile landscape of the south while swelling his war chest with tribute from the rulers and gathering hot-headed volunteers from the Regni, Atrebates and Cantii tribes. The men who joined his columns came with smiles, gratitude and a benign grace, but the kings sighed as they assessed their depleted winter stores, diverted to feed the High King's ravenous warriors. However, being pragmatic rulers, they reasoned that Constantine would honour his debts and protect them when the Saxons resumed their incursions in the coming spring.

At Dubris, the army took ship in what became a long and tedious shuttle that took men, horses and supplies over the short stretch of the Litus Saxonicum to a landfall at Gesoriacum in the land of the Franks. An invading army of this size took weeks to move, even over such a short distance as this narrow strip of water, so the resultant delays in communication forced extended periods of inaction for the High King and his officers. Gesoriacum had seen armies come and go, and the population was unimpressed by this latest claimant who sought the throne of the Western Empire. Meanwhile, the merchants of the town fleeced Constantine and his men outrageously.

Once Constantine arrived with the advance contingent, he

was forced to cool his heels in an unlovely bivouac that his advance party had prepared outside Gesoriacum, a port that was unapologetically devoted to trade and brisk, untrammelled commerce. Unfortunately, anything that disturbed business was frowned upon. The city elders knew that warfare would eat into their profit margins; warrior kings from Britannia caused trouble, so the presence of a foreign army was always accompanied by large ripples in the smooth-flowing river of goods that passed through the port.

Weeks passed as Constantine despatched scouts to assess the terrain and establish the presence of possible enemies along the probable route that would be followed by his army.

Then, while his army was assembling outside the port, Constantine despatched envoys to the Germanic tribes to broker meetings that could forge an alliance. He needed allies such as these barbarians at his back, fierce leaders who could secure the frontier and minimise the chances that his Romano-British force could be attacked by opportunistic savages when passing through the land of the Franks.

The Germanic rulers met with Constantine under leather in the far north of Gallia while his army languished in the bivouac at Gesoriacum. Fortunately these fierce warriors had the same resentments against Rome as the more civilised Franks, Goths and Visigoths. Truces were proposed and quickly agreed to.

In his triumph, Constantine had forgotten to discuss his plans with Britannia's most pressing enemies, the Saxons, who were offended when they found themselves ignored by this new claimant to the purple. The river of blood that would flow from this oversight was an unfortunate consequence for the innocent victims who would suffer at the hands of the northerners in the coming decades.

Meanwhile, two messengers had also been sent to Cledwyn, son of Conanus, in his sanctuary at Armorica. Cledwyn had no reason to love Constantine or Severa, his father's killers, but nor did he rest easily under the tyranny and taxes meted out by the decaying empire. As an intelligent young ruler, Cledwyn was ripe for alliances with any men of power prepared to assist the British presence in Armorica. Without a need to resort to threats, Constantine reasoned that its young warriors would flock to his cause, for his banner represented a victorious future rather than the demands of a dying empire that was Rome's legacy.

Other couriers were sent to the Franks, the dominant tribe within Gallia. As most of Rome's troops along the frontier were Frankish tribal warriors, Constantine appreciated the value of seeking favour with the many small kinglets co-existing within the Frankish lands. The warlike Visigoths of the south were also allies of Rome but they, too, chafed under the arrogance and pretensions of their Roman masters. Nor was their pay regular or generous. The emperor and the senate had bred slow-burning resentment in Gallia over the past century and had been careless of the desires and aspirations of those Franks and Visigoths who were an integral part of Rome's continued survival.

Yet here was a Roman, with an army at his back, who had the wit to make treaties with the greatest enemies of the Franks. The kinglets looked towards Constantine, remembered Maximus and decided to risk the enmity of Rome.

'Those pretenders who rule us from Rome have always treated the tribal lords as stupid barbarians over the years,' Constantine explained to Paulus. 'The patricians persist in believing that all men and women within the empire are no better than slaves if they aren't born into their exalted class. They also look down on any Romans who don't reside within sight of the Palatine. We know the slurs that are cast upon us, without fear or favour, by any Roman with any pretence of breeding. You must remember Marcus Shit-head!'

'Ugh!' Paulus grunted. 'My old pater served in the legions in Egypt, and his father served Rome before him. In the old days, some of us were born in Rome, but most of Rome's soldiers drew their first breaths in some stinking hole on the very edge of civilisation. As we were classed as plebeians, we were fated to stand a bare step above the slaves who served our betters.'

'Yet Roman soldiers remain proud of their legions and their positions within them,' Constantine allowed. 'At least our legionnaires know themselves to be the best soldiers in the world, regardless of the gratitude shown to them by the senate and the sodding patricians.'

Constantine had spoken with pride, but cynically too, as if men like him were fools to have spent their lives for so little reward or appreciation.

Paulus grinned in his usual dry fashion.

'Yes, master, my old father always said he'd been all kinds of fool during his long life. He always thought it better to try his chances in the arena or hire himself out as a bullyboy, rather than die in some shithole over nothing at all.'

'Aye!' Constantine replied slowly. 'I was a lucky lad when my father ordered me to learn my letters. Only the favours won in battle by my father secured my schooling among the group of lads who were the sons of senior officers in the Roman command. I was the token charity lad, and was made to feel like one. But when I seemed likely to become rebellious, my father told me that there was only one way to break out of the rigid class system. I took in my father's common sense and ambition with my mother's milk.'

This burst of candour embarrassed Paulus, although he recognised the reasoning and strength of purpose that had solidified Constantine's fervent ambitions. The decurion mulled over his lord's meaning with great care. But he kept his mouth shut and made no dangerous errors in judgement. A clever man knew when to listen in silence.

'The empire will fail without us,' he finally said. 'Like it or not, Rome survives on our bodies; rises above the barbarians on the tide of our spilt blood and has only seen the wonders of a huge world through our eyes. Change is coming fast and we, as usual, will have to be in the vanguard. But what if the empire should ultimately fail? How will those of us who live in the West continue to stand without our withered and ungrateful mother to succour us?'

'Fucked if I know, Paulus! But I don't intend to fail in my ambitions, regardless of what happens to Rome. I've made an irrevocable decision to throw the dice, exactly as Caesar did all those years ago. Only God can know which way the dice will fall.'

Constantine's rare confidences left Paulus with much to ponder. For the first time, the decurion was looking beyond the urgent demands of the present in order to consider what his actions of today might mean for tomorrow.

As the army gradually assembled in the bivouac outside the grimy walls of Gesoriacum, couriers and scouts began to return to Constantine's war tent. The news they carried varied from man to man and was, predictably, mixed in its effects on the High King's temper and plans.

Given its past history, Armorica remained stubbornly angry at the circumstances surrounding the death of Conanus. However, its young men would answer Constantine's call for assistance, now that he had finally come to Gallia. Cledwyn made his feelings abundantly clear in a memorised message that was passed directly to the High King, late one afternoon just as the lamps were being lit. The pungent stink of fish oil had permeated every corner of the tent and set Constantine's teeth on edge.

The courier began by begging Constantine to forgive him for the tone of the message that he was about to repeat. Although the High King readily agreed, his eyes snapped in anger at the expectation of an insulting rebuff.

But Cledwyn of Armorica was not so foolish. His message to Constantine was simple.

Hail to the High King, formerly the centurion, Constantinus.

I remember you well and I remain mindful of the circumstances of our last meeting. But nor has our province rested easily under the control of the emperor. Taxes are exorbitant and are taken from my people in a manner that offends them.

Therefore, regardless of our past history, Armorica will come to your assistance in the hoped-for victory over the rag-tag legions that are aligned against you. I do, however, reserve the right to leave your service at any time, if our safety and the benefits to Armorica are placed in jeopardy.

My warriors will pass through Lutetia within the week, and I will expect to meet with you in Arelate as summer ends. I trust that our association will be more mutually advantageous than our last encounter.

From Cledwyn of Armorica.

By his scribe, Demetrius of Antioch

No gracious welcomes! No respectful phrases! And definitely no hint of trust!

Any pleasure that Constantine could have hoped to receive from this curt message from Cledwyn paled into insignificance at its underlying tone. The High King bit on his lip and forced himself to ignore the thinly veiled contempt.

Meanwhile, cautious messages were delivered to Constantine from local kings and warlords, although no one was prepared to give unqualified support to a British High King who had once been a humble centurion.

Nor did they thoroughly trust him. The couriers reported that the High King's marriage to Severa, daughter of Flavius Magnus Maximus, was probably the actual reason that no tribal leader refused to support Constantine's ambitions. Maximus's memory still held the power to generate favour, but the tribes were wary of the disruption that occurred after the great man's demise. However, the tribal rulers knew that ruthless tribes of barbarians were clustered together in unholy alliances along the Frankish northern borders and these warriors were staring towards the soft, fecund lands of the south with avaricious eyes. And these were the same northerners with whom Constantine had made alliances. The more prudent kings called their men to war and, suddenly, the sluggishly moving army was swelled as the Franks made up their capricious minds.

Only a fool would give total trust to an unknown quantity such as Constantinus; but only a dangerously arrogant ruler would ignore a commander who possessed the golden touch.

And so a new feeling of confidence was conveyed to all the tribes and towns that were likely to supply men, gold and stores to the army from Britannia.

THE LINE OF MARCH FROM GESORIACUM TO ITALIA

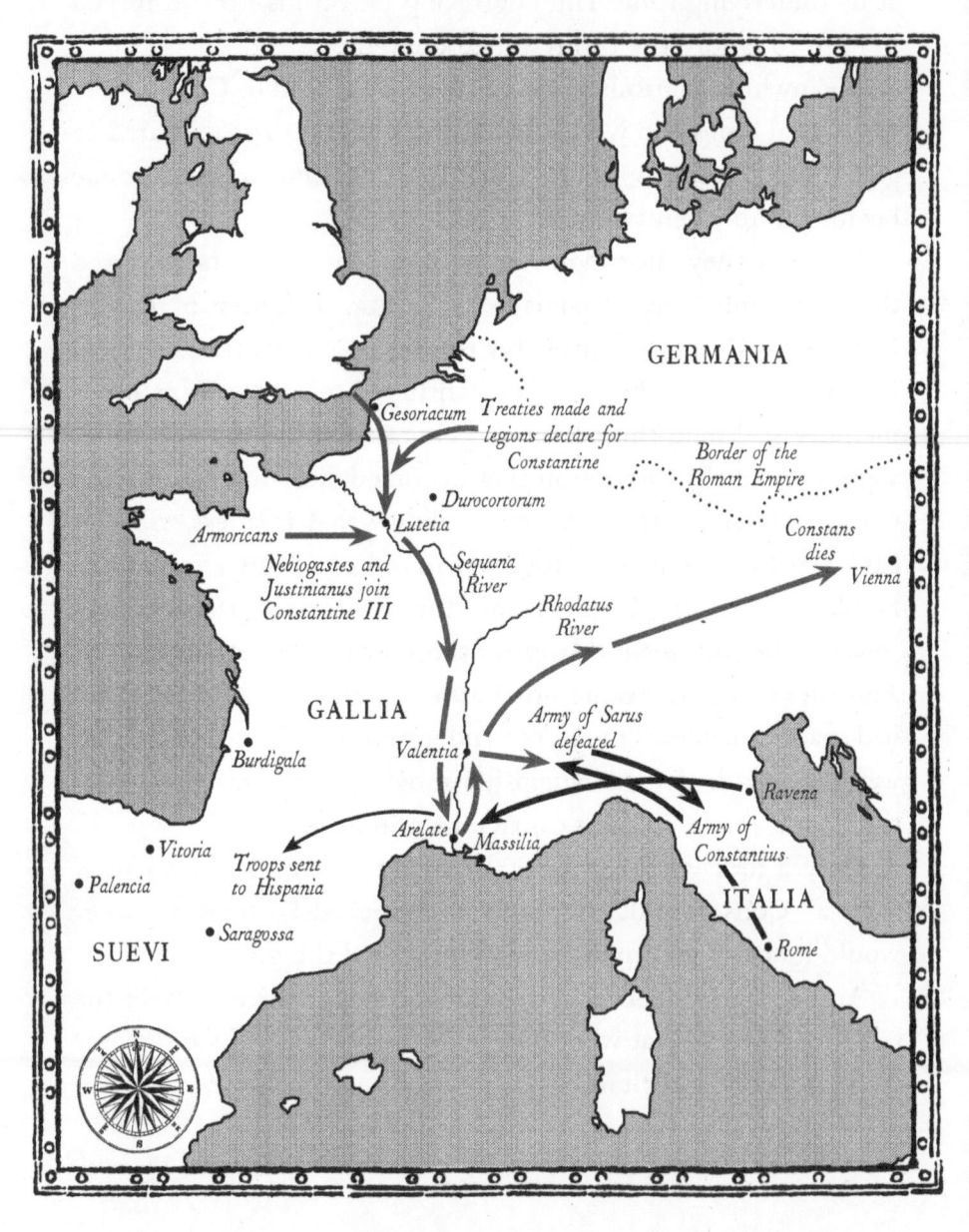

GERMANIA

Gesoriacum *Treaties made and legions declare for Constantine*

Border of the Roman Empire

• *Durocortorum*

Armoricans Lutetia

Constans dies

Nebiogastes and Justinianus join Constantine III

Sequana River

• *Vienna*

Rhodatus River

GALLIA

Army of Sarus defeated

• *Burdigala*

Valentia

• Ravena

Army of Constantius

• *Vitoria* *Troops sent to Hispania* Arelate Massilia

• *Palencia*

ITALIA

• *Saragossa*

• Rome

SUEVI

CHAPTER XX

A WOMAN'S PRICE
IS ABOVE RUBIES

Every day we die, every day we are changed,
and yet we believe ourselves to be eternal.

St Jerome, *To Heliodorus*, Letter 60

As her husband's army began the long and arduous march
through Lutetia, Severa waited, watched the regent carry out his
duties and experienced the taste and smell of maternal fear.

Constantine had scarcely set sail for the continent when
Vortigern began to strengthen the powers of the throne in Venta
Belgarum, through the simple expediency of forcing the tribal
kings to provide the High King, in absentia, with either men or
gold for what he deemed to be an *Army of Protection*.

After the demands that had already been made on them, the
kings resented Vortigern's high-handed manner from the beginning. But even the most foolish of them looked to the empty
Roman fortresses and the wide, deserted seas that surrounded
Britannia and protected the Britons from their barbarian

neighbours, and began to feel the first stirrings of alarm.

'We've been open to attack from the moment that Constantine stripped the land bare to pay for his adventure in Gallia. It's time to sacrifice more of our wealth to protect our lands and our citizens, until such time as the master returns,' Vortigern explained with an understanding smile. 'I must do my part as well as you, although the Demetae tribe is small and our lands aren't fertile. No man shall be exempt and no tribe can expect to receive favourable treatment.'

Regardless of how the tribal kings felt about the High King, they understood the unspoken warning that Constantine might not return.

Each of the rulers knew that Magnus Maximus had sailed away from Britannia and had never returned. But, deep within their secret hearts, many felt that Constantine wasn't comparable to Maximus, although the new pretender seemed strong enough.

And so the tribal leaders scoured their lands for youths who could be sent to Vortigern for training. In the process, they stripped their farming communities of the sons needed to work the fields and make them productive. Those tribes who had suffered the brunt of the barbarian attacks in the past, and who subsequently had no suitable men or boys to send, had to unearth their long-hidden gold so that mercenaries could be purchased. Forced to comply with these demands, the citizens were careful to ensure their masters' backs were turned before treasonous words were uttered.

Consequently, farms were worked by wives and daughters, while old men were co-opted to toil in the fields long after the strength of their legs had vanished.

Across the land, hunger came before the onset of winter, for strong men were needed to till the soil, tend the crops and gather the harvest. Apples rotted on the ground, while vegetables and grain went to seed unharvested. Small children worked like little adults and exhaustion fought with illness, as death came to the land before autumn was half gone.

Still, few new workers were forthcoming but the farming folk had to answer the demands made by the great ones, without complaint.

But should the rulers levy taxes on the crops and grain that were harvested with such painful effort and sacrifice? Even the most loyal of old men chafed under the injustices inflicted on Britannia's poor. The growls that came from the peasantry were finally heard as they spread across the length and breadth of the tribal lands. Vortigern heard them and his eyes became glacial.

'We've given our sons for wars that are of no concern to the people of these lands, so why should we starve for rulers such as Maximus? He is long dead and almost forgotten. Why should we suffer for a Constantine? Or a Vortigern? Neither of these men could stand in Maximus's boots, and neither will work beside us in the fields or serve in the ranks of the army. These men who would be kings see themselves as too fine to suffer as we do.'

Occasionally, an old man would offer a variation on this tirade, one that boded no good for Constans if his father should perish in Gallia. Severa heard the whispers through the gossip of her maid, Dilic.

'That Constantine isn't even a Briton,' one of the older folk was heard to mutter. 'He's Roman through and through, curse him, so why should he care what happens to us? His lady is half-British and is a good soul, right enough, but she's only a woman! At least this Vortigern is a tribesman, albeit one from Cymru, the cesspit of rain and sludge.'

Severa saw the sullen resentment in gaunt faces that had once smiled with the joy of living. She was afraid of Vortigern's plans, but she was unable to demur. No one would listen, regardless of her exalted status. After all, she was only a woman.

Yet Vortigern took pains to be respectful and gracious to Severa, deferring to her with open admiration as he displayed the outward loyalty of a devoted servant. He played with the boys and was a great favourite, even with little Uther who seemed to have been born with a natural distrust of human nature. To hear her sons chirping with laughter, as Vortigern tossed them high into the air and then, deftly, caught them as they dissolved into gales of giggles, made her frozen heart melt. But she could never trust the Demetae warrior, even though his desire to talk with her was more genuine than Constantine's had ever been in the days before his departure from Venta Belgarum.

Constans admired Vortigern with a boy's hero-worship and sought his opinion on all manner of subjects with a slavish devotion. Even when Severa attempted to warn Constans of the dangers posed by the Demetae kinglet, the lad refused to listen.

Into this world of resentment and bubbling tension came a number of dubious rumours warning the citizens that those who lived in the British lands were doomed. Severa heard the substance of this fear-mongering that terrified citizens of all ages and intelligences. Those families with means began to hoard food and coin for the troubled times that lay ahead; avaricious fortune tellers and charlatans convinced many of the citizens that the vagabonds who wandered through her lands were the true descendants of the Druids and, as such, were in possession of the Sight. The superstitious and the credulous became easy prey to these unscrupulous scavengers who sold dubious amulets, charms and worthless prayers.

Severa abhorred the activities of these obvious frauds. The educated persons in the community understood that their Roman overlords had twice ordered pogroms across the length and breadth of the British lands which ferreted out the last of these ancient lawgivers and religious leaders. For better or for worse, the Romans permitted none of the Druids to survive among the ancient groves where they offered prayers to their strange pagan gods in a doomed effort to save their people from the curse of history. Yet war and troubled times served to glorify their reputation and their demise erased the spectre of human sacrifice that had been an integral part of this ancient religion. The more gullible of the British peasants, fearful of the future, became easy marks for the rogues who wandered through their lands in dirty robes.

'We were born too late, Constans,' Severa told the youth after the first occasion when he delivered justice alone, Vortigern having undertaken a journey along the road to Calleva Atrebatum to meet with agents who would provide him with information on Tribune Maximo's plans for Isca. She had been encouraged by Constans's performance, although the boy was very conscious of his voice which, in the process of breaking, was occasionally unpredictable.

In response to the queen's congratulations, the youth raised one eyebrow in the manner of his father. Severa felt the nape of her neck shiver.

'If we had been born fifty years ago, we could have expected to live and die in relative peace and plenty,' she explained. 'But as God has decreed, Rome is failing in our time and the northern tribes of Germania are stirring from their dark forests to shatter the peace of our lands.'

'Father says that the demise of Rome is only a matter of time.

He's been saying the same thing for as long as I can remember, but when last we spoke, he swore that the time had arrived when all good men must do their utmost to stave off that terrible day.'

Severa nodded in reluctant agreement. Although she was half-Roman, her sympathies were wholly with the tribes.

'Yes, I suppose my Constantinus is right. He is wise in these matters. I suppose we must all try to halt the tide, although I fear we'll fail in this unequal task. It's easier to stop the sun from shining in the heavens than change the ambitions of avaricious and angry men.'

'My father's name is Constantine now, Mother Severa, and I'm sure that he has been chosen by Fortuna to become the next emperor,' Constans chided her gently, for he had developed a strong and unexpected affection for his stepmother.

Severa hated that shorter, assumed name that gave her husband the pretence of a talent that he lacked. Still, in deference to the lad's love for his father, she ignored her irritation and offered the boy proof of her own confidence in her husband's abilities.

'Aye, lad, I agree with you. But I fell in love with my Constantinus, a centurion, and the man who saved my life on so many occasions during our escape from Corinium. I loved the man who never thought to rule, although I suspect he may have cherished certain ambitions for a long time.'

She swallowed the words that came unbidden to her mind.

If the truth is known, I no longer love Constantine, for I know that he'll do anything that assists him in his quest to become emperor and rule in Rome. One way or the other, he will never return to Britannia.

A week later, after a self-satisfied Vortigern had returned and commenced the training schedules for the steady trickle of

410

youths sent to Venta Belgarum in response to his demands, a soothsayer arrived at Constantine's palace with the haughty arrogance of a man with an important message to report to superiors. This verminous man, wild of hair and eye, and clad only in a goat's skin, insisted on seeing the lords of the town. No threats, no cuffing about the ears or fierce promises of imprisonment deterred him in the slightest. After he had camped on the palace steps for two days, careless of where he urinated or moved his bowels, Severa finally ordered him brought before her, in order to warn the miscreant that he was risking her anger by persisting with his foolish and disgusting behaviour.

Unrepentant, foul-mouthed and with long hanks of grey, lice-ridden hair, the vagabond entered the King's Hall with a swagger, although his naked feet were cut and scabbed from half-healed sores. He was forced to depend on the assistance of a rough-cut staff of oak when he stood, without bowing or recognising the nobility of Severa, or even Vortigern, who joined her to examine this strange outlander. The seer pointed one arthritic, malformed finger towards Severa and spoke with such venom that spittle stained his yellow-grey beard.

'Beware, Woman of Straw, for your husband has ignored the warnings from God and his fate has now been sealed. As a bitch born of a Roman, you have no right to lord your birthrights over the people of these lands, so you will feel the lashings of despair before your sons are half-grown. Nor shall you raise them to maturity. Those who live will be forced to beg for their bread and know the shame of charity before they become men.'

Constans had entered the hall on silent feet while the eremite raved his words of warning at Severa. Now, incensed at the insults directed at his stepmother, the youth took a threatening step towards the old man, who seemed much stronger and more

411

terrifying than most of the usual charlatans who peddled their sick dreams for copper coins.

'Shut your disgusting mouth, old man! Your diseased rantings will be the death of you, unless I decide to have your tongue removed at the root. How dare you insult the mother of the British people and threaten my brothers with harm?'

The soothsayer turned his fanatical eyes towards the youth and snarled like a rabid dog.

'The gods have assured me, Constans, that you are the base scion of another base Roman. I warn you that you should heed my words. You must beware the man who smiles and smiles!'

Constans recoiled, but Vortigern drew his long knife from its scabbard. The soothsayer must have heard the hiss as the weapon was unsheathed, but he ignored the ominous sound to concentrate on the man who had drawn it.

'Do you intend to help me to reach my fate, son of the Demetae? You are the one who will betray our people and open the doors of Britannia to the Brothers of Chaos, so heed my warning to you. You must beware a white horse running and the Demon Seed!'

'By the name of Hades! What is this nonsense of which you speak?' Vortigern snarled, but his eyes had darkened with something more sinister than simple rage. Severa knew then that the Demetae king was false. She shivered and her heart sank.

'See! You've upset the queen, so take the fool away,' Vortigern demanded. However, as the warriors on guard duty attempted to approach the fanatic, the old man skipped away from their outstretched arms with the dexterity of an agile child.

'You shall pay for your treasons over the body of your first-born, regicide. Hear me when I say that these lands will run with blood because of you.'

Like an eel, the old man slithered through the grasping hands of Vortigern's warriors and ran behind Severa's chair. Her eyes tried to follow his movements, but she recoiled in shock when one of his greasy paws clutched at her own impeccably clean hands with a merciless, bony strength. His other hand, as strong as oak, gripped the back of her neck to stop her instinctive attempt to retreat from the heat and stink of his body. She felt his hot, rank breath in her ear.

'Never fear, daughter of Maximus! A child of your line will surpass your father, your husband and all your sons. You will be remembered down through the aeons because you refused to surrender to your fate. In fact, your sons will live to breed because you will dare to fight. You would have been a better man than your father *or* your husband.'

The old man shrugged.

'But the gods were unkind, weren't they?'

Then his laugh came raucously, like the shriek of a crow, and he danced away from her. 'You can't ask me to weep for you and yours, Severa of Britannia. Blood enough will soon be shed because of you, so you must permit a man who is soon to die to leave you with his curses.'

Whatever else that this strange and terrifying old man might have said was lost in a great spurt of arterial blood as Vortigern clamped one hand over his rotting mouth and cut his throat with the other. To her horror, Severa fainted away.

The arrival of the eremite, along with his subsequent death, upset the entire household. Vortigern remained on edge in case the man's ravings might be believed and was fearful of any words that the charlatan might have whispered into the queen's ear. Despite his overwhelming curiosity, Vortigern wasn't prepared to ask her what had been said. She might be led to query his motives.

Constans avoided Vortigern's presence and even shunned the company of Severa during the next few weeks, while he became a shadow of his former self. The queen guessed that the young man was embarrassed for giving credence to the maddened rantings of a soothsayer, leaving him reluctant to discuss his superstitions with her.

For her part, Severa wrote a long missive to Endellion in which she described the soothsayer, his prophecies and the means by which she might find a solution to the apprehension she felt for the future of her sons.

Vortigern was surprised that Severa should possess writing and reading skills, for he was forced to depend on a trusted priest to scribe for him. Grateful to discover that the tribal king read no Latin, Severa sent the scroll to her foster-mother with a reliable servant. She was forced to await Endellion's answer in an agony of indecision and anxiety.

The answer came in mid-autumn, at a time when Vortigern had almost forgotten the existence of the soothsayer or the dire prophecies that had been delivered in the King's Hall.

To the High Queen of the Britons,
Your Majesty, Severa,
Light of my life and sorely missed child.
Greetings.

I hope my courier finds you well and content, although your scroll speaks of fears and hidden motives that have given you reasons for concern over the safety of your boys.

Long have I wished to journey to Venta Belgarum once more, so I can meet your boys, Ambrosius and Uther, and hug them warmly!

But our own troubles in Corinium will keep me too busy to depart until the onset of spring. At that time, I shall be able to share my plans with you, for no mother should be afraid of the darkness.

Never fear, sweetling! An answer shall be found because Aeron wills it to be so. Even now, he is writing to a cousin in Armorica on a matter that is of concern to him, but I will say no more of this matter, in case others should read this missive and become cognisant of our plans.

I have my own concerns and so, unwillingly, I must ask for your assistance. My son, Pridenow, the strangest of my children, has reached the age of twelve years. Hence, your Vortigern requires him to present himself at Venta Belgarum for training as a warrior and an officer, as befits his birth. Or so I hope.

I don't believe that Vortigern is familiar with Pridenow or his skills, so I would ask that the British commander is informed that my son has already been schooled to a level far beyond what one would expect of a boy of his age. My son is quick-witted but, sometimes, the unusual paths his mind follows when solving problems puzzles his father. However, if you explain the situation to Vortigern, the commander might permit Pridenow some latitude, for our boy is far from ordinary. It might be worth mentioning that Pridenow has been trained in the use of arms and military strategies by Aeron himself, and the lad has shown ability in these fields of endeavour.

However, there is one special problem that worries me constantly. My son has grey eyes!

I imagine that you will think I am wanting in my wits. Grey eyes do not usually create any difficulties for the person possessing them, although they are quite rare. As you are aware, I am the daughter of Caradoc (praise to his memory) and Saraid, the wise woman of the Red Wells. Certain difficulties have been passed into Tintagel's bloodline from their union, but this scroll would need to be very long to describe the talents of my birth mother, although I have no conscious memory of her.

Without entering into a long explanation of a complex prophecy from Saraid that was passed on to me by my father, Caradoc, I must simplify my message by saying that no boy child of our line with grey eyes should be permitted to leave the shores of Britannia.

My father was convinced that disaster would follow, if that day was to dawn.

Caradoc treated his warning so seriously that both my brothers were required to swear an oath that no boy with grey eyes within the family line would ever be given permission by the Dumnonii kings to leave our shores. Caradoc insisted that, should the grey-eyed lad not appear in our children, then Cadal's heir should be sworn to abide by the same oath. Unfortunately, Pridenow was the first issue to be so marked at birth.

I was never told what would happen if the grey-eyed lad should sail away to foreign lands, but Caradoc was insistent that such a risk must not be taken. My father held grave fears for the consequences of a disregard for this prophecy, so that threat is enough for me. Besides, I love my boy dearly and would not willingly see him travel abroad.

I beg you to take my son into your home if you can do so, and watch over him if you are able. Your Vortigern is often described as having a hungry look and is apt to lick his chops, much like a wild dog that my brother, Cadal, once tried to tame. I must admit that I hold no trust in Lord Vortigern.

Pridenow is a good boy and he's not remarkable in any way that can be easily discerned. But I truly believe that his grey eyes will place him in danger and, perhaps, his eccentric way of looking at the world around us might also bring him to harm.

He has only just left Corinium for Venta Belgarum, so he will

*soon be with you. I wish with all my heart that I could travel with
him and protect him from harm, but Vortigern and Pridenow himself
would never permit me to keep him cosseted.*

*I think of you and your little ones almost every day, so I look
forward to the spring when I can hug you all.*

My love will always be yours beyond question. Farewell.

From the hand of Endellion.

Queen of the Dobunni tribe

Severa clutched the scroll to her breast with all her strength.
Whenever she was reminded of her childhood, she felt a frisson
of regret at the absence of her foster-mother.

She could recall those carefree days at wind-torn Tintagel
before Aeron returned from Gallia, wounded and exhausted
after the failure of Maximus's ill-starred attempt to conquer
Rome by force. Later, she would experience an idyllic youth in
Corinium with Endellion and Aeron.

All the prayers of all the priests in all the provinces of the
Empire could never restore the quiet, contented peace that she
had lost.

'Dilic!' Severa shouted now, as she put her scroll to one
side.

Severa's maid practised selective deafness at times, especially
when she was talking to a personable young guard, so Severa was
often irritated at Dilic's tardiness.

'Dilic! I need you! Now! Not in the near future, but right *now*!'

Even Dilic was unlikely to miss the edge in her mistress's
voice. A female squeak came from one of the storerooms where
woven fabrics were kept, and Severa's sharp ears heard the sound
of something large and metallic being dropped.

'Yes, mistress, I'm coming,' Dilic answered breathlessly.

She ran through the doorway, while attempting to straighten the plaits that had escaped the pins on top of her head. The state of her bodice told Severa that her earlier suspicions were probably accurate.

'I've just learned that my foster-mother's son, Pridenow, is coming to Venta Belgarum. He will reside here for some time, so I want a room prepared immediately for his use. I shall need tutors to assist with his education, as well as an expert warrior to supervise the programme of physical and martial training that Lord Vortigern will arrange for him. See what you can discover in these matters, Dilic.'

Severa watched sardonically as Dilic's cheerful face clouded over with dismay.

'I realise you have no idea how to find a tutor, but neither do I. Still, given your large coterie of friends in the guardroom and in the officers' quarters, you will be able to discover talented tutors with far more ease than I could. Also, I imagine that several of your grateful swains might be happy to assist in such a task, if only to win your smiles and favour.'

'Madam!' Dilic protested, shocked at Severa's lack of delicacy and bitchiness. Actually, Severa had surprised herself by her blunt speaking. Then she shrugged. She needed tutors, so Dilic would be given the task of finding them. Why be coy about the means employed?

Then, on impulse, Severa hugged her maid, who was thoroughly confused by her mistress's familiarity.

'I'm sure you'll quickly discover how to go about solving my problems, Dilic, given that you have such a natural talent at sniffing out useful people. I could never win the affection and friendliness that you seem to earn so effortlessly, even from casual acquaintances. I fear that I'm far too stiff and untrusting.'

'You're being unfair to yourself—' Dilic began, but Severa remained unrepentant.

'I've no one to blame but myself if I'm unhappy, Dilic. I could have married a man other than Constantinus, because my foster-parents would never have forced me to wed against my will. I married for the love of Constantinus in the end, and I'm beginning to believe now that the poets are right – love and passion can rob men and women of their wits.'

'We ordinary folk are far luckier than you and yours, mistress. Yes, life can be hard, but the common people aren't property, as you seem to be. When I marry, it will be to a man who wants to cherish me and protect me for the rest of my days. I'll be happy if I find a man I can talk to, one who wants to share a friendship with me.'

Severa felt hot tears prickle behind her eyes.

'For the moment, I'll be grateful if you could just find a tutor for Pridenow, Dilic! You could ask the steward for assistance, because Jerome might know a likely person.' She smiled as bravely as she could and thanked Dilic for her efforts.

The maid left the bower with a heavy heart. She would find tutors for her mistress if she had to tear Venta Belgarum down around the townsfolk's ears.

Arelate was so close to the sea and the great port of Massilia that Constantine could smell the salt that hung in the air long before the army set up a bivouac. The large river that Constantine's force followed to reach this wealthy Roman town, the Rhodanus, was wide and sluggish and, downstream from the Roman encampment, it flowed into a complex area of swampland that was prone to stinging insets and clinging mud.

The journey across Gallia from north to south was very slow

and unsatisfying, although troops, native volunteers and the sons of the local peasantry swelled the ranks of his army as it ground its way along the route that would take him to the city on the banks of the Middle Sea. But Constantine was far from happy. Nothing seemed to be happening in accord with the complex plans that had been forming in his mind for so long.

As always, Constantine's engineers were given the task of constructing the walls, gates, revetments, water storage cisterns and other essential facilities needed to maintain life in a semi-permanent Roman bivouac. When the long journey across Gallia came to an end, Constantine surveyed the damp, grey skies of winter with distaste. So much wasted time!

Thus far, the decision of his men to declare him Augustus seemed scarcely important, except to tease at the innards of his ambition.

Constantine's grand army was irretrievably bogged down in Arelate and the delay might keep him here for another two months. He had been forced to call a halt at the first sign of the winter sleet, although they had met no resistance from Rome and the army had swelled to more than twice its original number after a steady trickle of Goths, Franks, Visigoths and the Britons from Armorica had joined it. Despite the occasional sighting of armed horsemen, obviously couriers who were riding hard towards the south, the army of Rome was keeping itself as far as possible from the British forces.

Yet his glum irritation was premature. By his very existence, the High King had lured so many of the emperor's legionnaires to the rebel cause that Honorius's tribunes were fearful of their men's loyalty if they should come into contact with Constantine's army.

The Roman emperor was proving to be ineffectual and

anxious as he sulked in his preferred city of Ravenna, especially now that most of the legions of the West were calling for the elevation of Constantine to the role of co-ruler of the Western Empire.

Yet the emperor still had some support. One large Visigoth force under the leadership of Sarus, a competent commander, was an obvious threat to Constantine's plans but, so far, this army had remained in Italia and had not ventured forth from their bivouac.

Forever anxious, Constantine watched the Roman roads leading into the east with trepidation, for he expected to see Sarus at any time.

Conversely, when his army had been making its slow way along the banks of the Rhodanus, two talented commanders had appeared as if by the hand of Fortuna. The first of these leaders was Nebiogastes, a Frankish general, who met with the High King's army on a dusty section of road shortly after they left Lutetia. Accompanied by a squadron of seasoned cavalrymen, the general was mounted on a huge roan warhorse.

Constantine was warned of the approach of the Frankish column when his force was in bivouac, so he had barely enough time to intercept the impressive Frank at the entrance to the encampment.

'Your name, my lord?' Constantine demanded, but only his height and his manner marked him as a man of rank within the legions. Not surprisingly, the huge Frank pulled on his luxuriant blond moustaches and stared down contemptuously at Constantine, believing him to be an envoy of the king.

'I am Nebiogastes, and I seek Constantine who would be Augustus. Take me to him at once!'

Standing behind Constantine, Paulus snickered with

amusement, a reaction that caused Nebiogastes to sit bolt upright in the saddle. Affronted, he pulled his red cloak around his shoulders as if Constantine's presence might contaminate him.

'Then you're in luck, sir. I assume you're a Frank by your bare chin, although I've been led to believe that most Franks are civilised and charming gentlemen. I am Constantine, but I don't fetch for anyone!'

The surprise on Nebiogastes' face was palpable and he jerked on his horse's reins in a reflex reaction that caused the roan to rear indignantly and bridle with affront.

After this embarrassing exchange, Nebiogastes attempted to regain some semblance of equanimity.

'I offer my apologies, Highness! I didn't suppose for a moment that you would greet me personally when I'm covered in the dirt of the road.'

Neatly done, good sir! Constantine thought with a grin of appreciation. The Frank dismounted immediately, approached the High King and knelt in the dust.

'I've ridden many miles to join you, my lord. Honorius has insulted and bled his Frankish subjects dry for many years. Not since the days of Maximus have my warriors held expectations for a better tomorrow, so we are prepared to fight to the death for you and yours, if you allow us to join you.'

Constantine welcomed the Frank into his inner circle without hesitation, for only a fool would have allowed his personal feelings of irritation to override his common sense.

The other newly found ally was a Roman called Justinianus, a man who displayed such fervent passion that Constantine's instincts warned him to take care. With this officer came elements from a number of the legions in Gallia who leaped at the chance of casting off the yoke of their Roman masters.

Justinianus's followers, proud men in glistening Roman armour, were elite warriors in the western legions, although their long braids and facial hair would have marked them as barbarians in the eyes of their masters in Rome.

Constantine had won supreme control of Gallia without having to lift his sword, despite his need for Honorius to accept that he, a legionnaire who had been a lowly centurion only scant years earlier, was now the co-emperor of the Western Empire.

Constantine had arrived in Gallia at a time when the people of the province were demonstrating their disgust with Rome. Yet, despite the political advantages open to him, the High King still felt that time was slipping away from him . . . day by day.

Provisioning such a large army had proved to be a never-ending problem, one that had inevitably caused some resentment with the local population. Now, at their winter camp at Arelate, Constantine was careful to insist on paying for every chicken and side of beef required by his men, so his war chest was being depleted at a rapid rate. But his forces were yet to strike a single blow against the forces of Rome.

Consequently, his temper became mercurial. Even Paulus felt its lash when he reported several cases of the unpleasant illness known to the legionnaires as *the squirts*.

'By all that's holy, Paulus, what are your junior officers playing at? Dysentery is always caused by poor hygiene. Some of the men must be fouling the river upstream of the bivouac. I've seen that happen before, even though it sounds like the mistake of a tyro.'

Paulus grimaced.

'I think I've been caught out by a supply of dried fish that might have been contaminated. We purchased some barrels of fish at Gesoriacum and, at the time, I thought the price was far too cheap. I should have known that those shifty bastards give nothing away. Ultimately, it's my fault so I'll have to take responsibility for the outbreak.'

'You'll need to put your mistake to rights then, Paulus. I suppose we can't trade the barrels of fish for something else? Or should we keep them, and force our enemies to eat them when they finally show their faces?'

Paulus's face supplied an answer which made Constantine even more irritable because he knew his proposal had been unworthy of him. 'No, I suppose we can't, in all good conscience, do something like that. We'll dump the shite and see if our best hunters can track down some game that will keep the men fed. These men don't take well to inaction when they're in bivouac so, with luck, hunting might keep them occupied.'

Once Paulus had stomped off, offended and irritated, Constantine reviewed his complaints against fate and good luck. He had been delayed at Gesoriacum and his forces had been transported to the continent at what seemed like a snail's pace. Then, the army of Rome had melted away and remained decidedly elusive. Still, he had made some useful allies in the north, so the weeks at Gesoriacum weren't entirely wasted. His scouts had found traces of enemy reconnaissance parties and the wide Roman roads had seen the movement of an occasional courier who took to the woods at the first sign of interception by Constantine's forces during their journey down from Lutetia. But, apart from a few small war parties that retreated into the distance at the first opportunity to escape, his men remained unblooded and were as nervous as he was. Somehow, the initiative of the whole enterprise was slipping away from him.

What do you want, you fool? You have a large army at your back, one that is eager to advance your interests and win you the empire, he thought to himself in the emptiness of his campaign tent. You have won the support of all the major tribes of Gallia and Hispania who will support your claim to the throne. Be patient!

Constantine was avoiding the real cause of his anger and anxiety. Of even more importance than winning the throne for posterity, he desperately wanted to prove to the world that he was worthy to be a ruler, a high king and an emperor. He had heard the whispers that were hissed around the fire pits as logs burned to ash and men finished off their husbanded liquor supplies, tongues loosened.

'Constantine married the throne. Before he met his wife, he was only a lowly centurion, a nothing! What a lucky bastard! He gets a pretty, fertile wife who not only gives him living sons, but she also hands the whole province of Britannia into his hands. He has become the heir of Maximus through a provident marriage – and he didn't have to lift a finger to get it.'

The whispers were ugly and, perhaps, only a few malcontents were ready to speak in such a deprecating way, but Constantine was beginning to see enemies under every tent and behind every tree. Worse still, deep down he doubted his own worth. As his fears grew, the memory of the old prophet, his dirty hair and his ugly warnings were replayed in Constantine's imagination.

He must defeat Rome's army, or everything he had won would be dust in his hands, ash that could be blown away by the cold winds of chance. He must win a great victory that would quieten the whispers and win respect in the eyes of the Roman patricians and the kings of Britannia.

Most of all, he must wipe away the fear and doubt in Severa's eyes.

Now that he was alone in his campaign tent, he could admit that the silent reproach on his wife's face had almost driven him to madness. He almost hated her, because he knew that he still had such a great need for her. Not only was she the source of his power and stability, but some atavistic part of himself realised that she still owned him. Worse still, she understood the internal workings of his mind.

At this moment, an unseasonal snowfall was coating the terrain in a gentle white blanket that caused the warriors to light fires and fill the cracks in their makeshift barracks with moss or old rags that would discourage the draughts. Constantine could have slept in the wooden barracks that the army had constructed within their temporary fortress, or he could have commandeered a small hut for himself, but he never countenanced doing so. He was the leader of this campaign, so he was determined to sleep under sagging leather. By playing the role of a lowly field officer, he was showing his men that he was a man for all seasons.

In truth, the whole army, including Paulus, thought that he was slightly mad.

Wrapped in a bearskin that he had accepted as a gift from a grateful merchant in Lutetia, Constantine wandered to the tent flap and surveyed the camp. Sentries manned the four gates; the shadows cast by pitch torches created grotesque, giant shadow-warriors who could have been Titans that had come, once again, to make war on the gods.

This fort had the eerie, empty feeling of a settlement falling into ruin or a town long deserted by its inhabitants because disease had come, bare-footed, to steal away their lives. Beyond the camp, the trees clustered together for warmth, groaning and cracking under the weight of unlikely ice on their branches. A hunting owl shrieked with triumph as it grasped its kill in iron-fisted talons.

'Spring will soon be upon us and the way to the east will soon be clear. Italia lies naked before me and, by God, I will have my victory,' Constantine vowed.

The owl shrieked again and, with its unearthly cry, a sudden breath of cold air came in from the sea. Constantine pulled the bearskin around his shoulders and refused to accept the taste of fear that, like ashes, was soiling his mouth.

CHAPTER XXI

THE BOY WITH GREY EYES

Let us take warning from another's wound.

St Jerome, *To Furiaso*, Letter 54

Severa had not seen Pridenow since he was a young boy and, as a girl of marriageable age, she had tended to ignore the stripling with all of a young girl's scorn. But, now that he would soon be living in her house, she wondered just what had become of this strange, enigmatic child.

More than anything, she recalled his boisterous nature and the vital physicality he had inherited from Caradoc's line, although she had always guessed at unexpected, secret depths in his nature. Invariably ready for fun and mischief, Pridenow had shown signs of becoming an incorrigible scamp. She also remembered his very white teeth, mainly because he always seemed to be smiling at the world around him.

Severa also had recollections of the boy's strange fits, convulsions presaged by violent headaches that laid him low in his pain-filled bed. In the grip of these afflictions, his dreams had such strange imaginings that the servants relied on their amulets to ensure that evil passed them by.

She had never seen the boy when those dreadful fits struck him down, but she understood why Endellion was afraid. What would Vortigern make of such a boy?

A week after the courier announced Pridenow's imminent arrival, a small group of young men entered Venta Belgarum with the Dobunni prince at its head. The three bodyguards escorting the prince were young and cheerful, and they were obviously close to the lad. Behind the riders, a wagon carrying the prince's personal possessions was trundling along in their wake, driven by a slightly older lad, Emlyn, who was the prince's friend. This young man was the offspring of a Corinium merchant who wished his son to be educated into the warrior class.

When Severa saw the small party enter the city through the western gate and commence the short journey to the King's Hall, she straightened her hair and robe and hastened to greet them.

Pridenow may have been only twelve, but he had assumed a natural gravitas in the intervening years, a trait that made him appear older than he was. He dismounted easily and then, followed by his companions, he approached the queen who was waiting on the steps of the King's Hall. He bowed low so that his tow-coloured hair fell forward over his face.

'There's no need to stand on ceremony, Brother Pridenow. Come! Let me see your handsome face and give you a hug,' Severa demanded with a natural smile.

Pridenow rose to his full height and grinned engagingly. He took three quick steps and hugged her fiercely with a boy's complete lack of ceremony and self-consciousness.

'I can remember you as a young and very pretty girl, Your Majesty. You would chide me and throw your slippers at me whenever I came too close to you.'

Pridenow ushered his companion forward.

'This is Emlyn, Sister Severa. He's my dear friend, who has chosen to join me for the duration of my visit to Venta Belgarum. He yearns for adventure and intends to become a warrior in Vortigern's army, so we look forward to meeting with the great man. Is he here?'

'I bid you good day, Emlyn,' Severa responded evenly, while ignoring the latter part of Pridenow's speech. 'I pray that you'll both enjoy your time with us and that you'll treat Venta Belgarum like your own home.'

She smiled once more at her visitors, leaving Emlyn to blush under her close scrutiny.

As the boys followed the steward to their assigned rooms, Severa watched them and tried to make a dispassionate assessment of her young guests.

Emlyn was as dark as Pridenow was fair. His blue eyes were almost the colour of the midnight sky, and his long, bony frame reminded the queen of a colt that had yet to grow into its long legs. His delicate hands were far too beautiful for sword-work, being long-fingered and sensitive. Yet, when the boy smiled, he was transformed from a gawky youth into a charming young man who hovered on the brink of adulthood.

By comparison, Pridenow's facial features seemed very youthful, despite his adult manner. Although he was tall, his face was still soft with the chubbiness of boyhood and his skin was golden, like the layers of his sun-kissed hair. However the colour of his eyes was the only detail that Severa truly saw. She felt a moment's atavistic fear, as if wights from olden times had appeared before her and beckoned her to follow them into the Otherworld.

Pridenow had shark's eyes of pitiless grey, their irises as naturally flat and featureless as an icy-cold, becalmed sea.

She felt as if her breath had been taken from her for a moment when, like a wild beast with razor-sharp instincts, he suddenly turned back to look at her after feeling her steady regard concentrating on his back. For a short moment, queen and boy gazed at each other in silence, but then Pridenow released her from his mental grip with a happy laugh.

'I do like Venta Belgarum, Sister Severa. There are seagulls here. I saw them circling as we rode towards the gates, so they almost made me feel as if I was back in Tintagel.' His enthusiasm wiped away her fears, so she wondered if she was becoming over-imaginative in these troubled times. Pridenow was a precocious, twelve-year-old boy, not a changeling.

'They'll be scrambling through the midden outside the city gates,' Severa replied, then regretted her casual response when his face fell with disappointment.

'If you wish, and if Vortigern allows you a leave of absence, you could ride to Portus Adurni and obtain excellent views of the sea,' she added, in order to return some humour to their discussion. 'But I must say that it's tamed water in our part of the world, rather than the maelstroms that are seen at Tintagel.'

'There's no such thing as tamed waters, Sister Severa. I love the sea, but Mother has told me that I'm forbidden to cross it. She insists that terrible things will happen if I disregard her warnings. Do you understand her reasoning? I don't!'

Severa swallowed hard. 'Such explanations must wait for later, when you've changed your tunic, Pridenow. Or do you still plan to meet Lord Vortigern covered with grass-stains, dust and charcoal – as you always seemed to be.'

The boys continued to squabble with each other, mainly about seagulls, as they followed Jerome into the heart of the palace and climbed up to the maze-like corridors that had grown

431

with each new Atrebates incumbent. Confused, elated and a little worried, Severa watched the two boys disappear into these rabbit warrens.

Winter retreated, leaving behind a rime of snow that was rapidly turning to muddy slush when Constans ran into Severa's bower. He was red-faced with excitement and incandescent with joy.

'Constans! What's amiss? Why the smiles? I swear that your haste is unseemly, young man.' Severa had decided to reprove him with mock irritation.

'Mother Severa! I must tell you! I have received the most wonderful missive from Father. I am to join him in Gallia, and he thinks I'm old enough to go into battle with him. I am so happy. He even thinks I'm old enough to marry. Somehow, I have never considered being wed, but if Father thinks I should marry, then so shall it be.'

Severa sat stock-still and stared at the lad, now nearly sixteen, with total incomprehension. Wed? Go into battle? What nonsense was Constantine thinking?

'So far, he tells me that all of Gallia has risen up in support of his elevation to become the co-ruler of the Western Empire. Isn't that fine, Mother Severa?'

'It's very fine indeed! It would seem that you are now entitled to wear the purple, Constans. I am truly happy for you. However, I am a little jealous of you because I received no such message from my lord.'

'Oh, I'm sorry, Mother Severa! I forgot! Father said he would be sending a missive to you shortly and will explain everything to you. But now, I must pack for the journey. Lord Vortigern has also been instructed to accompany me on the journey, along with a dozen of the best trainees as a personal guard. I must find him immediately and tell him of Father's wishes.'

'I agree, Constans! You must speak with Vortigern immediately, because there'll be a great deal for him to do.' Severa's heart was in her mouth.

As Constans sprinted away, Severa tried to understand the true meaning of Constantine's message. Obviously, his plans have met with some success in Gallia if the High King is sending for his beloved son. Also, if Constans is to become hand-fasted to a suitable patrician girl, then Constantine must be certain he holds the whip hand over his enemies in Rome.

'Never mind, children,' she said quietly to her own two sons, now a year older and strong in body and spirit. 'Fact is that I'd prefer Vortigern to be in Gallia with Constantine rather than here in Venta Belgarum.'

The words had no sooner escaped from her lips than a terrible thought occurred to her. Vortigern would lose his frail advantage if he failed to neutralise Constans, for a married prince could father a child and that would make any attempt to usurp the High King's throne more difficult than would otherwise be the case. Or was she simply lacking in trust because, at bottom, she felt nervous at the lascivious way that the Demetae king looked at her?

'But if Vortigern should enter the combat beside Constans during the battles that will take place, he might be able to achieve all his goals at once,' she told herself. 'Many men can perish without seeing the secret hands that strike them down, while an arrow from ambush can kill the most careful warrior. Perhaps Constans is in terrible danger.'

Her heart leaped as her mind chewed away at the possibilities that Constantine's missive had created. 'And what will happen to *our* children?'

Before her rational mind took command and argued away these new fears, Severa called for Dilic. The girl arrived, out of breath and clutching at a crumpled piece of mending.

'Yes, mistress?'

'Do you love me, Dilic? More to the point, do you love my children?'

Dilic stared as if the question presaged some form of dangerous trickery. Bewildered, she answered hesitantly.

'Yes, I do! I'd do anything for little Ambrosius. And the same applies to little Uther, as well. I'd still be serving at tables in Tintagel if it weren't for you, so I'll do anything you ask of me.'

'Anything at all?'

Dilic was certain now that the queen was trying to trick her, but she was at a loss to see why and Severa's odd intensity did warn the servant that her mistress was seriously concerned about some unmentioned matter.

'Yes, mistress. I'd be prepared to do anything you asked of me, as long as I wasn't required to sin against the teachings of God.'

'I may ask you, with very little notice, to take my sons to Corinium. This sad day will only dawn if I should learn that young Lord Constans has met with foul play, or if Constantine has been killed or captured by his enemies. As well, if we heard that Lord Vortigern was returning to Venta Belgarum, I might be forced to send the boys to some safe place of refuge. Do you understand me?'

Slowly and inexorably, Dilic realised the dire possibilities that faced her charges. 'Oh, mistress! You can't believe that . . .'

'I must plan for every eventuality, Dilic. If my husband and his son should die, the regent would become the king in all but name until such time as Ambrosius has grown to maturity. If such an event should occur, I doubt that my sons would have any chance of survival.'

'But what will happen to you?'

'I would be the widow of Constantine and the daughter of Maximus, so I would remain the route to the throne for any unscrupulous man who wanted to achieve his ambitions. Perhaps my suspicions about Lord Vortigern are wrong, but I must be certain that my sons are safe.'

'But Corinium is so close to Venta Belgarum. Anyone who wanted to harm your boys would surely find them quickly if you sent them to Queen Endellion. Any competent assassin would expect the boys to be sent to your foster-mother's palace.'

Severa nodded. Good! Dilic's peasant common sense was beginning to assert itself.

'My foster-mother, Queen Endellion, has already made arrangements to spirit my boys to a place of safety in Gallia. If that grey day should dawn, I must ask you to accompany them to their final place of refuge. I'll be entrusting you with the most precious of all my possessions, so you mustn't let them forget me if the worst should happen.'

'I'll do anything you ask of me, mistress, but I'll be hoping that none of these terrible things ever happen. Perhaps we might still remain comfortably in Venta Belgarum for the remainder of our days.'

'Perhaps you're right, Dilic. But I don't believe in luck, so I'll base my plans on the worst acts of treason that can beset us.'

Then Severa hugged her boys so hard that Uther began to wail indignantly. But Ambrosius remained silent, his eyes wide, so Dilic took him from Severa's grasp and smothered his face with kisses.

But Ambrosius's eyes never left his mother's face.

* * *

Before the week was done, Constans and Vortigern were ready to leave with a hand-picked guard of freshly trained young men. Constans was beside himself with excitement, so he was unable to partake of the special repast provided by Severa on the morning of their departure.

'Indeed, Constans, I am hurt! I had supposed that you were happy with us, after all of the time you have spent in our household,' Severa teased. 'You must be eager to leave me, if you're prepared to forego food to escape from my presence.'

The young man's face reddened and his stammered disclaimers caused Severa to kiss him soundly on the cheek.

'I've been playing a May Game with you, Constans, and I'm just teasing you,' she explained. Constans responded with a wide grin.

Vortigern also grinned but his smile was vulpine as his eyes examined every inch of Severa's form, as if he was trying to memorise the lines of her body.

'I'll miss your presence too, Lord Vortigern,' she assured the Demetae king. 'My boys have enjoyed your company and they'll be heart-broken when they realise you've gone.'

If Vortigern suspected that Severa was attempting to convince him that her sons were an asset, rather than a liability, he made no sign of his thoughts. But his smile was wider than usual.

'You're too kind, Queen Severa. I hope that you'd want to see both of us again. For myself, I expect to remain hale and hearty until the day I return!'

'Of course, Lord Vortigern. We have come to know and understand each other very well during the year of your regency. I must admit that I shall miss your common sense and good judgement in the Hall, when I must once again dole out justice in the place of young Constans.'

How easily I have learned to lie since I married. Did I always prevaricate so readily when I was a girl?

Vortigern extended a forefinger and ran it down the length of Severa's face. Somehow, she was able to control the overpowering desire to recoil from his importunate familiarity. With a great effort, she dredged up a natural smile. Vortigern must not suspect her discomfort nor, worse, recognise her utter contempt for him.

'I shall return, Severa. That's a promise, and the Demetae kings always honour their oaths.'

Then Constans gave his stepmother a huge hug, so Vortigern backed away and mounted his horse. His bright eyes never left Severa's face as she went through the motions of making her farewells to her stepson in a vague state that seemed to turn her brain to fluff.

'Don't forget to give my scroll to your father,' she reminded Constans, who showed her the slim scroll-case stuffed inside his tunic. 'Take care, Constans! Trust no one and nothing, other than those things that you know to be true.'

Constans gently prised her hands away from his neck which she was gripping so hard that her knuckles showed white.

'I promise, Mother Severa. You'll see! I'll be back before the year is out with a beautiful young wife for you to train in the intricacies of running a household. Kiss the boys for me.'

And then he was gone.

Their departure was so quick that the roadway seemed to swallow the small troop whole. Severa prayed that God would be kind to this fine young man and that she would see him again in this life. But, even to *her* ears, this wish sounded hollow.

CHAPTER XXII

A MOTHER'S CURSE

Caesar had rather be first in a village than second in Rome.

Julius Caesar, taken from *The Advancement of Learning*,
Francis Bacon

In Arelate, the bulk of Constantine's force was ready to move when spring came tardily on a wave of flowers and bees. Scarlet poppies and swathes of yellow and white daffodils clustered beside the roadways and around the ploughed furrows that held the first green shoots of grain crops. Where trees grew, they sprouted new leaves and fragrant blossoms.

But Constantine took little pleasure in such beauty. His thoughts turned inward, for he was searching for some means of cementing his first year in Gallia, so that Honorius could no longer continue to ignore him.

His son, in company with Vortigern, had made the crossing to Gesoriacum with relative ease. They had ridden hard and fast to cross Gallia and reach Constantine's side, arriving in Arelate long before they were expected. The High King nodded in satisfaction. His boy seemed to be inches taller and wider in the shoulders than Constantine remembered, so he felt a sense of proprietorial pride.

As for the scroll that young Constans had carried for Severa, Constantine was far from satisfied. Within its careful wording, the king realised that his wife was very unhappy.

From the hand of Severa, Wife of Constantine,
To her husband, High King of the Britons.
Greetings.

I hope you are well, Husband, and you have succeeded in your ambition to claim the throne of Rome. I remain well and your two younger sons continue to grow quickly. Ambrosius will soon be four years and is a little prince in all ways.

Since you have chosen to leave me ignorant of the victories you have won, I suffer terrors for your safety. I was pleased to learn of your successes from Constans, who is a dear boy and one who is likely to make an excellent king, but I yearn to receive a missive from your own hand.

Vortigern has laboured hard to rebuild the guard and train an army to protect our island, but sometimes his hand falls too heavily on your subjects and they grumble under his rule. I regret to say that they will be happy he has journeyed to Gallia with Constans.

I realise that affairs of state must preoccupy you, especially as you now hold all the lands of the Franks in your hands, but Britannia made you a king. I would caution you that if the Saxons should return, there will be no one to stop them. You may return to a land that is aflame from end to end and no throne left to claim.

I ask that you send word of your plans to me so I will no longer suffer in ignorance. Your sons hunger for your return, as do I.

Severa,

Written at Venta Belgarum.

'Lying bitch!' Constantine whispered as he threw down the scroll after the fourth reading. 'You've always been a woman with strong opinions, so I know full well what's passing through your mind. You think that I don't intend to return to Britannia.'

Constantine had no intention of returning to Britannia, either now or in the future, so Severa's fears had hit a raw nerve. But the accuracy of her words only served to make him even more resentful.

A month can change the world, Constantine thought morosely, as he replaced the scroll in its case and threw it into a chest in the corner of his tent where it would be hidden from prying eyes.

Constans and his small party had arrived with full panoply. The eyes of the young prince had been full of stars and, before he had the time to consider his situation, he found himself married off to the daughter of one of the Frankish kinglets. When Constantine was impelled to undertake a task, the speed of his actions was dazzling and, within two weeks, Constans had been sent off to the court of the Frank king where he would take care of business for his father. He had left his new wife behind.

'I hope the boy has enjoyed his beautiful young spouse during their short marriage because there don't seem to be many enduring pleasures in the place where he'll be living for the next few months,' Constantine said aloud, and laughed.

The girl in question was a pale-faced child of thirteen, who looked like a doll in her stiff robes. She had looked terrified as the Bishop of Arelate had hand-fasted her to this strange young man with the kind eyes.

Constantine laughed again. The boy would discover quickly that females, regardless of age, tried to exert power over their menfolk. Let the boy beware!

In all respects, Constantine had little to complain about in the north, for one of his legions was guarding the frontier while, with the assistance of barbarian mercenaries in Germania, his allies conspired to keep the other tribes at bay. Honorius was preoccupied with attacks from a Vandal army that was rampaging, with little opposition, through the softer lands to the north of Italia. As these Vandal warriors carried out their opportunistic raids, General Sarus remained ensconced in the relative safety of his bivouac near Rome, while Stilicho, another talented Roman commander, was unable to help Honorius with his defence of the Roman lands.

'What else can we do now, master, for the Western Empire is yours in all but name,' Paulus had been fond of saying. 'Honorius must weaken soon and he will beg for peace.'

'I intend to make Honorius refer to me as the Augustus. And I want the senate to recognise me as the sole emperor of their precious city. I want to beat the shite out of them all, so that they will be forced to beg for mercy. And the bastards will realise that they've been beaten at the self-same moment that I cut Honorius's throat.'

The world can change in a heartbeat when frightened and greedy men come together to discuss the accumulation of power.

Constantine summoned Nebiogastes and Justinianus, the two senior Roman officers who had defected to his cause, to discussions where they were ordered to mount a reconnaissance in strength into the north-east that would take their forces through the easily approached coastal strip leading into Italia. If the advance undertaken by these generals proved to be successful, the remainder of Constantine's army could march on Rome with minimal opposition, a move that would culminate in a triumphant entry to the City of the Seven Hills.

After this success, Constantine would no longer be overlooked.

But strategies that are easily thrown together during long nights of planning can still go awry when rash tactical decisions are made by flawed commanders with limited strategic ability.

Like a precarious tower of flat, un-mortared stones, Constantine's planning began to collapse before his eyes. His first presentiment of trouble came with the arrival of a desperate courier, sorely wounded and staggering, from the direction of Valentia.

The man was pale from fatigue and loss of blood, but he forced himself to stand proudly erect on his own two legs to complete his allotted task. Two of his three horses had died from exhaustion during his desperate ride.

'I beg you to forgive the tongue that brings bad news to your ears,' the courier began, an indication that Constantine would be angered by his report.

'You will be treated like the superb soldier that you are,' Constantine replied stiffly. He felt trouble itching its way along the back of his neck.

The young cavalryman lowered his head in remorse. 'The generals, Sarus and Stilicho, have brought a Roman army to the fields outside Valentia, where the tributary joins with the Rhodanus River.'

'Yes, I'm familiar with those lands. We came that way during our own journey into the south.' Constantine's hand wanted to inch its way towards the maps that were kept on his desk. He stilled his fingers with an effort and forced himself to concentrate on the courier's message.

'The Frank general led his men in a direct frontal attack against the main force of Sarus's legionnaires,' the courier began.

'The general ordered his cavalry to charge at the very centre of the advancing Roman army where their foot soldiers were concentrated. I'll not deny the Franks' bravery, but they were riding directly into a trap that had been set for them.'

Constantine grunted in annoyance and snapped out a response that caused the cavalryman to whiten in fear. 'It isn't your place to criticise officers.'

'But this was the strategy of a fool, master! Your soldiers observe your tactics and we all know that you have forced your enemies to fall into traps on many occasions. One hundred men, correctly led, can prevail against a much larger attacking force, and these Roman legionnaires were led by officers who knew exactly what they were doing.'

Constantine gritted his teeth, for he could imagine the sequence of events that was about to be described.

'Nebiogastes was killed in the first wave, my lord. Justinianus took command of the survivors and he managed to prevent a total rout, but he was forced to retreat within the walls of Valentia where he is besieged. He sent six of us to bring news to you of the disaster that had befallen him. We escaped by walking through the sewers, stealing horses and then riding like hell to reach Arelate.'

'You're the only man to arrive, so Sarus must have captured the other couriers. We're lucky that you're such a determined young man, so you will be well rewarded for your efforts,' Constantine replied flatly.

Strangely, he was beginning to feel more confident, now that he had an assailable enemy.

'See to this young man's hurts, Paulus, for he needs a healer! Then find Gerontius and Edobichus for me. They want to show me that they're equal to the task of crushing Honorius, so they can start with this Sarus who, at the very least, has sufficient initiative to come out of hiding. For all that, Stilicho must also be nearby. He'll be a dangerous opponent. I've heard of his military prowess – even if the bastard is a patrician,' Constantine added with a sneer.

Then he assisted the wounded courier to rise to his feet. His solicitude was real, for it was the sympathy of one fighting man for another, and the young cavalryman almost wept with gratitude. His head drooped with his exhaustion as two guards hurried forward to lift him up and bear him away.

'Well, Paulus! We finally have an enemy to fight.' The indecision and frustration that had plagued Constantine for months was lifted from his shoulders and he seemed to be reinvigorated by the courier's message.

'Aye, sir,' Paulus replied crisply, grateful that his master had found a living, breathing enemy to fight.

The older soldier had long suspected that his commander could sometimes be a rash leader when he was dealing with intangibles. All those years when he was forced to obey the orders of others, Paulus decided, were now acting against the initiative of the High King.

Gerontius and Edobichus, two generals from the defecting legions in Gallia, came to their commander's tent as soon as Paulus's message reached them.

Why any man who had risen so high as his master would choose to dwell in such draughty conditions as this tent defied Gerontius's imagination. Perhaps the Roman shared his scorn with many of Constantine's officers, but he was one of the few men who might dare to speak of this tent aloud, and to Constantine's face. It said much of his personal courage, while demonstrating a flaw in his assessment of the High King.

Paulus held no trust in the seasoned Gerontius, because something in the man's manner betrayed an ambitious nature that might flare up at some point. Besides, once a turncoat, always a turncoat.

'Good! It's pleasing that you haven't kept me waiting, gentlemen,' Constantine said as soon as they passed through the tent flap. 'Has Paulus discussed the latest debacle with you?'

Edobichus saluted and then nodded, but Gerontius saw fit to elaborate on the topic of incompetence.

'Aye, sir.' His eyes roamed over the spartan camp stove and desk, and he raised his eye-brow at the neatly made camp bed in one corner. 'I've heard that the Frank has thrown his life away in a pointless display of suicidal idiocy.'

Offended that Gerontius was so obviously scornful of someone he considered beneath him, Constantine slapped the presumptuous officer down swiftly.

'For all the Frank's faults, Nebiogastes was a brave man. I might add that he has delayed Sarus's planned attack on our forces, an action that might have caught us napping, especially if he was to make an advance on our rearguard. We were given the boon of having more time to prepare our armies once Justinianus had the sense to retreat into Valentia, so you'll now have an opportunity to show your mettle and provide him with relief of the siege. You, Gerontius, will take Sarus out of our path, along with his legions, and relieve our legionnaires who are trapped inside the town. Edobichus will command your cavalry! I'm placing a great deal of faith in both of you, so don't let me down.'

Then, with a wave of his hand, Constantine dismissed the two men. Both were patricians by birth and, if Constantine enjoyed his small exercise of power over them, his tightly closed face revealed nothing.

* * *

In the months that followed, Severa still heard no word of her husband, apart from vague rumours that came to Britannia from traders in Gallia. Endellion made her promised visit and enjoyed a brief holiday with her son, Pridenow, who was excused from military training for the duration of her visit.

Nor did Endellion arrive with empty hands. On the second day of Endellion's visit, the Dobunni queen approached her foster-daughter as they sat companionably in the ladies' bower to watch her grandsons as they played among the climbing roses.

'Watch out for their thorns, Uther. Those red roses will hurt you if you pull at their stems, so be gentle. That's a good boy!'

Severa exchanged a rueful smile with her foster-mother.

'Uther is always grasping at things that take his fancy. He doesn't seem to mind the pain.'

'He's a strong boy, Severa. I hold no doubts that his life will be long and he'll carve out a place for himself, despite your fears.' Severa wondered if her foster-mother was seeing his future through that queer internal vision of hers.

'Ambrosius is much like his name – sweet and thoughtful. The boys are so different. It's a wonder, isn't it?'

Endellion nodded, and then pressed a small piece of linen into Severa's hands.

'What is this, Mother Endellion?'

The small packet was opened to reveal a golden amulet with the incised outline of a fish upon it. The gold was warm to the touch and the outline of the fish was only partially visible, but Severa was surprised that such a venerable object should be wrapped so carelessly. Then she realised that the stiff linen had been written on in some kind of black ink. The whole was addressed to Apollodorus, a vintner in Falencia in the province of Hispania.

'I don't understand, Endellion. What have this charm and this vintner to do with me?'

'They would mean little to you at the moment, but they might become important to the safety of your sons in the future. My Aeron knew the son of Apollodorus, a young man who was killed while serving with the remnants of the British cavalry when Maximus was defeated in Italia. Although the vintner's son, Andragathius, wasn't a close friend, he was a part of the detachment that assisted Aeron to escape from Italia after Maximus's defeat. Aeron swore to Andragathius that he'd take word of the man's love to Apollodorus during the return journey to his homeland. Although this task extended an already long journey, my dear old man kept his word. Apollodorus feels beholden to Aeron and the amulet is proof of that debt.'

'But I still don't understand. What can this Apollodorus do for me and mine?'

'If the time should come when your sons must flee from Venta Belgarum, they must be taken by ship to the Suevi lands in Hispania. Once there, they must be transported by a man called Daire, who owns a fishing vessel called *Neptune's Kiss*. His boat can usually be found at a fishing village called Burdigala. Many of our people live in the Suevi lands, and Daire has agreed to transport them to Apollodorus for a fee in gold. Aeron has arranged all these details in advance. This Daire will not willingly sail during the season of the winter storms, but he will make suitable arrangements to keep your boys safe from those that would harm them. Aeron says that Daire is trustworthy and my husband is a good judge of character. Once they are safely on his boat, all that would be needed would be to send word to Apollodorus, who will come for them.'

'Who is this Daire, and why should I trust my sons to him? I have no way of knowing what will happen to them,' Severa asked anxiously.

'He, too, served with Maximus and Aeron in Gallia, so he is prepared to do whatever is required to ensure the safety of the grandsons of Magnus Maximus,' Endellion stated.

'You've gone to much trouble to assuage a woman's formless fears,' Severa said, while clutching at Endellion's loom-scarred fingers.

'Pish, Severa! My father was your father's closest friend and trusted companion, while you are almost blood-kin to me. Above all, you are the High Queen of the Britons. Any service to our rulers is minute, when calculated against the grand schemes of the world.

'You must memorise everything I have told you and keep both the amulet and its wrapping close at hand in case there is an urgent need for them to make good their departure at short notice. Perhaps there will be no need for the precautions that we have discussed, but the boys will thank you if Fortuna were to cast her dice in the wrong direction. If danger should threaten, the boys must be able to make a successful escape.'

'I wish I could believe that no danger exists, but shadows are massing in the east of Gallia. I am afraid.'

'As are we all,' Endellion replied and the two women hugged each other for comfort as the children played at their feet in a shower of rose petals.

A messenger eventually arrived from Portus Adurni, carrying a scroll and a small waterproof pouch from Constans in Gallia. Disappointed that the missive wasn't from Constantine, Severa opened the pouch to discover that it contained a pair of heavy golden earrings with large pins to hang them from her earlobes. Large red stones were set into the earrings, but she believed her earlobes would tear before they could safely bear such a weight.

The missive, although it was short, was cheerful.

To Severa, High Queen of the Britons,
At Venta Belgarum.
Greetings.

What a time we have had, Mother Severa, and how exciting it has been. I am fortunate indeed to be the son of the co-emperor of Rome, and Emperor of the West, Constantine III, who is your husband.

Yes! After all this time, Emperor Honorius has submitted to the obvious good, and has agreed to Father's demands. I have enclosed a congratulatory gift from Father to you, jewels befitting an Empress of Gallia and Hispania that can be worn in your ears. I hope they reach you and that you like them.

Severa looked up from the page as tears clouded her vision. Endellion had left Venta Belgarum a few weeks earlier, so the High Queen had no one but Dilic with whom she could share her disappointment. Constantine left it to his son to inform her of his great victory over the might of Rome.

She bowed her head to the scroll once again.

So much has happened that I scarcely know what to tell you first.

Sarus, Honorius's general, was soundly defeated by a composite force led by Gerontius and has been chased back into Italia with his tail between his legs. Father set to work with a will and undertook a series of efforts to consolidate his tactical and strategic position. He left Arelate to secure all the passes that lead into Gallia from Italia. Honorius cannot outflank us now, without our full knowledge of his intentions.

We have made Arelate the capital, so Father has decided to give up living in his campaign tent, thank heavens. He has taken over the magistrate's villa, where we are quite comfortable, except for the magistrate. Apollinaris has been compensated, however, for he has been appointed to the position of prefect. He is the grandson of Sidonius Apollinaris, so Father is very pleased.

Severa looked up blankly. Who was this Sidonius Apollinaris? Was he a patrician? Or perhaps he was one of Rome's great generals? Constans was so enthusiastic in his praise that he forgot to explain any of the details that would give sense to the narrative.

'Mama! Mine!' Uther had found one of her new earrings in her lap and was now playing with it in the light, so that the red stone glowed richly like a drop of freshly spilled blood. 'Mine?' he asked hopefully.

'No, darling! These earrings are a gift to your mother from Father.' Distracted now, she dropped her eyes to the scroll and her stepson's large, vigorous handwriting.

Father has given me a special task to carry out, so I will be leaving in a week with Gerontius. I am fortunate indeed to have the advice of such a man who is devoted to my father.

Emperor Honorius has family who are ensconced in Hispania where they are well placed to attack the rear of our forces, if we allow them to live unchecked. I have been ordered to capture them, bind them and then send them to my father for judgement. I am confident that I will succeed in this task, if God helps me. Pray for me, Mother

Severa, and I know I will not fail in complying with Father's wishes.

Lord Vortigern's worth has been recognised. Father has appointed him to be his seneschal. Vortigern is pleased, although I sometimes find it difficult to tell exactly what my teacher is actually thinking.

I will write again when I have completed the task that Father has given me. Meanwhile, I can assure you that he has won a great victory without having to wage a pitched battle.

Farewell.

From Constans, Son of Constantine III, Augustus.

At the hand of the scribe, Laertes

Severa's heart was filled with loss for what might have been, for herself and her husband. But at least Constans had not forgotten her need for family connection. The duties of caring for those British people who lived under Constantine's protection weighed heavily on her shoulders.

But Severa was also able to judge her own worth through the service that she provided to the citizens of their kingdom. With the assistance of Cadal and Aeron, she had ensured that there was a military presence in and around Venta Belgarum that provided security to the inhabitants of the town and its environs. When her husband eventually returned, he would soon discover that the day to day administration of his kingdom had been carried out to his satisfaction.

But would he care?

Autumn arrived and, with it, the first of the bitter winds. Winter followed inexorably and, in the miserable pattern of the past few years, the cold weather in the south was unseasonal and excruciating. Venta Belgarum shivered within its walls and drew its skirts around itself in a vain attempt to obtain some precious warmth. Constantine had taken the stores of grain and essential supplies for his army, so wives, children and orphans were starving in cold crofts with few males capable of providing for the needy. The bishop of Venta Belgarum donated the entire grain store owned by the church, but the number of empty mouths mocked their remaining providence. Death came with the solstice, until Severa felt the forces of doom weighing heavily on her.

Then, when spring finally released the earth from winter's iron grip, dreadful news reached Constantine's city.

A merchant brought the first news of piratical barbarians, having barely escaped with his life from the port of Anderida.

'Saxon pirates struck our town as soon as the sea-ways were open. They burned and killed at will, for the garrison was unmanned. I fled into the swamps with the other families who knew that we had no chance of fighting the bastards off, and we returned after the fires of Anderida had finally died down.'

Severa sat on her hard chair in the King's Hall and twisted her hands together in the folds of her robe. 'And?' she asked, her harsh voice betraying her concern.

The merchant paused while he tried to respond with a definite answer.

'Do the Saxons still hold Anderida?' she asked again, while she tried to conjure up a strategy that might drive them out. Alternatively, she needed to know whether the barbarians intended to remain in Britannia for an indefinite period of time.

'No, Highness! They left Anderida in their wicked boats as quickly as they arrived. They killed every living thing, even the dogs, and they took every usable item they could find. They left a young boy to greet us on our return, but his grip on life was only sufficient to give us a message from the leader of the Saxons. The boy's eyes and hands had been removed, and they only spared his tongue so he could repeat their grisly warnings. The thane said that Constantine had refused to include the Saxons in his alliances in Gallia, so the destruction of Britannia would become their answer to his insults. I wish the High King had never sailed away, Highness, for he has left us naked and friendless to face the storm that will surely come to us during spring and summer.'

'Do you know where the Saxons went after they left Anderida?' Severa asked. 'Did they threaten Portus Adurni?'

'No, Highness! They sailed into the east, for they seemed eager to plunder Londinium and her sister cities before the summer is done. I don't believe they'll come to Venta Belgarum.'

A stream of refugees began to flow into the western tribal areas, and the new arrivals carried what little they were able to salvage from the Saxon scourge. All told the same tale, of Saxon insult and a land that had been left naked by the High King's absence.

Severa was beside herself, and remained so until Pridenow suggested that he could be sent as a courier to Constantine in Gallia. Once there, he would beg for the men and arms needed to send the Saxons scurrying back to their own lands.

'No, Pridenow. Your intentions are sound, but I'll not betray my oath to your parents by allowing you to cross the Litus Saxonicum. I do have an alternative proposal. Although you're not yet a warrior, I will permit you to lead a select group of six trainees and carry out a patrol of Anderida Silva, especially the higher terrain between the forests and the coast where Saxon activity can be expected. I need some good, reliable intelligence about any Saxon movements around the outskirts of Anderida.

Meanwhile, I'll send a missive to Cadal and beg for the loan of sufficient men from his reserve forces who could replace you in Venta Belgarum while you carry out this mission for me.'

Although disappointed, Pridenow vowed to discover exactly what the Saxons were about.

'But you mustn't put yourself and your other lads at risk, for we are in dire need of every man and boy we have. I want you to swear that you'll exercise restraint and be sensible with this important task you have been given.'

With some reluctance, Pridenow gave Severa his word.

'Insofar as Constantine's forces are concerned, I will not allow the doom contained in Caradoc's prophecy to be inflicted on our people, not even at the risk of further Saxon attacks.'

'But someone must alert the High King to the danger in which we have been placed,' Pridenow continued to insist until, eventually, Severa acknowledged that he was correct.

Fortunately there was no dearth of volunteers prepared to make the dangerous crossing from Britannia to Gallia. King Aeron, newly arrived on a visit from Corinium, agreed to lead a small contingent of his own men across the waters, for he had a detailed understanding and knowledge of the provinces of Gallia, Italia and Hispania. Severa accepted Aeron's offer regretfully, for she knew that Endellion would have no peace until her man returned. And so Aeron and Pridenow departed on desperate missions. Aeron would carry a lengthy scroll to Constantine, while the good wishes of the citizenry of southern Britannia would be resting on his still-square shoulders.

As for Pridenow, he and his friends rode away in good cheer, his eyes even more devil-may-care than usual.

Then, as another autumn came, the court of Venta Belgarum waited.

With a milder freeze and little snow, winter came late and finished early, yet no word came to Venta Belgarum of Aeron and his contingent. The weeks dragged by like years, until Severa could feel the weight of the crown bending her head and crushing her spirit.

A further spring came, along with more Saxon pirates who, blessedly, contented themselves with sacking Camulodunum, Venta Icenorum and Branodunum in the north. Blood stained the coastal towns and Constantine's officials were driven out of the city of Verulamium by its own people. This town had always been used as the bureaucratic heart of the Roman province by the British kings, so Severa began to think that there would be little of Constantine's kingdom left to obey his dictums once he did return.

Yet the people found no fault with Queen Severa and the kings of the west supported her reign. As best she could, she gave succour to refugees and citizens alike. Meanwhile, Pridenow matured under her guidance, and he rode far and fast in the saddle as he became her eyes and ears in the eastern parts of Britannia.

Still, no word was heard from Aeron. Nor were there any rumours or discussions about the king in any of the ports that could be expected to hear word about him. In Corinium, Endellion was privately fearful that her husband had met his death.

As the summer sun beat down with an unusual heat that baked the earth to the consistency of solid stone and the flow of water through the streams was reduced to a mere trickle, a small group of riders disembarked from a Frankish vessel at Portus Adurni and began the short ride to Venta Belgarum. Severa was informed of the imminent arrival of the contingent before they had covered half of the dusty miles that led to her gates. In an agony of dread, she waited at the ramparts. Pridenow understood her suspense, telling her he had dreamed last night of two ravens found dead in a midden, but nevertheless urged her to rest while she could.

'When Aeron and his troop dismounted in the forecourt of the King's Hall, she was the first to meet them and could scarcely wait for the courtesies to be completed.

'What has happened, Father Aeron? Where is my husband? How is Constans?' She was barely able to control her speech as she suffered an agony of impatience. Aeron's hooded eyes refused to meet hers, so Severa knew that the information he carried was grave. Instead, he embraced his tall son, now man-sized after more than two years of living in Severa's house and serving in the new frontier areas of Britannia.

'Let me wash away the dregs of the road from my throat, Highness, and I'll answer you as best I can,' he replied formally as he relinquished his son's arms. Then, once he had drunk a goblet of wine with the barest shadow of a smile, he asked to be taken to some private place where they could speak in comfort.

Flustered and frightened, and with only Pridenow at her side, Severa led her foster-father and his son into her own private apartment. She ordered Dilic to arrange food and drink for Aeron's guard and then to position herself outside the closed door so the privacy of those inside the room could be protected. Then, with her own hands, Severa poured another goblet of wine for Aeron, who gulped it down gratefully. Satisfied, she waited in an anxiety of stillness until her foster-father was ready to speak.

The tale related by Aeron was worse than anything her fertile mind could have imagined.

'At first, everything that Constantine touched was golden, as if the old gods had decided that he was worthy of holding the seat of power in Rome. Constans was sent to Hispania with Gerontius and their contingent returned with two of Honorius's cousins, Didymus and Verinianus, whom they had captured. Unfortunately, two other members of Honorius's family were able to escape from their clutches. Lagodius made his way to Rome, while Theodosiolus followed an even longer route that took him to the court of the Eastern Empire in Constantinople. Each man gave a detailed account of Constantine's attempted coup, a base strategy that raised the ire and disgust of the Eastern Emperor. It would have been better if Constantine had left these four men be, for there was no evidence that they had been plotting against him. But your husband had grown fearful of unseen enemies, so he acted foolishly.'

'What did my husband do with the two prisoners captured by Constans?' Severa asked, her heart sinking at the possible outcomes of Constantine's ill-considered fears.

'I'm afraid he was enraged and ordered them to be executed out of hand. Neither man was any real threat to Constantine, but he was certain that they would foment a revolt if they were permitted to remain free and unfettered within the Hispanic lands. His fear of treachery was a great mistake on Constantine's part, for his actions hardened the hearts of those rulers who opposed him. By all accounts, Constantine's reaction had been swift and brutal, so it became obvious that Honorius would never forgive such an insult.'

Severa lowered her head in despair. 'My husband has always had a streak of rashness when he is crossed by others, but I'd been told by Constans that Constantine had already been accepted as the co-emperor in conjunction with Honorius.'

'True!' Aeron agreed, and then he shrugged. 'Hard on the heels of Constans's return, word came to Constantine that the patrician, Stilicho, had been executed at Ticinum in Italia. Units of the Roman's army had rebelled and its legionnaires had declared themselves for Constantine, so your husband ignored any advice from Apollinaris or Gregorius, men who had been vocal in their reluctance to pursue Constantine's strategies. Your husband believed himself to be invincible, so Apollinaris found himself replaced as prefect by Decimus Rusticus, a Praetorian, and God only knows what happened to the Watcher. It's unfortunate, but your husband becomes dangerously wilful when he believes he is being manipulated by his advisers.'

Severa nodded, painfully aware of Constantine's flaws in this regard.

'Then, at the time of our arrival at your husband's bivouac, Constantine's plans began to unravel. Armorica rebelled and their troops left your husband's service. Their warriors simply melted away during the night. Constantinus decided to roll the dice and follow the example of Magnus Maximus. He marshalled his legions and marched on Italia, but several decisive battles were lost. Constantine was forced to retreat back into Gallia and Honorius was given an excellent example of Constantine's greatest weakness. When pushed, your husband acts too quickly for rational thought and tends to fall back on the use of force rather than employ diplomacy and good negotiation skills.'

Severa nodded in agreement. 'My husband was always the centurion, Father Aeron. At bottom, he truly believes that the use of brute force will achieve most of his goals.'

'Aye! But the troubles that were about to punish Constantine were still in their infancy. At this crucial time in Constantine's campaign against the power of Rome, Gerontius decided to elevate his own son, coincidentally called Maximus, to usurp the political position adopted by Constantine. Gerontius and Maximus came out of Hispania to crush your husband through a treacherous attack on his rear.'

Aeron paused as he considered his next words.

'I regret to inform you that we received reports that Constans had been killed by Gerontius's troops in Vienna. This information was followed by believable rumours that the young man's wounds had been inflicted on the back of his body, so many among us believed that Vortigern was directly responsible for his death. I have no knowledge of the whereabouts of the Demetae king, then and now, but I have heard from my sources that every member of Constans's Gallic family-by-marriage had been assassinated during the following weeks. His little wife was already pregnant, but she was killed anyway, despite being harmless in all ways.'

'Poor Constans! He could never see the danger in following the stars of his father with such open trust. He was too loyal and too trusting of everyone he knew, including me.'

Severa began to weep for a young man and his even-younger wife who would receive no other mourning from any other soul.

Then Aeron's final words slipped into her conscious thoughts and she realised that Vortigern's actions had signed a death warrant for her own sons. She blanched with fear.

'My God! My own children will also be at risk when that monster returns to Britannia. He has removed any family members that could be considered kin to Constans. My boys are the only impediment between him and the throne of the High King of the Britons.'

She turned to Aeron with a pleading expression on her face.

'As Constantine's regent, the other tribal kings will consider

Vortigern to be a potential saviour when the Saxon menace increases in the coming spring. You know that I'm right to be fearful, Aeron! The British kings will accept anyone who is prepared to fight for them and protect their fiefdoms. My sons can't defend themselves, so he'll kill them without hesitation – and then marry me! If he has any doubts about these actions, he will wed me first and then cause them to vanish. What can I do?'

'I will take them with me to Corinium when I leave,' Aeron stated in a determined voice. 'If Vortigern should return to Venta Belgarum, I'll send them away to my friends in Gallia, exactly as we have planned.'

Aeron's calm assertions soothed Severa, who was fast becoming hysterical.

'All will be well, daughter, and I swear that no harm will come to them. It's your own safety that is causing me the greatest concern.'

Severa knew her position demanded that she keep a cool head on her shoulders. She called on the shades of Maximus and Caradoc, and willed her heart to slow its breakneck pace.

'Is Constantine still alive, Aeron? Don't try to spare my feelings, for there is much that has to be done if we are to save the people of Britannia from Vortigern's assault on the throne. It's unlikely that any of the legions will return to our lands, so we must look to our own resources.'

'I agree with you, Severa. The legions have gone – and they'll never return to our shores! In fact, I spied Tribune Maximo at Portus Adurni when he was taking ship for Italia, so the rats are leaving the sinking ship. But we'll not go down without a fight. Britannia is still rich and trade will continue to flourish, so we'll learn to depend on ourselves rather than some Roman overlord.

We've been acquiescent for far too long. Our people will sink or swim, and the Saxon menace will remain unchecked until such time as we find ways to counter their incursions.'

Aeron paced around the lavish apartments, his eyes blind to the fine silks and wools on floors or walls.

Eventually, he gave the queen the last, and the worst, of his news.

'Small bands of our warriors may return from Gallia, but I have little hope that they can survive. Constantine is encircled by enemies now and I barely escaped from Arelate before it was besieged by Constantius, one of Honorius's better generals. Your husband had already despaired, for word reached him that Gerontius had been defeated by Rome before committing suicide. At this time, Decimus Rusticus, the Praetorian, had done what men of his ilk do best by abandoning Constantine to his fate. At the last minute, the remaining legion guarding the Rhenus River, a large force that Constantine had hoped to rally to his cause, followed Rusticus on to the side of Honorius. Constantine is finished!'

'But did my husband survive the battles?' Severa asked with a dim ray of hope still visible in her eyes.

'He's worse than dead! I've been told that he relinquished his position as co-emperor by impersonating a priest, of all things. No doubt he hopes that this pretence will save him from the wrath of Honorius. I have no expectation that this ploy will work, for the emperor loved his cousins and he will exact his revenge for their murders. Constantine played a dangerous game with Fortuna, but she has prevailed by rolling her wheel and pulling him down to disaster.'

'So there's no hope,' Severa replied. Aeron wished that he could tell a kindly lie, but Severa remained the High Queen. She

461

must face facts, if the people of Britannia were to have any hope of survival.

'In my opinion, Severa, Constantine was neither the man nor the soldier that Maximus was. Yet, he succumbed to the same hubris and he was doomed from the moment he left our shores. Sadly, the birds of prey will feed on the corpse of our lands.'

Severa nodded dumbly.

'Do you intend to come with your sons when I leave here, Severa? Endellion and I can also protect you at Tintagel.'

Severa rose shakily and looked out at the quiet town of Venta Belgarum that was laid out below them. The sun glared on the Roman-tiled roofs and threw light back from whitewashed walls and marble columns. The whole town seemed peaceful and at rest, but she knew that this calm was only an illusion that preceded the arrival of the summer storms. Her duty was with her people, whatever her heart told her. She knew that any claimant to the throne of High King would pursue her, for she held the route to power in her slender body. Should she decide to flee from her fate, then she would endanger her sons.

'If my sons are gone, Vortigern might ignore them for the greater prize: myself! No, Dilic will accompany the boys until such time as they are settled into their new homes in Gallia. She knows what is required of her.'

Aeron rose to join her and placed a hand on her stiffening shoulder. Under his fingers, Severa's body felt brittle, as if it could easily shatter under the slightest blow.

Then she turned and faced her foster-father with a hint of her old courage.

'You must leave in the morning, Father Aeron, in company with Dilic and the children. Their nurses will accompany the boys on their journey to Corinium before returning to Venta

Belgarum. I will see to their packing. I ask that you provide suitable protection for the journey that will take them into Gallia. Meanwhile, I will continue to do what is expected of me as the High Queen. Any joy we wrench out of life must be paid for, and my sons have been my blessing as well as Constantine's only gift to me that holds any worth. With luck, we will be left in peace in Venta Belgarum and my boys might eventually return to Britannia and their home. Pray for us all, Aeron.'

The packing of clothing for two terrified children, their possessions and their servants took some little time but, finally, all was completed.

On a grey day when the long-awaited summer rains finally came to lay the dust, Severa knelt in the mud to kiss her sons and make her farewells. Ambrosius's eyes were wet, but he was trying manfully to be brave for his mother's sake. Uther wailed with four-year-old gusto and beat at Dilic with his clenched fists as she tried to calm him. Mercifully, Aeron ordered the wagons to depart in a bid to end the children's suffering.

'All the portents have come to pass, Pridenow,' Severa said sadly to the youth standing beside her. 'Your two ravens are dead and only the living will remember their names in the years to come. And I? God only knows what will become of me.'

'Heaven alone can be certain of the accuracy of the prediction that one of your descendants will save our world. Perhaps the seers who give us these prophecies are right, Highness, and all this suffering will be seen to have some tangible purpose.'

Severa looked into Pridenow's grey eyes and saw with surprise that, no longer cold, they glistened like sun-warmed glaciers. She began to take heart.

'My sons are in Aeron's safe hands now, so I have nothing to fear. Whatever comes will come! Nothing worse can plague me, so Vortigern can have whatever is left of me, if he should still want the dregs.'

'And may the bastard take some joy from his success,' Pridenow responded sardonically, causing Severa to laugh at the emptiness of men's ambition.

Severa and Pridenow stood in the rain at the gates for some time after the small cavalcade had disappeared from view and the falling droplets covered the landscape in a veil of tears.

EPILOGUE

The road to Ravenna was almost empty of traffic by the time that the general, Constantius, called a halt in mid-afternoon. Clad in a dusty black robe belted by a simple rope tied around the waist, and wearing sandals that were grey with dirt and stains, the general's prisoner sank down in the chains that attached him to the rear of the leading wagon.

Constantine had been forced to walk behind his conqueror's wagons from Arelate, where he had been captured. During the long and dusty journey, his captors had refused to meet his eyes for fear that Fortuna's bad luck might be transferred to them. As he drank from a pannikin of water offered by Constantius's decurion, Constantine asked about the clerical position he could expect within Ravenna's administration. He had been promised this employment before his surrender, and the offer had sustained him during the long, weary miles as he considered the prospect of a comfortable future. Something might yet be salvaged from the mess that had been made of his life.

The decurion made a trifling reply, but refused to meet the gaze of the erstwhile emperor.

What could any true fighting man say to a leader who had possessed the numbers and the opportunity to decisively crush the power of Rome, yet managed to squander all his advantages?

What had this dishevelled man done to turn the face of God so adamantly away from him? If the High King's shame was catching, then this decurion wanted no part of it.

Behind their hands, other legionnaires smirked or grimaced at the foolishness of this black-robed man who had gambled his all on one last attempt to usurp the throne of the emperor. Priest or no priest, this idiot wouldn't be rewarded for his treasons.

General Constantius had already sent a confidential message to Emperor Honorius, in which he requested explicit instructions for handling this difficult prisoner. Without direct orders, the general would refuse to execute the fool who was lounging in the filthy garb of a priest on the soft grass along the verge of the road. Constantine had been promised sanctuary if he surrendered, but the general knew that such a promise would never be honoured.

Constantius spat scornfully on to the roadway.

The prisoner rolled onto his back to gaze at the blue sky. He stared up in wonder, like a man who has been asleep and dreaming for years, and then woken suddenly after his long slumber. His mind remained intentionally blank as he absorbed the blue sky above him with its drift of fuzzy white clouds. Constantine's demeanour was calm and he seemed convinced that his new status as a priest could protect him from harm.

Then, in the distance, a dust-cloud indicated a fast-moving horse, although it would be some time before the rider came into clear view. Constantius began to hope that the dust indicated the approach of a courier from Honorius's court.

Since the siege of Arelate, Constantius had been torn. He had been ordered to defeat the upstart, Constantine, by any means necessary. But he was also instructed not to lose his military assets. Belatedly, Honorius finally understood that all his legions were either dead or had defected to the usurper. As such, the Vandal army could destroy the Holy City of Rome without a sword being lifted in its defence. Even peaceful Ravenna might yet be destroyed and the emperor could be burned alive in his favourite city. Suddenly, the men that Honorius had scorned to pay had become important to Rome's survival, so Constantius had been ordered to take whatever action was necessary to capture or kill Constantine, but with minimal casualties.

Constantius kicked at a loose stone with venom. The emperor had no idea what lies his general had been forced to tell to save his army from involvement in a protracted and costly siege. Constantius had promised Constantine everything that usurper asked for, in the full knowledge that he meant none of it.

Constantius knew he was only a pawn, but he would be forced to carry out this man's execution if Honorius signed the man's death warrant. During every day of the long trek from Arelate, Constantius had been faced with his personal loss of honour whenever he looked at the prisoner; he knew that he was unable to bear the strain for much longer. He had reached the end of his tether, so he would refuse to enter Ravenna with Constantine in chains behind his wagon, because he shuddered to think what the other men would think if they saw the proof of his lies. Constantius had hoped that he could enter its walls without the High King of Britannia in his charge.

Perhaps he could forget his empty promises if he was spared the sight of his captive. Bile and spite, aimed at his emperor, rose in Constantius's throat and he spat in disgust. The globule of spittle raised a little puff of dust from the roadway.

'Have you ever been to Ravenna, Constantius?' the usurper asked.

'Aye! I was at court with Stilicho. He was my friend and

commander, and he was sent to deal with you while I was recovering from a bad bout of the coughing sickness. I recovered in time to learn that he had been executed by his own men who wanted to win your favour.'

Constantine raised one narrow eyebrow and a shadow crossed his dark eyes. The general's face gave no hint of his resentments.

'I never asked for Stilicho's death,' Constantine replied in as natural a voice as he could muster in these circumstances. 'I would have saved him, if I had known. Fighting men should never be treated as pawns, or dishonoured by their enemies.'

'Indeed? You might be speaking the truth regarding Stilicho's death, but you ordered the deaths of Didymus and Verinianus, two men who hadn't shown any signs of aggression towards you. You killed them because they were kin to Honorius, the legitimate ruler of the Western Empire.' Constantius's voice was sharp with disapproval and Constantine bridled at his tone.

'I'm persuaded that you would have taken the same approach to those men as I took, so you needn't treat me with such censure. I was trained from my earliest days in the legions to leave no one at my back who could become a danger to me and my men. I might add that I've been forced to deliver kind deaths to my wounded comrades rather than leave them to the torture of the enemy. I did what war dictates, and you've done the same thing on many occasions. War sometimes creates dishonourable consequences. If my young sons had been in Gallia with me, they would have met Honorius's strangler already, so where is the honour in the murder of children? At least, Honorius's cousins were full-grown. If they had any sense, they would have left Hispania months earlier.'

'I agree that your sons would have been long dead if they were in Gallia. But, as you say, such is war. At any road, I had just finished a long convalescence in Ravenna when the emperor summoned me to his presence. Honorius asked me if I was prepared to lead the last of his legionnaires into Gallia to face your army. He told me that I was Rome's last roll of the dice. I agreed, for I have no truck with men who seek to further their personal ambitions at the cost of innocents. Where are your legions now, Constantine?'

The prisoner stared fixedly at his ragged sandals and dirty toes. The man who would be emperor had finally been trampled into the dust. All that remained for him was his life and the promise of a safe passage to Ravenna.

Oh, Constans! Where are you now? Even your little wife – and the child she carried!

'My men are dead! I know what I have done in the pursuit of my dream, Constantius. Might I suggest that you look into your own heart and take care that you don't travel down the same road, for you'll learn what choices a man has to make when he's caught like a rabbit in an iron trap. When that day arrives, you'll learn exactly what a man will do to stay alive. He will chew off his own foot, repudiate his lifelong scruples and trample on his honour. You must take care if you ever decide to aim above your place in the good Lord's scheme of things.'

'Me?' Constantius blenched. 'I hold no ambition that will place me in another's boots, and I'll always remain a loyal Roman. You insult me, Constantine.'

'But so was I, Constantius. I served my masters well for twenty years, but the patricians never reciprocated. Does Honorius treat you with the respect you deserve?'

The general clenched his fists. 'Only a fool would insult a man who controls his destiny. You're worse than a fool, Constantine, and I'm beginning to believe that you're courting death.'

'I'm a fool who has finally given up all hope, General. Only my life can be taken from me now, so I'm warning you of the pitfalls I faced in my search for glory. I wish you well, General Constantius, for our names are very much alike and you remind me of myself.'

The distant horseman's outline was distinct now and Constantius could see that the rider was wearing the emperor's livery. The general longed for an answer, especially one that would stop the mouth of this man whose every utterance made him acutely uncomfortable.

By the time the wagons were ready to trundle down the empty road once again, the rider had reached the column and presented the general with a small scroll cylinder. Constantius broke the wax seal and read the few terse words that sealed the prisoner's fate.

Execute him immediately and leave his body for the scavengers.

An ugly order for a dishonourable death, but this sin will no longer sully my soul, Constantius thought, so he summoned four men to assist him, including one giant Visigoth who had served in Stilicho's force and was still mourning his dead commander.

When Constantine saw the approaching men, he could tell that the legionnaires were marching in step. He realised immediately what was to take place and rose to his feet with a curiously untroubled expression on his face.

'I understood I'd been given safe conduct,' he said loudly in the vain hope that he could attract some sympathy from the legionnaires who were resting in the shade of the tree-lined road.

'The clemency no longer applies! Honorius has revoked the safe conduct so that the shades of his cousins may be at peace. The emperor has ordered your immediate execution. There is no appeal!'

Constantius spat out these words sharply, but the doomed man thought he saw a flicker of pity in the general's eyes.

'Balbas?' Constantius called to the tall Visigoth. 'Your sword is sharp?'

'Aye, master! It has been especially cleansed for the killer of General Stilicho.'

Constantine wanted to retreat to the very end of his chains and tug at the iron links as if his frail human flesh could break them. But the last traces of the centurion within him made him reluctant to beg for his life.

'Come, Constantine! Do you wish to be held down like a woman? Honorius has spared you from the indignity of the strangler in recognition of your status as an emperor. Your death will be speedy, for Balbas has honed his blade to a fine edge. Be a man, sir, and don't force me to batter you into unconsciousness before we send you into the shades.'

Some last shred of courage stiffened Constantine's spine and he ceased to struggle with himself. He consented to kneel in the dust while one of Constantius's legionnaires pulled his cowl and the neck of his robe away from the back of his throat. Another man bound his hands behind his back.

Constantine turned his face towards the general and spoke clearly, so that the whole detachment could hear every word.

'I forgive every man who takes part in my execution, so that my shade will not await them at the hour of their own deaths. You, Constantius of the legions, are absolved from any guilt, or lies, and I only ask that you remember me from time to time.'

471

'Do you have any final words for the emperor?' Constantius felt constrained to ask. 'Or for your kinfolk?'

Constantine merely shook his dust-covered head.

Oh, Constans! Would that I could have saved you!

Then, scorning to look down at the earth, he raised his eyes to stare out at the distant mountains on the blue horizon, with their snow-capped peaks that pointed out the route he would take to reach the heavens.

Constantine thought of Paulus, of his children and, finally, he recalled Severa, far away and safe in Britannia.

Then he thought no more.

AUTHOR'S NOTES

There is a significant amount of confusion surrounding the figure of Constantine III, so much so that I found it difficult to extract a real man from the limited amount of recorded material associated with this strange warrior during the passing of the years.

Was it coincidence that the same general who presided over Constantine's execution was eventually elevated to the purple as Constantius II? Was it hubris? Or was it just another cautionary tale that paralleled the story of Constantine's rise and fall?

The many years of famine, disasters and armed conflict that occurred in Britannia during the Dark Ages destroyed many of the records kept in monasteries, handwritten scrolls that would have simplified our understanding of early British history. Unfortunately, the Saxons and other raiders from the northern climes spared little of the Roman and Celtic history of these times when they burned the churches which were the repositories of records. This period will always be *truly dark*, for modern historians can never really know what happened during these years. The records of heroes who lived among the British inhabitants have been irrevocably lost. Or altered, either by design or accident!

I have always wondered, however, why a man who was capable

of conquering the province of Gallia, a man who was fully cognisant of the mistakes made by Flavius Magnus Maximus, would repeat the same errors of judgement displayed by his predecessor. I would have thought that Constantine would have learned from Maximus's mistakes.

I endeavoured to show my Constantine was a talented man who, for the large part, was thrust into extraordinary political situations where his wildest dreams seemed to come true.

But I found myself liking my early hero, Constantinus, an able man whose only weaknesses were a deep-seated resentment of the patricians of doubtful talents who controlled the legions, coupled with a long-held, secret desire to prove that he was as worthy as any other Roman of good birth and selective breeding.

Of course, such a man was always doomed to fail. In part, the prejudices of my Constantinus made him blind to Severa's talent, although she was an aristocratic woman in her own right. He could never understand the pitfalls of rubbing patricians' noses in the dust, and he couldn't gauge the capacity of all men to be dishonourable. Those men whom Constantinus trusted brought about his downfall, and they included the turncoat, Gerontius, and the Praetorian, Rusticus, both of whom were higher up the ladder of caste than he.

Once Constantinus became Constantine, he appeared to change, but as a legionnaire and a centurion, he was always capable of necessary acts of cruelty. He was eventually trapped by his own total power or, as has often been said: '*absolute power corrupts absolutely.*'

Most men who are blessed by chance would consider themselves fortunate for any opportunity to achieve greatness, but they would choose to remain, perfectly safe, within the security of their homes and hearths. But a man who possesses secret dreams, one who marries a woman who was the daughter of an emperor, would consider himself to be blessed by God and Fortuna. I can imagine such a man being swept away by his own importance and, eventually, acting rashly.

This novel covers a wide expanse of ground, one that is much larger than in most of my previous novels. It is also peopled by a panoply of real characters who have been passed down to us from the histories of ancient Britain and Rome as shadowy figures that lack flesh, blood and motives. Their names come to us through the murk of the ages with a distressing lack of detail. I have tried to flesh them out to suit my storyline, so I apologise to any of those old shades who might be offended by my guesswork. Even Severa, a few brief lines in old Latin script, is an enigma who was difficult to unravel. To me, she is a woman of her times, trapped by conventions as a baby machine and a source of earthly power, while possessing little of her own.

I made her a silly girl, a besotted wife, a tortured mother and, at last, a queen. I hope that I've given her a soul.

Most modern women would look at my Severa with contempt. She makes no attempt to run away from a conflict, for she knows that there is no escape for her and few enemies would deign to lift a sword against her person anyway. The position of wealthy women in those days would be incomprehensible to most modern women, except those females who are still seen as property in the less enlightened parts of the world. I tried to make her believable, rather than heroic, so she presents as a woman who endured because she had little or no choice.

Two places in Britain call to me whenever I fly into Heathrow from far-off Australia, two places that have captured my heart above all others. These are the town of Glastonbury and the ruins of Tintagel castle. The first scarcely has any fences, let alone a wall that must be scaled, while the other is an impregnable fortress. Both sites are ancient and are misunderstood, for they sleep now in the peace and quiet of the British countryside. Of all the places I visit in the British Isles, I am always surprised to discover how few of our English cousins have visited these two important historical centres.

Once again, these two remarkable places have found their ancient way into my narrative. For what it's worth, I can still feel the ghostly presence of Britannia's past with every step I take when I am in Tintagel or Glastonbury.

I believe that the educated reader will find flaws in this novel, but I have done my best to make sense of a time of turmoil and power-hungry men who survived on the edge of extinction. I can see unfortunate parallels with the present day, for history is repeated again and again. I hope too, that some of the readers who wind their way through this tale will visit Glastonbury and Tintagel, strip away the commercial nonsense that permeates them and picture the faces and places as they would have been in those times, 1,500 years distant, when the characters that live in my novels were young and vibrant. Think, too, about two of Fortuna's fools who walked the cobbles of these ruins as you can still do to this day. Flavius Magnus Maximus and Constantine III gambled for the throne of Rome but, ultimately, they lost everything except their place in the history of a great nation.

Ave.

M. K. Hume

Brisbane, 2015

GLOSSARY OF PLACE NAMES

Abus Flood	Humber River, Lincolnshire, England
Albis River	Elbe River, Germany
Armorica	Brittany in Europe (then Gallia)
Anderida	Pevensey, East Sussex, England
Anderida Silva	The district surrounding Anderida
Antonini Wall	A Roman defensive wall in Scotland
Aquae Sulis	Bath, Somerset, England
Arelate	Aries, France
Branodunum	Brancaster, Norfolk, England
Caer Fyrddin	Carmarthen, Carmarthenshire, Wales
Caerleon	Newport, South Wales
Caernarfon	Carnarvon, Gwynedd, Wales
Calleva Atrebatum	Silchester, Hampshire, England
Camulodunum	Colchester, Essex
Castra Exploratorum	Netherby, Cumbria, England
Causennae	Ancaster, Lincolnshire, England
Constantinople	Istanbul, Turkey
Corinium	Cirencester, Gloucestershire, England
Cymru	The Celtic term for Wales
Deva	Chester, Cheshire, England
Dubris	Dover, Kent, England
Durobrivae	Rochester, Kent, England
Durovernum	Canterbury, Kent, England
Dyfed	A kingdom in the west of ancient Britain
Eburacum	York, Yorkshire, England
Fosse Way	A Roman road that linked Exeter (Isca Dumnoniorum) in south-west England to Lincoln (Lindum Colonia) via Ilchester, Bath, Cirencester and Leicester
Gaul (Gallia)	An ancient Celtic area in Europe that

	comprised most of France and parts of Germany and Spain
Gesoriacum	Boulogne, France
Glastonbury	Glastonbury, Somerset, England
Glevum	Gloucester, Gloucestershire, England
Hadrian's Wall	The Roman defensive wall that protected Britannia from the Picts
Hibernia	The ancient name for Ireland
Hispania	Spain
Isca Augusta	Newport, Wales (Caerleon). The major Roman garrison in Wales. It was generally referred to as Isca
Italia	Italy
Lindinus	Lichester, Somerset, England
Litus Saxonicum	The English Channel
Londinium	London, England
Lutetia	Paris, France
Massilia	Marseilles, France
Metaris Aest	The Wash, England
Middle Sea	The Mediterranean Sea
Navio	Brough, Yorkshire, England
Portus Adurni	Portchester, Hampshire, England
Portus Lemanis	Dympne, Kent, England
Ratae	Leicester, Leicestershire, England
Rhenus River	The Rhine River
Rhodanus River	The Rhone River
River Styx	A river in Greek mythology that is the boundary between the earth and the Underworld (Hades)
Rutupiae	Richborough, Kent, England
Tamesis River	The River Thames, England
Tanatus	Thanet Island, Kent, England
Ticinum	Pavia, Italy
Tintagel	A fortress in Cornwall, England
Valentia	Valence, France
Venta Belgarum	Winchester, Hampshire, England
Venta Icenorum	Norwich, Norfolk, England
Venta Silurum	Caerwent, Monmouthshire, Wales
Verulamium	St Albans, Hertfordshire, England

GLOSSARY OF BRITISH
TRIBAL NAMES

Atrebates
Belgae
Brigante
Cantii
Catuvellauni
Coritani
Cornovii
Deceangli
Demetae
Dumnonii
Dobunni
Durotriges
Iceni
Novantae
Otadini
Ordovice
Regni
Selgovae
Silures
Trinovantes